Danny Miller was born in Brighton, and studied English and Drama at Goldsmiths, University of London. He started his writing career as a playwright and his plays have been performed at the National Theatre Studio, Bush Theatre and the Theatre Royal Stratford East. As a scriptwriter he has worked for the BBC, ITV and Channel 4.

His first novel *Kiss Me Quick* was shortlisted for the 2011 CWA John Creasey (New Blood) Dagger award.

Also by Danny Miller

Kiss Me Quick

THE GILDED EDGE

DANNY MILLER

Constable & Robinson Ltd
55–56 Russell Square
London WC1B 4HP
www.constablerobinson.com

First published in the UK by Robinson,
an imprint of Constable & Robinson Ltd., 2012

Published in this paperback edition by C&R Crime, 2013

A copy of the British Library Cataloguing in Publication
data is available from the British Library

ISBN 978-1-47210-186-0 (paperback)
ISBN 978-1-78033-555-1 (ebook)

Printed and bound in the UK

1 3 5 7 9 10 8 6 4 2

PROLOGUE

London, 1965

The King was in residence: a glossily white-walled Georgian town house, four storeys high and three bays wide, with a classical Ionic-pillared portico. The house sat proud in one of the grandest squares in London, and in one of the most prestigious addresses in town. Tucked away in the basement of this plum piece of Belgravia real estate, a bead of sweat had just dripped on to the King's eye. Johnny Beresford glanced down at the smiling King, who looked up at him and, with his bulging and magnified eye, bashed him a wink. Johnny Beresford expelled a short mirthless laugh that sounded more like a snort of derision. It was, of course, merely an optical illusion, because the King in question was the King of Spades. But right now, to Johnny Beresford's mind, there really wasn't anything to be laughing about, never mind shooting off cocky little winks.

Johnny Beresford held him fanned out alongside four other equally worthless and mismatched cohorts. This mocking King was a redundant King, and ultimately a deadly King who was not about to grant him any pardons or favours. He gave the King — and all the King's men — another glance, hoping they might change into something else, something to beat his opponent's lavish line-up of a straight flush. Nothing changed. They stayed the same. They stayed a bad hand of cards.

1

He took the almost drained bottle of single malt that sat on the table beside him, and tipped a splashing glug of it into the crystal tumbler. He wasn't drunk. No, that happy mindless state seemed unattainable to him these days, no matter how hard he tried – and he did try, for his industry on that front could never be faulted. But, for all he'd imbibed, he couldn't dispel the new sobriety that was now settling in on him – and fast. Things were changing and there was no going back, and also nothing he could do about it. He seemed to be moving through time with a lacerating lucidity. The gambler's optimism was disassembling itself before his eyes like fragmenting clouds. And there was no azure sky, no bright sunlight beyond, and no rainbows with pots of gold at the end of them. Just a dead hand. Unable to bear looking at the reality any more, he threw in his cards. After a moment, he gathered up the rest of the pack and shuffled them, hoping for the chance to deal out another dose of optimism.

But all the King's horses and all the King's men . . .

'What do you say, sport, another hand? Just the one? Come on, you owe me that, no?'

Sport stayed silent. Whoever sport was, he was being very unsporting, and clearly didn't want to play any more.

Johnny Beresford realized this, squeezed his eyes shut, balled his fists and banged them on the table in a drum roll of percussive powerlessness. More sweat fell from his brow and on to the cards, but it was tinged with red this time. The nasty-looking gash on his forehead, which had earlier dried and congealed, was now liquefying and being carried through the wound on his saline sweat.

He deserved better, he always had. He had the pedigree and the prestige. From his moment of his baronial birth, Johnny Beresford had sat at the top of the pile: fast-tracked and first in line for everything in life, due to his predecessors' successful efforts in snaffling up great swathes of this green and pleasant land. His family, known as 'the Battling Beresfords', were a historically bellicose brood. Murderous loyalty, in the service of the kings and queens of England, had run rife. They had set sail and seen off armadas, shot off arrows at Agincourt, aimed muskets at Roundheads in muddy fields in Essex, gone over the top at Flanders, and taken to the skies and spat fire over the white cliffs of Dover. And, although there were no written records, it wouldn't have surprised Johnny Beresford to learn that his ancestors had steadfastly refused to hail Caesar, cut up rough with Cnut, and said a big fat 'No!' to the Normans in 1066. With the Beresfords' ability to do the business on the battlefield, at court and eventually in the board-rooms, by the time Johnny Beresford had eased his way into the world, the work had long been done.

With such prestigious lineage stacked up behind him, he had been able to live a life of opulent entitlement. He thus bowled through life working on the principle that money begat money, and good fortune begat good fortune. So when the turn of the cards came, he naturally expected them to come up good. They always had.

'Come on, Johnny. Let's do it!'

He registered the instruction and laid down the cards. He knew that he'd played his last hand. He also knew what came next. He'd strung it out for as long as possible, and lost four on the trot. It was official: he'd moved into *bad luck* and saw little sign of moving out of it. There are those who say that in poker luck has little to do with winning or losing; it's all about skill. And, time and time again, they're proved hubristically wrong. Because luck has a lot to do with everything in life. Especially when it comes to dying.

'Do it, Johnny. *Do it!*'

In another part of town, and in another world, as the large hours of Saturday night dwindled effortlessly into the small hours of Sunday morning, Marcy Jones walked up Lancaster Road towards her home in Basing Street. The surrounding streets were deserted and uncharacteristically quiet. Even the house on the corner where resided a collective of young musicians – who lived like you'd expect a collective of young musicians to live, and were constantly being told to turn it down during their weekly Saturday 'happenings' – was quiet. All Marcy Jones could hear was the click of her own stilettos on the frosted pavement.

Tall terraced houses lined the street, some in bare ash brick, some painted in city-soiled white. Black slate roofs like the scales of an old fish held untidy chimney stacks and spindly TV aerials that serrated the skyline. This part of Ladbroke Grove was thrown in with Notting Hill, and its once grand houses had always been a little unfashionable, a little too far away from the centralized action and affluence of Belgravia, Knightsbridge and Mayfair. And now they had met their inevitable fate, been slummed over, sectioned off, partitioned, truncated and turned into tight little flats and broom-cupboard bedsits. It was a part of town where there were not even signs hung in windows that read: *No Blacks, No Irish, No Dogs*. Everyone was welcome in this parish, and Notting Hill accommodation offered cheap rents that, once moved into, rose steeply without much rhyme or reason, and deposits that once deposited would never see the light of day again. It was an area controlled by landlords who ruled with iron fists and turned off the heating at the first sign of complaint.

This part of London sang its own song of immigration and unrest. Because when people talked about immigration, they invariably seemed to talk about unrest, and ultimately always pointed to Notting Hill as the example. The so-called 1958 'race riot' had put it on the map, and fuelled all future arguments.

But this neighbourhood was home to Marcy Jones. Her family was one of the first West Indian families to settle just after the war. She'd grown up here, was schooled and churched here, but she knew it wouldn't be her home for much longer. She had her plans, her dreams, and almost enough money to make them come true.

The taxi had dropped her off on Ladbroke Grove, and, as she walked the rest of the way to her flat on Basing Street, as she was in the habit of doing lately, she took in these streets she'd known all her life with fresh eyes, committing the images before her to memory. Collecting snapshots of the streets she had trodden all her life, in preparation for a time soon when she would be far away from them. Melancholy and memories were mixed with the joy of a fresh start and a new life.

She pulled up the fur collar of her long dark woollen winter coat. The mid-January air held enough of a chill and a bite that she could see her breath exhaling in front of her face. She wanted to be home now; she wanted to make herself a cup of tea, draw a bath, then relax and soak the night away.

Marcy Jones climbed the four steps leading to the street-entrance door of the four-storey terraced house. Her attention wasn't on the dark green door but on her handbag, as she fished around for her key. The overburdened bag was stuffed with sundry beauty and grooming products: a hairbrush, some hairspray, a comb, a card of hair clips, two shades of lipstick, several mascaras, some nail polish – also two spare pairs of black stockings, a pack of chewing gum, bus tickets and tube tickets and sweet wrappers and a half-read paperback. She tutted and chided herself as she searched a bag badly in need of a clear-out – a good purging to lighten its load. Her slender red-tipped fingers eventually came upon the shiny brass Yale key, the new key that replaced the one she'd lost. As she turned it stiffly in the lock and opened the front door, her mind was still focused on her untidy bag, so she didn't hear the man behind her until she *felt* him behind her. And heard his jagged, panting breath. She turned sharply, awkwardly, her hand still attached to the key which was secured in the lock. Her flawlessly pretty face creased into confusion.

'*You?*'

There was no reply as a black leather-gloved hand went up to cover her face with such force that the movement slammed her head back against the open door, then pushed her through into the tatty gloom of the communal hallway. One stiletto heel caught in the exposed webbing of the cheap threadbare carpet and, with her hand still gripping the trapped key in the front door, for a moment it seemed to Marcy Jones as if the entire building was working against her. Like a conspirator in her murder.

His left hand gripped the top of her skull and tugged at her hair like he was tearing a hat off her head. The long shiny tresses, worn with a short fringe, came away with ease. Without her wig, Marcy Jones's pig-tailed and corn-rolled hairdo made her look younger; it made her much commented-on eyes look even bigger and even more luxuriously lashed and gorgeous. But right now they were dilated and struck through with terror so as to be hideously distorted out of shape.

The first blow from the ball-peen hammer took away her voice, but not her life – not all of it anyway. The blow was dealt with such a force that the ball of the hammer lodged in her skull. And, just like Marcy Jones had forgotten to let go of the key in the door and run, somehow now she forgot to lie down and die. Instead she sat bolt upright, her back ramrod straight, her legs splayed and stretched out before her, looking as stiff as a porcelain doll propped against a plumped-up pillow. Her body began to quiver and judder, as if waves of electricity were being sent through her by the executioner's hand.

The killer squeezed his eyes half shut as he went about his task of closing Marcy Jones's eyes for ever. The hammer beat down on her shattered skull five more times, to complete the six of the worst. With the job now done, the killer straightened up out of his murderously hunched position of attack, and took on board some heavy panting breaths. He could feel the warmth of her moist body curled lifelessly around his ankles.

The child stood on the top of the first flight of stairs, on the landing. She was no more than ten years old, wearing a pair of brushed-cotton jimjams with daisies dotted over them. She gripped the comforter of a well-worn teddy bear in one hand. She yawned, then balled her other fist and rubbed blunt little knuckles into her eyes to dispel the gritty cobwebs of sleep. Another yawn and a sigh, and she was now wide awake. In the gloom of the landing she stared at the nightmare laid out before her. It was one she would never wake up from.

It had been the sleepy sigh that alerted the killer to someone's presence on the stairs. He registers the much-loved teddy bear with its glass-bead eyes, its leather-button nose, its matted golden mohair fur and one padded paw clasped in the little girl's hand; the daisies on the cotton jammies; the brown toes curled over the stair edge. The sheer heartbreaking bloody innocence of it all. But the killer can't see her face, and he wonders if she can see his. Is she committing all this to memory, like some nightmarish negative that will be fully exposed in the cold light of the day – and then printed on to her consciousness for ever? But then, in a blink of the killer's eye, the little girl has disappeared from view. For a moment, he questions if he even saw her at all, questions if she ever existed. Was this some ghostly and guilt-ridden presence; the innocent child witnessing an adult murder?

The killer wasn't about to take that chance, though. With the very real hammer gripped in his gloved and pulsing hand, he took the stairs two at a time.

CHAPTER 1

'Don't make me stand up, Philly. Don't you make me do it!'

'It's a pair of threes, Kenny! You're making a fool of yourself, but you're not making one of me, you fuckin' hear me?'

'Gentlemen, gentlemen . . .'

'Come on, Mac, I see what's going on here!'

'Gentlemen, let's keep a lid on it. Let's keep it civilized. It's just a friendly game . . .'

Detective Vince Treadwell lowered his copy of the *Evening News* and studied the scene before him, which was a card school. The game they were playing was Kalookie, a form of rummy – and currently all the rage for achieving a quick turnover in profit and losses. It wasn't much of a card school: two members hadn't turned up, and two players had already dropped out. DI Bert Jennings, a detective from Vice, who headed up the squad that looked into the illegal gambling activities centred in and around Soho and Chinatown, had done all his money and gone home to the wife in sleepy Dulwich. The other player was Dr Clayton Merryman, one of the most experienced and respected white coats in criminal pathology, and a degenerate horse player and gambler to boot. Doc had been fortuitously called away earlier; he'd been losing all night, going belly up with some dreadful hands, so a trip to the morgue was probably to be viewed as some light relief.

Of the three players left, DCI Maurice McClusky was the highest in rank, and also a calming voice of reason in the room.

'Gentlemen, gentlemen, let's keep it civilized . . . no need for any unpleasantness . . .'

Mac, as DCI Maurice McClusky was readily, if somewhat predictably, referred to, was soothing the ire of the two other remaining players, who were shaping up over a pair of threes. They were the redoubtable double act composed of DS Philip 'Philly' Jacket, and DS Kenny Block. Philly was accusing Kenny of cheating. It was subtle, unpremeditated, spur-of-the-moment cheating, but cheating none the less – some dealing from the bottom and some doubling up on the laydown. Mac already knew that Kenny cheated on occasion, so he always went in low when he was dealing. And he let it pass and didn't pull Kenny up about it, because he found it mildly amusing and it also gave him an advantage. He could tell when Kenny was cheating, because Kenny had a series of gambler's 'tells': he couldn't look anyone in the eye, sweat bubbled up on his forehead and his whole face went capillary red. He might as well have been wearing a sign. Philly, who should have known that Kenny cheated, clearly didn't and had just found out, hence the tête-à-tête.

Vince considered the two men, who were now standing up, with Mac pointing firmly at both. The reproving gesture was enough to stop them in their tracks. Philly and Kenny were both medium height, medium build, and medium-talent detectives. They were in it for the duration, but unlikely to rise much above their present positions. Both in their mid-thirties, both solid-looking fellows with the blunted features and the cautious eyes of coppers who mixed easily in the pubs and clubs and environs of villains, they'd been partnering each other for as long as anyone could remember, and worked well together. They were so similar in appearance, dress and demeanour that, when they were questioning a suspect, the potential perpetrator soon realized there was no good cop or bad cop in the room: just Block and Jacket. An insurmountable brick wall of sameness, as the two coppers shot off their questions, the suspect's head would swivel from one to the other like the observer of an especially fast rally in a tennis match, soon realizing there was no way out. It became a blur, and it was the inevitability and monotony of it all that wore the offenders down to confess their sins.

And that's exactly what Block and Jacket had been doing about three hours earlier. In a salacious case that had made all the papers, a schoolteacher had murdered his wife and her lesbian lover, who just happened to be the school's lollipop lady – the alliteration alone was enough to crack everyone up. The schoolteacher himself was out of the country at the time – a keen philatelist attending a convention in Germany – when the killer broke into the home of his wife's lollipop lady lesbian lover and splattered both of their brains all over the hire-purchase furniture with a twelve-bore shotgun. Salacious soon became farcical. The schoolteacher was discovered to be enjoying underage relations with one of his pupils. The girl's father had found out about the affair and confronted the teacher with a twelve-bore shotgun. And, somewhere in the calming-down process, the teacher and the factory-worker father had come up with the idea of killing the teacher's wife and collecting on the insurance and on her not insubstantial savings.

Vince and Mac had successfully joined the dots and brought the case in, whereupon Block and Jacket had extracted the confessions. For Mr Chips it had seemed like a good idea at the time, rather like in the film *Strangers on a Train* – but without the train, of course, or even the strangers.

After their case had been put to bed, still too jagged on strong coffee and victory to go home to bed, the coppers had decided to hang on until morning and thus cop for some more overtime, while playing a few hands down in the Inferno.

'Unbelievable,' spluttered Philly Jacket.

'Sit down, Philly,' said Kenny Block, 'it was a mistake. You're just overtired, you've had too much coffee, and now you're overreacting and making a prick of yourself!'

Every feature on Philly Block's face widened as incredulity took hold. 'A mistake? Coffee? Tired? Prick? You were *cheating*!'

'The cards are gummy, must have got stuck together, you prick!'

'Again with the prick! Who you calling a prick?'

'Easy, take it easy,' said Mac, standing between them and jabbing his index fingers in both their chests in turn. 'Let's play nice now, or not at all.'

'What did *you* see, Mac?' asked Philly.

'What are you asking me for?' Mac replied, wisely wishing to stay out of it. 'Ask Vince,' he suggested, sitting back down at the table before gathering up the cards and shuffling them.

'He's not even playing.'

'Exactly, therefore he hasn't got a stake in this game. Both you mugs owe me, and I'm not siding with anyone.'

In unison, Kenny Block and Philly Jacket looked at Vince. 'You been watching the game?' asked Kenny.

'Uh-uh.'

'Then why d'you come down here?'

'The scintillating conversation.'

Philly and Kenny looked at each other, then back over at Vince. They wanted to take their frustrations out on the young detective.

'Don't drink, don't gamble. What *do* you do, Treadwell?'

Vince glanced over at them and winked.

'I bet he does,' said Kenny, 'the little bastard! And lots of it. A face for the ladies has Treadwell.'

Vince considered winking again, but realized the two men were very tightly wound up and looking for an excuse to hit someone – anyone – and were happier for it not to be each other. So he just smiled and carried on reading his paper.

'Don't worry,' said Philly Jacket to Kenny Block. 'Those looks won't last, not in this job. Someone will knock that smile off his face.'

'Until that day comes, gentlemen, until that day comes . . . ' said Vince in a distracted sing-song voice.

'Oh, it'll come, and sooner than you think,' muttered Kenny Block to Philly Jacket.

'Don't take it out on me because you can't win a hand,' said Vince. 'Which, by the way, I was listening to and believe me, Kenneth and Philip, you can learn as much about a game by listening as you can from watching. Just by hearing how the betting goes.'

'You know nothing about gambling.'

'I know everything about gambling. That's why I choose not to do it. And I know what I heard.'

Block and Jacket's eyes met in silent conference, both looking for verification of this fact. And, like a mirror image, both faces drew a blank. So they turned to Mac for guidance. Mac weighed it up, and seemed to nod encouragingly in Vince's favour. Mac then sparked up another Chesterfield.

'Go on then, enlighten us. What did you hear?' demanded Block with a begrudging and cynical grimace.

Vince was perched on a cardboard box that was crammed full of files, with his feet up on another box which contained more of the same. The contents of a hundred or so similar boxes should have been either destroyed or filed away long ago, but no one had yet got around to it. And so the sagging containers had been turned into reasonably comfortable furniture, making up the stools the men were sitting on and the table they were playing at.

The four coppers were currently in a storage room located in the basement next to the 'Tombs', the old holding cells of Scotland Yard. The bright red NO SMOKING sign was habitually ignored, and the smoking was regularly accompanied by lots of drinking and gambling. Ground-out cigarette butts studded the floor. Discarded matches were tossed over shoulders with drunken abandon. All of which could be viewed as more than a little careless, considering the place was a veritable tinderbox of cardboard boxes filled with parched old files, therefore likely to ignite at any minute. Someone had once commented that this basement storage room had the smoky and hellish atmosphere of Dante's Inferno. The name had stuck. No one, Vince suspected, had read that epic poem, but they were all pretty sure that hell must be something like it — especially when you were on the end of a losing hand of cards.

Vince considered the other men, felt the weight of expectation on him, the potential for a punch-up, and the shredding of a reputation. And the opportunity for a good wind-up. He pulled a wicked grin internally, but externally remained poker-faced. He finally put down his paper, swung his legs around and planted his feet firmly on the ground, striking a Rodin pose as he gave the enquiry some serious rumination.

'Come on, Treadwell, what did you hear?' barked Philly Jacket.

After a hefty sigh, Vince said, 'Well, gentlemen, from what I heard, I reckon . . .'

Vince was saved by the bell. The fire alarm. And soon that was all that any of them could hear. Its repetitive note ricocheted around the room, almost sending ripples through the fug of smoke in the Inferno.

'Ah, what in the sweet name of?' cried Mac, standing up, shaking his head, and stubbing out his Chesterfield in the coffee dregs in a Styrofoam cup.

'What's all this about?' demanded Kenny Block, doing the one-footed twist as he ground his Benson & Hedges into the floor.

'Unbelievable! Un-fucking-believable!' crowed Philly Jacket, chipping a just-lit Rothmans and putting it back in the packet.

Vince didn't smoke — he didn't need to with the amount of time he spent in the Inferno.

The alarm stopped as suddenly as it had started, and PC Barry Birley, the most lanky and long-limbed copper that anyone had ever seen, stretched his presence into the room.

'What's it all about Shirley?' barked Mac. The Birley/Shirley joke had happened to the lanky copper's surname a long time ago.

'The Guv's idea. He assumed you lot would be down here.'

'What's Markham doing here, Shirley?' pressed Philly Jacket, looking at his watch, and not liking what he saw. It was 8 a.m.

Mac threw Philly Jacket a stupid-question look. He knew exactly what the Supe – a church-goer, then an avid golfer – would be doing in the office at 8 a.m. on a Sunday morning.

'Where is it, Shirley?'

'There's two of them. One in Notting Hill, one in Belgravia.'

CHAPTER 2

The murder of a black girl of limited means in a not too salu-brious part of town, and the murder of a very well-heeled and very well-connected white male in a very salubrious part of town? No one dared say that one murder outweighed or took priority over the other but, given institutional thinking in places like the Met, Vince couldn't help but be quietly satisfied at having been handed the Belgravia caper (every crime was described as a *caper*, from gruesome murders to frauds and thefts). All things being equal, Vince, being Vince, might rather have got the Notting Hill caper. He'd spent time in that area, while working Shepherds Bush, his first posting, and still had friends and contacts there. But being thrown the Belgravia caper did tell him one thing: that, after being in CID's Murder Squad for all of four months, he was now trusted with a high-profile case.

But, of course, he was partnering DCI Maurice McClusky, an officer with an outstanding record. And, over the three months they'd been working together, he'd not only learned an immeas-urable amount but had grown fond of the older detective.

Mac was a tall slim man, who, though only in his late forties, looked well north of his late fifties. He had a slow burn about him: professorial, methodical, walking with meandering stooped gait. He reminded Vince of the actor Jimmy Stewart, who, with his willowy frame and cautious demeanour, always managed to look older than his years. Mac had a long, gaunt face with deep lines running down it, like the folds in a theatrical curtain, all of which just accentuated his serious expression. His skin had an ashen pallor, perhaps accounted for by the constant haul of smoke he took on board through his beloved Chesterfields or his trusty pipe. Smoking aside, he wasn't the type to get flustered and red-faced, and Vince had never seen him break into anything resembling a run, never mind a sweat. He took everything in his stride, seeming the most measured man Vince had ever met. Mac had a full head of thick wavy hair that was now salt and pepper in colour but impressively white at the temples; like a dove had perched on the back of his neck and was hugging his head. And he always wore the same grey flannel suits, always a crisp white shirt and a black tie. With this monochrome appearance, he looked as if he'd stepped out of a black-and-white film into a Technicolor world. Or from Kansas into Oz, if you will.

Vince wheeled his shimmering petrol-blue Mk II Jaguar out of the car park and headed west. Hands planted at ten to two on the knotted wood of the steering wheel, looking down at the burr-walnut dashboard that framed the polished binnacles housing the various dials with their jolting needles, Vince gunned the engine to a steady purr as he made his way around Oxford Circus, along Park Lane, down to Victoria then finally Belgravia. He kept the Mk II at a sedate pace, allowing them to take in London's pomp – its history, its vanity, its palaces, its arches, its grand road-side gestures memorializing bloody battles – while roundabouting its stalled one-way traffic systems. Bronze eighteenth-century warriors sat proudly astride their mounts, looking down at First World War troops crawling all around an insurmountable stone block that marked their mass grave. They, in turn, were looking up at the Second World War Tommies standing aloft on their plinths, too occupied to appreciate their luck in being born a generation later because they were busily eyeing up a couple of scantily clad older birds: Britannia and Boudicca, rendered in marble and sitting safely in their squares.

★　★　★

16

Two uniformed coppers stood sentry before the columns supporting the portico of number 57 Eaton Square. Marked and
unmarked police cars were double-parked immediately outside.
Getting out of his car, Mac stretched and took in a deep and
sonorous sniff of the crisp morning air, then said: 'You smell that,
Vincent?'

Vince sniffed the air too, but nothing came to mind.

'Money,' Mac said. 'Unmistakable.'

Vince laughed. 'Any idea how much a place like this might
cost?'

'More than our public-sector pay packet could ever spring for.'

'Maybe I'll marry well.'

'Wouldn't surprise me. If you're in need of a butler, keep me
in mind.'

Vince couldn't actually smell it, but he could see it. There was
something coolly aloof about this square: the ordered affluence
perhaps. No kids playing out in the street – for that matter, no
one on the street at all. Even the litter seemed to have picked itself
up and put itself in the bins. And, for all the police presence and
the potential for excitement and scandal, there were no gawpers,
no rubber-neckers. Doubtless the neighbours were concerned, but
they were metropolitan enough not to appear openly surprised.
This was London – this was the middle of it – and it wasn't always
a box of chocolates. And even if it was, no matter how rich and
creamy the centre, there was always a hard carapace surrounding
it. So the local residents stayed secure inside their alarm-belled and
white-walled castles.

The two detectives unnecessarily badged the two uniformed
coppers, who had known who they were the minute Vince and
Mac had parked across the street and come striding over to the
house. Not that they looked especially like coppers – Vince himself was threaded-up in a Prince of Wales check suit, worn with
a pale blue shirt with faux French cuffs and a black knitted tie
subtly flecked with dark blue dots. A beige three-quarter-length
Aquascutum raincoat kept out the wind, which held a bitter bite,

and he was shod in a pair of black Chelsea boots polished to within an inch of their life, so the puddled pavement didn't prove too much of a problem. He was also road-testing a new haircut, for his black hair, normally worn swept back, was now worn with a side parting. It was more Steve McQueen in *The Great Escape* than Ringo Starr in *A Hard Day's Night*, and he liked it. He liked looking in the mirror in the morning and fussing around for a few minutes, trying to re-establish his parting as he thought about his day ahead. Cutting a dash seemed compulsory these days, and everyone was at it. Vince Treadwell could thus have been anyone he wanted to be, from a fast-talking Ogilvy & Mather's advertising man off to a pitch, or a suited and booted rock-and-roller attending a court appearance on a dope pinch. The boundaries were breaking up: this was the age of reinvention and upward mobility. Yes, in 1965 you could be anyone you wanted – or at least that's what the man from Ogilvy & Mather was selling you, and what the rock-and-roller up on a dope pinch was singing about.

No, it wasn't the duds that marked Vince and Mac out as a pair of detectives; it was the attitude, the way they crossed the road and walked up to the house. They were at work from the minute they got out of the car. They took in the street, their eyes subtly scoping and scouring and absorbing the scene, as they looked for people watching, curtains twitching, scaffolding erected nearby that might offer vantage points into the house itself, flower sellers, taxi stands, kiosks, tented builders digging up the road, checking on anyone who might have witnessed the ins and outs of the victim's home; anything that might just look out of place or provide a witness. And that was why Mac, the experienced and wily copper, kept to such a meandering pace, because he was assessing and assimilating the world he was entering, and capturing mental film footage that would be stored up for future reference. And Vince was absorbing Mac's movements and was learning to slow his pace, too.

Nice and easy does it.

CHAPTER 3

In one of the downstairs reception rooms, scene-of-crime officers were deep in discussion with the white coats of forensics and pathology. Clayton Merryman had already inspected the body and was making his preliminary notes. Nearby came the flash of magnesium, as cameras popped and pictures were taken. Details of the victim had been gathered, and teams of uniforms were being sent out to ask the neighbours what they had seen, or heard, or knew. Mac went straight over to join the huddle of coppers and white coats, while Vince hung back and studied the room. It was cathedral-like in its proportions, and the ornate decoration on the ceiling looked as if it had been piped on by a master cake decorator. Two stalactite crystal chandeliers, which wouldn't have looked out of place in an opera house, hung miraculously. Small, and not so small, expensive figurines stood in every available space on the richly hued mahogany furniture. A long-cased clock skulking in one corner of the room struck the hour with a gloomy chime. The gilt-framed paintings on the walls featured dark and serious portraits of men dressed for war, from a fey-looking Elizabethan in doublet and hose to a First World War officer encased in a greatcoat, amid warriors and soldiers from every war and imperial skirmish along the way. The women all looked the same: stiff and starched in lace and festoons, with powdered hair and alabaster doll's skin and brightly painted pinched lips. Meet the family! The whole room looked as if it needed a red rope sectioning it off, and a uniformed guide to talk you through the contents.

It wasn't until Vince looked more closely that he spotted the details that assured him he hadn't time-travelled back a couple of hundred years. Tucked away in a corner was a shiny hi-fi; a record sat on the turntable and some 45s, out of their sleeves, were scattered on the floor nearby. On a marble-topped coffee table stood two fluted glasses, one bearing the distinctive lipstick print of a woman – the colour was red. Vince spotted two empty champagne bottles by the Parian marble fireplace; another sat on the floor by a red-striped, silk-covered chaise longue. They all bore the eye-catching, wallet-thinning, burnished-gold shield label of Dom Perignon. Resting on a French marble-topped commode, next to an enormous bronze figure depicting the god Atlas supporting the world, about the size of a football, on his back, was a heavy cut-crystal ashtray. It was brimming with the butts of thirty or so thoughtlessly smoked cigarettes. Vince went over to take a look. Bending down, he saw that among the biscuit-coloured filtered butts were three hand-rolled joints smoked down to the roach.

Mac meandered back over towards him, and Vince said: 'It looks like our man had company last night. A little party? I bet it wasn't with his wife – if he's even married.'

Mac nodded in agreement, but wanted this deduction explained. 'What makes you say that?'

'When was the last time you and your wife got drunk and danced around to Lulu's "Shout!" – just the two of you?'

'You'd be surprised, Vincent, what me and Betty get up to. And she much prefers The Rolling Stones.'

'That explains it. Do you and Betty get stoned on pot, too? Because there's some reefer butts in the ashtray.'

Mac gave a concessionary nod to this point and said: 'His name was John Charles Samuel Beresford, but known to everyone as Johnny. And an Honourable, too. Thirty-four years old, ex-army man, officer class of course. His occupation now was City investments. He comes from a big-money family, landed gentry, so was mainly managing the family estate and its financial interests. And you're right, he wasn't married.'

Clayton Merryman came over and joined them, looking as if he had big news to impart. 'I think Philly Jacket cheats at cards,' he said.

'That's a hell of an accusation, Doc,' said Mac, as dry as you like.

'And it's wrong, anyway,' said Vince. 'It's Kenny Block that cheats at cards.'

Doc Clayton shook his head at this, as though a game of cards in the Inferno, for chump change, actually mattered. He was still shaking his nebbishy little head with its thinning crinkly red hair, a liberal sprinkling of freckles, and round wire glasses, when Vince prompted him for information about something that actually did matter.

'Where's the body, Doc?'

'Downstairs,' said the good doctor, leading the way with the sweep of a gossamer-gloved hand. On the way he filled in the two detectives, checking his just compiled notes during their progress. 'The maids found the body at seven thirty this morning. I won't know the exact time of death until I get to the lab and open him up but, by the freshness of the wound and the blood clotting, I'd say he was shot around midnight.'

'Does he employ live-in servants?' asked Mac.

'No, but he does have a team of three cleaners who come in twice a day to tidy up.'

'Is he that messy or just that much of a cleanliness freak?' asked Vince.

'He's just that rich,' said the doc, chuckling. 'But he does also like everything just so, apparently. He has fresh flowers delivered every day and everything has to be precisely in its place.'

Mac sighed and shook his head in amused disapproval.

'Don't worry, Mac,' said Vince. 'When I get to marry into money, you won't have to lift a finger on that score.'

CHAPTER 4

Downstairs in the basement were to be found a surprisingly small kitchen, a utilities room, a single bedroom, and a very large private study-cum-den containing the very dead body of Johnny Beresford.

'What's this?' said Vince, peering down at a nasty two-inch gash on Johnny Beresford's forehead.

'It's fresh,' said Doc Clayton. 'Not caused by a fall, though. It looks like he's been hit with something. There was blood on the base of one of the champagne bottles upstairs. When you're done here, we'll measure that up against the wound.' The pathologist looked at the two detectives with lively eyes and then offered, 'I bet it fits.'

There were no takers for this bet. But, nasty as the head wound was, it was clear to the three men standing over Beresford that the blow wasn't responsible for his death.

'As you can see, gentlemen, one shot to the right temple. It looks like the work of a 32 mil.'

Vince enquired, 'No exit wound from a 32, right, Doc?'

'Depends on the angle, Vince. In this case, it looks like the bullet was aimed upwards, sending it into the top of the cranium. Toughest part of the skull, so no exit wound.'

Vince considered the weapon, which was perfect for up-close work, but not powerful enough to blow the victim's brains out or make a mess on the walls. The bullet would just ricochet around inside and bounce off the walls of his skull, making its own internal mess by tearing through tissue and turning the grey matter into mush. *Did he feel it*, Vince wondered. *Did he feel his life being torn up behind his eyes?*

'Looks like a straight execution to me,' observed Doc Clayton, with an assured nodding of his head. 'Judging by how relaxed he was, sitting in the chair watching TV, he probably knew the chap who did it, I'd say.'

The two detectives stared at Doc Clayton, whose wire-framed and magnified eyes were fixed firmly on the stiff sitting in the chair. He looked as if he couldn't wait to get his hands on this cadaver: to cut it up and probe, and come up with further details of the death, and any other sinister little secrets that the body decided to give up. The white coats always thought they had all the answers, but it was Vince and Mac's job to come up with who did it and why they did it. And you didn't have to be a detective to come up with the notion that this victim knew his killer. Most of them did.

'Well, Doc, like with most things in life, looks can be very deceiving,' said Mac, as he ambled around inspecting the body. 'And dead bodies are the worst: they're full of lies and deceit. But, somewhere about them, the truth will be bursting to get out. Right, Vincent?'

Vince gave a distracted nod. He too had his eyes and attention solidly fixed on Johnny Beresford, as he lay slumped in a green leather button-back armchair. The TV in front of him hummed and thrummed away, and was hot enough to suggest it had been on all night. Glancing around the room, Vince noticed that where the upstairs was all Georgian panache, elaborate and grand, this room was Edwardian and cigar-chompingly masculine. In the oak-panelled room there was a moderately sized billiard table and laid on top of it was the horse-racing game Escalado, with all its little painted-alloy gee-gees set up for a race. Next to take Vince's eye was a large mahogany partners' desk. On top of it there were three telephones, a stock-market ticket machine, a green-shaded banker's lamp, and an in- and an out-tray, with more in ins than outs. Business papers, files, folders and documents were scattered about the desktop in the kind of ordered disorder that marked it out as a fully functioning workspace. Also fully functioning, and looking much used, was a small corner bar with three shelves holding serried ranks of booze bottles in various stages of depletion; while a selection of wines stacked in a forty-celled wine rack stood next to the bar. There was a side table in polished rosewood that looked as though it folded out into a dining table. This was borne out by the silver condiment set holding salt, pepper, oil and vinegar and the stack of six cork table-mats that sat on it. Four antique-style balloon-backed chairs were gathered around it. In a corner of the room stood another of those ominous-looking long-cased clocks, making a mechanical clacking sound, a racket that Vince knew he could never get used to.

As well as being the room that Beresford had died in, the young detective had a hunch that this was the room that Beresford did most of his living in: the engine room of the house, the epicentre of his life, the room he felt most at home and comfortable in, and the room that would probably tell them more about the victim than anywhere else.

The very walls called out his life story. Adorning them were paintings and framed photos of his regiment, the Coldstream Guards, including a portrait of the victim himself in full officer regalia. There were also lots of sporting scenes, a large print of a pair of eighteenth-century boxers shaping up: Mendoza vs Gentleman John Jackson, the pair striking a pose before they proceeded to strike each other. And oils depicting fox hunting, horse racing, shooting and fishing, and shiny-coated gun dogs clasping pheasants in their mouths. On the shelves were ranged many silver trophies and cups for various sporting achievements, from water skiing to leading the line for the first eleven. And Beresford wasn't the only dead thing in the room, which included a couple of very lively-looking stags with long fearsome antlers, who looked as if they'd just rammed their heads through the wall, while a seriously lethal-looking swordfish in his glass coffin looked as fresh and slippery as the catch of the day. But, impressive as they all were, the centrepiece of the room remained Johnny Beresford himself. Even dead, and slowly decomposing as he must be, he looked vibrant and anomalously alive; just ripe for the taxidermist's hand. Vince felt he could tap the dead man's shoulder and he would have sprung to life, as if awakening from a nap in front of the TV.

It was clear that the evolutionary process had been very good to Beresford. He was a big man, at around six foot three, and would be considered traditionally handsome with his thick flaxen hair scraped back from what Vince assumed would be classed as a noble-looking brow, and a strong jawline that was almost Desperate Dan in its solidity and confidence. The nose had a slight hook to it, and looked as though it had been broken at some time, perhaps at school, on the rugby field was Vince's guess, but it still fitted the proportions of his face perfectly. The wide and full-lipped mouth looked as easily suited to sensuality as to barking out orders on the parade ground or in the boardroom. Vince crooked his head, as if to bring into focus another slightly hidden aspect of the victim's physical appearance: the stuff that doesn't get written up in the reports, yet composes the metaphysics of murder. And, with this adjustment, Vince saw that Beresford looked almost contented. Even slumped and dead, there was a certain confidence in his posture, as if he was right where he wanted to be. Which went against everything one knew about death: *The last thing in the world we want to be, is the last thing in the world we end up being.*

Next to the corpse was a small side table with a phone and an open black notebook on it. In the notebook were written the names of what could only have been racehorses, and columns of arithmetic that included the odds regarding each of the runners. The question was whether Beresford had been backing or laying? Vince looked again over at the Escalado racing game set up on the billiard table. Only an innocent parlour game, a toy, but he'd known serious money change hands on the result of those little metal jockeys seated on their mounts being mechanically propelled along the green vinyl track.

'Go on then, Vince,' said Mac, 'talk me through it.'

Vince crouched down to take a look at Beresford's shoes: an exotic-looking pair of low-cut loafers fashioned out of what looked like crocodile skin. Vince wasn't just admiring them, he was wondering why a pair of bespoke shoes had both slipped loose at the heel. He stood up and considered the big man's posture.

'Doc's right, he does look relaxed and contented, like he knew his killer and wasn't expecting anything to happen. But . . . it looks wrong to me. Contrary to how it seems, I don't think he was killed in this chair. I think he was moved here. His shoes are off at the heel, like he'd been dragged. And look at his crutch.'

Mac and the doc leaned in to look, and saw how eye-wateringly tight and uncomfortable it looked.

Vince continued: 'The way all the material is gathered up looks like it's squeezing the life out the boy. No, you'd have done some serious trouser adjustment before you sat down like that and relaxed in a chair to watch TV. You'd have made yourself comfortable.'

'Yeah, he certainly does look uncomfortable,' Doc Clayton retorted with a smile. 'But who wouldn't with a bullet in their head? So he was killed upstairs? That's where all the action was, right, Vince?'

Mac shook his head. 'Vince is right, he does look like he's been moved, but my money's on him being killed in this room.'

'Me too,' agreed Vince. 'Upstairs may have been for the entertaining, but this is where Beresford did his business. This is where he kept his secrets.'

Mac, thinking obviously and out loud, said, 'So the question is, why bother moving him from the place he was killed, unless you want to distract us?'

'Yeah, and he's a big fellow,' said Vince. 'Whoever did it knew they had time.'

Mac said, 'Well, it's not robbery, because all the pictures in the house look in place according to the maids. And there's a couple of old masters hanging up that would definitely be missed – along with all the silverware and everything else. Plus the fact the place is fully belled-up and the alarm goes straight to Buckingham Palace Road police station.'

Vince then went over to take look at a collection of silver-framed photographs gathered on a shelf. There were a dozen or so of them, and all featured more or less the same cast of male characters in various locations: a shooting party on a country estate, a group on the deck of a large yacht with palm trees and a secluded white-sand beach as a backdrop, a team shot of them skiing in Klosters. The largest photo sat in the middle of the pack and featured Beresford and his five friends, in dinner jackets, sitting around the green baize of a card table. They all held cards in their hands. Of course Vince couldn't see the cards they were holding, but every one of them looked as if he was holding the winning hand – holding all the best cards that life's little game had to offer. They seemed so cocksure, pumped up and pleased with themselves. A shared sneering arrogance burned through the photo, which was both a little nauseating and compulsively magnetic. Vince reached into the inside pocket of his jacket and pulled out that most celebrated of detecting devices: the magnifying glass. Gone were the days of the ebonized handle and the big round lens, for this one was made of plastic, and about the same dimensions and with the same sliding cover action as a box of matches. He picked up the photo and, on closer inspection, all the above assessment was confirmed by the name printed in white on the green baize of the card table. It was the most exclusive gaming room in London, and probably in Europe for that matter. The Montcler Club in Berkeley Square.

Vince and Mac left Doc Clayton alone with his corpse and went for an investigative wander upstairs. There were fresh white lilies in every room, and the place was five-star spruced. The phalanx of maids that swept through the place, with their artillery of brooms and dusters, had certainly put their backs into the task.

Upon entering the master bedroom, the first thing to catch their eye was the bed. In a room containing a full suite of expensive French furniture stood a huge round bed designed to look like a giant open scallop, with a headboard covered in fanned pink satin to form the striations of the shell.

'Will you look at that?' gasped Mac, with a whistle.

The cream-coloured carpet was so thick and luxurious that it physically slowed down the two detectives as they waded across it. Mac pressed down on the mattress, which gave way with an undulating ease. The older detective pulled a face of supreme disapproval.

'It's a water bed, naturally,' Vince informed him.

'No good for me.' Mac shook his head. 'I need a mattress that's firmer than Doc Clayton's morgue slab.'

The bed itself was unmade, with the rumpled pearl-coloured satin sheets pushed over to one side and cascading on to the floor. They padded over to the en suite bathroom, which featured a shower cubicle and a circular bath that would have happily accommodated a five-a-side football team. Sandwiched between the washbasin and the toilet was something else.

'What is that?' asked Mac.

'A bidet.'

'A be what?'

'A be-day.'

'What do you wash in that, your feet?'

'Your jacksy.'

'You're kidding?'

'It's French.'

'What the hell's wrong with those people?' asked Mac, shaking his head in mild disgust.

'Sirs!'

Both men turned round sharply. 'Jesus Christ, Shirley! Do you have to shout?' demanded Mac.

The craning copper, Barry Birley, stood doubled up in the doorway, addressing no one in particular because everyone here was of higher rank than him, and therefore called Sir.

'Sorry, guv.'

Vince and Mac joined him back in the bedroom.

'Just got some information from the maids – not the ones who found him this morning, but one of those who was working here last night.'

Vince said, 'Mr Beresford had a visitor, a female?'

'That's right, his girlfriend apparently,' said Birley. He consulted his notebook. 'A Miss Isabel Saxmore-Blaine. She turned up at around six p.m., and was crying and upset. But apparently, according to the maid, that was nothing new or unusual.'

'Turning up at six p.m., or crying and being upset?' asked Vince.

Birley gave a quizzical frown, then hesitantly said: 'Crying and being upset . . . I guess.'

'You *guess*? The devil's in the details, Shirley. The devil's in the bidet.'

CHAPTER 5

Isabel Saxmore-Blaine lived in Pont Street, Chelsea, a brisk ten-minute walk from Beresford's Eaton Square house. The proximity didn't surprise Vince, who reckoned you could throw a net over Belgravia, Mayfair, Knightsbridge, Kensington and Chelsea, and snag up most of Beresford's cohorts – if they weren't away for the weekend at their country seats. Pont Street was composed of rows of very tall Victorian red-brick terrace houses that had been mainly converted into spacious luxury flats and maisonettes.

As Vince and Mac walked from the car towards Isabel Saxmore-Blaine's flat, Mac said: 'I've been thinking, Vincent, and I want you to take the lead on this one.'

Vince gave a neutral nod. He could see that, with retirement looming, Mac wasn't losing his enthusiasm for the job; he was just ceding control, slowly but surely. All good murder detectives are ultimately control freaks: they like to have power over every aspect of the investigation. They're like the killers they hunt – they like to play God. Vince noted a melancholy in Mac's voice. This man was going to miss being a copper. Mac had his family, a wife and two daughters, one of them at a private school and the other at university. And he had his hobbies – reading and tending a garden in Friern Barnet that was alive with colourful roses – but he was already getting the jitters about retirement.

He wasn't one of those coppers who joined the force because of job security, early retirement and a handsome pension, or because he liked pushing his weight around. He did it because he loved and understood the art of detection. On his days off, when he sat in his easy chair smoking his pipe with a book in his lap, the book was invariably a work in the area of criminal psychology, the expanding field of forensic science, and occasionally a hard-boiled American detective novel. But they all had something to do with the crooked human condition and the unearthing of unpalatable truths. He'd lent Vincent various books over the last few months, the most recent being a work of fiction, *The Moonstone*. With its opium-induced otherness, Vince was surprised to learn that it was the book that first fired Mac's imagination as a kid. Vince hadn't got around to reading it himself yet, but he would.

Under Mac's tutelage, Vince felt that he was being well and truly schooled in the subtler, less prescriptive and more intuitive arts of detection. Mac wanted Vince to know what he knew and read what he read. He wanted to retire safe in the knowledge that Vince was going about things the way he would have done them himself. Of course, that could never be the case, as the two men were too different. But Vince appreciated the fact that Mac saw qualities in him that were worth nurturing, and made him worth passing the torch on to. And he knew Mac wanted him to take the lead in this case, possibly Mac's last, so he could gauge and critique his junior's performance. As Vince put these facts to himself, he gave an involuntary roll of his shoulders like a prize fighter, the young contender, limbering up and stepping into the ring.

As they approached the big house in Pont Street, there was a ripple of net curtains on the ground floor flat – always a good sign. Vince rang the bell but no one was in, or at least no one was answering. He went to press the bell again, when the front door sprang open and out she popped: the neighbour who policed the whole building and knew the movements of its every occupant. A walking, talking (far too much) and breathing burglar alarm and information bureau. Always in, always watching, always alert and, as far as the two detectives were concerned, manna from heaven. Vince let Mac deal with the old bird. And Mac, with a flash of his badge and some second-generation Irish charm, elicited all there was to know.

Isabel Saxmore-Blaine had not been seen in a month; she was away somwhere. Her younger brother, Dominic Saxmore-Blaine, had been staying there and was looking after the flat for her. There were lots of late-night comings and goings from the young man, who was just down from Oxford and obviously gadding about town and enjoying London's nightlife.

The nosy neighbour adjusted the eagle-eye-shaped glasses that were wedged on to her beaky nose, and wanted to know what was afoot. Mac, who had won the old crow over by now and had her eating out of his hand, spun her some enticingly harmless yarn, gave her his card, and told her to call that number as soon as Dominic Saxmore-Blaine turned up again. She chirped: 'You must think I spend my whole day at that window.'

Neither man answered that, but they knew she would be nailed to her perch, peering out through the gauzy net curtains and awaiting the return of Dominic Saxmore-Blaine, and would then get straight on the blower to report what she'd seen, hoping to quench her thirst for a narrative of other people's misfortunes.

As the two men walked back to the car, Vince suggested they take a quick look in at the Notting Hill caper, to see how Kenny Block and Philly Jacket were getting on.

'You're the boss,' said Mac, with a smile that suggested Vince was slipping easily into Mac's sure-footed and industrious steps.

CHAPTER 6

'Pretty girl.'

'She's a nurse – worked at Charing Cross Hospital.'

Vince stood with Mac and Philly Jacket in the communal hall-way of 27 Basing Street, now a taped-off crime scene. They were looking down at the face of Marcy Jones, who was strapped to a gurney that was about to be taken to the morgue. Her head had been covered by a blue paper cap, to mask and also preserve the horror of her skull injuries. All that was available to the detectives was therefore her face. But the masking of these injuries didn't extend to the walls or carpet of the hallway, which pretty well told the story. It looked like the scene of a massacre.

The three men were standing over the dead girl with heads bowed and hands clasped in front of them, as if they were offering up a prayer for her – and maybe they were. For as the news had filtered through that the victim had been a nurse, there was a collective sigh from them, in unconscious beatification of Marcy Jones.

Philly gave the two men attending the gurney the nod, and they moved it solemnly into the waiting black windowless limousine.

'Twenty-four years old,' said Philly Jacket. 'She's got an eight-year-old daughter.'

'Where's the kid now?' asked Mac.

'The neighbour said she usually stays with her grandmother when Marcy works night shifts at the hospital. We're contacting the grandmother now.'

'What was the weapon?' asked Vince.

'Pathologist says, for now, that the wound looks like a hammer blow. Struck with some force too. There was no messing about, and whoever did it meant to put her away for good. And it's no robbery, either. Her handbag was with her, and she had sixty pounds in her purse.'

This sum got raised eyebrows from Mac and Vince. They turned and walked up the stairs into the dead woman's flat, which turned out to be a maisonette taking up two floors. The lower part featured a decent-sized living room with a little dining room to one side, and a galley kitchen. Vince noted that the flat was in stark contrast to the scruffy communal hallway: it looked freshly decorated, with nice crisp curtains and fitted carpets. The three-piece suite looked plump and new, while the dining chairs still had their plastic coverings on the seats. Taking up pride of place in the living room was a shiny new Radio Rentals TV set in a faux walnut-finished cabinet. It looked as though nurse Marcy Jones must have been caning the HP.

A quickening clumping sound echoed up the stairs, and Kenny Block came huffing and puffing into the flat. Flushed and out of breath, he'd taken the steps three at a time. 'Guess what?' he asked, not waiting for an answer. 'Marcy's mother, Cecilia Jones, says Marcy didn't drop the kid off last night. She hasn't seen her since Thursday night, which was the last time Marcy worked a night shift at the hospital.'

'Marcy was dressed up,' noted Philly. 'High heels, nice dress, and she was wearing a wig too. Must have been out for the night?'

'Where's Cecilia Jones now?' asked Mac.

'With the doctor and two WPCs. She's in pieces. And she suffers with a heart condition. I thought she was going to keel over and fuckin' die on us.'

'Watch your mouth, Philly!'

'Sorry, Mac.'

'So who was looking after the kid?' Kenny and Philly shrugged heavily in unison. 'Looks like you've got an abduction on top of murder, maybe worse.'

'Before the doctor gave Cecilia Jones a sedative,' said Kenny, 'I got some interesting stuff from her. Seems Marcy used to go out with a right villainous spade called — and get this — Tyrell Lightly. Ring any bells?'

No bells rang, and it was certainly the kind of name that would ring them.

'How about this: Michael de Freitas?'

Vince clicked his fingers. 'That does. Real flash, used to dress like Al Capone — white fedora with a feather in it and snappy purple suits. He worked for Rachman, collecting rents and general terrorizing.'

Kenny Block: 'Tyrell Lightly got six years and the birch for cutting a PC who broke up a fight he was involved in on the All Saints Road. He got out of the Scrubs six months ago and got shipped back to Jamaica. He slipped back into the country three months ago. A right vicious little fucker, cut you to pieces if he got the chance.' Kenny looked at Mac, to check his language again. Mac was deep in thought, however. Kenny rightly assumed that Mac only disapproved of swearing in the context of talking about grandmothers and little girls. But blade-wielding rude boys who cut up coppers were ripe for some colourful language. 'Michael de Freitas has quite a little team working for him. They're into everything from screwing warehouses to controlling all the drug dealers in the area — plus he gets a pension from most of the spade pubs and clubs. De Freitas fancies himself the King of Notting Hill, and Tyrell Lightly does most of the heavy work for him.'

'So what was Marcy the nurse doing with a lowlife like him, Kenny?' asked Vince.

'Marcy met Lightly when she was still a kid, and they split up years ago, but Marcy's daughter Ruby is Lightly's. He didn't have anything to do with her until recently, but apparently he's been hanging around Marcy, trying to get back into her life. But, get this, Marcy was planning on moving out of London, as she has family in America . . .' Kenny Block consulted his notepad, 'living in a place called Trenton, New Jersey. Marcy was sure she could get work as a nurse out there, so she wanted to make a fresh start for herself and the kid. Lightly found out about that, and all of a sudden he didn't like the idea of losing his daughter, so he started making threats.'

Then, with a click of his fingers, Mac snapped out of his deliberation and took control. 'Okay, here's what we're going to do. We need to find out who Marcy Jones was out with last night . . .'

Vince left Mac in a huddle with the two detectives, and went upstairs to look about. A crayon drawing of a teddy bear tacked on to the door alerted Vince to Ruby's room. The teddy-bear theme carried on into the room itself, with teddy-bear wallpaper and hanging mobiles and lampshades. But there were other toys, lots of toys. In fact there was a piratic haul of goodies spilling out of a wooden toy chest in one corner of the room. Again, this all confirmed the presence of money coming into the house. In Marcy's bedroom there was a wardrobe with a full-length mirror as its centre panel. Vince checked himself out in it: he looked frayed. He hadn't slept in twenty-four hours, and the fuel of adrenalin and strong coffee was running its course, and exhaustion was catching up and kicking in. He sat down on the bed and could have easily sunk back on to it and caught forty winks. So he did, just to rest his eyes, until someone would call for him. As he lay back, the bed made a squeak. A squeak of surprise? A squeak of distress?

Vince sat up again quickly. Then he stood up and examined the bed. Around the mattress was a polyester covering as frilly as a petticoat and serving much the same decorous purpose. He lifted it up to expose a box-spring frame that included two concealed storage drawers. He then slipped his fingers into the groove that worked as a handle for one of the drawers, and gave it a tug. It wouldn't budge. He got down on his knees to get more leverage and yanked at it again. It opened a couple of inches, then quickly closed again. The bed was alive! Vince flipped the mattress off the bed, grabbed the drawer with both hands, put his back into it, and yanked it open. Inside the drawer, a stack of folded bed sheets quaked and quivered. Vince lifted the sheets gently and found the tear-streaked face of Ruby Jones.

She lay curled up in her burrow, as small as she could make herself, and peered up at Vince as if not knowing what to expect from him – because now she knew fully what grown-ups were capable of. The little girl squeezed her eyes shut. Salted tears had dried and crystallized to leave white powdery deposits on her hot brown skin, and she had soiled herself. As Vince lifted her out of the drawer, there was no resistance, no fight in her. Yet he felt a current of fear run through her that gave a tremulous hum to her sweat-soaked little body. She gripped her companion, a teddy bear with large button eyes, who looked equally terrified. Holding the little girl close, Vince closed his eyes and intoned softly, 'It's okay, it's okay, darling, you're safe . . . no one can hurt you now . . .'

But even as these words fell from his lips, they sounded implausibly hollow, even for impromptu words of comfort. And Vince had the feeling that such reassurances had come far too late for little Ruby Jones.

Far too late.

CHAPTER 7

The curtains twitched as Vince and Mac again approached Isabel Saxmore-Blaine's flat in Pont Street. The old bird in the ground-floor flat had come up trumps and phoned Mac's number to inform him that Dominic Saxmore-Blaine had re-entered the house. The message came just after a traumatized Ruby Jones had been taken off to hospital. It was clear she was suffering from severe shock, of a kind she might never escape from.

Before Vince had time to press the bell, the front door swung open, and there stood a thin-faced young man. On a hunch, Vince asked if he was Dominic Saxmore-Blaine. He confirmed that he was, and that he was just on his way out. Vince and Mac badged him.

Five minutes later, Dominic Saxmore-Blaine was perched on the scrolled arm of a long white sofa, holding a fully charged tumbler of whisky and soda, to steady his nerves, as he claimed. He'd just been given the news that Johnny Beresford was dead. It had been delivered in the solemn tone of informing the next of kin; and not with the urgency of chasing down his sister because she was the main suspect.

Vince considered the visibly shaken young man before him. He was about five foot nine and rail thin, all his features small and slender apart from his eyes, which were now large and startled. In fact, on further consideration, he had one of the narrowest faces Vince had ever seen; it looked as if it might snap in two if any-one punched it, though Dominic Saxmore-Blaine didn't look the type to get involved in that kind of rough and tumble. His hair was a stand-out feature, however: a sumptuous shade of chestnut brown with a shine that looked like a mirror finish; public-school floppy with one of those swooping fringes that constantly needed a vigorous half-head rotation, or a continuous raking with the hand, to keep it out of his eyes. Its impressive impracticality annoyed Vince; just looking at it made him want to reach for a pair of shears. But maybe that was the haircut's main purpose, its aesthetic flamboyance being a lesson in loucheness. The floppy foppishness of it matched the rest of his garb, for he was wearing a suit of deepest blue velvet, a waistcoat of mustard-yellow silk with gold braid blazingly checking through it, and a bow tie of flushed red taffeta. He'd obviously been out for the night, and still had the acrid tang of stale booze and oozing spirits wafting about him; which he was even now topping up with a generously poured single malt and a quick burst of soda. He drank deeply, then said, 'Poor, poor Isabel. She'll be devastated, absolutely devastated.'

'Where exactly is your sister, Mr Saxmore-Blaine?' asked Vince.

'She's been away staying with some friends.'

'For how long?'

'I don't really know . . .'

Vince, for the benefit of Saxmore-Blaine, creased his brow as if in confusion and threw a consorting look over to Mac, who was seated in a boxy-looking armchair. Mac played along with him, and batted back an equally confused glance that appeared more than a little tinged with disbelief.

Saxmore-Blaine picked up on this exchange, and was quick to continue: 'She was abroad, you see, for a few weeks, and then she came back . . . I think.' He put his whisky down on the side table, then put his head in his hands, sinking long fingers into the lustrously thick veil of his fringe. Then he scraped the whole lot back from his face to reveal red-rimmed eyes glistening with tears.

'I'm sorry, gentlemen, but I have to go out now. As I said, I'm meeting my father for lunch.'

Mac and Vince made no effort to move or indicate bringing the conversation to a close. Vince glanced down at his watch and saw it was just gone 1 p.m. Then he scoped the room: obviously not as luxurious and grand as Beresford's place, not fifteen minutes' walk away, but a nice set-up none the less. And it looked like the furniture and décor were chosen by Isabel herself, and not inherited off some aunt who had read Jane Austen on its first publication.

There were some big floor cushions scattered around, covered in panels of bright-coloured silk, while lots of Aztec and Mexican-style throws covered the furniture. On the floor lay Moroccan and Indian rugs with naps so deep you could hide out in them. Around the room were other knick-knacks and ornaments from those countries too, like the large bronze figure of the elephant-headed Indian god Ganesh sitting heavily on the mantelpiece. Running up one of the walls was a range of fine pencil drawings of ballet dancers, and a large bookcase was bulging with paperback and reference books on dance, fashion, travel and the arts. There was a modern glass and chromium-tubed desk against a wall, with a blue Underwood 5 typewriter resting on it alongside a well-thumbed *OED*, a frazzled-looking *Roget's Thesaurus*, and stacks of text-covered typing paper. Next to the desk was a long magazine rack packed with glossies. On almost every available flat surface stood framed photos featuring Isabel Saxmore-Blaine on her travels, and invariably posing with Johnny Beresford. She was decorously draped around him in exotic and expensive locations, and they made for quite an eye-catching couple. Dressed up or dressed down, caught mid-laughter or unawares, from every angle she looked as though she oozed class. It was as plain as the perfectly poised nose on her face that this woman was on very good terms with the camera – it lapped her up.

'May I ask,' said Vince, picking up a picture of the happy couple on holiday in Sardinia, 'how long had Mr Beresford and your sister been going out with each other?'

The swathe of Dominic Saxmore-Blaine's hair was yet again hiding half his face. Vince glanced briefly at Mac, as if to check with him what the rules were regarding annoying haircuts, but from Mac's neutral expression, apparently there weren't any. Vince would soon change all that once he ruled the world, but right now he contented himself with watching as Saxmore-Blaine did the mental calculation, then his pinched little mouth twitched into life as he spoke.

'Oh, gosh, let me see. They met around about the time I first went up to Oxford . . . so about three years now.'

Vince put the photo back on the shelf. 'It's very important that we talk to your sister soon. Do you have the phone number of the address she's staying at?'

'No . . . no I don't.'

'You're staying here in her flat, yet you don't have a number to contact her? Not even in an emergency?'

'I'm sorry, but she always calls me, you see, so I don't. I'm sorry.'

Vince noticed that Mac was noisily lighting up a Chesterfield, almost as a means of disguising the fact that he too didn't believe a word he was hearing. 'Okay, Mr Saxmore-Blaine,' said Vince, reaching into his jacket pocket and handing him his card, 'when you next talk to your sister, can you tell her to call us straight away?'

'Yes, of course I will.'

Dominic Saxmore-Blaine stood up and walked the two police-men to the door. Vince turned sharply to face him and said, 'You're not driving, are you, Mr Saxmore-Blaine? Because it's recom-mended that if you've been drinking, you really shouldn't drive. Apparently they're even thinking of bringing in laws against it.'

'No, no, of course not. I'll get a taxi.'

'Where are you meeting your father?'

'The Ritz.'

'Of course. We happen to be going right past Piccadilly, right, Detective McClusky?'

'Right past it, Detective Treadwell.'

'We'll give you a lift.'

Dominic Saxmore-Blaine did that annoying thing with his hair again, a sharp upward jolt of the head, and, for good measure, dealt it a double scrape back with both hands. 'No, no, but thanks. That's awfully kind, but I need to get changed first, you see.'

Vince made a show of checking out young Dominic Saxmore-Blaine's duds – and, yes, he could see that. They left him to it.

Vince and Mac sat in the Mk II opposite the Pont Street flat, waiting for Dominic Saxmore-Blaine to emerge.

'You allowed him a choice,' said Mac, shaking his head.

'I know that.'

'Why?'

'Because, "Can you give me your sister's number?" is a leading question, because I've made the assumption that he does have her number, because it's a logical conclusion – because of course he does. By posing the question, "*Do* you have her number?", there's no assumption, no following logic, and he has a choice. And it's the choice he then makes that nails him.' Vince studied Mac's reaction; the older detective smiled and nodded in agreement. 'But you knew all that already, right, Mac?'

Mac lit a Chesterfield and said: 'She's quite a looker.'

Vince rolled down the window. 'Who?'

'The big sister – who else?'

'Really? I didn't notice.'

'*Really?* I thought you were about to eat her picture.'

'I noticed something else, too. She had lots of photos of Beresford there, but I didn't see any of her in his house. And it's a big house.'

'That's right. And they've been seeing each other for three years – but not so much as engaged? And she's twenty-six. They get broody at that age.'

Vince gave a slow distracted nod at this; not that he necessarily agreed with Mac's old-world view, but in this case he could find no strong opposition to it either, because Isabel Saxmore-Blaine and Johnny Beresford fitted it so well. They seemed to represent the embodiment of the establishment. And another thought had occurred to Vince, too: Isabel Saxmore-Blaine was the kind of girl you'd get a ring on as quickly as possible. But what distracted Vince from voicing all this was the sight of Dominic Saxmore-Blaine trotting down the steps in the exact same outfit he was wearing when they left him fifteen minutes earlier. Just as they had predicted. What took him so long, they suspected, was the phone call he'd been making to his sister.

Despite the advice that Vince had given him, Dominic got into a car, a snappy little Volkswagen Type 14 Karmann Ghia – badly let down by the colour orange. They followed him west, out of central London towards Hounslow and into London Airport. The sky was criss-crossed with the contrails of aeroplanes, some solid as sky writing, some fading like old smoke signals. In Vince's immediate scope of vision he saw one plane lethargically coming in for landing whilst another was sedately nosing its way along for take-off; both in miraculous slow motion and both looking about as capable of flight as a pair of fat bumblebees in a beer garden.

At a safe distance, Vince managed to slip the Mk II in behind Saxmore-Blaine's little orange car as they wound their way up the spiralling concrete ramp of the newly built multi-storey car park. At the top level, Vince stopped at the brink of the entrance to check where the Karmann Ghia was, and saw it was making its first turn around the central reservation of parked vehicles. The car park was less than a quarter full and, much as Vince was hit with a sudden urge to floor the Mk II and hear the screech of tyres on the smooth concrete as he tore around the first bend like Fangio, he didn't. He drifted slowly around, stalking his prey silently, not alerting Dominic Saxmore-Blaine to their presence.

And there sat Isabel Saxmore-Blaine in a white, two-seater Sunbeam Alpine, with the roof down. Dominic slowed his car and parked next to her. She gave a perfunctory smile to her younger brother, but the tenuous grip the smile had on her lips quickly fell away as she saw Vince and Mac in the slowing Mk II. Paranoid and prepared for the worst, she had them pegged as coppers the minute she clocked them. Even in the grey concrete light of the car park, Vince could see that the refined, unflappable features of Isabel Saxmore-Blaine looked tense and tormented, like she was tuned to alert, and *everyone* looked like a copper.

She bent down to pick up a red patent-leather handbag, and flipped its interlocking double-G-shaped metal clasp.

Her brother, probably still groggy from the night before, and unaware that Vince was right behind him, went to get out of his car. Isabel, meanwhile, had found what she wanted in the bag, and pulled out a .32 snub-nosed Colt revolver.

Vince slammed on the brakes and boxed in the Alpine.

Dominic Saxmore-Blaine shouted, 'Izzy . . . NO!' as Isabel took the revolver and stuck the stubby muzzle in her mouth, as though she was sucking on a straw.

Vince was out of the car and running over to her. Mac followed.

As Isabel glanced up briefly from this suicidal pose, she saw Vince running towards her and her eyes widened. Then her finger curled around the trigger. She squeezed her eyes shut.

Vince dived for her head first, his clenched fist extended and leading the way before him.

The report from the gun cracked and echoed around the concrete cavern of the car park with the sharpness of a rimshot drum roll.

CHAPTER 8

Five days later, Vince sat at his desk reading William Hickey's lead on the Beresford murder in the *Daily Express*. The column was written in that high-and-dry gossipy style so favoured by society columnists, as though the ordinary world didn't apply to them. Vince skimmed the facts: sketchy as they were, they laid out a précis of the two principal players in the scandal that was playing out. Beresford had all the advantages life had to offer, expensively educated at Eton, off to Sandhurst, then serving without much distinction in the Guards. He did better in the City, making money and filling further the family's already abundant coffers. But he earned his real reputation on the green-baize gambling tables of London and Europe, as a ferocious and fearless and, more importantly, winning gambler. As a staunch member and stalwart of the Montcler Club and considered very much part of their 'set', he played and beat some of the richest and most powerful men in the world.

Isabel Saxmore-Blaine's family stock, and her life, seemed to mirror that of her 'victim'. She was educated at Cheltenham College, but a promising career as a dancer with the Royal Ballet was stalled after an injury. She moved to America, her mother's home country, and took a degree at the prestigious Vassar College in upstate New York. She then took up journalism and became a respected art correspondent for *Tatler* magazine, and a free-lancer for various other upmarket publications. Her father, now a widower, came from a long line of distinguished ambassadors and diplomats, and had himself been ambassador to Washington for five years, before retiring and going on to become a royal equerry. Murder at such close quarters to the Queen?

Vince put down the paper. There was more, lots more, but after the initial facts it spiralled downwards into salaciousness and innuendo, and looked as if it was gearing up to become the next Profumo Affair.

What became apparent to Vince was that, as well as the expensive education and all the other goodies of her gilded life, what money and privilege really seemed to buy Isabel Saxmore-Blaine was that most luxurious of gifts: time. For any normal citizen it would have been a couple of aspirin and then down to some gruelling questioning. Because Vince's fist had hit its target and knocked the gun out of Isabel's mouth, and knocked her out cold. With the hammer cocked, when the gun was punched out of her hand it hit the door and a shot was fired into the dashboard – not through the back of her skull.

But it was pretty clear – from the doctors' reports, the psychologists' reports and the journalists' reports – that Isabel Saxmore-Blaine had problems other than a bruised jaw. She was a depressive and a lush who had admitted to an addiction to pills of every description: uppers, downers, prescription painkillers, the works. Even though she was on suicide watch, and under sedation on doctor's orders, in a private Harley Street hospital, details, stories, background and gossip about the case kept being leaked to the press – and all of them in her favour, running along the lines that Beresford was a bully who was violent towards her. Add that to the swelling tide of medical records documenting the state of her mental health, and it looked like, by the time she woke up from her stupor, she would have a well-marshalled argument claiming self-defence against aggravated physical provocation, with diminished responsibility thrown into the mix. Even though the motive and circumstances were all in place – it was the end of the romance, they got drunk and fought and, in the *Sturm und Drang* of it all, she had somehow managed to put a bullet in her about-to-be-ex-lover's head – Isabel Saxmore-Blaine still looked like walking free.

It seemed to Vince a perverse and cruel paradox that, while Miss Saxmore-Blaine was being kept silent under the chemical cosh in a private clinic whilst her expensive lawyers could rustle up a defence, little Ruby Jones was in hospital, mute through shock, and as the days slipped by it was becoming easier for her mother's killer to get away.

All attention in CID's Incident Room was focused on the Marcy Jones case. Prime suspect Tyrell Lightly was nowhere to be found. Rumour was he'd fled the country and was now back in his 'yard' in Jamaica. Rumour also was he'd got 'politics' and fled to South America, to fight on the front line. Rumour was he'd ended up in the cement being used for the new Westway flyover they were building.

'Got some news for you, Vince!'

Vince broke out of his reverie to see Doc Clayton standing before him. The good doctor grabbed up the newspaper lying on Vince's desk and turned to the racing section. Vince grabbed the paper back.

'I want to see what price they've got for Arkle in the Gold Cup!'

'It's the favourite, no value. What news, Doc?'

'Forensics found another set of prints on the gun.'

'Yeah?'

'Partial prints mind, but prints none the less. They belong to Beresford.'

Vince frowned. 'How's that news? It was his gun.'

'It's news because we also found carbon traces, gunpowder, on his trigger finger. Fresh ones, too. Which would strongly suggest that he himself fired the gun that night.'

Vince considered this point. As Doc Clayton awaited Vince's opinion, he couldn't help himself from grabbing up the paper again to check the racing section. Vince let him read it whilst he theorized, and postulated: 'So, Isabel and Beresford got drunk together. They had an argument. Beresford gets a gun, waves it about for dramatic effect, maybe fires it into a wall to scare her? And then Isabel clobbers him with the champagne bottle . . . snatches the gun and puts one in his head?'

'Sounds good to me,' said Doc Clayton, eyes still fixed on the racing page.

'But why move the body?' asked Vince, grabbing back the paper. Only a big fat shrug from Doc Clayton. 'And not only why move the body, but how? Beresford is six foot something and weighs in at fourteen stone something else. She's five foot eight and catwalk skinny. There's no way she could have lifted his dead weight and moved him. And anyway she was drunk and stoned.'

Doc Clayton arched a doubtful eyebrow over his wiry spectacles. 'You'd be surprised at the reserves of strength the human body has. If she really did shoot him, she would have been running high on adrenalin. There's lots of cases of people gaining three, four times their natural strength in a situation where their fear levels are raised. Or if their life is in danger. It's known as dynamic tension.'

'Like a pumped-up athlete?'

'Exactly! They say that's why the Russians are so good in the Olympics, because they're scared they'll end up in Siberia if they lose!'

'What does Mac say about it?'

'He says to refer everything to you first, as you're running the case.'

Vince smiled, swung his feet off his desk, and picked up the paper and ditched it in the wastepaper bin. 'Okay, let's get a team down to Beresford's place and try and find that bullet.'

Vince and Doc Clayton were able to rustle up three PCs, and two forensics, and headed to Eaton Square. First of all they swept the ground-floor living room where Isabel and Beresford had their little party and, predictably enough to Vince, found nothing. And then they concentrated on the basement study where Beresford's body had been found. However much Vince bought into Doc Clayton's theory of her adrenalized body gaining extra strength, he doubted that Isabel could sustain the amount of strength necessary to drag the corpse out of the drawing room, along the hallway, down the stairs and into the study. And, with the bloody head wound he had incurred, she certainly couldn't have done so without leaving some kind of visible trail.

In the study, Vince and the team fine-toothed the room wall to wall, floor to ceiling. They even took down the books from the shelves to see if the bullet had got lodged in any of the tomes, which mostly dealt with history, finance, military exploits, hunting and fishing and shooting and gambling, along with a twenty-four piece leather-bound encyclopedia and some signed copies of Ian Fleming's James Bond adventures. But, fitting as that might have been, there were no bullets to be found in 007. Vince got up on a ladder to give the two mounted stags a quick autopsy, to check that neither of the poor souls had copped for yet another bullet. Every inch of the room was searched, and nothing found. Far from the case being cut and dried, Vince was determined – family money or no money, personal contact with the Queen or not – to wake up Sleeping Beauty and ask her the questions that needed to be asked.

Before Vince left the room, he was drawn again to the photograph of Beresford and his five friends at the Montcler Club. He suspected he might be needing it, so he took the photo out of its cantilevered silver frame and slipped it in his pocket.

CHAPTER 9

It was around 5 p.m. when Vince parked the Mk II in Kensington Church Street and walked towards Notting Hill Gate. For the last three days and nights, he had been hanging around the same area to pick up whatever information he could on Tyrell Lightly. Photos of him showed a snappily attired Negro with sharp good looks, a pencil moustache, and a petulant slyness in his eyes. Back home in Kingston, Jamaica, Tyrell Lightly had put his looks to good use as the lead singer in a calypso outfit called the Gayboys. He was a heartthrob crooner by night, but by day he was a gun-toting rude boy aligned to the Spanish Town Posse. Like all the Jamaican gangs, the STP had politics in their blood, as well as other rackets, and they composed the muscle behind the right-wing Jamaican Labour Party, and were in charge of getting the vote out. When the JLP lost the '57 elections to their main rival, the left-wing People's National Party, the Spanish Town Posse – and Tyrell Lightly in particular – had left too many bodies lying on the street to be brushed under the carpet, and had made too many widows and too many enemies to be given a government pardon. So Tyrell Lightly had swapped Jamaica for England, Kingston for London and Trenchtown for Notting Hill. He'd stopped crooning by then and was now pure muscle: a bantam-weight of wiry knife-wielding venom poured into an electric-blue tonic suit topped off with a red felt Homburg hat sporting a peacock feather.

Vince had been regularly visiting places like Frank Crichlow's El Rio Café at 127 Westbourne Park Road, where West Indian and white kids hung out together and listened to the new Blue Beat and Ska craze on one of the best-stocked jukeboxes in London. Other favoured haunts, such as the Calypso and the Fiesta One Club, both on Westbourne Grove, were equally busy with hustlers and players. Then you had Johnny Edgcombe's Dive Bar on the Talbot Road, a jazz club that seemed to never close, and was a favourite with both the artist and the junkie crowd. And not forgetting either all the shebeens in Elgin Crescent, Latimer Road and Oxford Gardens. All these were establishments that Tyrell Lightly's boss, Michael de Freitas, either ran, had an interest in or took a 'pension' from. Vince even played a hand or two in a de Freitas-run spieler in a basement on the Talbot Road, so he blended in easily with the crowd.

To the rest of England, after the so-called '58 race riots where a couple of hundred white Teddy boys gathered under the lightning-bolt symbol of British fascist banners, and started beating up as many black people as they could find, Notting Hill was seen as a no-go area for, ironically, white people. In reality the disturbance just fired everyone's imagination and it became *the* place to go. At any given time, in those illicitly smoking rooms, it was packed with writers, artists, models, musicians, film people and thrill seekers of every description, from well-heeled Chelsea-ites slumming to East End villains exploring fresh territories and letting their Brylcreemed hair down.

Detectives Kenny Block and Philly Jacket thought Vince was wasting his time, for Lightly was bound to have skipped Notting Hill, skipped London if not the country, and was probably back in the yards of Kingston. But Vince wasn't so sure: sometimes hiding out in plain view was the best place of all. Lightly would feel safe in Notting Hill, and also his boss, Michael de Freitas, had the money and the muscle to protect him. Outside Notting Hill, Tyrell Lightly was just another 'spade', but in that de Freitas-run fiefdom – the City of Spades – Tyrell Lightly was if not himself the king, then certainly close enough to him to feel secure. So Vince decided to pay the king a visit.

But there was something else grabbing Vince's attention in that area. He'd spotted it three days ago in a music store on the Bayswater Road, near Notting Hill Gate. The shop girl had taken it off the shelf for him, and shown him how to apply his curled bottom lip and puckered upper lip to the beak of the instrument. After some huffing and puffing, nothing came out, so she told him to relax. He relaxed, and pretended he was Bird, Art Pepper, Trane, Sonny Stitt . . . and out it came. Just the one note. But it was enough. He was hooked. He wanted more. In his mind's eye he was already headlining at Ronnie Scott's. For aesthetic reasons alone, the alto saxophone was a winner, so damn cool. Bold and brassy, it hung in front of you and curled upwards like a king cobra about to bite. It wasn't cheap, but it was necessary. Learning an instrument was on his list of things he must do before he died; along with learning another language, and a slew of other things that tuned in and out depending on his mood. But the instrument and the language were two constants.

As Vince looked longingly at the alto sax in the window, the girl in the shop saw him and invited him to have another go. Vince explained that he was still just at the looking and longing stage, and needed more time to flirt with his potential new paramour. So he resisted going in, and just stood at the window ogling the shapely and brassy object of desire, until the girl put up the 'closed' sign.

Night was closing in as Vince made his way down the Portobello Road. The market stalls were being dismantled, wooden crates were being stacked, trestle tables were being folded and vans were being loaded; and all very loudly as the stallholders got in their last bits of banter to entertain the street and passing traffic. The light from the pubs and late night shops and restaurants and chippies kept the bustling centipede of the Portobello Road alive as, one by one, its multiple legs led off sideways to

Colville Terrace, Elgin Crescent, Talbot Road, and then the turning Vince wanted, Cambridge Gardens.

At this end of Notting Hill, things got slow and slummy. The shops and the lights died out and it was now tall terraced houses in various states of disrepair and the new low-rise concrete council blocks that already looked as if they were in rehearsals for becoming urban blight. Next to a brightly painted corner shop that sold everything from booze to bath salts stood another shop. This one was painted black and had a heavy black curtain covering the window – it was about as inviting as a funeral director's. The gold-letter writing on the window stated its intent: *The Notting Hill Brothers & Sisters Letting Agency – Incorporating Your One Stop Community Shop*. The letting agency/community shop stayed open till well past midnight, under the guise of serving as a local advice centre.

Vince had heard that this was Michael de Freitas' HQ, and not the spieler in Powis Terrace as everyone thought. Downstairs, he ran his burgeoning property empire, whilst upstairs he conducted card games, dice and dominoes. From here he also ran a bookmaking operation that ran unhindered by other West London villains because it catered for black punters only; and a private taxi and limousine service that delivered drugs and stunning black whores all over the city.

Vince remembered Michael de Freitas well, a tall Trinidadian with narrow suspicious eyes that were shaded by a heavy frowning brow. On a broad chin he bore the scars picked up in chiv fights, which he covered with a goatee beard that wrapped around a wide mouth that seemed to be permanently set in a scowl. His face was worn like a frightening mask, which for his purposes – having started out as muscle for the slum landlord Peter Rachman – served him well. Faced with Mikey de Freitas banging down the door, people did as they were told, which was either pay up, sell up or shut up! Before Rachman died in '62, he looked down favourably on the Trinidadian tearaway who had collected his rents and evicted people with such terrifying efficiency, and bequeathed him around twenty of his one hundred and fifty properties in the area. And now, with all his other rackets, Michael de Freitas was surely chewing on the fat end of a good few quid.

Black doors on dark nights, with no one around and only the low hellish sodium glow of orange street lights, are always a little intimidating. They reminded Vince of the great void, the end, and something you don't really want to go through. Standing at the door, Vince could hear laughter and the sound of dominoes being slammed down on a table, and sensed the rustle of money changing hands. *Them bones, them bones, them crazy bones!* What was traditionally seen as an old man's game played in backstreet boozers was a different proposition in these boys' hands. Like with mah-jong games in Chinatown, big money was played on the laying down of a tile. Vince rang the bell, then peered through the small round spy-hole in the glossily painted black door – and saw the light from inside quickly eclipsed. After the few seconds it took for the report to be carried back, the sound of laughter and dominoes stopped.

Vince counted to ten, then questioned if pitching up here on his own was such a good idea. He decided it probably wasn't – then had the decision taken out of his hands as the door opened. At around six foot, Vince was no midget, but he felt like one as he craned his head skywards to look up at the man in front of him. He was big and black, seven foot if he was an inch. With that height he could have been one of the Harlem Globetrotters – with that height he could have been two of them. His bigness and blackness was made to look all the more big and black because he was so unrelentingly swathed in it too: clad in a long leather trench coat and capped with a black beret. Though worn at an angle, the beret wasn't of the jaunty French type; it was the serious military kind. Dusk had dutifully departed and it was now officially night, but the tall boy was wearing sunglasses. No light from inside the building escaped because the solid figure was fitted into the doorway as tight as a jigsaw piece in a puzzle. Vince dispensed with the introductions and badged him. The man then stepped back and closed the door. This wordless exchange seemed surreal, so Vince decided to knock again and, this time, say something. But before he could do so, the door opened again and 'Tiny' – for that proved to be his nickname – gestured for Vince to come in. Not wanting to be considered a mute, Vince said, 'Thanks very much.'

The office looked about as innocuous as any cheap letting agency or advice centre he'd ever been in. There were two desks, with chairs in front of them, and chest-high filing cabinets. Overhead, strip lighting hummed away and made everything look jaundiced. On one wall was a large cork board holding a map of the local area with multicoloured thumbtacks dotted around; these were, Vince assumed, to mark properties that Michael de Freitas owned or had an interest in. Vince scanned the map for as long as possible, whilst trying to appear as if he hadn't even noticed it. He saw that there was an impressive number of pins spread liberally around the neighbourhood, with the largest cluster around the Tabernacle Church area of Powis Square, Powis Terrace, Talbot Road and Colville Terrace.

Also on the walls, besides a scattering of posters advertising local community events and flats and houses for rent, were framed photos of black leaders. Included in their serried ranks were Marcus Garvey, Elijah Muhammad, Dr Martin Luther King, Muhammad Ali and, taking pride of place, Malcolm X.

Vince looked down from the photos and towards the six men occupying the office. Like Tiny, they were all dressed in black, all wearing sunglasses. As unpleasant as the strip lighting might be, the wraparound shades really weren't, by any means, necessary. But in these surroundings, it wasn't they who looked incongruous. As the only white man and wearing a suit, it was Vince who looked like the enemy.

Two 'soldiers' were standing directly in front of one of the two desks, with arms folded, like a Praetorian guard blocking Vince's view of the man he was sure sat behind it.

'Police officer,' came the disembodied voice of the man sitting there, 'explain yourself and your presence here.'

'I'm Detective Vince Treadwell, Scotland Yard, and who are you?' asked Vince, knowing full well the who.

At that, the two men moved apart like a curtain to reveal the main player on the stage: Michael de Freitas himself. It was a theatrical unveiling and one, Vince suspected, that might well have been specially rehearsed for just such an event. Michael de Freitas was dressed in the same garb as the other men, and wearing the same black sunglasses. Vince looked for stripes on his black leather jacket, to signify his leading General status, but there weren't any. Nevertheless, it was clear he held the power in this room. He hadn't changed much since Vince had seen him last, being hauled into Shepherd's Bush station for questioning in connection with a murder. Nothing had stuck. But Michael de Freitas' reputation on the streets had ballooned after that incident, giving the real verdict as to his guilt or innocence. He was a light-skinned black man (just like his fellow revolutionary up on the wall above him, Malcolm X), his face now a little fuller, the goatee bushier and his hair longer and more natty. But the duds had definitely changed since then: the look was now Che Guevara revolution-ary, Marxist chic, rather than the rude boy gangster style of a few years back. The man looked relaxed and regally confident, sitting there in his high-backed black-padded swivel chair, his hands laced together in front of him.

'Mikey de Freitas,' confirmed Vince, with a smile and nod of recognition.

'Michael X,' he corrected with a steady and determined shake of his head.

'X?'

'You heard me, policeman. X. Just like my brother.' He gestured vaguely towards the framed photos on the wall.

Vince, without being invited, pulled up a chair and sat oppo-site Michael X. He glanced up at the photos on the wall again, his eyes falling admiringly on the picture of the handsome young world heavyweight champ. The victor stood over Sonny Liston, who lay sprawled on the canvas as the Louisville Lip goaded and mocked him. Vince looked back to Michael X and asked: 'Has Cassius Clay changed his name again?'

There was a collective and violent sucking of teeth, indicating a chorus of disapproval from all gathered there. Michael X unclasped his hands and pointed specifically to a framed photo of the *other* man, the original X, a smooth-looking Malcolm X in dark glasses and a slick suit.

Vince continued his wind-up. 'I had tickets for the Cooper fight, but I couldn't make it. Henry and his left hook put on quite a showing, but Clay—'

'There ain't no Cassius Clay!'

'Oh yeah, I forgot.'

'Cassius Clay was his slave name.'

'Sorry, Mikey—'

'And there is no *Mikey* either. Mikey de Freitas is dead – or should I say emancipated. And we will no longer be subjugated to the white colonization. We will return to the real power, the germination of mankind, the original source and a new truth . . .'

Vince glanced around the room. Heads were nodding in a harmonious rhythm of approval and accord. The giant Tiny was still standing by the door, an ominous and immovable slab blocking his exit. Vince spotted, in the corner of the room, a cardboard box housing a stack of black berets still in their plastic covers, and at least a gross of black sunglasses. Black Power had crossed the pond and reached Notting Hill, and they were obviously in recruitment mode. It looked as though this was going to be a long hot summer. As Michael X continued talking, Vince noted that he had now lost some of the relaxed patois of his Caribbean accent. His voice was clearly focused. He was getting into his stride now, and limbering up for some rousing rhetoric.

'. . . a new truth brought to us by the minister, the honourable Elijah Muhammad.' Michael X pointed to another framed photo on the wall of an older, almost oriental-looking man in a grey suit and a white bow tie, and wearing what looked like a fez but without the fringed tassel and embroidered with a crescent moon cradling a star. He continued. 'And we will smite those who will hold us back, the white oppressors, and the white Jewish conspiracy that has funded the world to enslave the black man and keep us down and send us chained to our graves. We will no longer be bound to the corrupt power of this evil axis, if you will. All corruption turns in on itself, festers, putrefies, and that is why we turn away from you and your mores, your corrupt white Christian and Zionist values. We will face Mecca. We shall speak of Allah. We shall speak of the truth. We shall speak of peace. We shall speak of freedom. We shall speak of revolution!'

Vince thought he was 'speaking' altogether too much, and wanted to suggest that he shut the fuck up and listen for five seconds. But he was clearly in the minority with this thought, so he wisely kept it to himself, at least until the full force of Michael X's diatribe, and the ensuing chorus of cheers exploding into the room, had subsided. For, right now, Vince was feeling incredibly white and slightly oppressed.

'Tyrell Lightly. Where is he?' he eventually asked.

'He's dead,' said Michael X.

'Yeah? Who killed him?'

'You did! The white oppressor!'

Not only did Vince roll his eyes at this, but he made an obvious play of rolling his eyes at this. With the oratory now on offer, he could have seen that one coming a mile off.

Unabashed, Michael X continued: 'Brother Lightly, too, is a follower of the righteous and the honourable Elijah Muhammad. He too is a Brother X. And until we find our real names, and write them in blood in Somerset House . . . until that time comes we shall all be known as X. Dig?'

They all dug. Some deeper than others, but they all dug. And they were all cheering again. Digging and cheering.

'If X marks the spot, he shouldn't be too hard to find then,' punned Vince, once the cheering had subsided. 'So why don't you just tell me where he is and we can save us all a lot of time by me not coming back here with more officers to turn the place over?'

'What do you want with Brother Lightly?'

Like he didn't already know. Vince dutifully filled him in. 'We need to talk to him regarding the murder of Marcy Jones.'

'Yet again the white wolf is at our door, hunting us down and baying for our blood.'

'Tyrell Lightly's no Goldilocks.'

'Brother Tyrell has sinned in the past – and he is the first to admit it. We are none of us without sin, Detective Vince Treadwell. We are all fallen. But now . . . now we are engaged in a greater struggle than personal wealth. We are concerned with change. He is an innocent man, and you, the police, are determined to put him behind bars. And we, his brothers, are determined that this shall not happen. The brothers will clean up these streets and we will bring about our own justice. We will not tolerate criminality in our community; that is not the black man's role in this world! That is a role forced upon us by the white infidels, and we shall not be subject to oppressive white law and to white corruption!'

Getting predictable now, getting sickening, more cheers, more 'Right on, brother's.

Vince thought it was his turn for some righteous indignation and tub-thumping. 'You want to clean up the streets, be my guest. Let's start with Marcy Jones, shall we? She had her head turned inside out with a ball-peen hammer. We counted six whacks to the head. Brains all over the hallway. How are you going to police that, *Mikey*?'

The loquacious Michael X had nothing to say on the subject. He angled his head up to regard his great leader and namesake on the wall. Vince followed his gaze. He could see the attraction to the original X: his charisma, intelligence and sense of purpose, by any means necessary, shone out from the photograph. Vince felt those qualities weren't necessarily present in all his followers – Michael X here being one of them.

'Marcy Jones was a nurse, did you know that?' said Vince. Still the great mouthpiece stayed tight-lipped. 'I hear Tyrell is quite the ladies' man and, the way I see it, a young, impressionable Marcy fell for the dashing gangster around town and ended up having a kid with him. No problem for Tyrell Lightly, he's sired a few in his time, so we hear. But Lightly doesn't like it when Marcy grows up and doesn't want to know him any more. Then he goes away for cutting up a copper. She's a smart girl, and she wants what's best for her kid, so she follows her childhood ambition and trains to become a nurse. She works hard and makes something of herself, makes her mother proud. She decides she wants a better life for herself and her daughter, so she decides to leave Notting Hill, make a fresh start so that her daughter won't make the same mistakes that she made and get hooked up with a lowlife like Tyrell Lightly.'

And still the otherwise verbose Michael X said nothing, but Vince could sense that the relaxed, controlled demeanour was tensing and tightening up. 'Michael X' was a new persona that Michael de Freitas was still working on, and it was a far cry from the edgy and energized gangster of a few years back; the metamorphosis from cutting-edge capitalist to conscience-ridden activist was not yet complete. The rackets he was still running were all testament to that, though he'd probably justify them as 'any means necessary' for funding the revolutionary coffers. But Vince had a gut feeling that Michael de Freitas, with the new beard and glasses combo, was just in fancy dress, like one of those all-in-one Groucho Marx disguises you get in joke shops. Yeah, definitely more Groucho than Karl, thought Vince, as he leaned in and put his arms on the table and knitted his fingers together. He could hear the men behind him rearranging themselves, but into what? Something violent? He didn't know, because he was too busy eyeballing Michael X behind his wraparound shades.

He said: 'Marcy's little daughter, eight years old, she witnessed the whole thing. She's in shock and she's not saying anything now, but she will. So, again, why don't you save us all some time and tell me where Tyrell Lightly is?'

'It's a fit-up.'

'Is this the party line?' Silence. Vince smirked. 'Talking about revolutions, Mikey, I wouldn't get your hopes up. Karl Marx used to live in Soho, so he knew a thing or two about England and the English. He said the best way to stop a revolution in this country would be to put up a sign saying it had been cancelled. But you're not kidding me, you're just a dope-peddling pimp in a fancy-dress costume.'

Vince could feel heat coming off Michael X as he briefly turned back into Mikey de Freitas. His heavy brow furrowed, his jaw jutted and he hunched over and grabbed the table edges with both hands as if to rip it up from the floor. Then he uttered, in a lethally hushed tone, 'Kill ya fwar dat . . .'

Vince's goading smirk widened into a victorious smile. 'That's more like it, Mikey. Now you're talking.'

Mikey said nothing as he took on board some much needed calming breaths and slowly composed himself. And after the composition was complete, he was back to being Michael X. He opened the desk drawer and slipped his hand inside.

On seeing this, Vince shifted in his seat and surreptitiously did likewise and slipped his hand into his coat pocket, where his fingers curled around the hilt and his thumb rubbed the button of the switchblade he was carrying. Not exactly standard government issue, but only a fool would come looking for Mikey de Freitas and Tyrell Lightly without a tool of some kind.

Michael X pulled out from the drawer a pair of black leather gloves and slipped them over his hands, then stood up slowly. Vince stood up with him, slowly. Michael X raised his clenched fist in the air. Vince heard a dull thud and a muttered curse, and he looked round at the men behind him. They were all standing in the same position, with fists raised in salute. The dull thud and the muttered curse had come from Tiny, who had almost put his fist through the ceiling.

CHAPTER 10

With news of the revolution still ringing in his ears, Vince left Michael X and his Brothers and made the rounds of the pubs and clubs in the area, hoping the confrontational cop-cutter Tyrell Lightly would have heard that Vince was after him, and wouldn't be able to resist showing his face. But that produced nothing, not a whisper. It was around ten p.m. when Vince decided to call it a night and walked back to his car, thinking about, of all things, the alto sax. Did he have the time to learn how to play the thing? Did he have the patience to learn how to play the thing? Or was it just going to sit in a corner of the room looking like a glitzy ornament, a conversation piece?

Then he caught a break. Standing on the corner of the Portobello Road, outside the Finches pub, was Vivian Chalcott. Vince and Vivian had followed each other's careers closely, in as much as Vince had had the pleasure of nicking Vivian at every turn in his career. The last time was while pimping in Soho for a Maltese firm, running a couple of black brasses out of two rooms in Berwick Street. And here he was now, standing on the street corner and up to no good. This wasn't just Vince being judgemental; this was him witnessing Vivian standing on the street corner and leaning into a Ford Zephyr and handing over a wrap of cannabis and getting paid for it. Vince knew he was on to a winner with this one. He waited for the transaction to pass, then collared him. Literally. By lifting the pint-sized drug dealer off the pavement and putting him against the wall, suspended by the felt of his collar.

'Well well well, Mr Treadwell . . .'

'Hello hello hello, Vivian,' said the laughing policemen as he rifled the dealer's pockets and pulled out a bag of ten golden cubes of finest Moroccan. 'What you doing with hash, Vivian? I thought you only smoked the weed in the Islands.'

'I'm from St Lucia – we smoke anything.'

Vince made a play of weighing the bag of hashish in his hand as if it was a dumbbell. 'We got about what? . . . about two to three years for this, I'd say.'

There was some sucking of teeth and some shaking of his head before Vivian said, 'Ah, shit, you reckon me gonna be doing some time now, uh, Mr Treadwell?'

'Not necessarily, Vivian, not necessarily.'

Vivian looked up at the smiling detective. He knew what came next.

Vince had collected the Mk II and was parked in Powis Square. His eyes were fixed on the top-floor flat of a four-storey terraced house, where a light was on. It was a red light. Vivian Chalcott had done the necessary for getting off what could have been, considering his form, a lumpy little stretch, and given Vince the lowdown on the whereabouts of Tyrell Lightly.

Michael de Freitas had opened a new drinking club in Powis Square that also ran brasses in the upstairs rooms. And that's where Tyrell Lightly was holed up, smack bang in the middle of Notting Hill. Vince had suspected the like, but he still had to admire the chutzpah of the man. So sure was he that his operation wouldn't get raided that de Freitas had decided it was the safest place to hide Tyrell Lightly. Not even somewhere north of the Harrow Road, in the dens of Willesden, Harlesden or Neasden, but right here in his own back yard.

Vince watched as the curtains were drawn shut in the red-lit window, and took that as his cue to go in. He got out the car and gave a roll of his shoulders. He had thought about calling this in, getting some back-up, some sirens and some flashing lights and some truncheon-wielding uniforms. But something had kicked in: the overwhelming feeling that he wanted to take Tyrell Lightly in on his own. The feeling that he had to do it for little Ruby Jones and her mother, that certainly played its part. The little girl he had held in his arms had left her mark. He thought about Mac and what he would do in these circumstances, with his calm head and measured objectivity. But it had taken Mac thirty years to reach that particular state of grace, and Vince figured he still had time on his side. He was forever being told that police work was, above all else, team work, and he wholeheartedly agreed. And tomorrow Mac and Kenny Block and Philly Jacket and Chief Superintendent Markham could do as they wished with Tyrell Lightly. But tonight, thought Vince, tonight Tyrell Lightly was his. His blood was up, and as he felt the adrenalin pump through him he was reminded of Doc Clayton's theory that a sufficient rush of it could give you extra strength, open up a whole new physical world of untapped resources. As he breathed in the spiced city air, Vince felt invincible. He had felt this hubristic buzz before, and knew it was not only dangerous but dangerously addictive. But it was a vice he allowed himself, for all work and no play . . .

The closer he got to the house, the louder the music got: Blue Beat and Ska with the bass and treble turned thunderously up. He took off his tie, unbuttoned his collar, dishevelled his hair, and affected the movements of a man who'd drunk a bellyful of booze, smoked a lungful of weed and ingested a fistful of pills. He caught another break as two dolly birds — one a bleach blonde, the other a copperish redhead and both largish ladies with seam-busting beams — came clicking towards the house on lethal stilettos and swollen ankles.

Vince smiled. They checked him up and down, and went out of their way not to smile back, as he was far too white for them.

But Vince bustled into the party behind them without too much trouble; all eyes were on the girls, who had as much going on up front as they did behind.

Vince, with the ladies leading the way, sank into the smoke-filled fug of the drinker. For the purpose of a prop, he bought a bottle of beer for an extortionate nine bob. He then made his way around the room. As shebeens went, this was a cut above most, for it had an air of semi-permanency about it, and bordered on looking like a legitimate drinking club. Red flock wallpaper crept up the walls. A proper-looking bar ran down one side of the room. A couple of one-armed bandits, a pinball machine and a pool table occupied another room. The music was paint-blistering loud, which Vince liked.

He played drunk and stoned, but played it carefully, not wanting to draw attention to himself or tread on anyone toes. Just wanting to look legless and harmless. It was the usual doped-up, speed-freaking, mixed cast of fancy-dress characters: gangsters and molls, tarts and vicars, rude boys and rude girls, mop-top mods and miniskirted bobbed brunettes in kinky boots, artists and actors and writers and all their representation, drag acts and property fat cats, politicians and prostitutes, and a doe-eyed skinny girl from Bromley who'd just made the front cover of *Vogue*.

As he scoped the room, it became clear that Tyrell Lightly wasn't in it. But Vince did spot four of the Brothers X with their black leather coats, black berets and, even now, in this most sunless of nightspots, their wraparound shades. They sat on two facing sofas and looked relaxed and off duty, with no military posturing. Three of them were nursing rums, smoking joints and laughing. Each of them had a stoned girl on his lap, looking like ventriloquists' dummies. The fourth Brother X provided the reason for the other three's mirth: his girl was on her knees before him with her head bobbing up and down in his lap, administering a blow job.

Vince made his way into the hallway and climbed the stairs. He spotted the two girls he'd come in with on the first landing – or their ample backsides anyway – as they disappeared into a room with two more of the Brothers X. Vince concluded that the revolution was taking a night off and getting itself well and truly laid.

He continued up the stairs to the next floor. Bathroom. Toilet. Two bedrooms; one was empty. The other was emitting a punter who was zipping up his fly with a less than satisfied look on his face. Vince carried on up the next flight. The stairs came to an abrupt end, presenting a half landing with a single door at the end of it, with a sliver of red light coming from under it. Vince put his ear to the door but couldn't hear a thing, as the swampy bass from downstairs was drowning everything else out. He gave a mental clearing of his throat, and attempted the patois of a Jamaican rude boy, which to his ear wasn't chilled and laid-back enough, but fast and impatient: 'Brother Lightly, I got a large rum for you!'

Immediately, an equally fast and impatient voice shot back: 'What you disturbing me now for, fool? You knowz I'm busy!'

Vince didn't care that the accent was lousy, just as long as the door opened. He went again: 'Open up, got something real special, brother!'

Vince heard hushed voices in conference inside, and he readied himself. His plan was simple: hit whoever answered the door as hard as he could, then take it from there. It seemed like a good plan, a simple plan, and was in place when the door opened. Vince pulled back his fist as far as he could and – *bang*! – struck a blow to the black face in front of him. Not that a lot of the face was available to him – a strip of about five inches – because the door had just cracked open a bit and then stopped. But it was enough for Vince to get his fist through without clattering against the sides of the door and the door frame and taking the power out of the punch. It was a clean blow that made a solid connect on the recipient's jaw. The stunned owner of the jaw reeled backwards, taking the door with . . . *her*!

She was a big girl, about six foot in most directions. Her enormous girth was cut in half, squeezed in the middle by a red corset that must have been of the old-fashioned whalebone variety, and surely culled from Moby Dick because the spillage from either side of this giant egg-timer was immense. When that garment was unlaced, all hell would be unleashed. Vince grimaced, mouthing 'sorry' to the wobbling figure in front of him. She then dropped to the floor, taking a dressing table and small wardrobe with her, and hit the ground like a felled giant redwood. The floorboards buckled, the walls groaned, the joists screamed, and ten years of dust exploded upwards in a mushroom cloud of energy from the crunchy old carpet.

The room beyond was big, and Tyrell Lightly was standing beside the brass bed. He'd managed to scramble into his strides and put his shoes on, a pair of shiny winkle-pickers that looked as if they needed avoiding. He was about five foot nine and all sharp edges, vicious crevices and knotted muscle. A long blade, about six inches, was already gripped in his bony-knuckled hand like a lethal sting. As soon as the big girl went down, taking all the furniture on one side of the room with her, both men had reached for their blades. But Lightly, a known knife merchant, was the quickest on the draw.

'The fuck are you, bad boy?'

'Detective Vince Treadwell.'

Anger flashed across Lightly's face, but on seeing the blade in Vince's hand, he smiled his handsome and expensive smile – expensive because every other tooth in his mouth was gold. He then spat venomously on the floor to mark his territory. 'Let's dance, eh, bad boy?'

Despite the invitation, Lightly didn't wait for a reply and lunged straight at Vince with his blade. Vince dodged to the right and raised his left knee into Lightly's gut, then grabbed his face with his left hand and slammed him straight into the wall. Lightly took the impact with a low growl, then twisted round in a flash, and lunged forward again, slicing at Vince's arm. Vince saw the torn arm of his jacket and felt the burning of cut flesh. He flexed his arm and realized the cut wasn't deep, no tendons or muscle, just a tailor's bill. Vince moved backwards, not part of his plan, but Lightly was fast and Vince felt a flurry of slashing movements whip past his face. A spiteful grin blazed on Lightly's mouth. He was fast, very fast, and he was now toying with Vince. And Vince was beginning to question his judgement in coming after him on his own, or at least coming after him without something a bit heavier than Lightly's weapon of choice. They danced, with Lightly leading, manoeuvring Vince around the room and away from the door with slashing motions and gut-wrenching lunges. Vince gave as good as he got, or tried to, and there were parries and ripostes. But time wasn't on Vince's side, and he knew he had to get the blade out of Lightly's hand as fast as possible.

Tyrell Lightly's slashing got closer: the knife cut through Vince's shoulder, across his breast pocket, then another slice down his lapel. Vince glanced down at the damage: material cut to pieces, its guts hanging out, the silk lining showing through. No amount of tailor's stitches would save the suit; it was dead. And Vince knew he had to act quickly before he himself followed suit; or before the suit was completely cut off him and Lightly started splicing and dicing and flaying and filleting him instead!

He grabbed the nearest thing to hand, a side lamp covered in a red shade. A questionable move, as they were now thrown into darkness, and his target had vanished. Vince muttered 'Shit' and threw the redundant lamp across the room at what he thought to be the darting figure of Tyrell Lightly. The lamp smashed against the wall, but not against its target. Vince waited for his eyes to adjust to the darkness, but they didn't. He still couldn't see a thing. He was groping in pitch blackness, and Lightly had somehow melted into it. A thick curtain hung over the window blocking out the nominal light from the street. Vince couldn't see his hand in front of his face, or the knife gripped in it. And, more worryingly, he couldn't see Lightly's knife either. Suddenly Vince was spooked, very spooked, and started slashing out around him, his blade cutting through the air, hoping it would connect with Lightly or at least ward him off. Was Lightly stalking him like he was stalking Lightly? Two hunters. Two victims. And one very big girl on the floor. But considering Lightly's skill with a knife, at least they were now more evenly matched: they were both fumbling around in the dark, so it would come down to who had eaten their carrots.

Vince reckoned that if Lightly went for the door, he'd see him, and his back would then be towards him. So he leaned against the wall and remained stock-still. Nothing but silence. Was Lightly doing the same against the opposite wall? The music downstairs was still playing, appropriately, Derrick Morgan's 'See the Blind'. Time was running out, since the two Brothers X would soon be through with their X-rated action with the two party girls. They didn't look like the kind of girls who would hang around – and nor would you want them to. Vince thought about cracking a joke, in the hope of making Lightly laugh so he could catch a glint of his gold teeth. He didn't know any jokes that funny, but the likelihood of it happening made him smile. Then he felt and heard the whoosh and whistle of a missile glance past the right side of his face, making a reverberative twang like a giant tuning fork as it stuck in the wall. It was Lightly's thrown knife. He must have taken aim when he saw Vince's white teeth as he smiled!

Then he heard a plangent groan rising up from the floor, which sounded like the big girl regaining consciousness. Then Vince heard a yelp; it was caused by someone standing on the big girl. The floor felt solid underfoot, so it wasn't him. Dark as it was, slowly Vince's eyes began to pick out a few details in the room. Shapes became apparent and he spotted a figure standing by the wall, right beside a heap on the floor. The spindly figure then darted for the door. Vince, with the big advantage of having his blade still gripped in his hand, pelted after him and pounced. There was a bony crunch as Lightly fell heavily to the floor. Vince grabbed his arms and pinned them down. Lying on top of Lightly as he was, it became obvious from the smell that Vince had caught him and the big girl post-coital, not pre-. The acridly bitter smell of stale sweat and other bodily saps made Vince want to retch.

DANNY MILLER

Vince saw the bulging white of the man's eyes, and Lightly saw the bulging white of Vince's. Tyrell Lightly's head shot up to deliver a butt to Vince's nose, but Vince pulled back in time. He smiled, because he had the advantage: he was on top. And he used that advantage, and the gravity that came with it, to propel his forehead down on to the angled bridge of Lightly's nose.

There was the crunch of bone. There was blood. There was a bark of pain. Then there was Lightly crying out: 'I'll kill you!'

'Not from where I'm looking, you won't! And it was your idea, Tyrell, after all.'

'You pig!' Lightly spat in his face, and he wasn't done yet. The wiry gangster began to wriggle, with great effect, in an attempt to get out from under. So Vince went for him again. Tyrell Lightly vigorously moved his head from side to side to avoid what was surely coming his way. Vince moved with him, this way then that, until Lightly's head slowed with exhaustion. And then Vince dummied him, took aim, cocked his head back like the hammer of a gun, and fired off another head shot. Say cheese! Again his forehead hit the target; again it was Lightly's rather finely sculpted nose that took the brunt – but harder this time, much harder. But there was no noise this time, either from the shattered bone in his nose or from the tongue in his mouth. The damage had been done, and Tyrell Lightly's face was mostly blood. Vince finally hauled himself off the supine gangster.

By the time Vince was on his feet, the white noise of violence had stopped, and so had the music from downstairs. He heard fast-approaching, heavy footsteps outside. As he put his hand inside his jacket pocket to pull out his ID, the door flew off its holdings. But still Vince was in darkness, as a wall of blackness blocked out any light from the hallway beyond. A scrimmage of Brothers X was jammed in the doorway. In the front of the pack stood Michael X. The great leader flicked a switch on the wall and the room lit up. As he quickly took in the scene, his face turned from scowling anger to a slow contemplative neutrality that eventually segued into a lavishly satisfied grin, as he remarked, 'Detective

70

Vincent Treadwell of Scotland Yard, and the Metropolitan police force, what in the sweet mother of goats have we got here?'

What we had here, and what Michael X was smiling about, was Vince standing with the knife in his bloodied hand, Tyrell Lightly on the floor with his lights well and truly out, and the big girl . . .

'Little piece of skinny white . . .'

Vince turned round just in time to catch the cannon ball that was coming his way, as the big girl's balled fist connected to his chin and sent him swiftly to the floor. Lights out all round.

CHAPTER 11

Vince stood before Chief Superintendent Ian Markham. He'd not been invited to sit down because, when he entered, Markham was himself standing up, looking cantankerously out of the window. With hands clasped behind his back, his inky-blue uniform appeared iridescent in the midday winter sun. Vince could see how, where Markham tipped his head back to address the gods, the oil from his brilliantine-black hair was seeping into the rim of his starched white collar. Markham clearly needed a haircut. A trim. A little tidy-up. This was noticeable because his hair was usually kept just so, a good two inches above the collar. It was now only an inch and a half, Vince reckoned. This was the kind of detail you pick up on when you're forced to stand and receive what seemed to Vince his annual reaming from his Chief Superintendent. Vince found himself glazing over, switching off and drifting around the room in some out-of-body experience. He desperately looked for points of interest around the room and eventually settled on a fly that was shifting its body irritably around on one wall. The fly took off, buzzed around for a bit, hovered over a light fitting, got hot, buzzed off again, and landed on the back of Markham's shoulder. This location, annoyingly, brought the Chief Superintendent back into view. Even though he was five floors up, Markham still managed to elongate himself to maximum height in order to look down his nose at *them* gathered below.

Chief Superintendent Markham was watching the protesters who were gathered outside Scotland Yard, led by Michael X and his Black Power Coalition. There, a troop of about twenty of them stood at attention in a well-ordered line, arms behind their backs, chests out, shoulders square (even Markham could appreciate the well-drilled military aspect and discipline). Michael X himself, equipped with loudspeaker, started to read out extracts of American black political writings and the works of his hero Malcolm X, whose assassination in Harlem three days earlier had added an urgency to the whole proceedings. They were soon joined by other protesters from the CND, TUC, LSE, SWP, NUS and BCP and, as soon as the TV cameras rolled up, the whole thing became a 'happening' as much as a protest. Showbiz luminaries, TV-friendly intellectuals and writers soon put in an appearance, along with some Angry Young Men actors and some kitchen-sink playwrights from the Royal Court Theatre, who delivered monologues for the cameras and, with their full and fruity voices, projected across the square the slogan: '*William Shakespeare, William Blake, We Are Doing This For Your Sake!*'

Apart from the charges of police brutality, their main gripe was that Tyrell Lightly was an innocent man being held and set up by *the man*. And *the man* at the centre of this shit storm in a teacup was Detective Vincent Treadwell. He had now become the unacceptable face of policing, and Michael X was stirring it up for all it was worth. He had as canny an eye for publicity and a photo opportunity as the most tawdry of door-stepping, baby-kissing, Westminster whores on the hustings hustle. The minute Michael X had opened the bedroom door and reviewed the scenario before him he'd known it was too good an opportunity not to grab. He drove a groggy Vince and a bloody Tyrell Lightly straight to Scotland Yard. Vince didn't protest. Tyrell Lightly wasn't too happy about it, but Michael X assured him that to be seen to be giving himself up was good for the cause and good for himself. Tyrell Lightly now sat in his cell refusing to say a word; in fact he was refusing to open his mouth at all: not to eat, drink water or swallow painkillers for his broken nose. With Michael X hanging over the proceedings, and offering counsel to Lightly, Vince thought the gangster-turned-revolutionary was hoping to have his first martyr for the cause.

'Look at them . . . the usual agitators.' Markham shook his head in withering disgust. 'There's a great unpleasantness moving through this land, Treadwell. Do you not feel it?'

'Not especially, sir.'

Markham turned away from the window and looked at Vince questioningly.

Vince shrugged. 'Freedom of speech, sir.'

'*Freedom of speech*,' Markham repeated with a slurry of contempt in his voice. 'It's you they want, Treadwell! You are the centre of their ire. 'Tis you they bay for. Does that not concern you?'

'Regarding their opinion, sir, they're wrong, but that's their right. It's what attracted me to the job in the first place, to protect their right to be wrong.'

Vince said all this with his tongue if not firmly in his cheek, then certainly positioned around that area. But sarcasm and irony had become his natural register when talking to the pompous Chief Superintendent. Vince wasn't looking at his superior as he said this, but straight ahead at the picture on the wall behind Markham's desk. The official portrait of the Queen was still in place, but she had been joined by a framed portrait of Sir Winston Churchill. Vince considered the great man, deciding there was a strange parallel between the photograph of the freshly assassinated Malcolm X hanging in the office of Michael X and Markham's portrait here of the recently deceased Churchill; and it wasn't just sharing the year of their death that drew them together. Both men knew how to coin a phrase, both men were flawed natural-born leaders, and both men were now hanging on the walls of men who, in Vince's opinion, weren't fit to black their boots. And yet, looking at the familiar image on the wall, Vince felt no more at home in Markham's Scotland Yard office than he did in Michael X's one in Notting Hill. He still felt like the outsider, the interloper waiting to be uncovered.

'Just like *he* fought for, sir,' said Vince, with a nod towards Churchill. He meant it, too, but also knew it would curry him some favour.

The Chief Superintendent was a big fan, and had taken the death of Churchill earlier in the year very badly. But he was determined to carry on the great fight, though the enemy had changed. Now they were not only on the beaches, and on the streets, but right outside his bloody window! Markham wanted them moved. Break out the white horses, baton charge them if necessary, but get them shifted on to the more traditional protesting patch of Trafalgar Square, which Markham had renamed 'Red Square'. But cooler heads and voices from higher up the chain of command, both authoritatively and intellectually, had prevailed, and successfully warned him against such action. But talk about parking their tanks on his front lawn, the very sight of them outside his window was tantamount to someone taking a big fat steaming dump right here in his office. And for this he blamed the young detective standing in front of him.

'You went rogue, Treadwell.'

'I was just carrying out my duty, sir.'

'If you'd have called for back-up, you wouldn't have compromised your position.'

'Like I said in my statement, sir, I didn't have time for that. I'd received information that might or might not have been true, and I had to act on it fast.'

Then there was the small matter of his knife, which Vince claimed he'd picked up in the mêlée in Powis Square. It was his word against Tyrell Lightly's and that of the Brothers X. But, with Lightly's form as a known felon with a penchant for knives and cutting up coppers, Vince was home and dry on that one. As for the protests, whether Markham liked it or not, something was moving through the country . . . how unpleasant it might be was yet to be writ.

There was a knock on the door. Markham barked 'Come in,' and Mac entered the room.

'We've just heard from Isabel Saxmore-Blaine's lawyer,' said Mac, who then nodded at one of the pictures immediately behind Markham, 'who incidentally are the same firm that represents the Queen.'

'I'm well aware of Miss Saxmore-Blaine's connections, Mac.'

'Well, she's made a statement and wants to talk to us.'

Markham gave a solemn nod to this news. He liked the sound of it. She had not needed coercing, had not even been asked. It confirmed one of the many attributes that he ascribed to the upper classes, far too many of them to list and all fawningly positive, but here was one of them showing that, by God, they knew how to conduct themselves.

'Good,' said Markham, gripping the hem of his jacket and giving it a tug, as though he was about to go on parade. 'This is another delicate situation and I have no need to inform you that Lord Saxmore-Blaine is a personal friend of the Commissioner, so this goes all the way to the top. Questions have been asked at Westminster, concerns expressed at the Palace. We shall need experienced and delicate hands in dealing with Miss Isabel Saxmore-Blaine.'

Mac looked at Vince. Vince looked back at Mac. This surreptitious and silent conference went unnoticed by Markham, who was still preening himself before putting his cap on. By the time he turned back to them, Mac and Vince had both wiped the smirks off their faces. Even the thoroughly professorial Mac was reduced to schoolboy mockery when it came to dealing with Markham. It wasn't even that Markham was all that disliked, or not respected. On the contrary, at times he was very fair-minded, gave solid orders and stood up for his men. It was just his oleaginous attitude to his perceived 'higher-ups and betters' that struck everyone as so humourless and self-defeating.

'Mac, you and I shall attend to Miss Saxmore-Blaine,' resolutely declared Markham. 'We shall take her statement, and we shall talk to her and assure her that—'

'Sir, she doesn't want to talk to us,' interrupted Mac. Stopped, and then stalled, Markham's face was a picture. 'She wants to talk to, and I quote, "the handsome young detective who punched me in the face".'

From the unacceptable face of policing to the handsome face of policing. Isabel Saxmore-Blaine had just saved Vince's neck – and he knew it. But it didn't stop him from wincing when he heard it. He'd never before hit a woman in his life, and, what with the big girl in the brothel, that made two in the space of a week. As if to compensate, he rubbed a thumb over his chin, which bore a murky bruise from the big girl's punch.

Markham turned slowly to Vince. His beady, bespectacled eyes narrowed in suspicion, and his whole face bore a look of grinding resentment. It was as if the young detective had just stolen his ticket to the dance. Vince's darkly lashed hazel eyes widened in innocence, and he gave a shrug that said: 'I can explain *everything*, sir.'

CHAPTER 12

London was at its best this morning: cold and bright. Vince liked this time of year, for winter suited London; it was its natural setting. Summer in this city always felt like an intruder, creeping around the edges of the buildings, skulking in the parks, the squares and the public gathering places like it shouldn't really be there, even though it was greeted with open arms and rolled-up shirt sleeves.

His destination that morning was the Salisbury private hospital in Harley Street. On entry, Vince saw that it was more akin to a swanky five-star hotel than a hospital. The only thing that gave away its true status was the white-coated doctors and blue-uniformed nurses – as opposed to pantomime-dressed bellboys and frilly-knickered French chambermaids. But Vince noted that even the medical staff had an unhurried and genial attractiveness about them, as though they were hand-picked extras milling around the set of *Dr Kildare*.

He was shown up to Isabel Saxmore-Blaine's room, where a uniformed copper sat reading a paperback outside the door. As Vince badged him, he went to stand up, but Vince said 'Relax' and knocked sharply on the door.

'Who is it?' came a woman's high-impact voice, its timbre a little husky, a little low, a little rich . . .

'The detective who punched you on the chin,' Vince announced, smiling at the uniformed copper who had looked up from his paperback with an expression bordering on astonishment. From inside, Vince heard some arguing, albeit of the very polite and hushed variety, which then hushed completely. The door eventually opened and there stood Isabel Saxmore-Blaine.

She took a deep breath, gave him a welcoming smile, and said: 'Come to admire your handiwork?'

He winced at the sight of the bruise on one side of her jaw. It had now reached its full apogee of colourfulness: a crescendo of tonic blues and purples fading into ochreous browns and yellows.

And then it was her turn to wince, as she noticed the bruise on the side of his own jaw. 'What happened to you?'

Vince's chin-shiner was nothing compared to hers, being just several different shades of black and blue. He couldn't tell her the truth; there was just no way of putting a good slant on that one. A list of appropriate mishaps ran through his mind: fell off his horse while playing polo, helping a lady out of her carriage, clumsily doffing his cap whilst neglectfully holding a croquet mallet. He shrugged out a dismissive mutter about an incident at work, par-for-the-course stuff.

So there they were, both wearing slight expectant smiles on bruised chins, as she invited him in. The luxury theme of the lobby had carried on up into the room, five-star all the way. The only thing to give it away as not being the presidential suite at the Dorchester was the high metal-framed bed with a clipboard of medical notes attached to the footboard.

Just rising from the sofa was a portly, elderly man in a double-breasted chalk-stripe suit, an old school tie and a gold watch-chain running from his lapel into his breast pocket. A corona of white curly hair skirted a bald head, which he now covered with a dark blue fedora, plucked from the arm of the sofa, before he struggled into a fawn covert coat with a collar of well-worn olive green velvet. Finally, collecting some papers from the coffee table, he slid them into his admirably distressed and monogrammed ($G\ D\ L$) pigskin briefcase, and fastened the brass locks.

'Detective Treadwell, this is Geoffrey Lancing, my lawyer.'

Vince offered his hand, and the lawyer grudgingly shook it.

'Pleased to meet you, Mr Lancing.'

'Likewise, Detective,' said the lawyer, not really meaning a word of it, while not taking his eyes off his client. 'Isabel, my dear, I must ask you once more to reconsider. This is not a wise decision.'

'Thank you, Geoffrey, but that really will be all.'

The lawyer turned to Vince. 'May I ask you for your professional opinion, sir?'

Isabel Saxmore-Blaine said: 'No, you may not.'

Vince looked between the two of them and said nothing.

She jumped in again before the lawyer could. 'I'll save you the time, Detective, as you know how long-winded lawyers can be. Geoffrey here is my father's lawyer—'

'Your family's lawyer for the last thirty-five years.'

'And a dear, dear friend for as long as I can remember.'

'Indeed.'

'*Indeed*,' she repeated with a gracious smile to the anxious lawyer. 'Geoffrey doesn't think it wise that I talk to you on my own, as anything I say might be taken down and used in evidence against me. Is that correct?'

'Yes, and I think it's good advice he's giving you, Miss Saxmore-Blaine.'

'Isabel, please. Call me Isabel.'

The lawyer threw her a reprimanding look, as if she was fraternizing with the enemy. Which, at this stage, she was. But he needn't have bothered, because Vince had no intention of calling her by her first name. The way he saw it, she'd already had more than her share of preferential treatment.

'But it's your choice whether or not you choose to have counsel present,' he confirmed.

'Come come, Detective Treadwell,' interrupted the lawyer, 'in circumstances as serious as these we both know it's not just highly advisable but imperative that Isabel does have counsel present.'

'Spoken like a true lawyer, Mr Lancing, and I was just about to make the same suggestion before I was interrupted. But Miss

Saxmore-Blaine hasn't been either charged or arrested in relation to this matter. I'm here just to pick up a prepared statement, I believe.'

'Correct,' said Isabel Saxmore-Blaine.

'Then that's all I shall do. And then I'm heading back to report to my superiors, who will read this statement and then decide how to proceed.'

Isabel Saxmore-Blaine looked at the lawyer with a kindly smile that would have melted the heart of the hardest litigator. 'Geoffrey, I thank you for your concern, but really I just want to thank the detective personally – after all, he did save my life.'

Isabel Saxmore-Blaine linked arms with the lawyer and marched him to the door, and saw him out with noisy kisses on each cheek. It was one of the most impressive acts of disarming strong-arm tactics Vince had ever seen. He could see how her charm and beauty could pretty much get her whatever she wanted. And he was determined not to get worked over in the same fashion: the satin-covered cosh, the velvet-gloved fist.

With the lawyer gone, she breathed a sigh of relief. Reaching into the pocket of her pearl-coloured silk robe, she pulled out a packet of cigarettes and lit one from a book of matches. She went over to the window, crumpling the cigarette pack and putting it back in her pocket. The window was locked and had bars across it. But even the bars looked five-star: they were fancily cast gilt metal, made to look like branches and foliage. She concentrated on her cigarette, sucking down a large percentage of it with each visit to her lips. Vince sensed that there had been a strained effort at normality in dealing with her lawyer, an old family friend, who was obviously under the direct employ of her father and would be promptly reporting back to him. The endeavour not to appear broken and cowed had taken it out of her.

Standing by the marble coffee table, Vince looked down at the neatly piled folios of A4 white embossed paper. They contained Isabel Saxmore-Blaine's prepared statement, signed by her and counter-signed by Geoffrey Lancing. And they were covered in some of the finest penmanship he'd ever seen. The handwriting slanted to the right, like rippling waves, but never fell into disorder: each letter, each word looked perfectly balanced and almost hypnotic. This was not the scratchy scrawl of a nervous suicidal wreck.

'I suppose I should give you that thank you now, Detective Treadwell.'

Vince glanced up from the statement towards Isabel Saxmore-Blaine. Her hair was shoulder-length, golden in colour and thick as honey, with blonde streaks running through it from the sun. Her skin was taut and lightly tanned, stretched over high cheekbones that gave her face its inherent structural beauty. With this combination, the rest of her features didn't have to work so hard in the looks department, but they all pulled their weight. A lineless forehead showed off plucked dark eyebrows that arched over large brown eyes. A slender nose, nothing much to report there; it looked just as it was meant to be, and fitted effortlessly into place. The mouth was rather shapely, not narrow and pinched, and looked as if it could easily open out into a broad and welcoming smile – just not right now. And all this was cradled on a faultlessly defined jawline. The only visible flaw was the bruise, but that was Vince's imprint, not nature's. Isabel Saxmore-Blaine's was a subtle beauty, nothing overpowering and pouty. It was demure, classy. It drew you in, made you want to lean forward to take a closer look. Somewhere about her, maybe in the eyes, she held a puzzle, an innate mystery you wanted to solve, a missing piece you wanted to find . . .

'You don't have to thank me,' said Vince. 'Trite as it might sound, it's all part of the job.'

'I only said I wanted to thank you because I wanted to clear Geoffrey out of the room.'

Once the initial shock of her up-close and in-the-flesh beauty had been appraised and applauded, Vince noticed that she was looking at him as though he was a hat stand; something in her line of vision but no more. The widely set eyes were now hooded, and Vince couldn't tell if this was a withering look or maybe the effects of the tranquillizers she'd been on. But since the departure of the lawyer, he felt things in the room had become decidedly frosty.

'But you really shouldn't have bothered, and it would have been easier and quicker if you hadn't. I wanted to die,' she said, seemingly without moving her lips or modulating her tone in any way.

Vince considered this. When it happened, he hadn't believed she wanted to kill herself. She had the gun in her bag and had plenty of time to squeeze off a shot before he arrived. Killing yourself is always the *final* – and you can't stress that enough – the *final* option. Vince and Mac turning up on the scene just accelerated her options. He hadn't saved her; if anything, he'd almost killed her.

A thin blue thread of smoke rose up from her cigarette as she gestured for him to sit down, which he did, on the floral-patterned sofa that the lawyer had been sitting on.

'I wanted to see you because I want to tell you everything I remember.'

Vince gave a cautious nod to the written statement lying on the coffee table. 'It's not already written down?'

'Yes, the facts as they are – as I remember them. But I read it all through, and it's not quite enough. Do you understand?'

Vince understood. Without turning a statement into a poem or a novel, it would be what it was – just a record of the facts. And somehow they never managed to tell the full story. 'Then Mr Lancing was right,' he said, 'and I need to advise you that it would be best to have a lawyer present.'

'I don't want one. I don't need one. I'm assuming I'm guilty, and I'm assuming that I'm going to be arrested for murdering Johnny. Am I right?'

Again Vince gestured towards the statement. 'Depends on what's in this. I take it your statement was prepared with Mr Lancing present?'

She nodded.

'And is it true?'

'Yes, it's true. And, if you read it, I'm sure you'll agree that it makes a very good case for me being innocent, because Geoffrey is one of the finest lawyers in the land . . .'

Although her voice was low and infused with a smoky decadence, it was still cut-glass in its precision. Nothing got lost or trampled on; every syllable was pronounced to within an inch of its life. He also noted the slight American accent.

'So I hear, but it seems that you're not so sure?'

She looked away from him, down to her hand holding the cigarette. It had burned down to the biscuit-coloured filter. She walked carefully over to the handbasin. Vince noticed that her movements were slightly mechanical. She ran the tap and extinguished the butt, took out the empty crumpled cigarette packet, put the butt inside it, then returned it to her pocket. She re-joined Vince and composed herself on the sofa. Not as cosy as it sounded; the sofa was as big as a boat and she was seated starboard, he was port.

'I must warn you, Miss Saxmore-Blaine, that if you wish to talk to me about the suspected murder of Mr Beresford, I'll need to first inform you of your rights.'

'I don't care about that – about the law.'

'You should, because the law will care about you, and in all the wrong ways. You're in a very precarious position since, as far as we know, you were the last person to see Mr Beresford alive. Also you had in your possession the gun that killed him.'

With her hands clasped in front of her, she sat very still, taking deep controlled breaths. And for the first time he clearly saw the hangover from the medication. It was slowing Isabel Saxmore-Blaine's world and keeping everything manageably unreal for her, freezing up the delta of tears that was now backing up behind those lustrous dark eyes. So dark that the pupil and the iris were almost indistinguishable. Her voice was so precise because it was overcompensating, reacting just a second or so too late.

She said: 'I have to tell you what happened. Because I need to know myself if I killed Johnny.'

Vince saw that she was ripe to talk; she wanted to unburden. He'd seen that look before with suspects, and it had always resulted in eliciting the truth. She began to talk, oh so carefully.

It was all pretty much as they had picked up on, anyway, from family and friends and the investigation they had conducted. For the last month or so, Isabel had been out of the country, staying with friends on the sleepy Balearic island of Ibiza. She had wanted to get away from Johnny Beresford and the high-octane social whirligig of the London party scene that she had been caught on for the last few years; just to clear her head and do some sober thinking. She was convinced that her future no longer rested with Johnny, and had returned to London to tell him so. When she arrived at Eaton Square, he had been all charm and affection, kisses and cuddles, stating his love for her and how much he'd missed her, and how his night-owl days of gambling and carousing were now over, and how he wanted to settle down with her and raise a family. But it was obvious that he'd been drinking, and he soon confessed that he'd been drinking all day. Johnny Beresford had an almost superhuman capacity for handling industrial amounts of booze: he could out-drink a poet on payday or a gang of sailors putting into port.

Isabel looked ashamed as she confessed that one thing had led to another, and they ended up popping open some champagne and getting drunk together. One last hurrah, perhaps? She knew it was a bad idea, having been on the wagon for almost three months now. Things had soon changed, as things are apt to do when people get drunk. The inhibitions slipped away and the old grievances and animosities resurfaced. As they argued, Beresford started getting abusive. He'd been abusive before, but she'd never seen him like this – till she feared for her life. It was as if he was losing his mind. That's when she hit him with the bottle, to protect herself when he came at her. But then she blacked out. Next thing she remembered was seeing him dead in the armchair, and the gun lying on the floor . . .

'Do you smoke, Detective?' she asked suddenly.

'No, but I could go downstairs and get you a pack,' he said eagerly, not wanting her to lose her train of thought through the distraction of a nicotine jag.

'No, no,' she said, with a resolute shake of her head. 'I'm not allowed to smoke in this room, of course, and I'm trying to give up anyway – you hear such stories these days.'

'Were there other women in his life?'

At this question, her face registered that she thought it was if not impertinent, then certainly a distasteful one. 'Why do you ask?'

Vince matter-of-factly responded, 'The life you described, it goes with the territory.'

She gave a conceding sigh, then said, 'One would assume so, but I don't know any names in particular. For Johnny and his friends it was not just perfectly acceptable to have a mistress; it was deemed dreadfully *un*acceptable not to have one.'

'You weren't married.'

'Correct. Not that it makes it any better. In fact, that makes it slightly worse – right, Detective?'

Vince got on to safer territory. 'What was Mr Beresford doing with a gun in the house?'

'Johnny loved guns and hunting almost as much as gambling. Almost, but not quite.'

'Was that the other woman? I've known a few gambling widows in my time. He was a member of the Montcler Club, I believe?'

'A *member* is an understatement. A devotee and an exalted one of the brethren, I'd say, but yes, Detective, you're right. Very perceptive of you. That place has been responsible for creating more lonely widows than a reasonably large and very disastrous war. And yes, Johnny's gambling had been a point of issue between us. Not that he lost that much. On the contrary, he seemed to win rather a lot. But it was the amount of time he spent at the club. I had sort of resigned myself to it, because that's what he was, a gambler. He'd been doing it long before he met me – as he pointed out – so I knew the score, or the *deal* I should say.'

'So tell me about Mr Beresford and guns.'

'I won't say they held a fetishistic obsession for him, but some-times Johnny would carry one when he went out at night – going to the Montcler Club to play cards, or to a party, or a business meeting. It amused him; maybe it turned him on in some way. Can you see that, Detective?'

Vince indeed could see it: something forbidden and deadly lurking within the polite society. 'Did he keep it tucked in his cummerbund?'

'I'm assuming that remark was humorous, Detective, but it's also pretty well spot on. A macho affectation, a childish accessory and, yes, completely ridiculous.'

'Did he actually fire the gun at you that night?'

At this she recoiled, as though it was the most ridiculous thing she'd heard in the world. 'No, of course not.'

'Don't look so shocked Miss Saxmore-Blaine. You said you were both drunk. You said he was acting erratically and you'd never seen him like that before. Then you hit him over the head with a champagne bottle and he ended up with a bullet in him. Con-sidering how things panned out that night, and his penchant for macho affectations, it's not such an outrageous question.'

She immediately ceded the point and looked shamefaced at the litany of behaviour laid before her.

Vince continued. 'Okay, the gun . . . you say you blacked out and woke up to find him dead in the chair, the gun lying at his feet?' She nodded. 'Had you passed out in the basement study?'

She put the fingertips of each hand to her temples, as if trying to focus her mind. Then, after a meditative pause, she lowered them and shook her head in failed resignation. 'I don't know what I was doing down there. The last thing I remember was being in the living room. I remember hitting him . . . hitting him with the bottle . . . and then I blacked out. Next I was down in the study. I had the gun in my hand, and there was blood on it. I must have gone looking for him, and picked it up . . .'

'Why didn't you call the police, instead of picking up the gun and running out of the house?'

'Maybe because . . . because I knew I was going to kill myself?'

'Because you'd killed him?'

He saw the anxiety and uncertainty gathering on her face, almost reaching the tipping point into tears.

'I don't know . . . To say anything else would be a lie. Because I swear to God, I just don't know.'

'Well, unless we can find out more than you've revealed, it's looking cut and dried, Miss Saxmore-Blaine. You killed Johnny Beresford with his own gun, then ran out of there.'

She stood up quickly and strode back over to the window. Vince stood up, but didn't go over to join her. She wasn't running away from his questions, and she wasn't denying that she had killed Beresford. She just wanted confirmation of the fact, either way.

With her back to him, Vince watched as she straightened up and inhaled some strenuous breaths. Gazing out at the winter sun breaking through the clouds that hung portentously in the London sky, she said with a certain cheerful resignation, 'That's it then. I did it. I killed him.' She turned round sharply, her chin up, defiant. Her eyes weren't even moist. She was determined not to cry, as if she didn't want such emotion to cloud his judgement of her.

Vince reached into his jacket pocket and pulled out the photo of Johnny Beresford seated at the gaming table with five other players, and handed it to her.

'Could you tell me something about these gentlemen?'

She didn't need to study the characters, she'd seen the line-up a thousand times before and knew them all well enough. And as she considered them, her stoic expression soured into aversion.

'I'm sure I could tell you lots, Detective Treadwell, but in the interests of objectivity I'll stick with the facts. First up, top of the table is James Asprey, known to all his chums as Aspers. He owns the Montcler Club. Like most professional gamblers I've met, he can be an incredibly cold-hearted bastard when he wants to be. The trouble with Aspers is that he wants to be that way most of the time. He's a monkey-loving misanthrope who likes animals more than people. So much so that he's even building himself a private zoo. I would describe Aspers as the leader of the pack.

'The fellow to the right of him is Simon Goldsachs. Born in Paris to an English father, who was a politician and later a millionaire hotelier, and a French mother. The Goldsachs family, much like their relatives the Rothchilds, were merchant bankers dating back to the sixteenth century. The only reason I know all this about him is because he insisted on telling me all this about him over a game of chess one day, whilst he was trying to seduce me.'

Vince raised an eyebrow at this. She lowered it with: 'Don't read too much into that, Detective, Simon tries to seduce everyone; it's almost a reflex action. I surrendered my King to him, but not my virtue, and made my escape. Simon Goldsachs is a greedy, arrogant, vengeful philanderer, and a completely magnetic charmer to boot. He's also by far the richest man sitting at that table. Next up is Dickie Bingham, or – to give him his full title – the seventh Earl of Lucan. He's never done a day's work in his life and probably wouldn't be good at anything anyway because, as the joke goes, he's not so much an idiot-savant as an idiot with servants.

'This fellow next to Lucan is Guy Ruley. I always thought Guy was somewhat in awe of Johnny, used to want to be like him. He's something in the city, and also something of a bore. The only interesting thing about him is that his father was a scrap-metal dealer or something like that, who struck it rich and could afford to send his son off to Eton. And that fact's not really about him so, no, nothing interesting at all.'

As Isabel reached the last member of the Montcler set gathered around the table, her robotic rat-tat-tat of dismissive commentary stopped, and a warm smile arrived on her face.

'And that's the lovely Nicky DeVane – the very talented photographer and one of my oldest friends.' She gestured towards the dozen roses in a vase on the bedside table. 'He sent me those. Of course I've not heard from any of the others. They've closed ranks, as usual.'

'They were Mr Beresford's friends but not yours?'

'Apart from Nicky DeVane, no. I think they view me with suspicion. You see, Detective, I was neither a wife nor a mistress, and those men have both. I was in the hinterland, and they never quite knew what to say to me. They were forever getting on to Johnny to do something about it: either marry me and get himself a mistress, or marry someone else and have me as the mistress. Or, preferably, marry someone else and get another mistress. They don't feel comfortable around educated women with opinions of their own.'

'Why didn't you two get married?'

She stuck her hands in the pockets of the robe, her hand scrunching around the dead packet of cigarettes, obviously wishing there was a fresh one in there. She shrugged and went over to the sofa. 'I think that ship had already sailed for us,' she said, sitting down. 'It's strange, but we'd reached a stage where we'd become pals more than anything. I loved him, and the attraction to him was as strong as ever – and his towards me, I believe. But too much bad behaviour had passed between us. We'd seen each other at our worst too many times. We needed to start anew. Does that make sense, Detective?'

Vince joined her on the sofa. 'So you went around to Eaton Square intending to finish it with him?'

'Unfortunate choice of words, but yes. I was planning on leaving London for good, and going back to New York.'

'And what did he say to that?'

'I don't know, as we never actually got around to the subject. Avoiding mature life decisions was a forte of his. No, that's unfair – it was both our fortes.'

'So what did you talk about?'

'The past. The good times. Of which there were many, I have to say.'

'Yeah, I saw the photos of you two together at your apartment.'

A slight smile positioned itself hesitantly on her lips; it was one of those oblique smiles that the rest of her face wasn't that convinced about, therefore didn't join in with.

'Johnny and I did holidays very well.' At the mere mention of his name, the tentative little smile slipped away. 'We both knew it was over. That's probably why we got drunk, because it was all too painful to face sober. And then, after we got drunk, it got even more painful. Turned nasty, with recriminations. Then . . . well, you know the rest.'

Vince looked at the photo one more time before he slipped it back into his pocket. Nicky DeVane's gesture of sending a dozen red roses struck him as a strange choice, considering the circumstances. Vince had heard of DeVane, and knew him to be a celebrity snapper. Photographers seemed to be the new thing, and they were cropping up everywhere and making it into the fashion and society pages almost as much as their subjects. But his name was famous for more than just that.

'DeVane? He wouldn't be related to *the* DeVanes, would he?'

'Yes, he would.'

Vince pulled an expression that passed for impressed, or at least intrigued. The DeVanes had been a political force in the country since the Roundheads and Cavaliers. He couldn't remember which side they'd been on; both probably at one time or another, if their longevity and political savvy were anything to go by. The DeVanes had produced two foreign secretaries, four home secretaries, two chancellors of the exchequer, and a strong candidate for prime minister – until Spanish flu claimed him in 1919. Nothing much since then, but still a power in the upper house.

Vince continued: 'Outside of the problems you two were having, did Mr Beresford have anything else he seemed worried about?'

'Such as?'

'The usual. Money worries? Business worries?'

She looked genuinely confused, then she gave an ironic little smile at the thought. Vince understood straight away: Beresford didn't suffer the slings and arrows experienced by mere mortals: the fear of the brown envelope dropping doomsday-like through the letter box, the HP payments on the new three-piece suite not being kept up.

'Obviously I've been to his house,' he said, 'and seen the lifestyle, but appearances can be deceiving. The big money deal gone wrong. The outstanding tax bill accruing interest. Death duties in the family. Big money brings its own set of problems, I imagine.'

'If there were any, he wouldn't have told me, because he wasn't the type to complain. Why do you ask?'

'Our people in forensics believe that Mr Beresford fired the weapon himself that night. We've searched the house thoroughly and haven't found a bullet hole, and you yourself say you didn't see him fire the gun.' There was a sudden spark of renewed attention on her face. 'His type of wound, a shot to the temple, is most commonly found with suicides.' She seemed genuinely shocked and very confused by this revelation, and was still shaking her head in disbelief as Vince continued, 'Like I said, Miss Saxmore-Blaine, it's just a possibility, like so many found in a murder investigation – and we have to look into all of them.'

Sounding firm and confident, she said, 'No. He wouldn't do such a thing.'

'If I were you, Miss Saxmore-Blaine, I wouldn't jump to conclusions. But, if I may say, I would certainly jump all over that one. I know your lawyers will.'

At this, she sat up and stiffened, indignation bristling through her and seeming to make her taller even sitting down, certainly tall enough to be able to look down her finely shaped nose at him.

'From what I've read in the papers,' continued Vince, 'your lawyers are already doing their job. It's common practice for law firms to put out stories – or leak facts as they call it – that will benefit their clients.'

'To what are you referring?'

'I take it you haven't read the papers?'

'No, they've been kept from me. And I can't say that I mind.'

'The story that you were both drunk and he got violent has made the society columns. And, of course, there're other anonymous sources who have come forward with pithy little quotes to back that up.'

'Who's said this?

'That's the trouble with anonymous quotes, they can't be held to account. That's why such stuff gets dumped into the society pages: it's gossip, it's hearsay, it's scandalous, but it's good copy and sells newspapers. And that's why the society and gossip pages are getting fatter, and the factual ones are getting thinner. No one wants boring facts; they want salacious fiction.'

'Thank you, Detective, but I'm not in need of a lecture. I do have some experience with the journalistic profession.'

Now it was Vince's turn to bristle, for it was all said in the tone of the lady of the house rebuking a tradesman. 'Then don't look so outraged, Mis Saxmore-Blaine, when I tell you that the idea of suicide will appeal to your lawyers. They, and all the people on your bench, are just trying to do the best for you. I've seen cases like this get pretty dirty, and for things to be good for you they will have to be bad for Mr Beresford.'

'Can they get any worse?'

'I'm talking about the only thing he now has left, his reputation.'

'I know what you're talking about. I was just being horribly facetious. I know how much these things matter to men like Johnny and his friends.'

'So in many ways, I'm sorry to say, having committed suicide would be the best outcome for both of you.'

At this there seemed to be a perceptible collapse in her indignation. She said, 'And would that also be the best outcome for you, Detective Treadwell?'

'No, the truth would be,' he shrugged, 'but that's just me.'

'And me, too. I loved Johnny and I won't slander him. He was funny, charming . . . sounds trite, I know, but you'll hear that said about him a lot, because it was true. Yet there was another side to the raconteur: he was gentle, kind and, for a while, my best pal.

93

Whatever happened between us, he deserved better than that. And I really need to know if I killed him.' She took a long pause that seemed to imbue the room with an uncomfortable significance, and Vince couldn't really think of anything to say to dispel it. Eventually she stepped in with, 'I'm not looking for excuses, or a way out. I'm looking for the truth, and I'm looking for forgiveness. Not from you or from the police. If I'm guilty, Detective Treadwell, I'll take my punishment and be glad of it. And then, hopefully, that way I'll find some forgiveness.'

Vince gave a considered nod to all this. It seemed strangely old-fashioned, but was said with such sincerity that he believed every word of it.

He stood up. 'My advice is, don't give up on yourself too quickly, Miss Saxmore-Blaine. And as someone once said, get off the cross, we need the wood.'

She wasn't so pious that she couldn't laugh. But she wasn't so irreverent that it could last too long either. Vince collected her prepared statement off the coffee table.

'Oh, can you do me a favour?' she asked, standing up and reaching into her dressing gown to pull out the crumpled pack of cigarettes and a book of matches. 'We're not supposed to smoke in our rooms. They've been so kind to me here. Would you mind?'

'Of course.' Vince took the empty cigarette packet and the book of matches and slipped it into his jacket pocket.

She walked him to the door and opened it for him. 'You never did call me Isabel, did you?'

'No, I never did. Maybe next time.'

CHAPTER 13

It was 9 p.m. and Vince was back in his castle: a one-bedroom first-floor flat in Pimlico. The spacious pad had darkly polished floors covered in thick Moroccan rugs that he'd picked up while travelling in that part of the world a couple of years back. The freshly painted walls were adorned with three large oils on canvas. This triptych of impressionistic jazz-playing figures, splashed on the canvas in vibrant primary colours, had been picked up through a friend of a friend who worked in a West End art gallery specializing in young American painters. Vince got them at a snip, but they were still the biggest purchase he'd ever made, and came in with the kind of price tag that made him constantly question their artistic merit, his own aesthetic judgement, and his economic acumen. At different times and in different moods, they either put a smile on his face or gave him an anxiety attack.

Vince had a shower and a shave and stared contemplatively into the bathroom mirror as he located the parting in his new haircut, and took the time to reflect on his day. It had been long, and as untypical and unpredictable as his untypical and unpredictable job allowed. Which was why he loved it.

After he had handed in Isabel Saxmore-Blaine's statement to Mac and Chief Superintendent Markham, the powers-that-be decided that she should be questioned further in regards to the death of Johnny Beresford, and therefore bailed on a Habeas Corpus Proceeding. This was all legalese to lessen the blow that she was in fact the prime suspect and was being booked on suspicion of murder. With the bail she was putting up, her family connections and her contrite attitude she was not considered a threat of flight, but she was still considered a risk to herself, and so was put under house arrest – with terms and conditions – at the Harley Street hospital.

He pondered Isabel Saxmore-Blaine. There was a lot to ponder. Externally she was easily put together: tall, slim, blonde, beautiful and privileged. That the genetic gods had been very good to her was plain to see. The other stuff that needed working out wasn't so plainly evident. The guilty or not guilty? The mad or not mad? The blackout drunk or not blackout drunk? The lover or the killer? Of course the answers to everything, and all of the above, probably lay somewhere in between, hidden within the crevices and curves, and dimmed in the shadows hanging over this case.

And if Isabel Saxmore-Blaine's contriteness, confusion, tortured conscience and seemingly selfless desire to square everything were all an act, then it amounted to a pretty convincing one. Vince believed it, and he could see it flying with a judge. And what with her diminished responsibility and Beresford's threat of violence towards her, and the fact that he had been killed with his own gun, never mind Geoffrey Lancing on the case, she would never see prison bars – just the ornate gilded ones offered by private hospitals like the Salisbury. A beaten down manslaughter charge, then off to a nunnery until the scandal faded, and the gossip columns had cooled down.

But what about Johnny Beresford? The dead man was curiously quiet, suspiciously silent. Dead men don't talk, but they are usually accompanied by a chorus of chatter with enough speculation buzzing around them to match the babbling of a séance conducted on amphetamines. But Beresford's family and friends had kept what most would describe as a dignified silence. They were all keeping their counsel, in public at least, and seemingly closing ranks. Ranks that Vince was going to try to break through tonight. Because there were still too many questions to be asked about the golden couple that had been Johnny and Isabel. Like when did it all start to tarnish? Isabel Saxmore-Blaine could probably have discussed the subject at length, but she currently lacked the necessary objectivity to answer things properly. And friends always have more fully formed opinions about other people's woes, more so even than their own, and they *love* to discuss them at length.

Vince selected a midnight-blue evening suit, a crisp white shirt, a knitted black tie. He then went into the kitchen and boiled up some water in a small saucepan. Opening his coffee can, he heaped a generous scoop of Jamaican Blue Mountain on to a spoon, dumped it into his French press, and then brewed himself up a cup of strong black coffee. As he did all this, his mind shifted a few postcodes north-west of Eaton Square and Belgravia, to the other side of the socio-economical tracks, and the enclave of Notting Hill.

Unlike Isabel Saxmore-Blaine, Tyrell Lightly had been solidly and unambiguously charged with murder; there was no 'Habeas Corpus Proceeding' for him. Regarding this, he broke his silence long enough to consult his political and moral mentor, Michael X, who then called in a lawyer. Both men decided Tyrell Lightly should talk, and talk he did. Lightly could explain his movements on the night of the murder. At the time the crime was being committed, he was out, like a true criminal recidivist, committing another crime. His alibi was that, with a team of three cohorts, he was robbing a warehouse in Park Royal, west London. Lightly gave up his three accomplices, and they were all picked up with relative ease. And, likewise, following criminal courtesy, for reduced charges they all gave Lightly up too. And thus unwittingly provided him with an alibi. If they'd had any brains, they wouldn't have given him up at all but merely said he wasn't there, and let him stew on a murder charge. But brains weren't at a premium with this mob, as the outcome of the robbery clearly illustrated. The job went wrong. At around midnight a guard, freshly armed with an Alsatian dog, spotted them clambering over the fence. After coshing the Alsatian to death and the guard unconscious, Tyrell Lightly and his mob were clambering back over the fence when the alarm was raised and the Alsatian's three brothers, dragging along the guard's three colleagues, came snarling and snapping at their heels. Lightly and his mob, however, made their escape, and spent the rest of the night at a lock-in in a boozer in Battersea.

Vince parked the Mk II in Bourdon Street and walked around the corner into Berkeley Square. The Montcler Club wasn't hard to spot, for it was undoubtedly the jewel of the square. A large four-storeyed Georgian town house, it was a 'town house' only in the loosest sense of the term. It was a house and it was in town, but so was Buckingham Palace. Whilst it obviously fell short of the palace's dynastic dimensions, and was terraced, Vince reckoned 'mansion' would be a more appropriate description.

Low-slung and elongated luxury cars – Bentleys, Bugattis, Rolls-Royce Shadows and Wraiths – and hackney carriages glided up and disgorged capped chauffeurs who loped around their polished steeds and opened doors with springy servitude, to evacuate aristocratic and carefree young couples dressed in furs and finery. These then made their way down to the basement of the Montcler, which hosted the exclusive nightclub called Jezebel's.

The young detective's interest was focused on the upper floors. The traffic into the casino was just as well-heeled and well-dressed, and consisted mainly of men, though not exclusively. The women that entered wore expensive furs too, perhaps as much for collateral as for warmth, but the casino crowd tended not to smile as readily as the nightclub crowd, and they looked about as carefree as Christians entering the Coliseum.

Vince approached the front door and it was opened by a fat man in a pea-green brocaded greatcoat and matching top hat, with a fulsome waxed moustache twizzled and sculpted skywards. The reception was the deep oak of a gentlemen's club, not the red plush of a Vegas-style carpet joint. Vince was greeted by a man in his early forties, who was elegantly put together: over six foot with oiled brown hair swept off a lean face that now creased into a well-practised and welcoming smile, exposing movie-star teeth as white as the dinner jacket he wore. But he wasn't simply twinkly eyes and sparkly molars, for there was lean muscle beneath the fine clothes and the meet-and-greet mannerisms. He introduced himself as Leonard, and was quick to tell Vince that he knew all the members personally, and didn't recognize him. Vince cut the conversation short, badged him, and asked to speak to James Asprey. There followed a phone call made from the reception desk, where Leonard cupped his hand over the mouthpiece, and a longer than necessary conversation ensued. Leonard finally put the phone down and, with a curt smile, swept a hand before him in a gesture for Vince to enter.

As they made their way up the magnificent double sided stairs, with their gilt-scrolled balustrades, Leonard gave Vince a potted history of the place, which was built by William Kent in 1744. Horace Warpole considered it one of the finest buildings in London in scale and execution but, for all its period panache, the games conducted in its rooms were the same the world over, only played on Chippendale tables. They included various forms of poker, including three-card or punto banco; there was blackjack, roulette and craps. But it was chemin de fer – or just chemmy, as it was known – that was the real star attraction of these rooms. Easy to play, and fun, with its quick returns and losses, and very addictive.

It was Baudelaire who declared that the devil's best trick is to persuade you that he doesn't exist. The best trick James Asprey pulled was convincing his punters that they weren't punters at all, but guests at a grand country house, enjoying a little harmless sport in the games room, instead of going belly up and flattening their wallets, draining their bank accounts, losing inheritances and in some cases their estates, to a high-octane, casino cash cow. Much has been said about the atmosphere of gaming rooms and casinos: the clawing and cloying desperation, the heady and binary opposites of raw cynicism and lethal optimism, the dead air and stilled time. The Montcler inverted all of that. It made you feel that you were exclusive, a special guest, and that you were lucky to be there.

That you were even lucky to be losing your money there. It's a general rule that there are no clocks in casinos. Not so with the Montcler, where there were lots of them. There were ornate Swiss timepieces on mantelpieces, long-case clocks standing up against the walls, even amusing cuckoo clocks in the dining room, all of them chirping, banging and ringing out the time. Because time in the Montcler was special, it was privileged, and each hour you spent there was to be celebrated. This was the time of your life.

The Montcler reminded Vince of Beresford's home in Eaton Square: the same schema, just on a grander scale. Like a home from home. As he was led through the club he scoped the rooms looking for members of Beresford's set, and immediately spotted two of them. Lord Lucan sat studying his hand of cards, wearing a troubled and none-too-bright expression on his face. It wasn't a poker face, because his moustache seemed to twitch and bristle involuntarily, giving away the fact that Lord Lucan either didn't like what he read on the cards or he just couldn't read them, full stop. But dim as the good lord looked, Vince wasn't going to judge Lucan, or any of the Montcler set, merely on Isabel Saxmore-Blaine's say-so. She clearly viewed them all as the enemy.

The other member of Beresford's set sat playing backgammon at a table with another man. A small crowd had already gathered around the pair, giving an indication of the stakes they were play-ing for, and the skill with which they were doing it. Simon Goldsachs was hunched over the table in intense deliberation but, unlike Lucan, he seemed to know exactly what he was doing. And he clearly enjoyed doing it, and thus concentrated fully on the task in hand. As Vince passed by, Simon Goldsachs glanced up at his audience while he loaded the dice into the cup to take his throw. It was the eyes that struck Vince most. They looked as if they could not only bore right through you, but sum you up in a second and then bury you on the spot. His opponent looked Mediterranean, and Vince could almost tell by the cut of his suit that he was Italian. The gesticulating hand movements backed this up, even in the act of smoking a cigarette or throwing the dice. Vince particularly noticed the Italian's watch, because it was meant to be noticed: a gold chronograph, an Audermars, with all its sub-dials and pushers. What made it so noticeable in a room probably packed with Pateks, Perregauxs and Rolex Presidentials, discreetly hidden under French cuffs, was that this man wore the watch fastened *over* his cuff.

'Is that Simon Goldsachs?' asked Vince.

'Yes. He's playing with Mr Agnelli, the owner of Fiat.'

Vince gave a nod of recognition, then shook his head in condemnation. 'I once had one of those. I spent half the time standing at the side of a road kicking the tyres.'

Leonard continued smiling, but not laughing.

'Enter' came the command, and Leonard opened the door warily. Vince noted the man's nervousness, which worried him. Because not looking nervous, flustered or showing any emotion at all was part of Leonard's well-practised stock-in-trade. Vince entered, and the door was quickly shut, with Leonard wisely staying behind it. The thing sprang at him from the floor, its eyes flashing a demonic emerald green. Its gaping twisted mouth growled, exposing a long purple tongue rough enough to scrape the flesh off your dead bones, and it had teeth and claws big enough and sharp enough to get you into that sorry position. The tight-packed muscle down its back and across its shoulders and shanks rippled under shimmering black velvet fur.

'Settle down, Zarra,' said James Asprey, pulling on the long leash that secured 'Zarra' to the radiator. Zarra was a panther. Not a fully grown panther, but not a cuddly kitten chasing a ball of string either.

'Do excuse Zarra, Detective, she has terrible manners. Obviously thinks you're after her steak.'

'Just as long as Zarra doesn't think I *am* her steak.'

Asprey was seated behind his desk, and before him sat a sirloin steak with all the trimmings. Asprey cut it into slices and handed the plate down to the big black cat.

'It's time for her walk, you see.'

'Where do you walk her?'

'Around Berkeley Square,' replied Asprey, in a low languid drawl.

'I bet that gets the nightingales singing.'

'That's why I have to feed her first. Last time she went out hungry, and ended up killing a bloody Jack Russell.'

'What happened to the owner?'

'He or she wasn't attached to it at the time, and I didn't hang about to hear their complaints. I dumped the dog in the basement, got in the motor and scarpered.' Asprey fixed him with a challenging look. But he needn't have bothered, since Vince wasn't on dead dog duties this week. 'I don't suppose I should walk her in public, as there's probably some law against it. But laws are made to be broken – that's how we change them, don't you agree, Detective . . . ?'

'Treadwell. Vince Treadwell. I know how you changed the gambling laws in this country by breaking them. I know quite a bit about you, Mr Asprey.' This stirred some interest in Asprey, in the form of a raised eyebrow that bade Vince to continue. 'You started out bookmaking whilst still at Eton, got sent down from Oxford for running card schools – and threatening to break a fellow student's legs when he wouldn't pay up on a wager.'

Asprey gave a short raucous laugh at this memory. 'Phileas Ainsworth. Modern languages. And he didn't understand the words "pay up" in any of them. The little turd thought it was all fun and games, until the credit ran out and it was time to stump up. A reputation is worth far more than a degree, and it's stood me in good stead ever since.'

'Back in London you decided against a career in the City, or in the Foreign Office, where the rest of the men in your family had distinguished themselves, and started working for the bookmaker Sid Amberg, to really learn the game.'

'Ah, Siddy, bless him, one of the finest desert dwellers to walk across the Red Sea and make it to Oxford Circus. Do go on, Detective Treadwell. The memories are priceless.'

Vince did something he wasn't invited to do and sat down on a red leather Chesterfield set against the wall. He deliberately forwent the chair closest to Asprey's desk. The room wasn't small, but it surely felt that way with Zarra at one end of it. She looked a lot more dangerous than the one Cary Grant had to contend with in *Bringing up Baby*.

Vince continued: 'You soon set up on your own book, with a share from Sid, and started running chemmy parties at various upmarket locations, the Ritz to name but one.'

Asprey's brow furrowed, weighing the detective up, reassessing him, then granting him a nod of approval. 'Well done. I'm a man who appreciates good information. As a bookmaker and layer of odds, it's key to success. And this is very good information you have, very good.'

'A lot of it's a matter of public record – if you can be bothered to dig. And I like to dig. You took a gambling pinch in '58. It made all the papers. Society amusement more than scandal. In fact, it made your reputation, as the rakish gentleman gambler.'

'Never my intention, Detective. My intention was to make money, and have some fun along the way. But mostly to make money.'

'And you made money – a lot of money. I heard you were clearing almost half a million a year.'

At last, Asprey looked something like surprised. 'And where did you get this information? Because *that* certainly isn't a matter of public record – not even my accountant knows.'

'I checked with a retired detective, DCI Teddy Maybury.'

At the mention of his old nemesis, Asprey stopped smiling. 'Retired indeed – retired on a pension supplied by me. I forget the amount of times Maybury broke up our little games. He was only looking for a pay-off, of course.'

'Of course,' agreed Vince, with a couldn't-care-less shrug. 'Teddy told me your mother, Lady Asprey, used to straighten them out. A formidable lady, so I hear.'

'My mother had a way with policemen, the common touch you might say,' said Asprey, smiling again. But it was the hooded, humourless eyes that Vince noticed as the owner of the Montcler Club delivered his next slight. 'She would convince them that they were being rather silly, very prudish and extremely boorish, and altogether living up to their reputations . . .'

This slight wasn't so slight, however. It was looking for – and demanded – a big fat retort. And Vince would have delivered one, both barrels, but for the fact he had been distracted. He was staring at Zarra. The beast was up on its paws now, its back arched, head bowed, fur bristling and trembling with a look of contorted concentration. Its tail was up and swishing from side to side like a windscreen wiper. It was taking a shit.

Asprey followed Vince's gaze, looked down unperturbed at his pet panther unpacking on the polished floor and, barely missing a beat, nonchalantly continued: 'But, of course, the police, though puerile and puritanical, were predictably and very punctually taking their cut. Yes, you could set your watch by Maybury and his mob from West End Central. But by that time things had really taken off. I had so many friends and contemporaries who were now politicians or in positions of power, and were gambling with me, that they really would have been arses to do anything other than make it legal. On any given night, there'd be front-benchers here from both sides of the Commons. Not to mention my ermined and robed friends from the upper house. You see, Detective Treadwell, the aristocracy of this great country have always gambled. It's their birthright, and gambling is the last bastion of honour in this country. In these straitened times, it's all we have available to us to test our mettle. And no mean-spirited little mercantile-class law was going to put a stop to it for long.'

With that, Asprey sighed and averted his languorous eyes from Vince; eyes that, by the end of his little monologue, were filled with antipathy for the world he found himself living in. He leaned back in his throne-like chair, hooked his thumbs into his waistband – and considered Zarra, curled around his feet like a discarded fur coat, as she licked her arse.

James Asprey was a tall, gaunt figure of a man. The dark blue three-piece suit he wore was covered in dried drool from Zarra. It looked as if it needed a good cleaning, or a good throwing out. But that was typical of Asprey's class: they never threw anything away. It all got handed down, everything from the grand houses they lived in, the furniture they sat on, to the three-piece Kilgour or Anderson & Sheppard suits they lounged around in. Asprey had wavy sandy hair and looked older than his thirty-nine years, with a face that was long and suitably equine-looking for an ex-bookie. The mouth was wide and fleshy and flexible, and could smile winningly if it needed to; like when meeting and greeting a big-money gambler about to spend it at his tables. His eyes, at the same time, remained hooded and glacially impenetrable. Vince had noted how everything that Asprey said and did seemed to take just that little longer than was necessary. His movements were slow and confident, and Vince had the feeling that James Asprey didn't hurry much for anything. He was working to his own personal timeframe and wouldn't be rushed, cajoled or stirred by the demands of the human race, a race he misanthropically refused to break a sweat for. Even with the animals he loved, he was the leader of the pack, and Zarra was going to have to damn well wait for her walk; and meanwhile could shit on the floor as much as she liked.

'That's all very interesting, Mr Asprey. Now you can tell me about Johnny Beresford?'

At this, Asprey straightened up in his chair, arranging himself in a more businesslike fashion. He reached into his inside breast pocket and pulled out a silver cigarette case, flipped it open and offered one to Vince. 'Bespoke blended, Turkish mainly.' When Vince declined, Asprey lit a cigarette for himself with a gold and enamelled Caran d'Ache lighter, and hungrily sucked down the pungent Turkish smoke.

Then he said: 'Johnny was a friend. One of the few. One of the best. I'd trust him with my life. Like all my friends, he loved to gamble; wouldn't be my friend if he didn't. Johnny was with me from the start. He was here at the club most nights and, un-officially, he was my floor manager of sorts. The rare occasions I'm not here, Johnny is, he takes care of any gaming problems that may arise. Everyone loves him, one of the funniest buggers I know. And he's a terrific card player, so he plays . . .' Asprey stopped, having caught his use of the present tense. Obviously still snagged on the past. He took what seemed a laborious breath to quell the emotion in his voice, and then gave a slight smile, as if to correct himself; he wouldn't be making that mistake again. 'Johnny played for the house. He brought a lot of players in. They wanted to play against him, pit their wits. They wanted to play the best. And for a long long time he was simply that.'

'A professional gambler?'

Asprey's head jolted back, as if struck by a humorous memory. 'When he left the army, he put down "gambler" as his occupa-tion in his passport. Probably not the wisest thing to do when you travel. People assume you're on the dodgy side, and of course it's not legal in a lot of places. But he thought it *rakish*, and didn't want to appear a bore, even to some chap at passport control. Putting down businessman on his passport he thought was ter-ribly dull. But, of course, it wasn't a complete affectation, as he did derive a portion of his income from gambling. How big the portion, even I couldn't tell you. He had lots of interests, fingers in lots of financial pies.'

'And enemies? I imagine a professional gambler with his fingers in lots of pies would make a few.'

Asprey looked genuinely surprised, then genuinely amused. 'Where do you think you are, Detective? A saloon in Dodge City full of twitchy-fingered cowpokes drunkenly accusing each other of cheating?' Then he shot out his hand, shaped it like gun, and mimicked the action of a fast-on-the-draw gunslinger. 'Good lord, no sir. We lose like we win, and vice versa, without celebration or commiseration but with dignity. It's just bad manners and bad form to do it any other way. If you want emotional catharsis, go join the herd and play the slot machines at Las Vegas – or Brighton. We're gentlemen here.'

'And yet Beresford still ended up with a bullet in his head – just like in Dodge City.'

'You have the culprit in Isabel, the wretched creature,' said Asprey, crushing out his half-smoked cigarette in the cut-crystal ashtray. He must have seen the look that Vince gave him, because he tempered his last statement with, 'A nice enough girl. Considered quite intelligent, I believe, but she clearly had her problems, as I'm sure you know. As I'm sure everyone knows now, if the papers are anything to go by.'

'Let's get back to Mr Beresford and his enemies. Everyone has them and, as one of his closest friends, I'm sure you would know who they are.'

'He's bound to have picked a few up, being a wealthy man. One of the lucky few, the silver spoon and all that. And he was a handsome chap, too. Money and looks can make a combustible combination, as people get jealous. No doubt the enemies were there, Detective, but none so spiteful as to prove a problem, and certainly none with the strength of feeling, or character, to put a bullet in his head. If I was a gambling man, Detective Treadwell, which of course I am, my money would be firmly on Isabel. But if I was going to bet the house, my money would have been on Johnny killing her instead.'

'He was violent towards her?'

Asprey wobbled his head from side to side in a gesture of weighing this up, then said, 'It was a volatile mix. Certainly had a temper on him, and he was a big chap. Spent five years in the army, boxed for the regiment, and knew how to handle himself.'

'I'd hardly call Isabel Saxmore-Blaine simply an adversary who needed handling, would you?'

'Yes, I would. She shot him, for God's sake!'

Vince let that one hang in the air. And he let Asprey hang with it. He watched as the gambler waited for Vince's confirmation of the fact, but Vince didn't give it to him. Instead, he asked: 'When did things start to go wrong between them?'

'Who's to say?'

'Take a punt. Six months ago? A year ago?'

'From day one, I'd say. There was something . . . something very show-offy about them. They had to be the centre of attention: either fawning all over each other in public or fighting. Acceptable behaviour in the animal kingdom, where they do it without affect-ation, but with those two it was just tiresome. They were as bad as each other, Detective Treadwell. And, of course, they were both drinking too much in the end. She's half-American you know, so of course she was taking drugs. Not the hard stuff, but uppers and downers and the like. Frankly, together, they were a mess.'

'So different then from the photos I've seen of them together, where they look like the golden couple. All cheesy smiles and expensive dentistry for the camera and the public. But, in private, deep resentments and tearing strips off each other. Is that right, Mr Asprey?'

Asprey gave an exclamatory knock on the desk. 'Exactly! Looks can be deceiving, Detective, and the camera often lies. I've got a chum, a professional photographer, who's paid a fortune to tell lies with his camera.'

Vince reached into his inside pocket and pulled out the photo of Asprey sitting with Beresford and the rest of the Montcler set. 'Like this, you mean? All smiles, and expensive dentistry?'

The smug grin on Asprey's face weakened, then fell away alto-gether. His normally languid delivery tightened as he said, 'Well played, Detective. I fell right into your hands.'

Vince pointed at the picture, 'And there's your photographer chum – Nicky DeVane, right?'

'That's him. So you don't think Isabel did it, do you? Then what are you suggesting, Detective? One of us?'

'I'm sure you understand, Mr Asprey. This is just procedure, nothing personal. We have to hedge our bets.'

'A gambling man too, are you?'

Vince shook his head.

'We'll never be friends then.'

'I always figure that likelihood into the equation when I meet people working a murder case. Did any of these men in this photo have a reason to kill Johnny Beresford?'

'I'm in that photo myself, Detective.'

'So you are. Then let's start with you. Where were you the night he was killed?'

'You think I would have let you in here without having a decent alibi? I was at home. Not in London, but my home in the country. It's near Canterbury. I'm usually in London during the week, but my camel was suffering from a compacted tooth that needed removing.'

'Camel – as in the animal?'

'Unless you can think of any other kind of camel, yes. As you may know, wildlife is a passion of mine. Everything else I indulge in is a vice.' Again he looked down lovingly at Zarra, who now lay stretched out with her eyes closed and was purring contentedly. 'I find animals so much more agreeable as company than humans. Most of the humanity crawling across this planet are vermin.'

'You should join the police, that'll warm your views.'

There was no witty rejoinder from Asprey. He was being deadly serious.

'Hitler, for all his little eccentricities, had some good points regarding eugenics. Did you know, Treadwell, it's been proven that higher-income groups tend to possess superior genetics? So joining the police would be out of the question, as I'm just not genetically built for the penuriousness of the public pay sector. I'm a capitalist with a big C.'

'The air's turning rank, Mr Asprey, and it's not all Zarra's fault either. I'm a little bored with the Übermensch philosophy, so let's just stick to what time you spent at home?'

'The vet arrived at about nine p.m. It was a reasonably simple procedure, but he's a chum and we then had a drink together and a game of backgammon, so he didn't leave until well past midnight.' Asprey smiled. 'Minus his fee for the camel's tooth.'

'After that, were you alone?'

'Yes.' Then, almost as an afterthought he said, 'Apart from my wife and children.' He gave a decisive shake of his head as if he'd suddenly come to a conclusion. 'No, Detective, I wouldn't kill Johnny. Not only was he a friend but he was a financial asset. Lots of people would come to the club to try and beat him, and they lost. He brought people in, so why kill the golden goose?'

'You're all heart.' Vince stood up. 'I'll now need to talk to two of your members, Mr Goldsachs and Lord Lucan.' Asprey gave him a quizzical look, and Vince firmly informed him: 'I saw them both downstairs as I came through.'

'You'll give us a bad reputation.'

'Rakish, I'd have thought.'

'This is a place of business.'

'Oh, I'll be incredibly discreet.'

'Yes, I'm sure you will.' Asprey stood up and looked Vince over, as if measuring him for a suit. 'I must say, Treadwell, you don't look like a policeman. I usually expect the rotten clothes, the flat feet, the haggard expression, the dull eyes, and ultimately the outstretched palm.'

'I've got all that to look forward to.'

'I'll draw you up some chips, on the house.'

'Like I said, I don't gamble.' But he knew that Asprey wouldn't have forgotten that little fact already.

'Like I said, you're most unlike a policeman. They always used to accept my chips, whether they gambled or not.'

Vince glanced down at Zarra, and her spiralling tube of shit on the floor. 'I bet the cleaner's glad you don't bring the camel in to work.'

CHAPTER 14

Vince and Asprey made their way down the stairs just as Leonard was making his way up – with some urgency. When Vince asked him about the whereabouts of Simon Goldsachs and Lord Lucan, Leonard quickly informed them that they had both left the club (no big surprise there: Leonard had obviously done his job). He then quickly revealed his real purpose for coming to see his boss: Isabel Saxmore-Blaine was downstairs, in Jezebel's. She had obviously been drinking and was demanding to see James Asprey, or any of his friends.

Asprey wanted to know: 'Why the hell did they let her in?'

Vince wanted to know, why the hell did they let her out?

The red silk rope was immediately unhooked and the detective descended into the basement club alone. Vince had been into downstairs dives before, but this wasn't one of them. The high Georgian style from upstairs didn't stop downstairs, which originally would have been used for the servants' quarters and cellars of the grand house above. Jezebel's took its name from Lady Belle Finch, who had lived at the Berkeley Square address circa the 1700s. Quite a beauty, and quite a gal in her time, she was rumoured to have been the lover of Frederick, Prince of Wales, hence the nickname from Belle to Jezebel. It was a name and a reputation she apparently, though very privately, revelled in.

Jezebel's, with its vaulted ceilings, gave you a sense that it was a cathedral of high class and good taste. All the fixtures and furnishings were period: silver Corinthian-columned candlesticks illuminated the rooms, and gloomy old Dutch masters adorned its darkly varnished wood-panelled walls, giving the club a sombre look. But every now and then your eye was taken by a flash of colour: a framed splashy abstract, a modern advertising poster of artistic merit, along with the odd African mask or South American tapestry. All this was tempered with fine dining, one of the best wine cellars in London, and the slickest cocktail mixers this side of Manhattan. Somewhere around there was also a dance floor, although it wasn't big enough to swing Zarra on. But for the members of Jezebel's, this was home from home. For visiting kings and queens and presidents and potentates it was a paradigm of English class and discretion.

And for Isabel Saxmore-Blaine it was a designated battlefield. Seated on her own, nursing a greenish-looking cocktail, she was in full plume. The thick honey hair was jooged and styled and shiny and luxurious. The lips were painted, the eyes mascaraed, the cheekbones blushed – all done with the lightest of touches, because hers was the kind of face that really didn't need a lot of work. She came pre-prepared.

She was dressed in a short shiny black and white outfit, something by Pierre Cardin just a little more modern than the gowns worn by the surrounding debs. To Vince's eye, and he considered his eye to be pretty damned good, she was easily the best-looking woman in the place. And maybe that's why she was being so studiously ignored. Out of jealousy? No, because she was being ignored by the men too. Therefore social pariah. How could she be anything but? And yet she looked as though she didn't give a damn, positively rising to the occasion and enjoying it. She sat bolt upright, defiant, as if she was challenging the room; which, of course, her presence was.

Vince sat down at the same table. He stayed calm and was all smiles, as though they were two friends meeting up for a drink.

Inside he fumed, though, and didn't quite know why. What did he care if they banged her up?

'What are you doing here?'

'You want a drink, Detective? I'm on the gimlets. They were a favourite of Johnny's. I soon developed a taste for them myself, like a good little faithful lush.'

Vince saw in her dark eyes that she was already well lit up. From out of nowhere a waiter magically appeared at their table.

'My handsome detective friend and I will have some more gimlets, please, and—'

'We'll just have the bill,' said Vince cutting her off. 'And that will be all.'

The waiter genuflected his way silently back into the ether.

'You asked what I'm doing here. Well, I could ask the same of you. No offence but they're very fussy about who they let in. I'm a member, so what's your excuse?'

He looked down at her three-quarters finished drink. 'Finish it up and let's go.'

'No.'

'Then leave it and let's go.'

'No.'

'You want to make a scene, Miss Saxmore-Blaine?'

'No.'

'That's an awful lot of nos.'

'I counted three, but there's a lot more where they came from. I'm drunk and I'll do as I please, Vincent Treadwell.'

'Drunk or sober, you're a spoiled, over-privileged brat who's been cut far too much slack, as far as I'm concerned. You want to make a spectacle of yourself, to be honest I really don't give a damn.'

Her head rolled back to emit a peal of laughter, then she banged the table in approval. 'Well said, Detective! I think you've hit the nail on the head with that summation, and I really don't give a damn either, so there!'

'Let's go.'

'I'm not ready to leave. Not until I've set eyes on one of the rats. Where are the rats? Are they here?'

'If you mean James Asprey—'

'King Rat himself!'

Heads turned at this remark. Isabel Saxmore-Blaine did the mature thing and poked her tongue out at them.

Vince could not resist a smile. 'Sitting here really isn't doing you any favours at all.'

'Oh, that's the joy of this place. Everyone so incredibly discreet. No one talks. No one will say a thing, for fear of being considered indiscreet and having their memberships taken away.'

'It's not them I care about.'

She leaned across the table at him. 'Your summation of me was about right, my dear Detective Treadwell, but with the money and influence my father has, until they tie a noose around my neck, I can do pretty much as I please.'

'Don't bet on it. I'm pretty sure the stipulations of your bail don't allow nightclubbing. If this gets out you'll be residing in another exclusive club, Holloway, with bull-dyke screws as hostesses and a mixed clientele of whores, junkies, shoplifters and murderesses. How does that grab you?'

The forced frivolity left her face, and a moroseness settled in. 'Maybe that's what I deserve.'

She looked as if she might start crying. Vince wasn't going to let that happen, so he said, 'No, no, and thrice no! You see, two can play at that game.'

A smile broke out on her lips. 'You're cute, as we say in Poughkeepsie. In case you don't know, Poughkeepsie is in New York State, home to my old alma mater, Vassar College. I was happy there, Detective, full of fun and ideas and ideals. Just before real life started. Did I mention you're "cute", as we say in Poughkeepsie?'

'And you're pissed, as we say in Pimlico. But beautifully so.'

Vince grabbed her by the arm before she could react or get into a self-pitying jag. She attempted to free herself of his grip, but soon realized that resistance was futile, as they say. He had already arranged her escape route with James Asprey, just in case any photographers were waiting outside. So, with a firm hold, he steered her towards the cloakroom and collected her coat, which wasn't a coat at all but a black fur cape, just like Zarra but without the teeth. Then through the kitchen and out the back way to where Vince had parked the Mk II.

He drove Isabel to his own private club: Gino's Café in Pimlico. It was an Italianate greasy spoon that did a good line in mama's homemade cooking, the meatballs with red wine sauce being the pick of the menu. Red plastic gingham-style tablecloths covered Formica tables that were screwed to the floor. Framed pastoral scenes from the old country covered the burgundy-glossed walls. Vince tucked into the meatballs with ravioli.

Isabel smoked and glanced listlessly at some slices of Welsh rarebit that seeped rust-coloured globules of grease on to her white plate. Both had fresh coffee in front of them.

'So, what did Aspers have to say?'

'Asprey? He thinks you did it,' answered Vince, looking squarely at her as he did so. Her head dipped and she let out a dispirited and deflating sigh, like the jury had just delivered the final verdict. Vince could see that, without the fuel of booze, which had given her the ability to stare down an entire room, she was far from insensitive to the opinions of others.

'Don't look so upset. What did you expect Asprey to say? And I imagine the rest of Johnny's friends will follow suit.'

'Nicky won't,' she said, with a vigorous shake of her head. 'He's a true friend.'

'If he killed Johnny, he will.'

She sat up straight and hoisted her black eyebrows to breaking point, as though this was the most outrageous thing she'd ever heard.

'Well, if you didn't do it, someone did.'

'Meaning you don't think . . . I did it?'

'I don't even think you really think you did it,' said Vince, eye-ing the small gold crucifix hung around her long neck. 'And you're likely to be your own worst witness for the persecution.' She looked confused, so Vince corrected himself. 'Witness for the *prosecution*. If you genuinely thought you were guilty, you'd be tucked up in bed now, instead of pitching up at Jezebel's dressed to the nines and drinking gimlets like Boudicca.'

She laughed, as if this was the second most outrageous thing she'd ever heard. 'Boudicca . . . with gimlets?'

Vince picked up on the ridiculousness of the image, and laughed too. Their laughter went on far longer than either of them intended. It gathered momentum and quickly turned into a fit of giggles that just got worse every time they looked at each other and tried to subdue it. It became infectious as heads turned. Even the three stern-faced old cabbies, who looked as if they'd been around the block a few times, and were silently fuelling up on steaming copper-coloured tea and meatball sarnies, cracked smiles that soon turned into chuckles. Breathless and flushed, Isabel finally took control of the situation and excused herself to pow-der her nose. When she returned, she found Vince soberly sipping his black coffee.

'Thank you for that,' she said. 'For making me laugh, I mean. It's been a while. For a moment there, I almost forgot about every-thing. But you're not going to let me do that, are you?'

Vince looked apologetic for about three and a half seconds, then it was back to business. 'Asprey and the others, did any of them have a beef, a problem, with Johnny – no matter how seem-ingly small, how seemingly slight.'

'They've known each other since school days. They were his best friends.'

Vince threw her a look over his coffee cup that killed off the last of such naivety, and in case it hadn't he backed it up with: 'Then they probably *all* had motives to kill him. I'm looking for

116

rifts, I'm looking for falling-outs and arguments . . . I'm looking for *anything*. Let's start with James Asprey.'

'He's your classic misanthrope, prefers the company of monkeys to most men outside his close circle of friends, and he thinks women have their place purely for breeding purposes. Believes they should drop the H bomb at least three more times, because a good culling is what the world needs. Thinks dictatorships are the only way to run things. Stalin had it right, but he was a red. And Adolf Hitler is preferable to Harold Wilson. I've heard all this being said without any hint of irony.'

'Me, too, some of it. Would he include Johnny Beresford in that cull?'

'They all fell out with one another at one time or another, but they always made up. Simon Goldsachs was the most recent, but I don't know what it was about. Johnny claimed it was nothing, just a silly spat. Before that he wasn't talking to Guy Ruley for a while, because of a business deal gone wrong. But they seemed to put it all behind them. As for Lucky—'

'Lucky?'

'Lord *Lucky* Lucan. A nickname, and deeply ironic to everyone but Lucky himself. Even as he watched his money drift away from him in hand after hand of chemmy or each throw of the dice, he still didn't get the joke. Johnny never fell out with him, because he was too busy beating him at the tables.' Vince's eyes flashed with interest. Isabel must have noticed this, because she quickly added, 'Lucky wouldn't kill him. He wouldn't have the brains to.'

'You don't have to have brains to kill people, you just need them to get away with it. And no one's got away with anything yet. But go on, tell me about Nicky DeVane.'

At this she gave a short derisive laugh. 'Impossible. Nicky wouldn't fall out with any of them. And they wouldn't fall out with him. He's impossible to fall out with.'

'He's more a friend of yours than of Johnny's, you'd say?'

'I've known him for years. Our families were neighbours when we were children. He and Johnny met at Eton. But I know that

Nicky wouldn't hear a word against me. Johnny told me that Nicky was intensely loyal to me.'

'He sent you the flowers, a dozen red roses. That could be construed as a statement of more than just friendship.'

'I like roses, and Nicky knows that. Johnny always preferred lilies, had them all over his house.' At the memory of this, her eyes squeezed shut for a moment. But Vince could see it was a moment intensely felt, and she wasn't savouring the recollection, instead was trying to rid herself of it. 'I can smell them now, pungent and cloying. The drifting pollen used to catch on my clothes and leave an orange stain. They're the flower of death, did you know that?'

Vince knew it and nodded, but he was preoccupied with an idea that was slowly but surely sliding into place. 'You've not been to Eaton Square since, have you?'

'No, of course not.'

She circumspectly picked up a slice of her Welsh rarebit. Vince took it out of her hand and said, 'Your biggest problem is your blacking out there. I know a little about blackout drunks.' Vince watched as her head dipped, and a shadow of shame passed over her face. But, heartbreaking as it was, he'd had enough of humouring her and pressed on. 'Blackout drunks are capable of anything. Jails are full of men who went for one drink after work and woke up the next morning with their wife lying dead next to them, and themselves holding the knife that did it. Yet they didn't have a clue how it happened. And saying you blacked out and can't remember anything is not a defence. From going around to Eaton Square and getting drunk, from fighting and clocking him with the champagne bottle, you're missing about six hours. If you want to prove you're innocent before a court of law, we have to find those hours.'

'But where? I *can't* remember.'

'Trust me?'

Isabel searched Vince's eyes. 'Why do you care about me, Detective Treadwell?'

'I don't, not especially,' he said, none too convincingly. 'Johnny may have killed himself. Maybe not. If not, which is my bet, then I want to find out who did. So, Miss Saxmore-Blaine, do you trust me?'

She nodded, and asked: 'What are we going to do?'

'We're going to wake up and smell the flowers.'

CHAPTER 15

It was around midnight when Vince drew up in Eaton Square. Isabel pulled out a cigarette and began searching her patent-leather clutch bag for a light. Vince opened the glove compartment and pulled out a book of matches, the same one Isabel had given him to dispose of when he'd seen her in the private hospital. The cardboard match sparked and fizzed into life, illuminating the car when its light caught the glint of the gold-coloured match book.

'Are you sure you want to do this?' he asked, examining what was embossed on the gold cover of the match book before dropping it on to the dash. She took a deep drag on her cigarette and plumed out a cylinder of smoke that, filtered through her fragrant lipstick, smelled better than any fancy-schmancy perfume he cared to mention.

She gave Vince an assured nod.

The plan was simple: to place Isabel back at the scene of the crime and have her retrace her footsteps on the night of the murder, and thus try and dismantle the fugue state she was now in. To throw light on what had happened that night: illuminate the blackout she'd fallen into and unlock the *thing* hidden in her subconscious. Just like the malodorous scent of the lilies had unlocked memories of Johnny Beresford. Vince had warned her of the dangers; it could prove her guilt just as easily as prove her innocence. There were obviously other risks involved in this 'experiment'. But seeing as Isabel had fallen off the wagon by her own doing that night, he felt those risks were calculated. Because,

to make it work, Vince needed her to replicate as closely as possible her state of mind at the time the murder was committed:
the setting, the mood and, naturally, her level of intoxication.
They'd bought a couple of bottles of champagne, and the plan also
meant Vince making a trip up to Notting Hill.

There he had collared Vivian Chalcott inside his haunt, the
Finches pub on Portobello Road. It was a gentle collar, a soft
collar, a velvet collar. Vince collected him from the bar and sat him
down in one of the pummelled red booths, where he scored a
couple of joints off him. With a sly smile, Vivian said that he was
always happy to 'turn on' members of the constabulary, and this
wasn't the first time he had done so. Vivian was about to disclose
who Vince's fellow policing potheads were when Vince raised a
halting hand and explained firmly that they weren't for him, but
for 'a work-related experiment'. Vivian nodded sagaciously, then
winked and nudged, and remarked that even the great detective
Sherlock Holmes had got high from time to time. Vince
then warned Vivian that if he ever started peddling the stuff
that Sherlock Holmes shot up with, relations between the two of
them would get decidedly frosty. Vivian gave him the ready-rolled
reefers for nothing, whereupon Vince said he owed him one,
and knew that, somewhere down the line, he'd end up paying
him back.

Isabel looked at the two rolled joints nestling in her cigarette
pack and said, 'I can't imagine this sort of activity being standard
police practice. How did you get to know about it?'

'I read it in a book. And now you're stalling. If we're going to
do it, we have to do it right away.'

On entering the house, they went straight into the main drawing room. As a crime scene, it had been done and dusted. The
place had been thoroughly swept for prints, and photographed,
and all the evidence they might need from the house had been
collected and bagged and recorded. So there was nothing here to
disturb. He watched as Isabel walked slowly around the big room,
breathing it in, eating it up with her eyes, a room she'd been in

a hundred times before that was suffused with memories and meaning – and hopefully, clues. The lilies in the room were over-ripe and ready to die, and their pollen was pungently rich.

She went over to the drinks cabinet, a converted black boulle-worked commode, and took out two tall stemmed and fluted glasses.

'Will you be joining me?'

'No thanks.'

'Scared I'll kill you too?'

'There's no nice way of putting this, but if the scientist got in the cage with the rats every time he did an experiment, where would we be?'

'You're right, there was no nice way of putting it – but you could have tried a little harder.'

Vince popped the first champagne bottle, and poured some of the fizzy amber liquid into her glass. It wasn't the same quality as the champagne drunk on the crucial night, and he had wondered if she needed the exact same brand to relive the true sensation. But she had assured him that she'd be okay with what they had. It seemed Isabel knew all about booze, not just from the per-spective of knowing the right wine to order with the right food in good restaurants, but from the perspective of a drunk, or a lush, to use the feminine designation. And no matter how hard the average booze hound or bottomed-out alcoholic professes to be a connoisseur of the grape or the grain, it's the ethanol alcohol they crave, be it in a bottle of Bollinger or a tin of silver polish. Both will eventually take them to the same place. You drink it and you drink it, until one day it decides to retaliate and drink you. Isabel knew this all too well as she put her lips to the glass and took the first sip: the first one that triggers the phenomenal crav-ing, and the compulsion to drink more and more of the stuff until it spiralled her down into the black pit, the blackout, the big nowhere.

She took the bottle of champagne from Vince, holding it firmly by the neck in one hand. In the other she held her glass of fizzing champagne, as she sat down in a blue velvet and gilt-framed chaise longue. Vince sat down opposite her.

'You want me to put on some music?'

'Why?'

'Because you were listening to music that night.'

She said not yet, and drank thirstily. It was the booze that had her attention now. In no time she'd drained the glass and poured another. And another. And another. She took the pack of cigarettes out of her bag and fished out a joint, lit it, and drew the earthy smoke deep into her lungs. She held it there without a cough or a splutter, then finally released it wrapped around a resigned sigh. Vince watched her with a scientific eye as she went about getting wasted in an almost workmanlike fashion. She drank deeply, she smoked heavily, and didn't seem to be enjoying any of it.

'I turned Johnny on to this,' she said, raising the joint between forefinger and thumb. 'I first smoked it at college.'

'They smoke a lot of pot in Poughkeepsie?'

'Oh, Detective Vincent Treadwell, you would not believe what they get up to in *Poughkeepsie*.'

She leaned back into the sofa, her lips curling into a lazily lascivious smile. Her dark lustrous eyes now held a glint, and it was a glint aimed right at Vince. It was an inviting glint, one that wanted him to join her on the blue velvet chaise longue. But, flattering and exciting as it was to have Isabel Saxmore-Blaine looking at him like this now, he didn't want her to be in the *now*; he wanted her to be in the *then*.

With three-quarters of the bottle polished off and the joint smoked, she said, in a voice now thoroughly smeared with booze and dope, 'You can put on the music now, Vincent.'

He went over to the hi-fi, where all the 45s were still scattered on the floor. There were albums featuring classical music, and some good jazz standards, and some Tamla Motown and Stax.

But it was the guilty pleasures that had been enjoyed that night. As if reading Vince's mind, Isabel said: 'Johnny could be pretty square about some things, but not about music. He'd listen to anything.'

The playlist had already been selected for Vince: it was all the 45s lying on the floor, out of their covers, all the platters that had been played that fateful night, like The Kinks' 'You Really Got Me'.

Vince sat back and watched as she danced for him, just like he assumed she had danced for Beresford that night. Her long body moved effortlessly with the beat. Inhibitions and class then went out the window when she climbed up on to the table. The dirty beat of R&B was obviously a great leveller. She didn't dance like an uptight and out-of-step little white girl, but like one of the Ronettes trapped within a wall of sound when 'Be My Baby' got played.

When he flipped on Eric Burdon and the Animals' 'The House of the Rising Sun', she produced some of her best moves.

Then came the killer track, and you'd have to have a pretty hard heart and feet of lead not to dance to this one. It was a little slip of a Scottish girl with the voice of a very big black man from Detroit inviting everyone to 'Shout!'

Grabbing the second bottle of champagne, she jumped off the table. Her eyes glazed over and, with her body plugged into the rhythm, she seemed possessed. All in all, she had already polished off a bottle and a half of champagne and, along with the gimlets she'd drunk in Jezebel's and the joint she'd smoked here, she was well and truly looking through a glass darkly and fast spiralling into blackout . . . Till she crashed and burned and hit the deck. On the floor she curled into a ball, seemingly wrapping herself around the half-empty bottle of champagne as if it was her lover.

Her body juddered and shook; her voice sounded breathless as she struggled to scream out: 'STOP!'

. . . 'Stop, Johnny . . . stop . . .'

She'd had tears in her eyes when she turned up the last time at Eaton Square. She knew it was the end of the affair, the end of the party. Same old Johnny stood at the door: all handsome charm and a beaming smile, and all the bonhomie of a one-man parade.

. . . 'You're back, darling. I've missed you so much. Don't ever leave me again,' he'd said, peppering her face with kisses, the smell of single malt potent on his breath.

. . . 'Stop, Johnny, stop,' she'd said. 'We need to talk . . .'

. . . But, in an ebullient mood, he pops open a bottle of Dom Perignon to celebrate her homecoming. Isabel refuses to drink. She's been off the booze for over a month, and now wants to keep a clear head. She tells him the score: they've been seeing each other for over three years, and she feels like she's wasting her time, wasting her life with him. It's too volatile a mix. She's going back to New York . . .

. . . He says he loves her, that he's sorry for the way he's treated her, his past sins, and that he doesn't want her to leave him. He tells her to have a drink — just the one, just the one. She is reluctant. He is persuasive . . .

. . . 'Stop, Johnny, stop . . .'

. . . Just the one. What harm can it do? For old times' sake. But it's never just the one, and pretty soon the genie's out the bottle. And one thing leads to another and the music goes on . . .

. . . Then his mood darkens. He becomes sullen, talks about his luck running out, nothing lasting for ever, and having a premonition of death. And now the one person he can trust is leaving him. She's never before seen him like this, the bravado and bluster vanquished. She goes over to him, she holds him.

. . . And then, like a summer day in London, he turns again. He pushes her away. He wants her gone, out of his house and out of his life. He grabs her by the arm and steers her towards the hallway, trying to get her out of there.

. . . 'Stop, Johnny, stop!'

. . . Vile abuse spews from his mouth. Isabel gives as good as she gets, she slaps his face. He slaps her back — hard. It sends her to the floor. As he looks down at her, an unbelievable cruelness comes over him. 'Look at you, pathetic.' He grabs her by the arms and hauls her to her feet. He squeezes her arms, as if getting the measure of her, the very depth and *breadth and substance of her. His solid muscularity against her slender suppleness . . .*

. . . She feels weightless, nothing more than a pitiable sobbing husk. And doesn't he just know it! He pushes her towards the sofa, but she stays on her feet. He goes towards her again, sure this charged moment will turn into something else, as it has before. The knife edge that he believes their relationship rests on always falls in his favour. Wasn't that the real push-and-pull: the excitement, the uncertainty, when feeling her body, her face damp with tears, pushing against him — when no really means yes, when stop really means go . . .

. . . 'Stop, Johnny . . . stop . . .'

. . . Her breathless mouth nuzzling his ear, while she's clawing and punching, little blows beating down on the trunk of his body, sending charges through him, driving him on . . . and then her body yields, sub-mits. That's the way it goes. That's the way it always goes . . .

. . . 'Stop, Johnny . . . Stop . . .'

'Isabel . . .'

Vince uttered it softly, her body still now, her shoulder-length hair spread out over her like a net. He bent down on one knee and put his hand gently on her shoulder as if to wake her out of her stupor.

Isabel recoiled from his touch with such vehemence, it was like she'd been pulled back by some external force. She raised herself up, her right hand gripping the neck of the champagne bottle like a tennis player about to serve.

'Get away from me, Johnny!' she hollered, her eyes rounded in fear, and then glowing in anger. With a two-handed smash, she brought the bottle crashing down on to Vince's head.

'I'll kill you! I'll kill you!'

Vince had been too transfixed by the hypnotic spinning saucers of her eyes to dodge it, and the onslaught had happened so fast. But somewhere in the wielding of the bottle, or in the service and delivery of the shot, she had lost her form, and the force wasn't enough to break the bottle, nor hard enough to knock him out. But it was hard enough to send him scuttling backwards across the floor, until he was stopped by the wall.

Clutching his head he let out an exclamation of pain that seemed like a massive understatement. 'Ouch!' He raised his hand to the spiral of his crown and dipped his fingers gingerly into the shallow tarn of blood. By the time he looked up, he saw that Isabel was staggering out into the hall. There were two of her, so that she looked as if she was being stalked by her ghost. But there were two of everything right now: everything had an aura, a simu-lacrum, or a doppelgänger. Vince climbed to his feet, of which there were currently four. A dull thud originating at the top of his crown seemed to slide down his face as he stood upright. His ears rang and he could hear the blood sloshing around inside his head. He kept his feet firmly planted in the thick carpet as his surroundings wobbled around him, and slowly his vision quivered back into focus. Eventually there was one of everything again; including Isabel now perilously swaying halfway up the stairs in a state of semi-consciousness.

Vince uprooted himself and ploughed on down the hallway, then darted up the stairs till he stood just behind Isabel, ready to catch her should she lose her grip on the banister. He was all too aware of his responsibilities: he'd got her into this state, and he would make sure he got her out of it – unharmed.

The booze and the dope now had her thoroughly sequestered in the blackout. She moved in a world of lost time, a realm of death and danger. Her long eyelashes flickered like the wings of a faltering bird. She kept up a constant stream of commentary, but it was hushed and slurred and altogether incomprehensible. Yet she seemed to know where she was going. On the first-floor landing she made her way along to the master bedroom. Vince turned on the hallway lights to illuminate her path. Again, the wilted lilies in their fetid glass coffins stank the place up, redolent of death and decay.

Isabel faded into the darkness of the master bedroom. Vince followed her inside and hit the switch, a dimmer device keeping the light low. Isabel headed straight for the imposing bed, fashioned like an open clamshell with its fanned silk headboard. To Vince this, at first sight, seemed like an especially uncharacteristic ostentation on Beresford's part, and out of keeping with the rest of the house. Vince had him down as a solid four-poster boy. But it wasn't until he saw Isabel climb up on the bed that Vince got the joke, or understood its effect: with her on the bed, it was like Botticelli's Venus. Beresford had found his immortal beauty, his Venus, and wanted to give her the setting she deserved. But why couldn't he keep her? Why couldn't he seal the deal? Why couldn't he close the shell?

Isabel lay down across the bed, then reached over to the bedside table, her hand patting the surface as if searching for something. Unable to find it, she let out a pained groan and her eyes closed. The tearful mutterings petered out into sleepy whimpers and nose-twitching little snores.

Vince looked around the room to remind himself that, apart from the odour of the dying flowers, it was just as he remembered it, room-service tidy, and five star at that. In the en suite bathroom things were also in perfect order. The porcelain shone so you could have slurped soup from the sink, drunk Bollinger from the bidet, and doused yourself in genuine toilet water.

Vince studied Isabel's position as she stretched out across the bed – the still unmade bed. He then went around to the bedside table she was reaching for. On the floor lay the same pile of silk sheets that had been pushed off the bed on the night of the murder. He then spotted a wire leading from under the bed into the same silken mound. He lifted it up, and there it was, hitherto unseen, hidden under the sheets: a small cream-coloured bedside telephone. Vince took out a handkerchief from his breast pocket and picked up the receiver. There was a red-coloured lipstick smear on the mouthpiece. He put the mouthpiece to his nose, and even after all these days, he could still smell Isabel's perfumed mouth on it.

Vince smiled, and not just because he loved the scent of a woman's lipstick.

CHAPTER 16

'*Jezebel?*'

'Jezebel's,' corrected Vince. 'It's a nightclub.' Then, by way of reassurance he said, 'It's very exclusive.'

'She's not supposed to leave the hospital, never mind go visiting nightclubs, no matter how exclusive!'

They were both in Mac's office. Mac himself perched on a corner of his desk. Vince stood contritely before him.

'I didn't take her to the club, Mac.'

'But you got her drunk!'

'She was drunk already. Ish.'

'*Ish?*'

'Drunk*ish*.'

'No such thing.'

'Okay, she was drunk. I sobered her up, then got her drunk again.'

'Oh, terrific work, Detective! Do you have any idea how this is going to play out with her brief? I kept nitto over Tyrell Lightly, because you were going to get it from Markham anyway. If he finds out about this, you're out, Not out-*ish*. Just out. On your arse!'

Vince knew better than to answer back. And Mac was right, he had given him a pass on Tyrell Lightly and the knife Vince was carrying. So Vince stood there with his mouth shut, penitently watching and waiting as Mac filled his pipe. Whilst Mac's nicotine habit wasn't quite as desperately urgent as for him to be grasping for the opium pipe like a degenerate doper, it wasn't to be sniffed at either. It was the whole routine and the paraphernalia that went with it: the ancient and oily leather tobacco pouch, the weeding it out, the filling it up, and the tamping it down in the bowl; and then setting fire to the little potted heap, all so ceremoniously assuring. And Vince knew that the pipe would have a soothing effect and cool the ire of the older detective.

He had just filled Mac in on the events of the night before, from interviewing James Asprey at the Montcler Club, to finding Isabel Saxmore-Blaine downstairs in Jezebel's nightclub, to taking her back to Beresford's house, and conducting his little experiment. He'd left out some details, like the diversion to Notting Hill to score two joints off Vivian Chalcott, and Isabel gyrating on the table as if she was a dancer on *Ready Steady Go!* As for the experiment itself, after Isabel crashed out on the bed, Vince had rolled her over into the recovery position, and swaddled her in silk sheets. She then slept like a baby – albeit a baby prodigiously embalmed in booze. Vince meanwhile sat on the chaise longue in the bedroom, drinking strong coffee. He needed to stay awake and watch over her, knowing that if anything happened to her whilst on his watch, it would put his pension in serious peril. *Ha!* They'd have buried him alive! He didn't want her sleepwalking and taking a dive down the stairs, or worse. Feeling the lump on his head from the champagne bottle, he was warily reminded that there had been cases, though as rare as rocking-horse shit, of people murdered in their sleep by people who tend to murder in their sleep . . .

'Grossly irresponsible, Vincent. You opened yourself up to all sorts of accusations and charges, and you put Isabel Saxmore-Blaine's life in danger too. She's borderline nuthouse and has an obvious booze and pill problem.'

'All of it played up by her doctors and lawyers to get her a softer sentence, because they're convinced she's guilty. But I think she's innocent, and I can prove it. I think I can find those missing hours,

Mac. Those hours that she doesn't know about, during which Beresford was killed.'

Vince waited under Mac's scrutinizing gaze. The older detective stood up and moseyed around his desk, which was habitually heaped and humped with papers and files, then sat down again. He opened a bloated desk drawer as far as it would go, knowing it would be an effort to close again, and stuck in his hand, groping around among the unyielding layers. Eventually he pulled out a single pink-topped match, and scraped it against the back wall, where Vince saw the pink skid marks of previously lit pipes, and fired her up. Twenty minutes later – or what sure as hell seemed like twenty minutes – through a cloud of bonfire smoke, like big chief Sitting Bull Mac asked: 'How?'

'When we first went to Beresford's house, you remember the bed in the main bedroom?'

'The shell-shaped thing? How could I forget?'

Vince nodded. 'The bed was left unmade, with a pile of sheets on the floor. From what we hear, Beresford was a bit prissy, and if the maids hadn't made up the bed he would have done it himself. He wouldn't have left it messy like that. The way I see it, Isabel hit Beresford with the champagne bottle then went upstairs. She was out of her skull, drunk and stoned and scared. I saw her eyes, Mac, and she was terrified. Beresford was—'

'Hold your horses, Vincent, you didn't see anything! Your little experiment, no matter what you think, means sweet fuck all!' Vince was visibly taken aback by this, for Mac wasn't in the habit of punctuating his points with profanities. 'And if you go around quoting it, you'll be laughed out the force!'

Vince raised both palms in a conceding gesture. 'I admit it wouldn't stand up in a court of law—'

'Ha! It wouldn't stand up in the canteen!'

'When you're right, Mac, you're right, and you *are* right. Isabel went up—'

'*Isabel?*' Mac took the pipe out of his mouth, his dense eyebrows circumflexed in an involuntary spasm of alarm.

'Miss Saxmore-Blaine went upstairs and crawled across the bed to get to the bedside table, because that's where the phone was. We didn't see it ourselves because it was hidden under the sheets. I'm getting a trace on the calls made that night, to find out who she was talking to. Her fingerprints are all over the phone, Mac, and so is her lipstick. I don't know how long it will put her in that room for, but it will put her up there at some time. This all goes along with Beresford's body being moved into the armchair after he was dead. Someone moved him there, and it wasn't her.'

Mac issued a long meditative 'Mmmmmm . . .' then said, 'There's no denying, she is a willowy thing, and he is a big old oak.'

Vince cracked a smile. In the all too real world of murder, Mac's metaphoric proclivities shone out every now and again, and he still had enough of the Irish in him to give things a nice lyrical twist.

'What are you smiling at?'

'I like your turn of phrase.'

'Don't brown-nose me, it doesn't suit you. You got any suspects?'

Vince reached into his inside jacket pocket and, with the rehearsed smoothness of a tired party trick, pulled out the photo of the Montcler set and placed it before his boss. 'We can start here, with Beresford's best friends. They're all in each other's pockets: work together, play together, gamble together. They know more about each other than anyone else. I've already mentioned I spoke to James Asprey, who owns the Montcler club, and took a pinch in '58 for running chemmy parties.'

'Yeah, yeah, yeah,' came the rat-tat-tat of recollection. 'I remember the case. Teddy Maybury at West End Central?'

'That's the feller. Asprey's chemmy parties put Teddy's kid through private school, according to Asprey.'

'Sounds about right. Who else have you spoken to?'

'There were two of the others in the club, but I didn't get a chance to talk to them. One was a businessman named Simon Goldsachs—'

'I've heard of him. I have some shares and read the *FT* every now and then.'

'Got any tips?'

Mac raised a be-with-you-in-a-minute hand, picked up his phone, dialled an internal number and, after three rings: 'Doc, could you get up here right away? . . . Thanks.' Mac put the phone down and said to Vince, 'You want a tip? Don't invest in Goldsachs' companies for long-term security, or because you like their product. He's an asset stripper. He buys companies and takes them apart, selling off the best parts and dumping the rest, all for a quick and usually very big profit. He's got quite a reputation, big money. Who was the other one in the club?'

'Lord Lucan. Heard of him?' Mac shrugged in the negative. 'But I didn't get to talk to either of them. As soon as they found out I was in the place, they bolted.'

Mac gave a considered nod to this. There was a knock on the door, and Doc Clayton swung in, all bug-eyed enthusiasm.

'Doc, tell Vince what you told me earlier.'

'About the two-thirty at Kempton Park?'

'No, Doc! About the . . .'

'Oh oh oh. I'm just preparing a full pathology report on that now.'

Mac impatiently waved his pipe in a circular flourish, like a conductor's baton, and said, 'Just give Vince the bare bones, as it were.'

'The wound is contact, with a good deal of distension from gas pressure. The eyes are exophthalmic from the same cause. The fresh carbon prints we found on the victim's right hand were dense on his forefinger – the shooting finger – and they matched up with the calibration of the gun. His prints are all over the gun and, from the physical evidence of the body alone, one bullet was fired to the head, and judging from the accessibility of the wound through his right hand, pathology-wise, we're happy to say that it all adds up to suicide.'

Doc Clayton smiled, and looked from Vince to Mac to Vince to Mac to Vince, until Mac ended the volley by saying, 'Thanks, Doc.'

'The three-thirty at Catterick?'

'No, Vince, the two-thirty at Kempton. Blue Lagoon, seven to two. And narrowing as we speak. It's a shoo-in.' Doc Clayton exited.

'Beresford shot himself,' said Mac, knocking out the knotted dead embers of his pipe in the ashtray. 'Isabel Saxmore-Blaine, who was upstairs as you said, woke up and found him, then panicked, took the gun and drove off . . . The rest we know.'

There was a dryness in Vince's voice as he said, 'Because it's the best possible result for everyone.'

'Because it's probably the truth and, yes, that is the best result.'

'Probably?'

'Don't get me into a debate on probability, Vincent. This looks an even better bet than Doc's shoo-in at Kempton Park. Almost a victimless crime. The next alternative, of course, is that *she* did it.'

Vince pointed at the photo. 'Or one of *them* did it.'

Mac frowned, perplexed. 'At first I thought you just wanted to get a pretty girl off the hook. That's a normal reaction for a young feller. Now she's off it, you want her back on it!'

'I just don't buy it, not yet.'

'You want motive for Beresford's suicide?'

'You don't have to tell me, Mac. It's all there. Ex-soldiers turn the gun on themselves almost as much as people in Sweden do, more rich people top themselves than poor. It's the modern condition, the ennui of existence . . .'

'You missed the most important point,' said Mac. 'Isabel Saxmore-Blaine was leaving him, and she's a very beautiful woman.'

'Yeah, Mac, I get it.'

'Yeah, you get it. Just won't accept it, eh?'

'I think someone might be getting away with murder, if we simply take the path of least resistance.'

135

Mac stuck both hands into the pile of papers on his desk, pulled out a fatigued copy of the *London Evening Standard* and handed it to Vince.

'Take a look. Marcy Jones, front page news. Isabel Saxmore-Blaine, page three. For all the money, influence and connections Isabel Saxmore-Blaine has, the funny thing is, the public are more interested in the killing of an anonymous black girl from a poor part of town. Who just happened to be a nurse, making the best of her lot, trying to raise her young child and contributing to society. And she's been brutally hammered to death in her own home. As opposed to Isabel Saxmore-Blaine, a beautiful, poor little rich girl with a booze and pill problem. Her plight has been relegated to the gossip column, because no one really gives a monkey's. A few years ago, a deb up on a murder charge would have wiped World War Three off the front page. Especially with her looks. Take Profumo, no one gave a damn about him; it was the two slips everyone was writing about and taking pictures of. But tastes change, and fast. We're used to scandal: disgraced toffs topping themselves, debs debauching themselves, politicians caught with their pants down.' And, with a warning edge to his voice, Mac added, 'And if you've taken a liking to Miss Saxmore-Blaine, take some advice. She's way out of your league.'

'I haven't taken a liking to her.' Vince picked up the photo of the Montcler Set, 'but I have taken a disliking to this little mob.'

'Because you're not in their league?

'Like you said, Mac, times have changed. We don't have a class system now, haven't you heard?'

The older detective's head jolted back, with a gruff dismissive laugh.

Vince continued, 'You *know* there's more to this case. And we don't work for Beaverbrook, so why do you give a shit about what goes on the front pages or what's in the gossip columns?'

Seemingly ground down by the young detective's enthusiasm as much as his argument, Mac gave a weary shake of his head and conceded, 'Okay, look into it. Talk to your rich boys, see what's under their fingernails. But just until the paperwork is done and dusted on Isabel Saxmore-Blaine. Then we're going with the *evidence*, and with death by misadventure, as no doubt they'll wish to call it.'

Vince smiled.

Mac tried to wipe it off his face with this: 'You've just doubled your workload, because Marcy Jones remains the priority case, and I still want you to attend all briefings on it, and put your shift in.'

He didn't succeed. Vince kept on smiling. And that's what Mac liked about him.

CHAPTER 17

The first person on Vince's list was Simon Goldsachs, to be followed by Lord Lucan. Vince reckoned, after their haste to leave the Montcler the night before, they'd have had plenty of time to work out their alibis by now, and would be expecting him. Shame to disappoint them, but disappoint he did. Vince was about to leave the Yard when a desk sergeant told him he'd received a call from a Mr Guy Ruley. Ruley had just flown back into the country from Hong Kong that morning, and wanted to speak to the investigating officer to find out exactly what happened, and if he could be of any assistance. Vince rang him back, but Ruley wasn't in his office – his secretary explained that he was currently at his club in Mayfair.

What set the Racquet & Ball club apart from other sedentary gentlemen's clubs in London, like White's, the Garrick, or Boodles, was the fact that you could lift weights in the fully out-fitted gymnasium, have a game of squash in one of the five courts, and finish off with a Turkish bath and a sauna in the basement. That's before you sank into one of the battered and buttoned leather armchairs, where genuflecting waiters ferried endless tumblers of booze to your Hepplewhite side table, and you drank yourself into a stupor in perfect peace, whilst admiring the Gainsboroughs and the anatomically precise Stubbses over the Adam fireplace.

At the reception Vince introduced himself, and was told that Mr Ruley was expecting him. He was promptly signed in and was led down the sparkly white granite stairs to the arched inner sanctuary of the building. On arrival there, he was given a white towelling robe and three warm towels of such a luxurious softness and heft that they immediately had Vince contemplating ways of trying to steal them. Once changed, and his own clothes deposited in a locker, he was led through to the Turkish baths, where men of all shapes and sizes lounged on slabs, or simmered and broiled in bubbling hot tubs, or got oiled and lathered up then rigorously rubbed down by muscular men with large nimble hands who could rid you of a rick, a twinge or a knot just by looking at it. There was a green oxidized copper fountain shaped like an heraldic jumping dolphin, which gushed some frothy-looking sewage liquid from its gaping mouth into a pool that was as murky as a garden pond, in which men floated and wallowed in the green slime. The towel boy informed Vince that it was a special algae developed in the baths of Budapest, and said to possess special restorative qualities. The pond life seemed to be enjoying it, looking as fat and happy as frogs, so there must have been something in it.

At the very end of the long room rose a series of spacious marble terraces on which men sat around draped in toga-like towels, like Roman senators. The higher up you sat, the hotter it got. Vince sat down on the bottom tier (which still felt like a griddle) and was informed that Mr Ruley was just having a massage and would be joining him shortly. He sat back and breathed in deeply, letting the steam work its magic.

Five minutes later, Guy Ruley emerged from the fog. At around six foot two, he looked as if he used the gym a lot more frequently than the soft leather armchairs in the lounge bar above. Packed with finely sculptured muscle, he was wearing the skimpiest of swimming trunks to show it all off to best effect. Vince noticed there was something of a resemblance to Beresford. He had the same thick flaxen hair, worn full and scraped back from a broad handsome face, but Ruley looked younger and a lot fitter. There was a refinement in his features that kept everything neat and tidy, short and sweet, and indistinctive. There was no bulbous nose, fat lips, buck teeth or bulging eyes to draw attention to him. In fact, he had the kind of face that could get away with things just because it defied description. Generically handsome? Ears a little too small; features a little too English-looking. The sketch boys back at the Yard would *not* have a field day with Guy Ruley; he'd end up looking as if he belonged in a passionate clinch on the front cover of a cheap romance novel.

After the introductions, and a firmer than usual handshake that implied nothing, no matter how hard it tried, Guy Ruley sat down right next to Vince. He sat uncomfortably close, decided the detective, who lacked the locker-room mentality enjoyed by men on the rowing team or in the first XV. In a bullish baritone, Guy Ruley declared that it was all 'a bloody bad show and shocking', then promptly told Vince that he'd been away on business for the last ten days, which effectively put him out of the frame. Guy Ruley explained how on the actual day of the murder he was in Dublin, a business venture having taken him to Tipperary in Ireland, to invest in a stable of horse-racing thoroughbreds. Then on to Germany, then Hong Kong.

'I hope I'm not wasting your time in getting you down here, Detective, but I just thought I should call and get the facts. Of course, I've already spoken to my friends about it, and read the papers, but better to get it from the horse's mouth, as it were.'

'You're not wasting my time, Mr Ruley. In fact, I was going to talk to you anyway.'

'If I can help in any way, Detective. But, from what I've already read and heard, it all seems rather fait accompli, no?'

'Really?'

'Isabel.' He shook his head, as if implying both sadness and disgust, but it was the disgust that really shone through. 'It's the sort of thing one hears about, reads about. It happens to other people, never to yourself. But at the same time, it comes as no great surprise, as they were such a volatile couple. Blowing his brains out though, *Jesus*. That said, Isabel's a crack shot. She used to go shooting with Johnny and could more than hold her own.'

'I didn't know that.'

'Her father taught her. Not the usual thing you teach girls, but what with her younger brother being, well . . .'

'Well what, Mr Ruley?'

'Young Dominic, he's a bit of a queer, isn't he?'

'I just thought he was public school.'

'I went to a public school, the best,' said an indignant Guy Ruley.

Vince let that one hang amid the hot vapour.

'I'm not judging, Detective, just making a point.'

'Tell you the truth, Mr Ruley, I'm more interested in your business dealings with Johnny Beresford.'

'What's she been saying?'

'Who?'

'Lizzie bloody Borden, who else? I read that she was smearing Johnny's name. She'll do anything to get herself off the hook.'

A loud sizzle echoed around the large room, a noise met with helpless groans of joy from those gathered on the terraces. Someone had just ladled some more water on to the white-hot sulphur coals. The effect was felt immediately, as the steam puffed and panted in clouds, and wrapped itself around Vince like a scorching cloak.

Once he'd acclimatized, he asked: 'So you're saying you didn't have business dealings with him?'

'You know I did. Okay, Detective Treadwell, I'll come clean. Aspers told me.'

'James Asprey?'

'That's right. He said you'd visited him, made enquiries. Said you're smart. Good for you, I say, because you're just doing your job.'

'Glad you appreciate it, Mr Ruley. I heard you had a falling out with Mr Beresford.'

Guy Ruley gave a nonchalant shrug of his broad shoulders and said, 'Not much of one, lasted only a few weeks. More of a spat. You want to know what it was about, right?'

'As quickly as you can. I'm beginning to wilt.'

'It was a reasonably sophisticated financial deal involving a series of smallish high-risk ventures that went pear-shaped due to Johnny's greed. Not huge amounts involved, but it all adds up. I won't bore you with the details, because I don't know them all myself. I'm not a number cruncher, myself. I studied physics and engineering at London. I'm a bigger-picture man, so I have a crack team of accountants to look after that side of my business.'

'But it was big enough to fall out with him, though not enough to kill him over, would you say?'

'I'd laugh, but I don't find it a laughing matter,' said Guy Ruley. Then he laughed.

'What changed your mind there?'

'I've just remembered something. Good old Johnny the Joker!'

'Johnny the Joker?'

'That's what we all called him at school. Loved practical jokes and funny stories. He was the consummate raconteur. And it looks like he's saved his best joke till the last. With Johnny dead, I stand to lose even more money. He held all his money for our deal in offshore accounts, with all the accounts in his head. That's what made him so good at the tables, that ability to commit to memory complex equations and figures. I gamble for fun, just the sociability of it. People like Johnny do it for the numbers, to beat the odds, beat the house, to come out on top. And, in a way, I guess he did this time.'

It seemed to cheer Guy Ruley that Beresford had gone out of the world owing him. But Vince couldn't tell whether he viewed this as a victory or a failing.

'How much was he into you for?'

Guy Ruley shrugged. 'Losing money in such ventures is all par for the course. High risk, big profits, and sometimes losses. Swings and roundabouts. What I lost with Johnny this time around, I was sure he'd make up the next time . . .'

Guy Ruley's brusque baritone trailed off, and he wiped his eyes. Vince was sure it was sweat, not tears. It would seem that Guy Ruley didn't kill Beresford, not solely because of the physical impossibility of it – being out of the country at the time – but, and the real clincher, was because he was at the end of a losing deal with him. Even though the mercury was rising to treble figures in this underground sweat hole they were in, Vince saw that Guy Ruley remained cool and calculating, operating with all the heart of a humming refrigerator.

And Vince told him as much: 'James Asprey shares your philosophy, said that he wouldn't have killed Johnny Beresford either, because he made too much money from Beresford playing for the house. Said it would be like killing the golden goose. Sentimental old lot, aren't you?'

With an indignant edge to his voice, Guy Ruley said, 'Look here, Detective, just because we don't go around bawling our eyes out, or emoting like a bunch of cheap actors, doesn't mean we don't care. I've known Johnny since school – how many old schoolfriends do you have?'

'Good point. Most of mine are in prison.'

'You put them there?'

'No, they found their own way there. So if it wasn't over money, what else did you and your friends fall out about? Women?'

'Yes, mostly. Johnny had an eye for them. But if you want to talk about women, it's Simon you need to talk to.'

'Simon Goldsachs?'

'He and Simon had a hell of a spat, when he took up with Simon's mistress, a model called Holly who was introduced to them by Nicky DeVane. You know him?'

'I carry around a picture of all of you.'

Through the steam, Vince saw Ruley throw him a sour look.

Guy Ruley said, 'Nicky's a photographer, very talented too.' There was another sour look, but not for Vince this time. 'If you can consider pressing a button and saying cheese a talent. He assures me there's more to it, but it's hardly oil on canvas, is it? No wonder there are so many cockney barrow boys at it, being money for old rope. The "dapper snapper" they call Nicky now. Anyway, this Holly, stunning-looking creature, I mean, unbelievable—'

'When was this?' asked Vince, mopping his face with the skirt of his towelling toga.

'About six months ago.'

'Simon was smitten with her, but she was a real beauty.' Ruley looked off somewhere into the middle distance, as if he could see the model herself emerging from the shimmering heat and swirling mist. 'I mean she was stunning, gorgeous, amazing—'

'You said that already.'

Ruley snapped out of it. 'Anyway, Johnny slimed his way in. I'm sure he did it just because he could, only to get one over Simon. I mean, for all her faults – which have proved pretty fatal – Isabel is a real beauty herself. Very attractive, gorgeous-looking thing—'

'So we've established,' said Vince, to stem Ruley staring off into the middle distance again. 'How did it go down with Simon Goldsachs?'

'Well, Detective Treadwell, you should have seen Simon. He's a man with a monumental temper on him, prone to legendary tantrums, and he was a study in apoplectic rage. Livid purple he was. It was a matter of Homeric honour, since Simon wanted her for his harem.'

'Where's Holly now?'

'Took up with a film producer and lives in Hollywood.' Guy Ruley stood up, breathed in swirling steam and announced, 'Time to shrink the trouser snake. Coming?'

Vince just looked at him blankly.

'I mean take a cold plunge. Bit of an initial shock, but it's invigorating as hell, and good for the circulation.'

'I'll pass.'

As Guy Ruley strode off, Vince considered him, and could see how Isabel would find Ruley a bore. But what did Beresford see in him? The long and the short and the tall of such friendships seldom rang true in Vince's experience. Men who hung together invariably – despite a few tics and traits – looked the same, dressed the same, talked the same and shared the same ideologies, values and sense of humour. Why? Because it gave them a greater sense of themselves. It was them not so much multiplied as squared. Guy Ruley dropping the revelation about this triangle of Goldsachs, Beresford and the model was no revelation, not even a surprise. They fucked each other's women because they'd probably like to fuck each other, and they'd like to fuck each other only because they couldn't fuck themselves. This coterie no doubt shared mistresses, shuffling them around like cards. Vince knew that the information Guy Ruley was throwing him about Simon Goldsachs was merely a chip to play with, and a very low-value one at that. But at least he now knew why Isabel didn't know about this falling out between Beresford and Goldsachs. It also meant that if she had found out about it or he'd told her about it, she would have had even more motive for killing him.

CHAPTER 18

Simon Goldsachs was at home. And home was a much publicized pile in Richmond Park. To get to Goldsachs' place, Vince had to drive through the park itself, where the deer and the antelope play. Well, if not the antelopes, certainly the deer. It was all enough to make Vince pull the Mk II over and get out and take a look. The deer were tame enough not to run away, but smart enough to keep their distance. Vince told himself he should get out of London more; communing with nature was good for the soul. He stood there for a good three or four minutes before getting bored checking his shoes for deer shit and getting back into the motor.

Vince exited the park and turned into the exclusive tree-lined avenue where Goldsachs lived. Stand-alone properties stood tall and proud and expensive and hidden away, with decorative iron-work gates, tall ash trees, and the occasional castellated topiary. As you approached Goldsachs' walled-off pile, all you could see of the house was the tip of the rotunda. The property that had existed there before Goldsachs arrived was much in keeping with the rest of the houses in the area: Georgian and early Victorian. Goldsachs had knocked it down and built his own vision in its place. The result had made all the papers, the locals calling it a monstrosity. Goldsachs called them backward-looking tiresome anti-Semites, and had walled the place off.

On being let through the solid metal sliding electric gates, definitely built for security not decoration, Vince drove up the sweep of the tree-lined gravel drive and parked next to a green Mini

Cooper, which was next to a muddy Ford shooting brake. Vince was expecting a Ferrari GTO, an Aston Martin DB5, and at least a spaceship or two. He got out of the car and stepped back to take in the scenery on the 'compound'.

The main house was a modernist block of concrete clad in a burnished orange stone, with stained-glass windows. Of the many striking features, the most striking was what covered the central body of the building. A huge golden dome. The less than vibrant winter sun still managed to catch various facets of this polished metal-panelled rotunda and set it on fire, making it jaw-droppingly impressive. It was a modernist Taj Mahal . . . or maybe a Martian palace. Vince couldn't make up his mind which, and that's what he liked about it.

'You should see it in the summer, it's pure gold.'

Vince turned round to see Simon Goldsachs striding towards him. Leading with his bullish chest and thrusting shoulders, he looked big and almost hulking. By the time he was within hand-shaking distance, which he didn't offer, Vince gauged he was about his own height, six foot or thereabouts. The man was in his mid-thirties, but his heaviness – especially around the shoulders – and a certain physical authority managed to put about ten years on him. The face was round, the nose flat and fleshy, and his skin bore that patina of success: a midwinter tan. His tawny hair was cropped short, and a broad smile was fixed on a thin-lipped mouth. But it was his eyes that held your attention, cobalt blue, glacial and dissecting. They held both fire and ice in their tractor-beam intensity. Tufty blond eyebrows arched imperiously over them, and Vince soon had him pegged as the 'Browbeating and Staring Down' champion of the world. No wonder he was the king of the hostile takeover. The aggression and chutzpah was writ large all over him. He didn't look like your average smooth business operator or bowler-hatted City gent; instead he looked downright pugnacious. You can take the boy out of the ghetto, but you can't take the ghetto out of the boy, goes the saying. Simon Goldsachs might be a good few generations out of it, educated and cultured to within an inch of his life, but still the old hunger lurked just beneath the surface. He was considered the man with the Midas touch, and already rumoured to be closing in on his first billion (whatever the hell that looked like). The boardroom was his boxing ring, his battleground, and he'd leave you bloodied and bruised and beaten on its carpet. Not in his normal battledress of a pin- or chalk-stripe suit today, he was casually clad in battered bottle-green cords tucked into muddy wellington boots; an elbow-patched blue cable-knit jumper over a Tattersall check shirt, with a red bandanna knotted around his thick neck. A muddy shovel was gripped in a well-tanned hand.

He said: 'Of course, it's not real gold. That would be altogether too tempting. If they'd pinch the lead off a church roof, imagine what they'd do with this lot!'

'Been digging in the allotment?'

'No, not today, Detective. I've just been murdering and burying an annoying neighbour!' Another smile shot across his thin lips, exposing perfect rows of squat calcium-rich white teeth that looked as if they could chew their way through a mountaineer's rope. Vince returned the smile, but made a mental note to check on missing persons when he got back to the Yard.

Twenty minutes later they sat facing one another on a pair of teak sofa chairs in Goldsachs' study. Drinks had been served by an athletically built Japanese man dressed in black, including traditional black slippers. An anomaly, he looked too relaxed to be a butler, too well dressed to be an odd-job man and too refined to be a bodyguard. Yet, as he served Vince his black coffee and then serenely genuflected away, Vince was hit with a vision of the Jap smashing his fist through three piled-up house bricks as if they were made of Styrofoam.

The brief house tour had left Vince in no doubt about Simon Goldsachs' wealth – some of which was stashed all over the walls. It ranged from young British artists like Blake and Hockney, and the brash and blazing big guns of American Pop, to the subdued realism of the masters. The alarm system was a work of art itself.

When Vince commented on the collection, Goldsachs dismissively told him that he had to cover the walls with something, and an art dealer friend of his had said they were a good investment. Vince got the message. This man couldn't cover his walls in junk bonds or money, so he covered them in art that would make more money, which he could invest in junk bonds to make more money, to buy more art to . . .

The 'study' situated at the top of the house seemed to take up an entire floor and was all blond wood, exposed concrete, and boxy modern furniture. A huge semicircular window provided a vista of the grounds containing a man-made lake with a bobbing flotilla of pedalos clustered on its banks, a maze, a folly in the form of the Houses of Parliament, and a very inhabitable-looking multistoreyed pagoda.

Goldsachs had now removed the muddy wellies and slipped into a pair of dainty-looking loafers tooled from crocodile hide. Vince noticed the shoes because they were practically identical to the ones Beresford had been wearing, thus proving Vince's theory about their friendship: they were, if not cut from the same cloth, then certainly shod by the same shoemaker. In one hand Goldsachs now held another accoutrement of success. The cigar, a cabinet-sized Bolivar, was as big and smelly and expensive as one of his factory chimneys. He fired her up with a long match; the only way to light a cigar was with a match, he informed Vince. So big was the cigar that Goldsachs' whole head resembled a pair of bellows as he huffed and puffed, trying to get the thing lit.

Once it was up and running, he laughed good and loud, saying: 'No, no, Detective, Guy must have been pulling your leg. I was never going to marry Holly. It's a well-known dictum that when one marries one's mistress, one merely creates another position. What else did he tell you about me?'

'That's all. The rest I found out myself. You made your first million at twenty-four by winning the franchise to bring low cost generic pharmaceuticals into the country. And you've made a few more of them since. It's a varied portfolio, everything from food products and baby clothes to a logging company in Canada. You enjoy the reputation of being a buccaneering greenmail corporate raider and asset stripper. I've got my boss to thank for all that info, as he plays the stock market and follows your career. He says you always make money in any new ventures.'

Goldsachs stretched his arm along the top of the sofa in a gesture of expansive ease as he savoured this reputation. Then he smiled his fat-cat smile and said, 'After that précis, you'll no doubt be wanting to know my whereabouts on the night of the murder, Detective Treadwell?'

'I intended to ask you the other night, when I saw you in the Montcler, but you left in a hurry. Not your usual practice, I hear. Nothing to do with me, I hope?'

Goldsachs fixed Vince with his big artillery – his eyes – and studied him as if he was examining something unpleasant on a Petri dish. Vince could see that the very idea that Goldsachs might alter his routine for a mere plod was anathema to him.

'I left the club early, Detective, but not in a hurry. And I left because I wanted to.' He made a little flourish of the hand that seemed to guide Vince's eyes around the room, embracing the surroundings, the wealth and the sheer *I can do what the hell I like* of it all.

Vince had met three of them now: Asprey, Ruley and Goldsachs. And, unless Goldsachs pulled something pretty spectacularly charming out of the hat soon, he felt sure he didn't like any of them. But he'd hold off final judgement on the Montcler set, as there were still three to go: Nicky DeVane, Lord Lucan and, finally, Johnny Beresford himself. But he would naturally come last. When Vince had found his killer and put the pieces together, then he'd finally meet the man.

Goldsachs continued, 'As for the night of his murder, I was at home with my children.'

'Your wife can verify that?'

'She could, but they're not her children. My other children, from another relationship, and their home is in Paris. But surely that's all an irrelevance, since I thought you already had your killer, Detective?'

'Isabel Saxmore-Blaine?' Goldsachs nodded. 'Not really, no. We'll keep on investigating until we're absolutely certain.'

'Wish I could be of more help.' The tycoon issued an approbatory little humming sound, and said, 'It's a funny thing about little Isabel. Such a sweet girl, and yet she's gone and done something all of us think about, all wish we could do. Commit murder. Didn't think she had it in her.'

'You think much about murder Mr Goldsachs?'

'One uses the language of violence so frequently in business – make a killing, liquidate, bury the opposition, blood on the carpet – that you do wonder if you've actually got the guts to perform the act itself.'

'Killing's quite a preoccupation with your friend Mr Asprey. Theoretically, of course, and on a grander scale. He proposes earthquakes, H bombs and homicidal despots to alleviate the problems of overpopulation.'

The magnate shook his head, more in a gesture of good-hearted patronage than in disagreement. 'Yes, what's it up to currently? Two hundred and fifty million?'

'Minus one, right now.'

Goldsachs made with the eyes again and delivered the dissecting stare.

'Save me your looks, Mr Goldsachs. This isn't the boardroom. Hitler had the same ideas, and your good friend Asprey is clearly a fan. Just wondering how that squares with you?'

'*Divide et impera.* Do you know what—'

'Divide and rule. Boccalini's defining principle for politics, warfare and economics.'

The industrialist, sitting so comfortably on his sofa, now looked uncomfortably wrong-footed. He weighed Vince up with fresh eyes.

'I read law at university,' said Vince.

'I knew there was something about you.'

Vince felt a tangible shift in the room. Not seismic, but enough to dislodge the look of distaste that Goldsachs had on his face for the young detective. He was now eyeing him up like a potential acquisition. He had assimilated and dismissed Vince too quickly, and he knew it. It was a mistake, and Goldsachs didn't like making mistakes.

'I wasn't a good student,' he confided. 'I left Eton at sixteen, had a couple of years in the army, then went straight into business. My plan was to make enough money that if I needed to know something, I'd pay some don to come and read to me in private.'

'Standing on one leg, I'd imagine. Money buys you everything.'

'But not friends. I'm loyal to my friends. And your little attempt to divide me and Aspers won't work. Ours is a cloudless friendship, a love that is forever May. You always make enemies in business, Mr Treadwell. If you're doing it well, that's par for the course; it's the free-market competitive nature of it. And me and my friends do it better than most. As for one of us being somehow responsible for Johnny's death − which, let's face it, is what you're sniffing around for − well, you just don't get it. Johnny was one of *us*. And there aren't many of *us* around. It's a tribal thing, Treadwell. We gambled together, fought and argued together, and occasionally shared women. But we were always the best of friends, who had each other's well-being very much at heart. And if I knew who killed him, well, I might satisfy that lingering curiosity of mine − by killing them myself.' Goldsachs gave three slow and solemn nods at the memory of his dead friend and continued, with some warmth in his voice, 'I shall miss him, the Johnny of old. He was damn fine company, and very, very funny when the mood was on him, which it was most of the time. That's why Aspers loved having him at the club, a supreme raconteur.'

'Johnny the Joker, I believe?'

'Yes, always the joker,' Goldsachs murmured wistfully. The tycoon then slapped his thigh as if to break himself out of this melancholy, abruptly stood up, and said forcefully, 'Let me show you something! You know, I had a favourite uncle called Vincent . . . your name is Vincent, isn't it?'

Vince said it was. He'd noticed how Goldsachs had slowly eroded the 'Detective' title over the course of their conversation.

'Yes, Vincent, I think you will appreciate this!'

He followed Goldsachs up some steps to the mezzanine tier of the study. Standing in the centre of the room was an oblong plinth-type affair, about the same size and dimensions as a professional snooker table and made out of a blond wood.

'You admired the dome on the house. Whilst its aesthetic value is priceless, it has a practical purpose too. Solar panels fitted to it provide energy, meaning, in laymen's terms, that it heats the boiler! It's new technology. The chief reason for making money, Vincent, is to make a difference. And that's why I make more than most, because I believe I can *do* more than most!

'The ecology fascinates me, not only as a member of the human race but as a free-market businessman. It is, quite literally, the future, representing a whole new global marketplace. Since the rise of the industrial age, we've been voraciously eating up our resources. The road to progress has ironically become an irrefutable march towards our own demise. Overpopulation, food shortages, energy crises – yet the earth is a precious and limited resource. Believe me, I've spoken to scientists the world over who are convinced that in thirty to forty years' time – if both sides can refrain from dropping the bomb on each other and we don't blow ourselves up – the energy crisis and the pollution of the very air we breathe will become the world's biggest issue! Are you with me, Vincent?'

Vince wasn't with him; he thought the man was sounding like a nut job. He'd never heard anything like it, but he nodded along. And Goldsachs, enthused and full of energy, just full of it, continued.

'Oil, that most precious of commodities, has its prices going through the roof, and its major source is an increasingly unstable region. Coal is unsustainable, since the filth it produces is gradually choking the world. So, we will need to find new energy sources – and there is only one place to look. It's the greatest untapped source of energy of all time: the one right at the centre of our solar system!'

With his fiercely beaming eyes, Goldsachs looked at Vince expectantly for the answer.

Vince took a wild guess: 'The sun?'

'That's what I'm looking into, Vincent. The sun.'

'It's recommended you don't, as it'll blind you.'

Goldsachs wasn't listening. Apart from heavily prompted answers to endorse his points, he really hadn't factored Vince into this one-way conversation.

'The sun indeed. That is where I intend to invest next – in technology and materials that can capture that ultimate energy. This house is just a prototype, a doll's house if you will, compared to the version I plan on building. It's here we'll gather together the finest brains in the field, in order to capture the power of the sun!'

'Didn't Icarus try the same thing? But without your budget, obviously.'

Again no reaction from the tycoon. Clearly his own vision wasn't just blinding him; it was deafening him too. His thousand-watt eyes were lit up brighter than the fiery star he was determined to win control of. He picked up a device that looked like a radio receiver and was about the size of a house brick. He aimed the long aerial protruding from it at the large boxy table nearby. On the press of a red button, the table top began to electronically slide open. A scaled-down model of what looked a coastal area slowly began to rise up until it rested flush with the table top. What became immediately recognizable was the type of house Vince was standing in. But the model on the table portrayed a larger version of it, a much larger version with not just one rotunda but six. An enormous dome rose in the middle, with five smaller ones orbiting it on the various wings of the house. There were other domes, too: three huge skeletal glasshouse structures, like circus big tops, that contained what seemed to be model trees and plants and foliage. Another area contained a zoo, even bigger than London zoo – more like a game reserve where the animals (plastic model figures) came in two by two. And a lake with a giant aviary sitting on an island in the middle. The whole place was a verdant paradise covered in lush foliage, tall trees with Tarzanesque hanging vines, and even a rocky waterfall. It looked like a Hollywood version of a jungle, or a tourist trip up the Amazon. Or just a lot of fun if you were ten years old and liked toys. But this was no toy.

'My new home. Offshore the country is oil rich, excellent for the short term. It's got good soil, mineral rich for sustainable farming and vegetation. And it's a perfect environment for the breeding of rare animals, and lots of . . . *Shit!* . . . *Shit! Shit! Shit!*'

That wasn't exactly how it sounded, for Goldsachs wasn't planning on breeding lots of shit. He was merely swearing at the table. Because the mechanism had obviously broken. Technology was letting the great man down. The model of Goldsachs' Xanadu was yo-yoing up and down.

Vince stood back and concentrated on scratching a fictitious itch on his nose, in an attempt to hide the grin that was spreading across his face, as Goldsachs began to frantically stab a stately finger at the red button. Nothing. It got worse, in fact. The table top began to open and close at a comical speed. Goldsachs' legendary temper then began to emerge. His golden tan became lavishly luminous, he was burning up, going through the entire colour spectrum of rage, before settling somewhere between puce and blue. His head seemed to hunker down into the broad bulk of his shoulders.

'*Damn! Damn! Damn!*' was followed by worse, worse, much worse.

It was then, obviously hearing the commotion and the swearing, that a very attractive, petite Frenchwoman with short black hair and big Betty Boop eyes, bustled into the room and ushered

Vince out of it. She was obviously the visionary's wife, or mistress, or secretary, or at least two out of those three, and had herself
the foresight to see that it would be best if Vince left now. As
she guided him by the arm, she explained in breathy broken
English (which didn't need fixing, because it sounded completely
charming and very sexy) that there was no use trying to talk to
Goldsachs now; once he was in this kind of mood, it was damage
limitation.

Vince saw what she meant. He left with the sight of Goldsachs
grabbing an expensive piece of modern-design furniture, meant
for sitting on and talking about, and hoisting it up into the air
and then sending it crashing down on to the model. The one blow
destroyed his Shangri-la, smashing his golden domes, and sent
Dinky Toy-sized figures of men and women and beasts of the field
flying into the air. Goldsachs' cold war nightmare (and everyone
else's for that matter) had come true. It was too late for the
scientists and their new technologies to save his brave new world.

Goldsachs had dropped the bomb.

CHAPTER 19

Another part of the city, away from the outer zone of picturesque Richmond, and right into the heart of the matter. The epicentre. Smack bang in the middle of *everything*. One of the most talked-about thoroughfares in London town. The place where the British Invasion came to arm and swathe itself. Carnaby Street, or just off. In Beak Street, to be precise, and the photographic studios of the Honourable Nicholas Raphael Evelyn DeVane. Of course, the name on his business card had slimmed him down to plain old proletariat Nicky DeVane.

It was four p.m. as Vince walked down Carnaby Street, and this rich little vein of central London was doing cracking business. Mods were still the order of the day, but the hair was well and truly creeping over the collars now, and the gear was getting a little louder, a little more lairy. There were braided military tunics, candy-striped boating jackets, Paisley-print shirts, and lots of things with Union Jacks on them. In fact Union Jacks seemed to be everywhere. England may no longer be a great power on the world stage, but it was finding new ways to assert itself and fly the flag, in music, culture and clothes.

Vince climbed the stairs to the Beak Street studio, and had one of those surreal little moments that capture time and place perfectly. Brian Jones, with his unmistakable mop of blond hair, and a girl (equally blonde) were making their way down the stairs. They both wore wraparound shades and were giggling as if they didn't have a care in the world, and to Vince's mind they probably didn't. Vince stood aside as they wafted downwards arm in arm, with broad smiles on their pretty little faces. Vince couldn't tell if they were smiling at him or just the planetary arrangements that had momentarily placed them right at the centre of everything. He watched as their stardust disappeared out through the door to the waiting car. It was exotic air Vince had breathed for that brief moment – they were both smoking joints. He imagined the pinch, and he wondered sometimes if he was cut out for this work, because most coppers would have been all over that little opportunity, and the publicity that came with it. But nicking pot-heads held absolutely no interest for Vince, no matter who they were. Two more long-limbed girls came down the stairs next, with bright-eyed and bushy-tailed enthusiasm. He assumed they were models; they had that sense of otherness about them that other girls just don't have.

Vince climbed to the third floor and knocked on the industrial-looking door. An unsmiling girl dressed in black, with black shades and a lopsided bob haircut, answered it with all the welcoming enthusiasm of a mortician. Vince introduced himself and stated his business, without flashing his badge, and was let in. Still she didn't smile, but she did ask if he wanted a cup of coffee. He said that he did, and she strode purposefully off to make it. And was never to be seen again, with or without coffee.

The studio was just as Vince had imagined it would be. Painted matt white with high ceilings and long windows. Lots of lighting equipment rigged up on the ceiling like a theatre, and tall free-standing arc lamps that stood around looking impressive, expensive and technical, with white and silver foiled umbrellas mushrooming off them, presumably for reflective purposes, not decorative, but they looked good anyway. There were painted backdrops and props, and racks of clothes and the occasional cigarette butt crushed out on the floor. Vince went over to where a very pleasing noise emanated, that of girls giggling.

Nicky DeVane was showing a card trick to two models dressed in identical long sequinned body-hugging gowns. They stood towering over him, drinking champagne from Styrofoam cups and sharing a long oily hash joint. Vince waited for DeVane to finish his card trick, which he did to gasps of wonderment and whoops and kisses and hugs from his gorgeously gangly and giggling audience. It was a neat performance.

'Mr DeVane, I'm Detective Vince Treadwell,' he said, stepping out from behind a rack of clothes and showing the now turned faces his badge. They froze like a freshly snapped photograph, and said nothing, but their mouths all formed perfectly shaped Os. Vince, by way of defusing their fear of being busted on a dope charge, stated his intention. 'I've come to talk to you about Mr Beresford, that's all.'

On this, and realizing it wasn't a stunt, they got all three-dimensional again and sprang back to life. The joint was quickly deposited in a Styrofoam cup, and long slim hands pointlessly fluttered the air in front of them, as if to disperse the illicit smoke. Vince smiled.

Five minutes later, he was standing in Nicky DeVane's private office, which was a partitioned-off section of the studio with a couple of folding metal chairs, a filing cabinet, and a long trestle table cluttered with papers, magazines and lots of photos of lots of gorgeous women in lots of different outfits.

'You don't look like a policeman,' said Nicky DeVane, who stood leaning against the trestle table. 'Which can be rather, uh, disorientating. I thought you were with one of the girls at first. You've got good bones. You'd take a good photo.'

'And you, if I may say, look every inch the photographer.'

Size-wise, Nicky DeVane was the runt of the Montcler litter. Depending on the extravagancies of his footwear, he was around five foot six, slender, sprightly-looking, but with a round cherubic face and large brown eyes. Shiny brown curls were gathered under a peaked corduroy cap. The rest of his ensemble consisted of a Paisley button-down collar shirt, a pair of tight blue cords matching the cap that he was wearing, and black Cuban-heeled chisel-toed boots with nifty side zips. This was all out of sorts with the rest of the Montcler set, with their sombre business suits, or those dinner-jacketed figures assembled in the photo. But this was Carnaby Street, and he was a photographer, so his fashionably flamboyant garb could be viewed as merely the overalls of his profession.

Nicky DeVane took off his cap and chucked it on the table. He then ruffled his curly hair and said, 'Well, yes, just keeping up appearances,' then almost apologetically, 'You have to look the part.'

'Speaking of which, was that who I thought it was on the stairs?'

Knowing immediately who Vince meant, DeVane said, 'Brian just dropped by. He's a chum. There's always a lot of people dropping in and hanging out here.' He gave an exasperated sigh. 'It's the location, of course. I'm thinking of moving actually, so I can get more work done.'

Nicky DeVane then took on a look of real concern to replace the seemingly frivolous one he had previously and asked, 'Isabel, how is she?'

'She's doing better now than she was. Mainly because she's beginning to believe she's innocent.' As Vince said this, he searched DeVane's face for a reaction, signs of either relief or of concern. But nothing came. 'She told me a little about you – and of course I saw your flowers at the hospital. A dozen red roses.'

Nicky DeVane caught the snag in Vince's voice. 'You think that strange, Detective? It's no secret that I love Isabel. Always have.'

Vince, equally matter-of-factly, 'Enough to kill Johnny Beresford over?'

'Let's just say this, if anyone tried to hurt Isabel, then yes, I would. *Anyone*. I've known her all my life. When you've known someone as a little girl, that never leaves you. They, and you, remain innocent, somehow, through it all.'

'She speaks very highly of you, too.'

'Do you know about her mother, Detective?'

'Only what I read in the papers.'

'Then let me fill you in on Isabel's mother Jessica. Jessica Dallowmain, to give her maiden name, was an American, of the famous Dallowmains of Boston. A frightfully rich brood, with a lineage going back, oh, about as long as the work desk I have in my study. But believe me, Detective, those Bostonians know a thing or two about being snobs – they can out-snob a Brit at a hundred paces! Anyway, Jessica left Isabel's father when Isabel was just eight or nine. She ran off with an Argentinian polo player. That was no surprise, because there were other men before that, lots of them. Spanish bullfighters, Ecuadorian racing drivers, Tunisian tennis players . . . She suffered from tuberculosis and, apparently, one of the side effects is that it makes you incredibly promiscuous. Whether that's true or not, I'm no doctor, but Jessica was recklessly randy, uncontrollable, and frankly mad. Lord Saxmore-Blaine had to go to extreme measures to cover it all up – because of scandal, blackmail, she was open to the lot. It was a full-time job keeping her misdemeanours under wraps. Poor old sod, there must have been a sense of relief when she did eventually end it all. She'd tried before, you see: various aborted hangings, a failed wrist slashing, and some underwhelming overdoses.

'Jessica was a stunner, just like Isabel. And, believe me, Detective, I have had the pleasure of snapping a lot of beautiful girls. But women like Jessica and Isabel have that other quality about them that can't be captured on camera. It's too elusive.'

'How did she kill herself?'

'She ended up sticking her head in the oven, Sylvia Plath style. She was the poet who killed herself—'

'By sticking her head in an oven.'

'Quite. The joke with Jessica was, to everyone's astonishment, that she'd managed to do it. That was not because of her other failed attempts. No, everyone was just astonished that she'd managed even to turn the oven on – because she'd never used one before.' He gave a short mirthless laugh, but it quickly faltered as a memory struck, and he fell into melancholy. 'Poor Isabel. I remember it vividly. And so does she, no doubt. It's not the sort of thing you ever forget or ever get over, I suppose. So you see, Detective Treadwell, there's a history there of unstable behaviour. And I always feared there was more tragedy in store for her, poor Isabel.'

'That's all very interesting, Mr DeVane, but I've already spoken to Ms Saxmore-Blaine in some detail,' Vince said with a guiding edge in his voice. 'It's Johnny Beresford's friends I'm interested in now.'

DeVane looked disappointed that Vince hadn't congratulated him on his gems of insight, whipped out his notebook and feverishly written down his words verbatim. The snapper huffily folded his arms, and said: 'Quite. You asked if I could kill Johnny, and I said yes, so let me explain. He was my best friend, and we've known each other since school, where I was a year below him. But there's a part of me that's glad he's . . . gone. Isabel always had her problems, but Johnny exacerbated them. He knew how to press her buttons, as it were. But I'm sure she's not capable of killing anyone. Not while sober anyway.'

'She wasn't sober,' added Vince redundantly. Because he knew DeVane knew that she wasn't.

'Quite.' DeVane paused for thought, then said determinedly, 'Isabel needs protecting, not persecuting.'

Vince weighed DeVane up. Was he himself protecting her or persecuting her? Vince came down on the latter. Out of Nicky DeVane's mouth, from her closest friend, came words as damning and loaded as that smoking gun in her hand.

'One last question, Mr DeVane.'

'Surely.'

'Where were you on the night he was killed?'

DeVane looked taken aback at this, and made a show of his displeasure by creasing his brow and putting a petulant little twist on his mouth. 'I take it that line of questioning is merely standard procedure? I can't imagine you think I'd kill my dearest friend.'

'You've admitted that, given the right circumstances, you could have killed him. I'm just checking to see if you did.'

'You misunderstood me, Detective. I . . . I just meant that I would do anything to protect Isabel. Do you not see that?'

Vince saw it, but didn't really buy it, and he didn't throw him a lifeline. His mouth stayed shut, but his eyes said: *Just answer the fucking question.*

DeVane muttered his astonishment at all this, then spun around and reached over to a large red desk diary and flicked through it to the appropriate page. 'Ah, yes, I was in Soho. Met some friends for drinks at Muriel's Colony Rooms, then on to the Whiskey-a-Go-Go in Wardour Street with Brian and Anita. Then we met up with John and George and some others and went off to Brian Epstein's party at Tiki's on the King's Road. I left at about three, with a friend called Gloria. She's on the cover of this month's *Vogue.*'

'You needed to check your diary to remember *that?*'

DeVane gave an immodest little shrug that verged on smugness, flipped the diary shut, and said: 'It's irrelevant anyway, Detective. I know what you're thinking, and killing Johnny wouldn't have done me any good with Isabel. I've always known she doesn't love me – not as one would wish. She clearly sees me as her brother, I fear. She fell in love with Johnny the first time she clapped eyes on him, I think. Of course, irony upon ironies, I even introduced them.'

You didn't need to be a detective to catch the palpable and barely disguised bitterness in Nicky DeVane's voice. But Vince was, and he did – and he exploited it. 'The dashing and daring army man, uh? And so tall and handsome. What was he, six-five, six-six?'

DeVane took an angry breath, then said guardedly, 'I don't know. I've never measured him.'

Vince decided not to mine this rich vein of antagonism and said, 'Did he know about your feelings towards Isabel?'

'Of course he knew. But we didn't talk about Isabel, nor would he say anything derogatory about her in front of me, because he knew how I felt. He respected that feeling. It was the love that daren't speak its name.'

'Not quite, though.'

'Quite. No, not quite. But you get the idea.'

Quite. Vince got the idea. And, on that, he drew the interview to an end. Outside, night was cramming in, as all the neon signs that spelled the end of the day were being switched on.

'Well, Detective Treadwell, if there's anything else I can help you with, do let me know,' said DeVane, leading Vince to the door. 'Oh, yes, and I owe you – for ignoring the indiscretion. I hardly touch the stuff myself—'.

'Don't worry about it.'

'Very enlightened of you, Detective.'

'I let the little things go, just so I can get on with the big things. It's more time management than enlightenment, Mr DeVane.'

'Quite.'

'Actually, you could do me a favour. Can I borrow your phone?'

'Of course. I'll leave you to it,' said the photographer before exiting the office.

Vince waited for the click of DeVane's Cuban heels to fade away before he dialled the direct number. 'Mac, it's Vince.'

Mac said, 'Got some news for you on Isabel Saxmore-Blaine.'

'Good or bad?'

CHAPTER 20

'This place is driving me crazy!'

'You could do a lot worse, and a lot of people in your position do actually do a lot worse,' said Vince, looking around Isabel Saxmore-Blaine' private room – or *suite* – at the Salisbury Hospital. It was 10.30 a.m. He sat drinking a cup of coffee, as she paced the floor with all the poise and grace of a professional dancer. She was dressed in a black roll-neck sweater that seemed like a tube of liquorice wrapped around her long elegant neck, black ski pants, and a pair of black leather ballet-pump style shoes. No make-up today except a slash of red lipstick that looked glossy and moist, like a fresh paint job on an Italian sports car. Her hair was scraped back into a polka-dot Alice band.

'Yes, I know I should be grateful,' she said. 'But even a gilded cage, at three hundred guineas a week, is still a cage when you can't go out.'

'Not without an escort, you can't.'

He said it with enough of a mischievous inflection in his voice for her to immediately stop her pacing and look around at him with a childlike expression, her eyes lit up in expectation like a kid at Christmas time.

So twenty minutes later they were in St James's Park, throwing stale bread to the ducks in the pond. All around them, London brooded under a dark sky, heavy clouds slowing, rearranging themselves against a stark background of a metallic winter light. The pond was busy with web-footed birds of all descriptions milling around as they looked forward to the impending rain. A magisterial swan with four fluffy grey cygnets in tow, like little tugs around a grand ocean liner, approached them for a hand-out. Isabel tore off strips of bread for this feathered family, while Vince merely viewed them with suspicion. He'd never liked swans, and he had the feeling they didn't much care for him either – or any of his species, for that matter. Swanning around as if they owned the place. And, with their royal connections and warrants, in this most royal of royal parks, they probably did. But with their vaunted violence, their venomously hissing leathery tongues and archangel wings, Vince viewed them as feathered velociraptors.

'Vincent!'

'Whoops,' he said drily, as the large lump of bread he'd just thrown caught the adult swan squarely on its beak and it ruffled its feathers. 'They say they can break your arm with one flap of their wings,' he observed.

'You don't believe that, do you?'

'Adamantly. I have first-hand experience. I got chased by one as a kid.'

'Poor you. It must have been terrifying.'

Vince weighed up the terror aspect of it. 'Humiliating, more like, running away from an overgrown duck.'

She laughed. 'And you've held it against them ever since?'

'Well, let's just say, if one tries to pull anything now, I'm ready.'

'You'll end up in the tower, seeing as they're the property of the Queen.'

'You think I'd let some law that was probably etched on to the side of a turnip in 1066 stop me?' She laughed some more. 'Anyway, your father could get me off the hook. I hear he knows her personally.'

'Before he became an ambassador, he was equerry to her father. So, yes, he does know her. It's my father I now feel sorry for. He's been through so much already.'

166

'Are you talking about your mother?'

Sadness sent a ripple through her voice as she answered, 'Yes, I suppose I am. And I take it, being a detective, you know all about that too?'

Vince shrugged in innocence and lied. 'Only what's in the papers, and I certainly don't believe everything I read in them.' Isabel swept her attention back to feeding the ducks, obviously not wanting to discuss her past, and Vince didn't see much point in that either, so he pressed on with the present. 'I've got some real news for you,' he said. 'We traced a phone call you made on the night of the murder, and for fifty-seven minutes you were using the upstairs line in his bedroom. You started the call at 10.12 p.m., and the operator finally cut the call at 11.09 p.m. That puts you upstairs around the estimated time of the shooting.'

Whilst he wasn't expecting her to fly into his arms through gratitude, he was certainly hoping to put a smile on her face. But it seemed the image of him getting chased by a giant duck was more pleasing to her than learning that she might be off the hook for murder. But Vince realized that all the damage that could be done to her had already been done. Innocent or guilty, his revelations were just cold facts to her now; and nothing much to celebrate, either way.

She asked, with a cursory interest, 'Who was I on the phone to?'

'A woman called Rebecca Flowers.'

She looked puzzled at first, and then the name suddenly clicked into place for her. 'Yes, of course, Rebecca. It's her surname that threw me. You spoke to her?'

'This morning.'

'How was she?'

'She was scared.'

Isabel looked concerned at this, and said, 'I've not spoken to her since . . . I was too ashamed. I'd let her down by taking that first drink.' She tore off another strip of bread and threw it to a comical-looking duck that had a Mohican haircut and a bulbous red roll on top of its bill. 'It's the first drink that does the damage, they say in AA, and I believe that now. If I hadn't taken it, I wouldn't have gotten drunk and . . . and Johnny might still be alive.'

First thing that morning, Vince had called the phone number he'd had traced, and arranged to meet a frightened Rebecca Flowers in a café not too far from the school in Hammersmith where she taught. Over several cups of strong sweet tea, Rebecca Flowers had shared her story. She had met Isabel four and a half months ago in a church crypt near Marble Arch, where they had hosted an Alcoholics Anonymous meeting. Through a fog of cigarette smoke, in a room full of beetroot-skinned Irishmen, swaying Scotsmen, bloated builders, addled academics, mashed musicians, cowed creatives and sallow stockbrokers, Rebecca Flowers had seen the beautiful Isabel stand up and announce, in a timorous, barely audible voice, over a soundtrack of hacking coughs, brimming sobs and the occasional bout of laughter: 'My name's Isabel, and I'm an alcoholic.'

Rebecca had given the newcomer an encouraging smile, and took her out for a cup of tea after the meeting. She then became her sponsor. Whenever Isabel felt the craving for a drink coming on, or experienced moments of anxiety and despair, she was to contact Rebecca and share the problem. It had all been anonymous until Isabel got herself splashed over the newspapers. Rebecca felt guilty for not coming forward then, but she didn't want to lose her own anonymity and possibly her job at the school. She hadn't even wanted to give Vince her name, but he insisted her secret was safe with him.

'What did Rebecca say to you?'

'She said you were very drunk when you phoned, and you were crying. You told her that Johnny had attacked you and that you'd hit him with a bottle, and that you thought you might have killed him.'

Pensively, she asked, 'What else did I say to her?'

Rebecca Flowers had told Vince that Isabel then talked about her mother's suicide, and how she felt that she too was losing her mind, and feared that she was drowning in the same gene pool, and was destined to follow her mother's fate and take her own life. But Vince just said: 'Until I hear from you otherwise, that's between you and Rebecca. The most important thing is that you didn't hang up on her. You spoke to her for about forty-five minutes, then you fell asleep with the phone to your ear and Rebecca could hear you snoring. She tried to wake you by yelling down the phone, and when that didn't work she hung up and went to bed. Then twelve minutes later the operator cut you off. This gives us pretty solid evidence that you were asleep upstairs when he was shot.'

Not expecting much, if her previous reaction was anything to go by, Vince watched as the news worked its way through to her, until something akin to a slight smile settled on her lips. It was worth it all just to see that. The weather broke just then, and the rain began to fall. The ducks quacked and motored busily around the pond like they'd been mechanically wound up.

'Let's go,' said Vince. He went to head back to the car, but Isabel just stood there unmoving. Vince wasn't expecting trouble, so he threw her a surprised look.

'It's almost lunchtime, Vincent, and I know a great restaurant near here we could—'

'I bet you know lots of great restaurants near lots of places, but I myself have work to do.'

'Can't I buy you lunch? I just want to thank you.'

'Consider me thanked.'

'I do owe you a meal, though, remember?'

'Nice try, but come on. I don't want to take you back to the hospital suffering with a cold.' He turned his back on her and stalked off. Isabel soon fell in step with him as they walked through the park.

'By the way, I met some of Johnny's friends yesterday.'

'Which ones?'

'All of the ones in the photo I showed you – apart from Lord Lucan, who I'll catch up with later today.'

'What did you think of them?'

'They lived up to your description – with bells and whistles.' When Isabel suddenly stopped, Vince looked round at her and said, 'I'm late as it is. You're not planning on getting me into trouble, are you?'

'One question. You could have told me all this on the phone. Or maybe you didn't need to tell me at all. So why did you?'

A clap of thunder sounded in the distance.

'I thought you should know.'

'Like I said, you could have phoned me.'

He shrugged, and offered up: 'I happened to be in the area.' Then he turned on his heel and carried on walking, confident she would fall into step again. She jogged up next to him and hooked her arm around his. The slight smile she'd worn earlier had grown into a barely disguised grin. She clearly didn't believe a word of it.

CHAPTER 21

As soon as Vince got back to Scotland Yard, he and Mac drove straight to the crime scene in Notting Hill. Little Ruby Jones had talked. She had eventually broken her silence and spoken to a young nurse. Detectives Kenny Block and Philly Jacket had immediately gone off to Great Ormond Street hospital, taking along the sweetest WPC they could find (for with their unnerving double act as inquisitors, Block and Jacket had no intention of talking to the little girl themselves, just collating the information). With them also went Dr Pamela Rodriguez, a renowned female psychologist favoured by the Yard, who offered the added bonus of having a Caribbean father, in the hope that she at least could talk to Ruby. Dr Rodriguez had a powwow with the other doctors looking after Ruby, and all agreed it was still too early to expose her to people she didn't know. And it was too early to start asking questions, that would effectively mean her reliving the horror, so they decided that the same nurse would spend the rest of day with the little girl, indulging her in whatever she wanted, in the hope that Ruby might again feel able to confide in her new-found friend. Specifically instructed not to ask Ruby any leading questions, the nurse would then relay to Dr Rodriguez any information the child offered of her own free will. Meanwhile, Vince and Mac were back in Notting Hill, verifying the information Ruby had earlier given to the nurse: *'I didn't see his face.' 'Whose face, Ruby?' 'The man who killed Mummy.'*

And at 27 Basing Street, Vince and Mac soon saw why Ruby couldn't see the killer's face. The chalk outlines of the victim's position were still visible on the carpet. Marcy Jones had been killed near the front door; she'd barely made it into the communal hallway when the first blow took her down.

Standing on the top step, Vince could only see the bottom of the stairs, his view ahead blocked by the sagging stairwell above him; a result of the slumming-over process that the house had undergone some years ago, when the original staircase was removed in order to allow more living space. It wasn't until Vince was midway down the stairs that he could see the chalked out-line of the victim's head, where Marcy Jones had fallen. Vince crouched down sufficiently to approximate Ruby's four foot two and called out: 'Go ahead, Mac.'

Mac stepped into position and brought down the rolled-up newspaper standing in for the murder weapon, suspected to be a ball-peen hammer. Again and again he brought it down, deliver-ing six of the best.

'What can you see?' he asked.

'I don't see your face. Just your feet and as far up as your knees, your arm only up to your elbow, and the weapon hitting its target.' Vince then saw another set of feet join Mac's – a pair of shiny-toecapped boots belonging to the PC who had been wait-ing outside by the squad car. 'DS Kenny Block wants to talk to you, sir,' he announced.

Mac and Vince went out to take the call over the car radio. 'This is DCI McClusky. Over.'

This is DS Block, came the static-crackling voice. *Mac, Ruby just told the nurse that the killer came into the bedroom, but again she didn't see him. But she did hear him. Ruby said that he sounded upset, like he was crying. Over.*

At this, Vince and Mac looked pensively at each other. Vince said, 'Crying? Last time I checked, tears meant feeling emotion. Would some psycho out prowling the streets on a random killing spree be upset about what he was doing?'

'At the prospect of killing a kid, he might.'

'At the prospect of killing his own kid, he definitely might. Tyrell Lightly – has to be him.'

Mac didn't dismiss this opinion out of hand, but threw Vince a look saying: *Give me more and give it to me quick.*

Vince obliged. 'Lightly's got an alibi for robbery which is a good cover for murder. He might do six months to a year for a failed robbery attempt, but murder means life. His so-called accomplices on that robbery are all witnesses to his innocence once they get bunged a few quid to make it worth their while.'

'The security guards were also witnesses?'

'But they didn't see their faces; the gang were all masked up, and they only chased them off. The whole thing's a put-up job. Lightly doesn't have the brains to set up a stunt like this, but Michael de Freitas does. He obviously told Lightly to keep his mouth shut until he worked something out. Maybe de Freitas knew the robbery was going down that night? Maybe the team involved were working for him? So he just puts Lightly in on the job, and gives him an alibi for when he's killing Marcy.'

Sounds good to me, Vince. Over.

It was 2 p.m., and Tyrell Lightly was tucked up in his pod, in his crib, in his yard. By the time the doors were kicked off their hinges and truncheon-wielding and tooled-up officers, led by Vince and Mac, entered the bedroom, the big blonde and the even bigger brunette sharing the wiry gangster's bed were trying to wake him up – Lightly being a heavy sleeper – with shrieking cries of feminine distress. On stirring eventually to find ten coppers standing at the foot of his bed, the first thing that the charm-school graduate Tyrell Lightly did was attend to his ladies' distress and assuage their fears with the magic words: 'Shut your big fat mouths, you bitches!' Very David Niven, everyone agreed – but effective. The wailing sirens did indeed promptly shut their big fat mouths.

Tyrell Lightly then reached over the big blonde, who was now sobbing plangently, and picked up a multi-papered joint, about the size of a traffic cone, that was docked in the ashtray on the bed-side table. The thing looked as if it must have half a pine forest stuffed in it. And when the torch was lit, and the giant jazz fag was fired up, its stems and seeds crackled and popped, and the whole room swiftly smelled like a bonfire. As Tyrell Lightly looked back defiantly at the coppers, and blew big billowy smoke rings in their direction, that might as well have been sky-writing spelling out: *Fuck You Coppers!* The uniforms looked at each other, and smirked and grinned and almost giggled at the prospect, knowing that there were four flights of stairs to descend, and knowing that Tyrell Lightly was going to feel every one of them, every step of the way.

'I ain't saying a t'ing!' he eventually said.

At that, Vince whipped away, not the burning bush from his mouth, but the book of matches he had lit it with out of his hand. He examined the gold cover embossed with the words *The Imperial Hotel*.

'Where did you get these?'

Tyrell Lightly gave a shrug and repeated, 'Not a t'ing. I ain't saying a t'ing!'

With his hand flattened like a paddle, Vince slapped the joint out of his mouth.

'Easy, Vince!' said Mac.

Vince got straight into the rude boy's face and repeated, with controlled urgency, 'Where. Did. You. Get. The. Matches?'

'I. Ain't. Saying. A. Fuckin'. T'ing!'

With that, Mac gave the uniforms the nod, and Tyrell Lightly was swiftly bundled out of bed, chafingly cuffed, risibly read his rights. Then enthusiastically *escorted* down the stairs.

Ouch!

Vince drove next to Gore Street, just off the Gloucester Road, not a stone's throw from the Royal Albert Hall. The Imperial Hotel was very much in keeping with its surroundings, and very much of its time. Victorian red brick was piled up in the grand Gothic-revival style, with turreted spires and arched windows. Inside it echoed the last years of the Raj with its faded grandeur and crumbling Empire. This impression was emphasized by the large brass and wood colonial fan that hung from the paint-cracked ceiling of the foyer. The lounge/reception area was beset with sagging sofas that looked as if they'd had the life sat out of them a good thirty years ago, and tables and chairs in dark teak that were ornately carved in that dust-catching Anglo/Indian style. The walls were covered in plum silk damask that had long faded to pink, while the well-flattened nap of the carpets was scabbed with cigarette burns, and all the paintwork was richly tobacco-tanned. To the left of the reception desk there was a bar, and a large dining room lay through some glass-panelled doors. To the right, a flight of streaky faux-marble stairs led up to the bedrooms extending over four floors.

Vince went up to the reception desk, currently manned by a young woman with an orange-bleached beehive hairdo, who was reading a movie-star magazine. She looked Arabic, in her twenties, and not unattractive – taking into account all the slap she was wearing. She had eyes like tarantulas due to the trowelled-on mascara, and pencilled brows that arched and flicked like a cracked whip. Vince flashed his badge and introduced himself. She looked at him stony-faced, not a dent in the foundation that plastered her pock-marked skin and gave her a greyish pallor. Her muted reaction spoke volumes. The natural reaction to a call from a copper was usually one of guilt, even if you were totally innocent, *especially* if totally innocent. It manifested itself in over-friendly compliance or flustered defiance. However, to the girl with the bleached beehive and too much slap it was clearly business as usual.

'What's it about?' she eventually asked in a monotone voice, and in an accent more Canning Town than Cairo.

'Someone's been stealing your complimentary books of matches.' Her powdered forehead crinkled and flaked in humourless confusion. 'And I need to speak to whoever's in charge.'

'The manager?'

'Is he in charge?'

She shrugged. 'He's the manager.'

'Terrific.'

With that flat little exchange over, she got up and disappeared behind a frosted-glass door into what Vince took to be the manager's office.

Vince strode over to the bar to take a little look-see. Brown leatherette booths lined the walls. Lots of palms in tall jardinières. A long, dark wooden bar with fixed swivel stools arranged in front of it. There were two girls sitting at the bar. He watched as one lit a cigarette with a gold match book.

It was the same kind of match book as Isabel had given him to dispose of, along with her empty pack of cigarettes, at their first meeting in the Salisbury Hospital. And just the same as the one Tyrell Lightly had used to spark up his joint only an hour ago. And they had both lit a path to here . . .

As Vince stood by the entrance, the girl next to the one smoking gave her friend a gentle nudge, and they both looked around and smiled at him. Nothing too unusual in that, so he reciprocated. He then turned on his heel and went back over to the reception desk. Still no manager in evidence. Vince reckoned he was taking his time to make a few phone calls. Vince was about to press down hard on the desk bell, but instead spun the reception book around to take a look. In its columns there were listed lots of Smiths and Joneses and Browns – and that was all. And each name had an initial inscribed beside it. This wasn't a checking-in book, it was a ledger. Vince scoped the reception area again with fresh eyes, and saw there were now two new girls sitting in the reception lounge, attractive and well dressed in their little black cocktail numbers and short fur coats and heels. At four in the afternoon, that was leaning towards over-dressed.

Vince was then hit with a hunch. It was a horrible hunch. A cruel hunch. One that he didn't want to be true, but one that couldn't be ignored, and one that was moving forcefully into focus and fitting into place with an unavoidable obviousness and a weight of evidence to keep it there. From behind the frosted-glass door of the back office he was aware of footsteps and voices getting closer. He didn't wait for it to open.

CHAPTER 22

Vince sat patiently in the Mk II, opposite the Imperial Hotel. He'd called Mac to tell him where he was, what he was doing and about the hunch he had. Mac had given him one of his extended 'Mmmms', but told Vince to go with it. Mac then filled him in on the Tyrell Lightly situation. He was pulling the same shtick as last time, and wasn't saying a 't'ing'. And meanwhile, to the continued consternation of Chief Superintendent Markham, Michael X and the Brothers X had again pitched up outside his front window, with their Black Power salutes and calls for revolution. But Michael X was no longer reading out the words of Malcolm X, but instead had opted for a megaphone and a selection of his own musings and poetry.

After his call to Mac, Vince had thought about calling Isabel to confirm where exactly she'd got those matches. But he didn't, because it was obvious she had got them from Beresford. And, if what he suspected was true, that it would all come out anyway. So he waited for night to fall. And watched the traffic at the Imperial come and go, which seemed to be predominantly male; but it thankfully included the beehived receptionist, trotting down the steps in bright red patent-leather pumps and a multi-buckled black leather motorcycle jacket, then straddling the back of her boyfriend's proudly polished Triumph and roaring off.

Vince watched as three dolly birds in figure-hugging satin pencil skirts, perilously high heels and predatory furs, sallied forth from their black cab and sashayed their way into the Imperial. He

178

immediately demobbed the motor, made his way across the street, and followed their perfumed vapour trail inside.

He headed straight for the bar, scoping the place and checking out the reception. Manning the desk was a middle-aged man. He was compactly put together, and wore a white dinner jacket with a red bow-tie and matching cummerbund. He, also, was of an Arabic hue – the beehived girl's father perhaps? He had a severely manicured moustache that looked as if it had been pencilled on. At first Vince thought he was wearing a black beret, but it turned out to be a wig – a very bad wig.

The dining room was closed, drapes drawn across the glass doors, which were roped off. In the bar, the three dolly birds he had followed in had quickly established themselves at a booth. Other young dolly birds sat around, entertaining men. They were the kind of men who normally wouldn't attract such birds of the dolly variety. They were of all shapes and sizes and ages, but for most of them thirty-five was a distant memory and so was hair, flat stomachs and possessing their own teeth. But they were expensively, if sinisterly, dressed, and as soft of hand as they were of belly. The stand-outs were two Arabs in full desert finery: flowing white gowns and glitzy keffiyehs. Their hands sparkled with hefty gold rings docking diamonds of at least five clean carats.

Vince sat down at the bar and ordered himself a club soda. No sooner was it put in front of him by the beefy-looking barman than the air turned fragrant. Vince glanced round to find one of the two girls he saw earlier sitting next to him. Again she had a cigarette in her hand, and she asked: 'Have you got a light?'

Vince took one of the books of matches out of the ashtray and lit her cigarette. In the gloom of the bar, the match illuminated a face that on the surface looked as pretty as a picture: a picture that was heavy on the paint and broad on the brush strokes. Cut beneath the paintwork, though, and there were layers of disappointment and tragedy all underpinned by a brittle hardness. As every other feature on her face folded into a well-rehearsed smile, the eyes stayed cold and businesslike. She had lambent auburn hair, not her natural colour but it suited her. She quickly introduced herself as Sadie and there followed some small talk, nothing really worth recording and nothing contentious like *are you married* or *do you have a girlfriend?* She asked how Vince had heard of the Imperial, and he told her a friend called Johnny had recommended it to him. She carried on smiling, and made some acknowledgement of that name. But Vince didn't read too much into it. Sadie was on duty, and smiling dutifully was all part of it. It took only as long as for Vince to drink a small glass of club soda before Sadie was asking him if he'd like to book a room for a few hours. And, as it so happened, he did.

They left the bar and went to the reception desk, where they were met by the Arabic fellow. Up close, it was plain to see that he was wearing, officially, the worst-looking syrup Vince had ever seen in his life, *ever*. It sat autonomously on his head, steadfastly refusing to blend into its surroundings, arrogantly refusing to assimilate. Neither wig nor an item of clothing, neither fish nor fowl, yet, looking very alive, as if it was in a constant state of flux, a constant state of take-off, always about to depart, always looking to hop on to the nearest hatstand or low-slung bough for a little exercise, a little respite from the giant pulsing brown egg it was incubating. Depending on the angle, it was either perched on top or sitting astride him, as its own private entity, if you will. Not covering his baldness, but drawing attention to it. The crowning glory was crowing it out loud and proud as it swooped and circled over the rooftops at night before returning to its perch in the morning to . . .

The bald Arab handed Sadie the key. Vince handed the rug-wearer the six pounds required for the room. Sadie told him to sign in under 'Brown'. He did so, and then she added her initial by his name. Forsaking the elevator, she walked Vince up to the first floor: a long red-carpeted hallway with rooms on either side. Their room was number 7.

Vince smiled and said, 'My lucky number.'

She smiled back, like she'd never heard that one before. The room had been revamped so that whatever charm of faded glamour was offered downstairs had been ripped out and renovated. It was bang modern, mirror-fitted wardrobes, deep carpets, dark wallpaper. But it would have been in poor taste to go on about the décor when you had Sadie standing before you, webbed as she was in stockings and suspenders – the stock-in-trade of upfront erotica. She sat down on the plum satin-covered bed, her soft milky breasts juddering and spilling out of a half-cupped purple bra that was fringed in black taffeta. She then went through the menu. By the time she got around to the eye-watering freaky stuff, which relied heavily on costume changes and props and was all reflected in the cost, Vince had whipped out his badge.

'You're bloody kidding?' she said.

'I kid you not, Sadie.'

She shook her head and pulled an ironic little smirk. 'Typical. I knew you were too good to be true.'

'Flattery will get you nowhere.'

'Well, let's face it, handsome, you don't look like a copper.'

'I hear that a lot.'

'And I should know, because they're some of our best punters.'

'Relax, Sadie, I'm not vice. I'm not going to pinch you. Not if I get the right answers.'

'I know nothing. All I do is turn up for work and . . .'

Vince shut her up by taking out a picture of Marcy Jones. It was the picture that had made the papers: a head-and-shoulders shot of her that said butter wouldn't melt in her mouth.

'Have you ever seen this girl?'

Sadie looked away from the photo, then said, 'No.'

'Everyone's seen this girl. She's front-page news. And every girl in this city has followed her story and wants her killer caught. What makes you so different, Sadie?'

'I said I don't know her. I didn't say I didn't want him caught.'

Vince's left hand shot out and he grabbed her around the throat. Not hard enough to stop her talking, but hard enough to stop her from looking away. 'Look again, before I take out the next picture, the picture they didn't put in the paper. The picture I carry around just to remind me how important it is to catch the twisted psycho who did it.' Sadie squeezed her eyes shut. 'Six whacks with a ball-peen hammer. It looked like she was wearing the back of her head inside out . . .'

Sadie shook herself free from his grip and blurted out, 'Okay, I know her!'

Vince saw that the switched-on, hard-as-nails, all-business look was fading fast. She stood up, grabbed her blue satin dress and got herself into it just as fast as she had got out of it. The room had chilled over, but it was the inappropriateness of the stockings and suspenders that she was currently feeling the most.

'She worked this hotel?' Sadie nodded to his question. 'She was a working girl, like you?' Again with the nod. Not good enough, Vince decided. 'I need words, Sadie, information. I need to know from day one until the day she died, and anything else that might help nail the bastard who killed her. So, she was a working girl and you two met here?'

'Working girl? I've tried to avoid that all my life. If you're going to use similes, I'd prefer the term *model*.'

Vince hadn't really copped her accent before now. Down in the bar it seemed playtime and sexy and husky and come-hither. Now he noted how she was reasonably well spoken, middle class. The reference to 'model' was ironic. It was clear that Sadie had a line in irony. Good for her.

From the chair she snatched up her clutch bag and pulled out a pack of Pall Malls and lit one with the ubiquitous gold-leaf match book.

'I first met her six months ago. Believe it or not, she started here just as a maid, earning a bit of extra money beyond what she got from the hospital. But, even as a maid, the money was good. Discretion pays a premium in this business, and all the other girls gave her good tips, so she was doing more than okay. Plus it was good having a nurse about the place, in case you picked something up – if you know what I mean.'

'So how did she end up on . . . I mean *in* the modelling game?'

'Money, sweetie, what else? Root of all evil, haven't you heard? Even though she did okay, she could see that we did better. And she wanted some of it, too. And she needed it quick.'

'Why quick?'

'She wanted to get out of London. She had her dreams, like everyone else,' said Sadie, a twist of bitterness replacing the dryness now. 'But, unlike everyone else, she was actually putting hers in motion. She wanted a new start, away from a vicious bastard of a boyfriend.'

'Tyrell Lightly?'

'That's the fellow. He'd just come out of prison, and she wanted to get away from him.'

'Was he her pimp?' She merely shrugged. 'Come on, Sadie, you can do better than that,' he prompted.

'All I know is that she wanted to get away from him.'

Vince considered the facts. Something didn't stack up here. 'From turning down beds for a living to lying on them for a living is a hell of jump, no matter how good the money. Did she know what was going on here before she got the job?'

There was another hesitant shrug from Sadie. Her head was dipped again. Not meeting Vince's eye, as she urgently inspected the carpet she'd seen a thousand times before.

Working for Vice in Soho had left its mark on the young detective. He'd questioned plenty of 'models' in his time, and been through the same grim routine when the occasional one had turned up dead or been cut to pieces by her pimp, or taken a beating from a sadist, when some S&M had gone painfully wrong. The girls had always rallied around and talked, because the underworld code of silence, fragile at the best of times, was completely shattered for the benefit of sisterhood and good sense. So why was Sadie now so cagey? Where was the sisterhood now?

'You know what I think, Sadie? I don't think Tyrell Lightly was her pimp. I don't think he knew about it – not when she first started here, anyway. I think *you* got her into the game.'

Her head shot up. Sharp and defensive, she spat out, 'That's shit!'

Bingo! 'That's why you're giving all the short answers, staring down at the carpet like it's so fascinating. Look me in the eye and tell me!'

'She was a pretty girl, so she had lots of offers. It was only a matter of time . . .'

'She was a very pretty girl, but wanna see how she ended up? It's not a pretty sight.' With his left hand, Vince grabbed her by the front of her satin dress and pulled her to her feet. With his free hand, he reached into his inside jacket pocket as if to retrieve the other photo of Marcy Jones he'd promised to show her.

'I'll tell you!' she yelled.

It was only a bluff. He didn't have Marcy Jones' morgue pictures in his pocket, but the gesture had the effect of pulling out a loaded gun. If there was any glint left in her eyes it was now completely extinguished by a wash of salted tears. And he doubted the irony would return either, since it's a tough act to pull off through a guilt-racked crying jag. Vince let the bunch of grabbed satin dress unravel from his clenched grasp. It flapped down, torn at the seam and the strap, as she sat back down on the bed.

He took a pause for some soothing breaths, worked up some equanimity and let the facts sink in. The confirmation that Marcy Jones had been a prostitute both widened and narrowed the investigation. Random killers and known killers became indivisible; personal and impersonal became one. Men can get as physically up close and personal as possible or permissible, simply by tendering money. Yet at the same time they remain impersonal, denied the intimacy of the kiss on the lips, the loving cuddle, the meaningful post-coital conversation or cigarette. And they can even disappear completely, blocked out, nullified from the girl's mind even whilst it's happening. They're known and unknown. They're merely James Smith, or Brown, as Vince himself had signed in as.

'I'm sorry,' said Vince, gesturing to her dress. 'I'll pay for it, of course.'

184

'Yeah, that's right, copper,' she said in an acid tone, 'it can all be bought and paid for.' She took a tissue from the box on the bed-side table and dabbed the corners of her eyes.

'Come on, Sadie, give me some answers.'

'She was a sweet girl. She wanted to get away from Lightly as fast as possible. For all sorts of reasons.'

'Name one.'

'Her daughter. She didn't trust Lightly around her, if you know what I mean.'

Vince did, but only from the tone of her voice. Because from what he'd so far witnessed of Tyrell Lightly's sexual practices, hav-ing busted in on him twice, all Vince could confirm was that the wiry gangster liked his women big. But then again, Marcy was just a slip of a girl, and was only fourteen when she had his child. So he said: 'Are you saying Tyrell Lightly is a child molester?'

'Not exclusively. That's just one of the things he likes. So you can understand why she wanted to get away from the bastard; he's a real sick dog. And working here was a quick way for her to earn money.'

'All the same, you must get more than your fair share of sick dogs coming in here?'

'No, we're strictly slap and tickle and a bit of pantomime. All harmless fun.' Sadie stood up, went over to the fitted wardrobe, and slid open its mirrored doors. 'You lot are well represented in here,' she said, putting on a policeman's helmet. 'Hello hello hello . . .'

Inside the wardrobe were WPC uniforms, WRAFs, Wrens, nurses, and even a traffic warden's uniform. But they were all shorter and more revealing than the standard government issue. Amongst the non-authoritarian civvy-street delights were PVC catsuits, leopard-print leotards, rubber corsets and masks, medieval-looking bondage gear, vicious-looking bull whips, fluffy handcuffs, leather handcuffs, rubber handcuffs . . . a pickelhaube helmet, a bearskin, a mortarboard, a nun's habit; and, on the very top shelf, a serried rank of dildos, double-enders, baby's fists and butt plugs.

'Everyone loves a gal in uniform – especially a nurse or a matron. Strong medicine, you see. How about you, Detective, what's your poison, pleasure or perversion?'

'I vacillate between Brigitte Bardot and Sophia Loren.'

'Why limit yourself? Why not both?'

'Why, indeed? But the likelihood of finding them stashed in your wardrobe is pretty slim. So let's get on with the business in hand.'

Sadie took off the policeman's helmet, put it back on the shelf and slid the door shut, then took her place back on the bed.

'Did she have regular punters?'

'It was different for Marcy. She was propositioned and offered a lot of money. She refused at first, then the money being offered went up. Plus the fact she didn't have to have proper sex with him.'

'What did she have to do?'

'Dress up, do a little dance for him . . . other stuff.'

'What other stuff?'

'Are you getting off on this?'

'How much did he pay her?'

'Fifty quid, sometimes more.'

Vince was surprised. 'That's a lot of money for a little dancing, especially when you're not even a dancer. Who was he?' Sadie shrugged. 'Was he a regular?' Sadie shrugged, again. 'I get it – keeping loyal to your punters, eh?' She didn't need to shrug, but she did need to start talking, so Vince turned it up. 'Where do you shoot it, Sadie?'

'I don't know what you're talking about.'

Vince winked knowingly. 'The brown, baby, the brown.'

Indignation ripped through her body as she proudly displayed her arms: milky white and untouched. Not even an imprint left from her kinky collection of handcuffs.

Vince shook his head, unconvinced. 'Not in your arms, Sadie, too unsightly. I hear that between the toes is a popular alternative. Take off your shoes and stockings.'

'You bastard!'

'That's right, I'm the bastard. You know what's coming next? All back to your place, surprise your boyfriend, who's probably got a bigger habit than you do, and is nodding out even whilst we talk.'

Vince saw the shudder run through her shapely frame as his words struck a chord. It was all so grimly predictable. A big fat cliché for a skinny little junky. All those nice middle-class girls he'd met who'd gone on the game didn't do it because they favoured the working hours, liked meeting people or had found some kind of mythical liberating empowerment through it. On the contrary, there was usually a bad habit enslaving them to it. And it was nearly always 'the brown', the heroin. The one that takes everything away – starting off with your soul, then working outwards. And the working girls didn't shoot up in their arms, because track marks might put the punters off. So they take it in the foot. After all, a vein is a vein; it might take a little longer that way to hit the spot, but it does hit the spot.

'What do you want?' she asked.

'Marcy's punter.'

'His name's Lucky . . . What's so funny?'

Nothing was. But as soon as he heard the nickname, it struck him like an axe and a big grin split his face. 'Tall, dark . . . droopy moustache, sort of stupid-looking?'

'That's the fellow. He sits in the House of Lords, when he's not sitting here.'

'How often is he here?'

'More than he's ever in the House of Lords. He's even got his own room.'

'Don't tell me, number 13?'

'Nice to see you've kept your sense of humour, officer.'

'Show me.'

'I don't have a key.'

'Not a problem.'

CHAPTER 23

Sadie led Vince up to the third floor, where Lucky Lucan kept a room. Vince sized up the door; a single Yale lock, no mortise or anything to really worry about. He flexed his right arm and girded himself. One – two – three, he ran at the door and *bang!* He felt the curved brass bolt and the metal holding bend and buckle. He stood back, did a windmill action with his arm to get some blood back in it. His shoulder fortunately was holding firm, a lot firmer than the door. He went at it again. The bolt burst its holdings this time, and the door flew open, with Vince falling into the room after it. Even with the door wide open and the light from the hallway streaming in, the room was still unyieldingly dark. It was like being sucked into a great black void. Vince hit the light switch by the door. Black paint covering the walls soaked up and killed the light. Thick black curtains covered the windows, blocking out the world and turning the room into a cell.

Vince's first reaction to the room was to leave it and leg it down the hallway. To get away from the evil that hung there, and away from the two men with their dead eyes, lifeless waxy pallors – and the Lugers they gripped in their smooth hands.

'Jesus . . . so, this is what he's into,' said Vince, as he scoped the room with eyes that were wide with shock and more than a little amusement. The two men holding the guns were mannequins, of course, although very lifelike ones, with articulated limbs arranged in an attacking pose, and realistic wigs – certainly more so than that of the Arab joker manning the reception desk downstairs. The

188

guns looked real enough, too. One of the dummies was dressed as an SS stormtrooper, and the other, his superior in rank, as a Gestapo officer sporting an eyepatch. The two Krauts were so realistic and detailed that Vince was tempted to flip the eyepatch over to check if his glass-bead eye was in fact missing. With their black uniforms, shiny leather boots, skull-and-crossbones decal and insignia, the fetishization of evil was overtly apparent. But, authentic as they were, they still looked as if they belonged in the wardrobe with the rest of Sadie's kinky uniforms, the PVC gear and the dildos. Nevertheless, taken in context with the whole room, Vince saw that behind its occupant's perversion lay a darker purpose.

The black-painted room was draped with Nazi flags: the black Swastika set in a white roundel against a red background. There were German military banners featuring gold eagles and wreathed skulls. Framed photos featured images of Aryan supremacy, involving massed crowds with frenzied faces and straight-arm salutes. And the main attraction was the Führer himself, captured strutting in various poses and stances. A portable record player predictably had an LP with music by Wagner on its turntable, and a hardback translation of *Mein Kampf* sat on the bedside table.

Once Vince had taken in this mise en scène, he felt a genuine chill pass through his bones. The air was thick and musty here, and the Nazi militaria – old, illegal, hated and hidden from view – carried a malodorous stench redolent of repression and evil. They say that in real life there are no genuine black hats or white hats, but, to Vince, this display seemed as pure a manifestation of evil as you could possibly get. The Hitler mob knew exactly what they were up to when they decked themselves out in these outfits and brandished these flags.

'So what was his interest in Marcy? I'd have thought he preferred blondes.'

'Superiority, what else? Sometimes he'd make her clean his jackboots. Other times she had to just stand there whilst he read aloud to her – educating her, as he saw it.'

'About the superior ways of the aristocracy?' said Vince, in a voice thick with irony.

'Exactly! He talked all sorts of bollocks, and he was pretty deeply into it all. He even told her how he respected her race, and so did Hitler. There was a purity about them and, according to Lucky, it was only when they came off the banana boats that they started to go wrong.'

Vince stared at her, incredulous. '*They* went wrong?'

'Oh, yeah, you couldn't take him seriously. Me and Marcy used to giggle about it all the time. Got to keep your sense of humour with some of the clowns who pass through here.'

'And that's all she had to do for her fifty quid?' asked Vince, but considering the room with its pervading malevolence, he now thought she had more than earned her money.

With a nonchalant shrug, Sadie added, 'He had the occasional wank, but that was about it.'

'Classy,' Vince said, wishing he hadn't asked. Because then maybe he would have heard the man entering the room behind him. Vince turned just in time to see the interloper's balled fist heading his way – he leaned back but still took a glancing blow to his temple, hard enough to throw him off balance and send him to the floor, on his hands and knees. As soon as he was down, in came an underside kick to the gut that jerked him up as if he was being yanked by his spinal cord, then sent him down again without a breath left in his body. Vince rolled over on to his back to get sight of his attacker, and saw only the tread of a large work boot zooming into view, and about to stamp its impression on his face. His hands instinctively shot up to protect his face, and grabbed the size twelve coming his way. He twisted the boot, then with his own right foot kicked away the man's supporting leg. The attacker fell to the floor with a considerable thud.

Vince clocked him for the first time and saw he was a big lump with a big greasy pompadour, and dressed like a lumberjack in a pair of grimy-looking Levis. He had a nose that had been pummelled so many times it looked like spat-out chewing gum under shoe leather. His mouth was just as unappealing, for a severe hare-lip exposed an upper row of snaggled and buck-toothed decay.

Vince scrambled to his feet, still gasping for air as he desperately tried to fill his compressed lungs. The greasy lump on the floor was faster than he looked, and he too was quickly up on his feet, with a wooden chair in his grasp that he sent hurtling towards Vince. He ducked and it crashed against the wall, splintering apart. Vince grabbed one of its dislocated legs, as the greasy lump let out a roar and came towards him with arms outstretched. Vince had the man sussed: he wasn't a fighter, he was a frightener; all pompadour and circumstance and not one precision punch in his repertoire. But Vince was also sure that, if the lump got hold of him, he could probably squeeze the life out of him. He lunged for Vince, who twisted nimbly out of the way, so the lump was left grabbing the air in front of him.

Vince cracked one sharp edge of the square chair leg on to the back of the man's head, with enough force to feel the skull bone judder beneath. There was now blood on the chair leg, and a deep red gash in the fellow's head, where the tight flesh had split open like a gaping mouth. Then, reckoning he didn't need it any more, Vince let the chair leg drop to the floor. The lump turned round, his face creased in pain, his rotten teeth extending from his mouth as if he was trying to spit them out, and his arms raised to grab at the back of his split crown. Vince took this opportunity to shovel some fast two-fisted jabs into the lump's gut, and get in some rib, liver and kidney work whilst he was at it, leaving the lump doubled up, with his arms crossed over his pummelled gut.

Vince took a moment to look around and see if Sadie was still in the room – but she wasn't. No surprise there. The surprise came in turning round to see the lump steaming towards him again, head first. Vince was cannonaded backwards, until he was stopped by the wall. There was a crack from either the plasterboard or his back, and he immediately suspected the latter. That took more wind out of his sails. The lump now had firm hold of Vince and spun him around like a rag doll, and then bull-charged again. What stopped Vince from slamming into the other wall was the bed. The landing was soft, but with the lump now on top of him, it was as uncomfortable a position to be in as any. The bed sagged as the lump grabbed Vince around the throat with both hands. He felt himself sinking into the mattress as though he was drowning in quicksand.

The lump's grip was solid, unmovable, and it was choking the life out of him. There was a grin on the man's face, and Vince saw drool collecting and pooling up in the sack of his bottom lip. The dam it provided was about to break, and all the sewage it held was heading Vince's way. He could see a thick cloudy rope of toxic saliva making its way over the lump's smooth chin, and it was set to impact around about the vicinity of Vince's mouth. Time to act, so Vince removed his hands, which were redundantly trying to loosen the man's grip, and arched them slightly.

Bang! In a clapping motion, Vince smashed both cupped hands against the lump's perfectly placed plug ears. He could hear a pop, like a firecracker going off, and feel the suction as he removed his hands. The lump immediately released his grip around Vince's neck, and grabbed at his own scorched ears, whereupon Vince wrapped his legs around his bulk and with a scissor motion twisted him off the bed, ending up with Vince on top this time. Standing shakily, Vince started to rub the blood back into his throat, and gasped some more air back into his lungs. The lump rolled around on the floor, letting out only a strange hissing sound. He then staggered to his feet, with his hands still over his ears, and stared at Vince with alarmed question marks in his eyes. Vince's hands must have felt like crashing cymbals or a couple of mallets beating against his eardrums but, either way, he was a consummate percussionist of pain. Vince put the man out of his deafened misery as, with his left hand, he grabbed the lump by his greasy quiff, drew back his right fist as assuredly as an arrow in a bow, then sent it flying at its target: the hopelessly exposed and hapless putty of his victim's nose. The lump fell backwards, barrelling into the fake Gestapo officer, and sending the pair of them crashing into the wall beyond.

Vince hovered over him, knuckles white and blood pumping, almost willing the lump to get up again, just so he could knock him down a second time. The lump didn't oblige, because he was out for the count. The Gestapo officer, whose head was now off and his limbs irreversibly twisted, had more chance of regaining consciousness than the lump did. Vince pulled a Swastika flag down off the wall and threw it over them, covering them up to conceal the unsightly mess they were. And for good measure, and in memory of Winston Churchill, he took the still-standing stormtrooper's head off with a right hook.

We shall fight on the beaches, we shall fight them on the landing grounds, we shall fight in the bedroom, we shall never surrender . . .

Vince exited. He sped along the hallway and down the stairs to the reception. Halfway down the lower flight, he caught sight of two men leaving the hotel. They were of middle height and build, and both wore beige trench-coat style macs. With their backs towards him, Vince didn't see their faces, and by the time he was down the stairs, they were out the door and gone.

And so was everyone else. The reception desk was empty. The girls previously lounging around on the sofas had vamoosed. Vince went into the bar, and found that too was empty. The barmen had absented themselves. Half-consumed drinks sat on the tables, cigars smouldered silently in ashtrays, no doubt the folding rings of their dead ash could have told Vince how long their owners had been gone, but he didn't really give a shit about such details – they were gone. Sadie had worked fast, and the proprietors and punters knew the routine, and had evacuated the place with the discipline of a preparatory-school fire drill. But Vince didn't expect to find them all lined up outside in the playground, awaiting a head count. He went back into the reception area, around the desk, and opened the office door beyond without so much as a knock.

Seated at his desk was the Arab in the white dinner jacket and the bad syrup. A small desk lamp lit the room. He looked up at

Vince with big brown, unblinking, sad eyes. But it was the wig, of course, that held Vince's attention.

'No doubt Sadie told you who I . . .' began Vince, before stopping, as the truth dawned on him.

The bewigged Arab didn't utter a word or move a muscle. Then, slowly, his head began to tilt forward. And, even more slowly, the syrup began to slide down his face, until it lay in front of him on the desk. There wasn't a hair to be seen on his burnished nut-brown head. Or a breath in his body. He was dead.

CHAPTER 24

At the Moncler Club, Vince was again greeted by Leonard. But once the young detective had stepped out of the street gloom and into the light of the vestibule, Leonard's front-of-house smile quickly dropped and he looked about as welcoming as a parking ticket.

There was blood on Vince's shirt, which had a torn collar and the top three buttons missing; a savagely yanked tie hung tightly knotted but loose around his neck, like a hangman's noose just before the drop. But it wasn't just the bloody and dishevelled duds that rang alarm bells with Leonard, and sent the usually unflappable front-man into a flap. No, it was Vince himself: the sunken brow, the fierce eyes, the snarling mouth. You can't wipe violence off your face like a smirk. It's a stain that seeps into the flesh, torques and twists the muscle and sinew, boils the blood and looks like what it is: undisguisedly and unrepentantly ugly. It would take a good couple of hours before Vince could fully shake it off and move a couple of notches back up the evolutionary scale. Leonard might have been tempted to say something stupid like, 'I'm sorry, sir, but you can't come in here looking like that.' But he didn't, as he wasn't that stupid. He clearly got the message written all over the determined detective's face.

'I need Lucan,' growled Vince, not paying Leonard too much mind as he was already through the antechamber and into the belly of the casino, with its well-phrased chatter, expensive cigar smoke, and calls from the croupiers to place their bets on the roulette tables, as well as the constant barking of 'Banco' at the chemmy tables.

Leonard stood nervously at his side, and proffered, 'I think he was playing over at—'

'I've got him,' snapped Vince as he spotted the deadbeat peer. He strode over to the blackjack table, where the feckless fascist Lord Lucan was twisting on a seven of clubs, a three of hearts, and an eight of spades. Vince dealt him the 'game over' card – by dropping his badge on the table in front of him.

But before giving Vince his undivided attention, Lucan cast a glance around at his fellow players at the table, and in an attempt at drollery, said, 'I'm reminded of the good old days at Aspers' early parties. These chaps were forever turning up uninvited and empty-handed, and leaving flusher than the lot of us, without seemingly playing a hand.' This got some muted laughs. He then looked up more closely at Vince, and read the detective's face, and his situation, about as badly as he had the cards. 'I was wondering when you chaps were going to get around to me.'

Vince wiped the smile off his face by slapping on the handcuffs. Unlike Lucan's attempt at humour, this did bring a genuine smile to the gamblers gathered at the table. Because the handcuffs weren't standard government issue. They were made of black rubber.

CHAPTER 25

Vince sat in Mac's office drinking black instant coffee, with three sugars, out of a polystyrene cup. Always sugar with instant coffee, and always three with Scotland Yard instant coffee. Mac's office offered a fairly unobscured view of the Thames running amok through the city. It was a rich vein of activity that morning: a rolling river working its way right through London, as little tugs and long vessels chugged up and down it, churning over the dark choppy waters. What monsters lay beneath didn't bear thinking about. If you were to dredge the Thames thoroughly, you'd be likely to find a king's ransom, more corpses than Highgate Cemetery, and the answers to half the crimes in London. But it was all best left alone, to mix and mingle and lie together lost in the deep. There was quite enough to deal with on the surface, with the murders of Johnny Beresford and Marcy Jones. The two murders, and the two worlds, now mixing and mingling. And lying, lots of lying – and now another murder in the mix.

At 9 a.m., in interview room one, sitting with his lawyer was Richard John Bingham, the thirty-one-year old 7th Earl of Lucan, known to all either as Lord Lucan or as Lucky by those who considered him a friend, and considered irony an essential element in sustaining that friendship. He'd spent the previous night in the cells, crying himself into a fitful sleep. When locked down in a cell, they say that the innocent never rest. Yet the guilty, lying on their concrete bunks, can sleep like tops. Lucan had slept somewhere in between and somewhere undecided, so the slumber jury was still out on that one.

The greasy lump Vince had tangled with in Lucan's hotel room-cum-bunker turned out to work for the hotel as a handyman/porter/bouncer and anything else that he might be called on to do. The Imperial employed three of these fellows, and it was clear that their main task was to protect the girls and eject any liberty-takers. The dead Arab, one Ali Azeem, fifty-three, was the owner of the hotel, or it certainly had that name above the door. But Ali was no ordinary hotelier – or ordinary pimp, for that matter. And, with a set-up like the Imperial operating in that part of town, Vince had to surmise that Ali Azeem had sleeping or silent partners who, at the drop of a hat or more likely a name, would no doubt awake from their muted slumbers and get very vociferous and volatile.

The lump said that he'd only been working at the Imperial for a week or so, therefore conveniently didn't know too much about the workings of the place. He was keeping tight-lipped, or as tight-lipped as his harelip would allow. When Vince and Mac had questioned him in the hospital where he was being treated for three broken ribs, a broken nose, a torn septum and a fractured cheekbone (Vince had to quickly explain to Mac how the pancake proboscis and split lip wasn't all his handiwork – he was like that before Vince met him), they could see that he was scared, very scared. When Mac flagged this up to the greasy lump himself, he immediately pointed at Vince, and continued talking to Mac as if Vince wasn't in the room.

'It's him I'm scared of! I thought he was gonna send me to my grave! There's something bad to the bone about him! He's got the devil in his heart!"

Vince laughed it off, said the description of him sounded like a list of overly familiar R&B records. But, either way, the greasy lump was scared of something, and was keeping shtum. As for Ali the Arab, owner of the Imperial and the worst wig in

Christendom, or in Mecca for that matter, he died from strangulation, garrotted with a length of telephone cord. It was clean, methodical and professional, with just the right amount of sustained pressure that it barely grazed the skin around his neck. It struck Vince as a curious killing, and not the normal method London villians used to dispatch trouble. They generally liked it louder, messier and quicker, coming tooled-up with the more traditional fare of guns and knives. These killers didn't come loaded, they came light and improvised, and used whatever was at hand to get the job done. And they seemed all the more lethal for it. As for the wig, it had been bagged up with the rest of Ali's possessions, to hopefully be reintroduced back into the wild at some later date.

Mac came through and broke off Vince's musings, telling him that they were ready to interview Lucan. Mac made it clear this was still very much Vince's case, so he wanted the young detective to lead.

Lucan sat there with his blue-chip lawyer, one Julius Cundy, a bony-faced fellow, whose skin was drawn so tightly over his face that he looked as if he could catch flies with his tongue. He wore thick-rimmed tortoiseshell glasses that sat accommodatingly on the ridge of a thin hawklike nose. From a small bony head plumed carefully attended strands of sparse red hair that were greased into place and arranged for maximum coverage, the desperate fronds clinging clawlike on to the weathered rock of his mottled pate. He looked sharp, and ready to intercede and interject at the drop of a hat.

Lucan sat choking back tears, swallowing snot, and hacking on what struck Vince as a longer than usual cigarette. Like James Asprey's choice of 'coffin nail', it was probably bespoke-blended and made to measure. From somewhere he had managed to procure a very swish-looking ebony and gold banded cigarette holder; and he really shouldn't have, because humility-wise it did his case no favours at all. Due to his frayed nerves, the extended cigarette and holder combination had about as much movement in it as a baton conducting 'The Flight of the Bumblebee'.

Vince and Mac sat opposite them. When Vince began the proceedings with a 'Shall we begin?', the quailing Lord Lucan started the interview predictably enough by protesting his innocence.

'No, no, no I couldn't . . . I couldn't kill anyone, let alone a woman . . . especially a woman . . .' he uttered in a faltering voice.

Julius Cundy's magnified eyes narrowed as he fixed the petrified peer with a hard look that said *pull yourself together, man*. Lucan took the prompt (and at Cundy's prices, he'd have been a fool not to), remembered his military bearing, and straightened his guardsman's back. Finally, realizing that the skittish cigarette in his hand made him look like some theatrical type up on a buggery charge, he crushed it out in the tin ashtray. He executed a traumatized swallow that sounded as though he was necking a well-knocked about tennis ball, and lamented, 'It's heartbreaking, a tragedy . . . but one I am not responsible for. I could not have committed such a cowardly act, of that much I am sure. Positive of that. I just . . . I just don't have that quality within me. On the battlefield I dare say I could do so, all things being equal. But a defenceless gal? No no no.' He took some meaningful deep breaths, did a job of arranging his features into something akin to humble sincerity, then continued, 'Over the brief time I had spent with Miss Jones, and I stress our liaison was very brief, I grew very fond of . . .'

Vince blew an audible blast of breath that flapped his lips as he listened to the opening bars of a speech that had no doubt been whipped up for him by Julius Cundy.

'. . . Miss Jones. We spoke at length about our respective cultures and she taught me a lot—'

Vince cut in sharply, 'When was the last time you saw Marcy Jones?'

'In the *Evening News*, I believe.'

Vince and Mac exchanged furrowed glances: *was he serious?* Yes, he was, gormlessly so.

'I didn't know she – Miss Jones, I mean,' Lucan carried on, 'was the gal mentioned in the papers until one of the gals at the Imperial pointed it out.'

Vince: 'Sadie?'

'Yes . . . yes, I think that was her. Although I can't be sure. I suspect they use fictitious names, you know. They're all sexy Sadies, or gorgeous Glorias. Never a Gladys or an Elsie around when you wanted one.' Lucan attempted a fraternal smile with the other men in the room, like whoremongering was a collective activity. From the heady heights of their moral high ground, the smile was met with cold disdain; especially by his brief, Cundy, whose eyes shot up to the ceiling for higher counsel.

Vince and Mac now had the measure of Lucan's intellect, and it was scraping somewhere along the bottom. And they also realized that by attempting to wrong-foot the good lord, you wouldn't necessarily reveal fruitful hidden truths, but simply enter a barren wilderness of confusion. This was a man who was permanently wrong-footed, stumbling around in the dark trying to find a switch to flick, and thus make sense of a modern world that was increasingly leaving him behind, increasingly not taking him seriously. The class clown of the Montcler set, and yet even his class was conspiring against him; he wore it so brazenly that it was almost fancy dress. Lucan had come to life's party dressed as a dim toff.

'Okay, Lord Lucan, tell us about Marcy,' prompted Mac.

'Lovely gal. Such a sweet gal. She looked so different in her nurse's uniform . . . so innocent.'

Whilst not matching the redoubtable double act of Philly Jacket and Kenny Block, Vince and Mac's physical aspects naturally lent them their own routine. Mac was the avuncular good cop, whilst Vince was the unruly ruffian who was going to beat the shit out of you the minute the uncle's back was turned.

So it was no surprise when Vince spat out: 'What are we talking about here, Lucan? The real nurse's uniform she wore to work at Charing Cross Hospital, or the rubber one she wears with fishnets at the Imperial? We've been to your room there, and spoken to Sadie. She told me all about your sick little routine. And, let's face it, getting togged up in a nurse's uniform is the least of it!'

'I must object, Detective,' said the lawyer.

'Object away, Mr Cundy,' Vince retorted, his eyes firmly clamped on Lucan.

'My client isn't denying he visits the Imperial Hotel—'

'*Visits?*' Vince's eyes now fixed themselves on Julius Cundy, as he gave an incredulous shake of his head. 'Let's cut to the chase, shall we? Lord Whore–Whore here has his own specially themed room there. It ain't exactly the bridal suite, unless you're Eva Braun or one of the Mitford sisters. It's decorated in the neo-Nazi revivalist style, all Swastikas and death's heads. We took some pictures and we're considering a feature in *Homes & Gardens*.'

Before Cundy, flushed with anger, could respond, Mac raised a halting hand – ironically, but not intentionally, like Hitler's favourite salute – then authoritatively announced, 'Personal turpitude isn't the issue here – it's cold-blooded murder. And it's cold-blooded facts we should deal in. I think it's best we stick to those, so we'll carry on with your movements, Lord Lucan. What Detective Treadwell initially wanted to discover was when you last saw Marcy Jones alive.'

'It was about a week before Johnny was killed,' said Lucan.

'We need specifics, Lord Lucan,' said Vince. 'What was it, seven days, six days? Do you have a precise date?'

'Let me work this out . . .' Lucan enumerated with his fingers, 'it was four days before he was killed.'

'So that would be the Wednesday.' Vince wrote down the date on the pad in front of him. 'Go on.'

'I was meant to be meeting up with him that same night,' said Lucan. 'It was to be a boys' night out. Me, Johnny, Aspers, Simon, Guy and Nicky. We all met up at the Montcler at about eight for supper. We weren't going to spend the evening there, as it was supposed to be a non-gambling night. But Aspers got himself involved in a backgammon game with Eddie Stanley—'

'Eddie Stanley, who's he?'

'A member of the club.'

Vince gave a wry smile. 'Sounds like a gangster.'

'Oh, how droll. No, no, Detective. Eddie is Edward John Stanley, the 18th Earl of Derby. Won the military cross and is an avid supporter of the Scouting movement.'

'Glad to hear it,' said Vince. 'Carry on.'

'Well, poor Eddie, Aspers smelled blood. He knew he could take him for a small fortune, because he'd already taken him for a large one the night before. So we all left Aspers and Eddie to it, and went downstairs to Jezebel's. It was a good night, with the usual crowd. It was someone's birthday, I seem to remember. An Australian chum of Simon's. He paid for all the champers.'

Vince, wanting to move things along: 'Apart from the gambling and champagne, did anything else happen at Jezebel's that's of significance to the case?' Lucan said no. 'Did you *all* go on to the Imperial Hotel after Jezebel's?'

'No, not all of us. Simon Goldsachs wasn't with us by then. If I remember correctly, he slanted off early with some blonde filly. Some married filly, at that.' On letting this slip, Lucan suddenly looked concerned. As concerned as Vince had seen him.

The lawyer instantly read what was now written all over Lucan's face, and he immediately turned to Vince and fired off, 'My client wants to know if he need mention any names in the liaison between Mr Goldsachs and a married woman? Surely, at this stage, considering the absence of Mr Goldsachs, there is no need to make life unpleasant for certain innocent parties.'

Vince took a moment to process this request, which told him much about Lucan and the world he operated in. The man was up to his eyeballs in murder, prostitution and Nazism, yet he was worried about disclosing someone else's social indiscretion, and thus breaking a confidence of the Montcler. He replied, 'If we deem it to be irrelevant to the case, we won't.'

Julius Cundy gave Vince a quick gesture of agreement, then nodded to Lucan as a prompt to continue.

'As I say, Simon left, so the rest of us went off to the Imperial.'

'What time?' asked Vince.

'Quite early, around midnight. It usually doesn't get interesting until after the clubs have closed, but it was now quiet at Jezzies, so—'

'So, once you were at the Imperial, you met up with Marcy Jones?'

'That's right. In the bar. Well, there she was and I couldn't resist. The others complained that I was buggering off too soon, but to be honest I was so well and truly oiled already that any more drinkies and I wouldn't have been good for anything. Especially for the thing I really wanted to do. So I slipped off.'

'You and Marcy Jones together?'

'That's right. Off to my . . . to my room.'

'And then what?' asked Vince. Lucan looked confused. 'Up in your room . . . what did you do?'

It wasn't a trick question, but it was received as such. The confusion on Lucan's face just deepened. He turned to his lawyer for guidance, and the lawyer gave another irascible nod to encourage him to answer.

'Well, the usual.'

'The usual? You see, Lord Lucan, there's nothing in that room of yours that suggests the *usual*. It all suggests very much the *un*usual. So we need to know what happened there.'

Lucan shifted in his seat. He picked up his cigarette holder, tapped it on the table until Julius Cundy told him not to, then said, 'Well, she took her clothes off. I put on some Wagner. Then she . . . she handled me . . . you know . . . did the necessary on my chap. And then I fell asleep. I woke up, oh, around nine in the morning, and went home.'

'What time did Marcy Jones leave?'

'Oh, she was gone by the time I woke up, so I haven't a clue.'

'I do,' said Vince. 'She probably left as soon as she could.'

Julius Cundy said, 'My client is cooperating in your inquiries, Detective Treadwell, therefore I see no reason for sarcasm.'

Vince continued, 'And was that the last time you saw Marcy Jones or had any contact with her?'

'Yes.'

Vince's and Mac's eyes met in conference: this wasn't what they wanted to hear.

Vince said: 'We believe that Marcy was at the Imperial the night she was killed. She hadn't been out for a drink with her friends, and there were no new boyfriends on the scene. We think Marcy put her little girl to bed around about eight, then sneaked out of the house to meet you. Like you said – as did Sadie, by the way – you were always quick. It was easy money. Too damned easy.'

Lucan said, 'I swear to God, that night I described was the last time I saw her. If you must know, I caught hell from my wife for staying out that night. I was given the three-line whip. Not allowed out for a week. Not all night, anyway.'

'And your wife can confirm that you were at home on the night of Marcy Jones's murder?'

Lucan's military bearing collapsed and he sank in his chair. He knew now the jig was up. His wife, the family, everyone would soon know about the contents and activities in his third-floor room in the Imperial Hotel. Lucan had role-played being on the losing side of the Second World War, and was now preparing himself for being on the wrong side in World War Three when that news hit the fan. Which he knew it would, for it was as inexorable as Hitler marching into Poland.

Lucan snapped the ebony and gold banded cigarette holder that he gripped in his hand and dropped the two pieces into the ashtray. 'Yes, I was with my wife. And my in-laws were staying with us, too, for good measure.' As he sat there ruminating on his future reputation, not rejoicing in the fact that, for now, the two detectives believed him, a silence hit the room. It was an unsatisfactory conclusion for all involved. Except for Julius Cundy, for whom it was just another payday. The satisfied lawyer was already recapping the expensive marblized Wyvern fountain pen that he'd been making notes with, and putting away his notepad.

By way of rounding things up, Vince asked, 'And was that the last time you saw Johnny Beresford, too?'

'Yes, in the bar of the Imperial along with Guy, Nicky and the other one.'

'The other one?'

'Yes, the boy just down from Oxford. Isabel's brother.'

Vince and Mac looked round at each other, and a series of double-takes took place, with even Julius Cundy in on the act. But not Lucan: he appeared impervious to the statement he'd just made, and was busying himself by studying his hands with an intensity that made Vince believe he'd only just discovered them. Julius Cundy gave a sigh that grew into a despairing groan, and the expensive fountain pen was dropped on to the desk from sufficient height to produce an exclamatory clatter.

Vince: 'Dominic Saxmore-Blaine was with you at the Imperial Hotel?'

'Yes,' said Lucan, looking up from his hands. 'It was his night, really.'

'How do you mean, *his* night?'

Lucan at last felt the sense of exigency that now surged through the room, and saw the faces opposite him looking expectant and impatient. He turned to his brief, but Julius Cundy realized it was now too late to guide his client. The pursed lips, the magnified and alert eyes, the attack-dog demeanour, all that seemed to imperceptibly collapse under the burden of the peer's stupidity.

Vince repeated, 'How do you mean, *his night*?'

'It was the night of his . . .'

Lucan acquired the countenance of one for whom something was slipping into place. You could almost hear the mechanics of thought turning over in that titled head of his. There was a palpable *kerr-chink* as the penny dropped. A bad penny. A terrible penny.

'. . . his blooding.'

CHAPTER 26

'*Dominic Saxmore-Blaine?*'

At Isabel's flat in Pont Street, Vince and Mac had been let in by the ever-accommodating downstairs neighbour, who'd already informed them that Dominic was in, and had been in for the last few days.

'*Dominic Saxmore-Blaine!*' Vince called out again, with his fist urgently banging on the apartment door this time. Again no answer. He sized the door up. Then stepped back, ready to kick it in.

Mac put an arresting hand on his shoulder. 'Let me try something first. It's an old trick I picked up.' He turned the handle and opened the door. 'Always worth a go. You see, not every one of them has to be kicked in, Vincent.' But both men already knew that the door being off the latch didn't bode well for what was inside.

The curtains were drawn. The ashtrays were full. Two bottles of Glenfiddich whisky had been drained; the same fate had befallen the brandy decanter, and on the floor it looked as if the wine rack had taken a beating too. On the coffee table was scattered a selection of pills, both uppers and downers. And on the desk, next to the pale blue Underwood 5 typewriter, was a neatly stacked pile of typed A4 paper.

In the bathroom, on the floor, was another neatly stacked pile – of clothes this time. A pair of new-looking crocodile-skin loafers sat atop them. Lying in the bath full of deep crimson water was

Dominic Saxmore-Blaine. From what was visibly on offer, it was clear he'd cut his wrists with the blade of a lady's safety razor. His supine alabaster body looked completely drained of the life force that drifted around his fragile frame. He was almost floating in a diluted vat of his own blood. Vince considerd Lucan words, 'his blooding', but of course this isn't what he meant. He had meant the night that Dominic Saxmore-Blaine was accepted into and gained full membership of the Montcler set. He'd been dead now a good twenty-four hours, and you didn't need to be Doc Clayton to work that one out. Although that's who Mac was already on the phone to.

As Vince rejoined Mac in the living room, he breathed in the stale residue of the four hundred thoughtlessly smoked cigarettes and the imbibed and sweated-out booze that had provided Dominic Saxmore-Blaine with enough bottle for the task ahead. He padded over to the desk again, and picked up the manuscript resting next to the typewriter. It was a signed and dated confession by Dominic Saxmore-Blaine.

Vince sat down at the desk and began reading. It became clear soon that Dominic Saxmore-Blaine was a graduate in English literature, for its forty-five pages weren't just a dull list of the events; indeed, some of the prose got pretty florid and purple in patches. Maybe, like his sister, he would have taken up the pen for a living, or maybe he harboured ambitions to write a novel. But, unlike others, he knew that would never happen, so this was it. His last hurrah, his last flourish: the tap of the typewriter keys playing out his exit tune. But, writerly as the narrative got at times, there was always an urgency to it: the urgency of the deathbed confession.

The account was pretty much as Lucky Lucan had laid it out. There were a few minor discrepancies, no doubt brought on by the vast amounts of booze consumed, and some different points of view. According to Saxmore-Blaine, John Asprey was playing a hand of poker with the Earl of Derby, not backgammon.

Downstairs, in Jezebel's nightclub, Goldsachs was canoodling with a tall handsome brunette by this account, not a blonde.

Then to the meat of the matter – and off to the Imperial Hotel. Dominic Saxmore-Blaine had visited the place before. Since he came down from Oxford, and with his older sister out of the country, Johnny Beresford had taken Dominic under his wing and introduced the young man to the wilder and not so polite side of London society. Within certain circles, the Imperial was a legendary playground of bacchanalia and debauchery, and by the time they arrived Dominic and the remainder of the Montcler set – Johnny Beresford, Guy Ruley, Nicky DeVane and 'Lucky' Lucan – were all well oiled. At the Imperial, Dickie Lucan was the next to drop out. As Dominic Saxmore-Blaine described it, one minute Lucan was quaffing convivially at the bar with the boys, the next he was gone. Dominic didn't know where he had gone to, and did not speculate on it in his confession.

In the bar, Johnny Beresford took Dominic to one side. His mood seemed to have changed, turning serious, if not grave. He told Dominic that, like most things in life, nothing is always as it seems, especially the world that Johnny and his friends operated in. And that it wasn't all fun and games. There was a serious purpose in their coming to the Imperial tonight. Beresford then told the young man that he was here on business – business of national importance. For Queen and country. Tonight Beresford was to meet a man called Boris Sendoff, a KGB agent operating in London. However, years of deep cover in the hub of Western capitalism had seen Boris Sendoff enjoying a sybaritic lifestyle in London Town that had turned him, if not into a double agent, then certainly into a very pliable and corrupt Russian one.

Beresford told Dominic that he was part of a planned coup, one that was to be partially financed by himself and the rest of the Montcler set. Their silent, and very secret, partners in this coup were the British government, and their target was a small country off the west coast of Africa that was oil and mineral rich, and currently in the hands of a communist dictator. Boris Sendoff had provided the ground plans for the operation, since it was the Russians who armed the small country concerned. Beresford explained to Dominic that he would himself be in charge of all the military aspects of the operation. He and a few other well-trained men − because he had men like that at his disposal, old army colleagues − would take over the island in a matter of days, if not hours.

He grasped Dominic's narrow shoulders in his large hands and drew him closer, drew him into his confidence, and in a con-spiratorial tone of contained glee told him: 'It's not only the opportunity to make our fortunes several times over, but it's our opportunity to hold power, *real* power, in our hands. The chance to run our own country.'

Still holding Dominic close, he assured the young graduate that they'd be needing intelligent and reliable men just like him. The excitement was infectious, and merely being held in the arms of Johnny Beresford, in the grip of it, as it were, gave Dominic a rush of blood. And Dominic assured the handsome ex-military man, the gambler, the bon-viveur adventurer, that he could count on him!

In the bar, the men were quaffing freely, as if there was no tomorrow. And there, in the hedonistic climate of the Imperial, who was to say there would be? This place had the edgiest edge in town: so easy to slip and fall. Check into one of its rooms, and never check out again. At various times, its patrons had been rumoured to have been asphyxiated in over-ambitious sex games that went awry; pooped out on cocktails of pills; and been bludg-eoned to death in booze-fuelled arguments. The free-for-all debauchery, and the rotating door of debauchers who swung anonymously in and out of the place, meant the Imperial had its price, and you took your chances.

All apart from Dominic Saxmore-Blaine, who was now sitting quietly in a corner. He had been instructed to keep a clear head. Or certainly not to get it any more fucked-up than it already was. So he stealthily sipped a club soda and awaited further orders. And watched.

He watched as Nicky DeVane was the next to drop out. The pint-sized snapper eventually collapsed under the weight of all the booze distributed about his small frame and passed out at the bar, face down in a bowl of mixed nuts. Next up was Guy Ruley. According to Dominic, his exit was a little more dignified but a lot louder (and a lot more interesting to the detective reading the confession). Johnny Beresford and Guy Ruley had been sitting in a booth at the back of the bar, having a heated discussion. This quickly turned into a raised-voice argument, then almost degenerated into a full-blown stand-up fist fight. The two men were eventually separated and calmed down by the attendant hookers. Guy Ruley then stalked out of the hotel, cursing Johnny Beresford as he went. Dominic, now completely committed to the cause, had asked Beresford what was wrong. Flushed with anger and embarrassment, Beresford dismissed it as merely a childish spat, a locking of horns, a pissing contest and nothing to worry about. They could do without Guy Ruley tonight.

Johnny Beresford then went to the reception desk to take a phone call. When he returned ten minutes later to the bar, he told Dominic that Boris Sendoff had arrived and was waiting for them in one of the rooms upstairs. The bridal suite.

Beresford tried to wake Nicky DeVane, who was now snoring on the counter, peanuts, lemon slices and cocktail cherries adorning his head to the amusement of the other revellers at the bar. Annoyed with the figure of fun DeVane was cutting, Beresford doused him with a soda siphon, but still he wouldn't stir. Beresford sneeringly summed up Nicky DeVane as 'a useless lightweight little twerp', then turned to Dominic and said, 'Ruley's gone. Nicky can't be relied on, so it's just me and you, old son. I'll need a good man to watch my back with the Russian. Are you game?'

'Yes, sir,' replied the young plotter. He'd never called him 'sir' before. But then again, he'd never been part of a military coup before.

CHAPTER 27

So Johnny Beresford and Dominic Saxmore-Blaine took the lift up to the bridal suite, where the meeting with the Russian was to take place. Dominic had never been up to the top floor before. The hallway carpet was deep blue panelled in red squares, and the paintwork seemed fresher than downstairs. Beresford knocked on the door three times. As if intrigue wasn't already the name of the game, Dominic was looking for significance in everything now, including the number of knocks. But he soon realized that the only real significance of the knocking was that it was the best way to get a door answered. And answered it was, by a man of unparalleled proportions, at least in Dominic's eyes. Filling the door frame was the Russian, and he *looked* Russian. He carried the size and bulk of that country about him. Its bloody and eminently fascinating history was written all over his face. Here was a brutal visage that had known great violence: gulags, Stalinist slaughter, Siberian terror camps and KGB questioning.

Johnny Beresford introduced Dominic to Boris Sendoff as a trusted friend. The big Russian said nothing, did nothing. He just stood there for an unnerving amount of time, weighing Dominic up with dead eyes that practically made a clicking noise, like an old adding machine, every time he blinked. Finally satisfied, he said something in what Dominic took to be Russian, and invited the two men in.

The bridal suite offered little in the way of romance, its main feature being that everything inside it was either a yellowing cream colour or a mucky magnolia. Not quite virginal white, but it certainly wasn't the biggest slapper in the building either. Dominic had visited those rooms, with their pushy and plush red wallpaper, hot and heavy velvet drapes and sweaty black vinyl furniture.

Once they were over the threshold, the ursine Russian's mood changed. His large fleshy features lifted and transmogrified into something comical as, in broken English, he told them that after their business was concluded they would enjoy the hospitality of some whores. Johnny Beresford and Dominic sat down on the long cream-coloured sofa, and Boris Sendoff poured out three generous tumblers of vodka. Dominic expected them to be turned into martinis, but they weren't. They were brought straight over, blindingly neat. Sendoff then raised his own glass, pronounced something unpronounceable and necked it. His guests followed suit. After the burst-geyser sound that exploded from both of them when the neat vodka had burned its way down their throats and scorched their oesophaguses, Sendoff said that now they knew why the local brew was referred to as the Siberian central heating system.

The big Russian then went over to a bedside table, opened up a drawer and retrieved an A4-sized manila envelope, which he then handed over to Johnny Beresford. The Russian assured him that it contained a detailed layout of the aircraft landing strip, and all the military posts and positions nearby. With pursed lips and serious eyes, the old Etonian ex-army man, and now leader of a proposed coup, inspected the three sheets of paper comprising the plans.

After a few moments of considered perusal, Beresford's pursed lips relaxed into a smile, then he nodded his head in approval and announced, 'With the men I've got lined up for the job, and these plans, this should be a cinch. We could secure the place in a matter of hours.' He put the plans back in the envelope and handed them to Dominic, his new partner in this operation. Johnny Beresford then excused himself and went into the bathroom.

Dominic sat on the sofa holding the manila envelope in both hands as if it weighed a ton, which in many ways it did. It held the lives of . . . He didn't know, but he was sure lives would be lost. And he was sure this was the heaviest and gravest and most important document he had ever held in his life. He turned it round and readjusted his grip on it because his clammy hands were now sweating, his prints penetrating the sheen of the manila envelope and soaking through. That was beyond incriminating; it was potentially deadly. What if the plans were now smudged? What if the smudge was mistaken for something else: a military installation, a machine-gun turret, a tank? No, this was without doubt the weightiest document he'd ever held.

Dominic rested the envelope on the sofa next to him and, as nervous as a new date, sat there under the heavy-browed gaze of Boris Sendoff. It was a gaze that was unrelenting, unsettling and unflappable. It was the kind of gaze that could crack you under questioning. It bore the heavy weight of violence without even lifting a finger. Dominic drew great comfort from the fact they were both on the same side, so much so that he considered suggesting to the big Russki that it was rude of him to stare. But he thought better of that, as it may have been interpreted as, *What are you staring at?* Those were words Dominic had never uttered in his life, but had once heard from a group of boys on the top of a double-decker bus, during one of his rare and youthful forays on to public transport. Of course, Dominic wasn't staring at them, quite the opposite: it was they who were staring at him, togged up in his Eton tails. He had tearfully alighted from the bus under a hail of gob. Dominic realized there would be no such childish pranks now, because this was big school.

So he kept quiet, and covertly considered the broadly smiling Russian: the heavy ridge of his forehead, thick eyebrows like brushes made of shiny black porcupine needles, the sooty slab of his solid jaw, the brutal hands of a seasoned brawler or a clumsy stonemason. The sheer daunting body mass of the Russian just accentuated Dominic's fragile hold on the world. The man was a perfect representation of the sheer mass of the Soviet Union. Meanwhile, Dominic sat there looking like England: slight and set adrift. But it was Boris Sendoff's very size that made Dominic now question his effectiveness as a spy, for he looked as if he'd stand out like a big red sore thumb anywhere he went. This cheered the frail young man, the thought that the spying game was open to all shapes and sizes. Of course, he'd heard about fellows at Oxford being approached and recruited by the security services, but he himself had never been approached. But now was his chance to live like his hero, Johnny Beresford, and to show his father once and for all that he too was a man of action, and not just an aesthete, an eternal stripling and a habitual disappointment.

Dominic smiled at the thought of it. Boris Sendoff smiled back.

And then he stopped smiling. Because just then, Johnny Beresford stepped out of the bathroom. The big Russian turned towards him, and the jovial grin on his face distorted into a grimace as the first bullet tore into him.

Dominic sat frozen on the sofa as he watched the big Russian grabbing at the bullet wound in his chest, as though he was trying to retrieve the slug with his big blunt fingers. But it was too late. Blood began to spread across his white shirt like ink on blotting paper. Slowly, in stages, like the professional demolition of a tall building, Boris Sendoff collapsed to the floor.

Johnny Beresford was holding the smoking gun. 'Here, take this,' he said, handing the gun to his young accomplice. Dominic held the gun in both hands, gripping the handle and the barrel as if it was alive, as slippery as a mink that could escape his grasp at any moment. He felt its deathly heat, the destruction in the pull of its trigger, but he said nothing. Was this the plan? Had he agreed to this, to commit murder? Did Johnny warn him that this was going to happen? For the life of him, he couldn't remember.

Johnny Beresford now knelt over the big dead Russian and, with an exertive grunt of effort, he rolled him over on to his back and began rifling his pockets. He relieved him of his keys, his wallet and a bulging bloodstained white envelope. He checked the contents – Dominic assumed it was a wad of money by his calculating stare and the way his thumb flicked through it – then pocketed the envelope—

215

—and the Russian grabbed him by the throat. The brutal hands fastened around Beresford's neck like a big muscled brace.

Dominic was jolted up out of his seat by this sudden action. The big Russian's hands had shot out as fast as a lizard's tongue taking down a fly. Seemingly subject to a new lease of life, as if invigorated by death, Boris Sendoff climbed back to his feet a lot faster than he had gone down. Dominic watched as the very much *alive* KGB agent took a firm footing in the room. And yet it made perfect sense that one bullet, just one little capsule of lead, couldn't take down the Beast from the East. No, you'd have to nuke this big bastard . . . or at least empty the gun and send a volley of slugs into the monstrously big old pump that kept the Boris Sendoff show on the road.

Since the Russian had risen again, things had moved on fast – over to the other side of the room, to be precise. With his back to Dominic, Boris Sendoff now had Johnny Beresford pinned up against the wall, huge hands firmly around his neck, the blood leaching from the Russian's knuckles as his grip intensified. It seemed like deadlock, for Sendoff would either squeeze the life out of him, or he would die trying . . .

'Kill him . . . Dominic!' gasped Beresford, with what sounded like the last breath in his body. 'Kill . . . him!'

Dominic had used a gun before, his father having been a soldier and being still a sportsman. The young man had grown up around guns and, with very modest success and very little enthusiasm, had bagged a little of everything in his time. But this was different, for this was big, big, BIG game. This was murder.

'God sakes, shoot him! Do it, Dominic, do it!'

Considering the hold Sendoff had around Beresford's throat, his voice still sounded surprisingly clear, surprisingly firm. Its gasping desperation was subservient to its authority: this was an order – an order Dominic knew he had to obey if they were to get out of there alive.

'Do it, Dominic. *Do it.*'

Dominic raised the gun into the killing position, and aimed it squarely at the broad upper expanse of Boris Sendoff's back. He had no qualms about doing a 'Robert Ford'; in fact, all things being equal, he would rather put one in the man's back than see his face. A wave of self-justification washed over him – the big Russian was dead already, wasn't he? He was already on his way out. It had to be done.

Bang! Bang!

The two shots went into Boris Sendoff's back before Dominic had time to fully think it through. It was a well oiled and well sprung hair trigger, even for Dominic's slender fingers. After the shots, a deep silence vacuum-packed the room. The air stilled. Time seemed to freeze. And so did the Russian holding Johnny Beresford up against the wall.

Beresford grabbed the Russian's hands, released himself from the man's grip, and slid down the wall. He took some deep breaths to fill his lungs, got up and went over towards Dominic. There was no time for thanks or congratulations, or even for Dominic to comprehend what he had just done. Because the Russian, who was still on his feet, had turned round and was moving towards them in robotic lurches. His murderous arms were stretched out in front of him, like those of a wounded grizzly.

Then came the instruction, as clear and urgent as before: 'You've already shown your mettle. Now finish the job. Go on, Dominic, do it. *Do it.*'

Dominic did it. Two more times into the chest. Straight into the red expanse of blood, the red flag now hanging from the Russian's neck. Boris Sendoff had soaked up four shots, but still he came on, Rasputin-like – a zombie emerging out of his country's horrific and deadly past. He barrelled his way towards Dominic, his dead weight gathering momentum until he was on the young assassin, his heavy ursine arms wrapping around him like a loved one, burying the frail young man in his bloodied chest. Crushed against Boris Sendoff in a bear hug, Dominic smelled . . . *antiseptic? Vodka?*

Then the big Russki released his hold, went into rewind, stumbled backwards and fell against the wall. The room shook as he slowly slid down the wall, and finally rested on the floor in a sprawled sitting position. His slow calculating eyes clicked over the scene one more time, then finally shut up shop. His dark head dropped forward, as though he was taking a nap.

Dominic stood transfixed, the gun now feeling lighter in his hand. He looked down and saw that his white ruffled Turnbull & Asser evening shirt was stained with the man's blood.

Johnny Beresford was suddenly at his side. 'Well done, Dominic. You're one of us now, one of us,' he uttered with a warm camaraderie in his voice. He then held his young accomplice's frail face in his hands and looked steadily into his eyes, as if savouring what he found in them. *The reflection of a killer, just like himself?* He wiped the blood from Dominic's blood-drained cheek, and assured him: 'It was vital that Sendoff didn't leave this room alive. For the safety of our operation and everyone involved, he had to die. Measures had to be taken. Do you understand?'

Dominic's body still felt frozen from top to toe, as if he'd been shot through with a huge dose of Novocaine. But he managed a timid nod of his head.

'Good man. Now go home and . . . well, you're a smart lad, so no need to say it, but I'll say it anyway. Tell no one about this. *No one.* Do you understand?' There was another compliant nod from the new assassin. 'Stay at home and await further instruction. I'll call you soon.'

Somewhere in the blanket of numbness, Dominic managed to find partial remnants of his voice. 'What . . . what about him?' he said, looking down at the dead bulk of Boris Sendoff.

'Don't worry about him,' said Johnny Beresford dismissively. 'It's all been taken care of. You think I'd go into a situation like this without the correct prep? I'll make sure his body is never found. He'll disappear and no one will ever know. Trust me, Dominic, it'll be like he never existed. And, as a double agent, in many ways he didn't. You get me?'

Dominic didn't really get him because, not knowing the ins and outs of espionage, he didn't fully understand the significance of Boris Sendoff being a 'double agent' and why that should make him more prone to disappearing than a *single* agent. But he did trust Johnny Beresford. Dominic just had to look up at that handsome face, radiating its confidence and sure-footedness, to know the big Russian would never be seen again.

'Now, off you go. And, remember, not a word to anyone, Dominic. The lives and fortunes of a lot of men depend on it.'

With that weight of responsibility resting on his narrow shoulders, Dominic Saxmore-Blaine backed out of the hotel room. He then noticed that he still had hold of the gun, his finger still curled around the trigger. He shuddered and shook it from his hand, as if it was some repellent creature that had attached itself to him.

He made his way along the hallway, along the blue carpet with the red panels, those panels about the size of the bloody wound on the Russian's chest. He didn't wait for the lift, because he wanted to run – run all the way home. He wanted out of there, and he wanted out of there now.

But he should have taken the lift. Because it was on the stairs that he met her . . .

'You? What have you been up to, Dom?'

'What does it say?'

Vince looked up at Mac, who was busy tamping his pipe. Things had moved on since Vince had picked up the dead man's confession, and the room was now a busy crime scene. Photos were being taken. Evidence was being bagged up and recorded. The bath had been drained, and Dominic Saxmore-Blaine's body had been loaded on to a gurney. The usual routine, but the sense of urgency that threaded through most crime scenes was lacking in this one. Because the chase was not on, since it was clear to everyone that it was a suicide. But Vince knew the next incident wouldn't be clear to *anyone*.

Vince stood up and answered Mac's question: 'It says we've got another body.'

CHAPTER 28

The Imperial Hotel was again swarming with coppers. They were energized and at it; with this murder the chase was now on. As they headed up the stairs, through the silent corridors and past the empty rooms, Vince had to wonder if this red–brick Victorian edifice dedicated to illicit pleasures would ever be back in business as a destination for well-heeled debauchery. Would the whores and hoorays ever return here? He doubted it.

The bridal suite of the Imperial was chock-full of forensics in their virginal white coats, fanning out and fine-toothcombing the place. Of course, if Dominic's deathbed confession was to be believed, and Beresford was as good as his word, Boris Sendoff would be long gone and untraceable. He clearly was, on both counts: no bloodstains on the carpet, no blasted bone fragments on the bedcovers, no dried scabs of bullet-strewn flesh on the wallpaper.

Vince and Mac stood by the door. Mac had been reading Dominic's confession, up to the point that had taken the group of men to the Imperial. He shook his head and said: 'It's well written, I'll give him that.'

Vince said, 'Nice to see that his expensive education wasn't wasted.'

'Reads like a novel.'

'A real potboiler. You've got spies, military coups, toffs, tarts – and with young Dominic Saxmore-Blaine featuring as its main protagonist, a psycho triple killer.'

220

'See where it takes us, Vincent,' said Mac, offering him the manuscript. Vince took it and read on.

After killing Boris Sendoff, the newly initiated assassin had stepped out of the bridal suite and legged it along the corridor and down the stairs. It was on the second-floor landing that Dominic had run into Marcy Jones, who was just coming out of Lucky Lucan's room. Marcy saw the blood on Dominic's shirt, and the fear stacked up in his eyes.

'You? What have you been up to, Dom?'

Dominic didn't answer. He pelted on down the stairs and out of the Imperial, and straight into a black cab. Once safely ensconced back at his sister Isabel's flat in Pont Street, he poured himself a large Scotch to rid himself of the taste of the vodka. It was a drink he'd always detested for its vapid nothingness, and now it tasted like murder.

And he waited, and waited, for his fellow conspirator, Johnny Beresford, to call. Hours fell off the clock, but there was no word. He paced, he panicked, he picked up the phone to call him . . . but didn't Johnny tell him to wait? The world of intrigue he had just entered offered too many potentially life-threatening options to risk disobeying orders. So he poured himself another drink. And pretty soon after that he found his sister's hidden stash of pills: a bottled balancing act of uppers and downers.

Night became day, and then turned back to night again. Two days passed and still no call from Beresford . . .

Dominic had made the mistake of looking at himself in the mirror, his narrow frame almost disappearing from view in it, like a vampire. The eyes felt lidless from lack of sleep, burning hot and cold, circled in black, sinking deep into his crumbling skull.

With the agents of sleep still paying him no mind, Dominic continued pacing the flat. It wasn't the pills and the booze keeping him awake, but the knowledge of what he'd done. He felt a rush of power mixing in with the poisonous fear. A potent cocktail. A perfect storm. His mind twisted and turned . . .

. . . The black whore . . .

She saw him. She saw the Russian's blood on his shirt. She saw the fear, the guilt in his eyes . . .

. . . What have you been up to, Dom? . . .

'Dom'. The diminutive of Dominic. Who the hell gave her permission to *shorten* it . . . to make it *smaller*? The cheap, filthy, mocking *black whore* . . .

It would all be so perfect now, if it wasn't for her. She'd seen too much. She knew too much. She knew *all* about him . . .

Dominic was sure he knew what Beresford and the rest of the Montcler set would want him to do. They were men who lived by their own code of conduct. Men of action. Men of power. Men of honour . . .

So, armed with a ball-peen hammer he'd found in a bucket under the kitchen sink, next to a perished plunger and a rusted hacksaw, Dominic Saxmore-Blaine drove to the Imperial Hotel and waited for Marcy Jones, so he could stave her head in. The girl he only knew as a black prostitute, there merely to accommodate the needs of men like Lucky Lucan. She was simply a serviceable slab of meat that could nevertheless end Dominic's glittering career and jeopardize the whole operation. Tuned-up on pills and booze, these were the thoughts than ran through Dominic's mind as he tried to dehumanize Marcy Jones. Tried to take away her life before he physically accomplished the job.

He knew she would be there, of course. She worked the Imperial twice a week, and tonight was regularly her night. He watched as she spun out of the rotating doors, the raunchily high stiletto heels clicking on the chequer-tiled steps, and then skipped down the stairs as fast as she could. She looked as if she couldn't wait to free herself of the Imperial and get home.

After she got in a waiting taxi, he followed the cab as it made its leisurely way along Kensington High Street, then up Kensington Church Street, on its way towards Notting Hill.

It was around midnight when Marcy Jones got out of the taxi and walked up Lancaster Road to Basing Street. She didn't hear the man behind her until she *felt* him behind her, his jagged panting breath encroaching on her. She turned round sharply, awkwardly, her hand still gripping the key, which was already secured in the lock. Her flawless, pretty face creased in confusion. '*You?*'

Vince skimmed through the following account of the murder of Marcy Jones. There were no surprises in Dominic's confession, no fresh facts. After he killed Marcy, he noticed little Ruby standing above him on the stairs, and chased her up into the flat. Unbeknown to him, Ruby had of course hidden in her favourite hiding place – the drawer under her mother's bed. Unable to find her, his mind twisted and torqued again as he became convinced she was just a figment of his imagination. She was a ghost born out of his own guilt that would haunt him for ever. Satisfied the child did not exist and fearful of being caught, Dominic abandoned the flat and drove from Notting Hill straight to Eaton Square, Belgravia.

There he told Johnny Beresford what he had done, giving a full report to his commanding officer. But Beresford was displeased with Dominic's actions, and they argued violently. Dominic killed Beresford, shot him with his own revolver, then left Eaton Square and drove back to Isabel's flat in Pont Street. Thus ended the confession of Dominic Saxmore-Blaine.

Vince weighed up the manuscript in his hand, and considered this unsatisfying and underwritten ending. For all its heft, vivid description and strong motive, there was still something rather unconvincing about it all. It had a beginning, a middle . . . but no end. A narrative that quite literally dropped off the bottom of the page and died.

So it was with a certain amount of irony that Vince now said: 'A deathbed confession. They don't come any better than that.'

Mac, well read, well versed and hard to convince at the best of times, picked up on Vince's tone. He gave a contemplative nod, and said, 'Let's talk to the other two.'

CHAPTER 29

Guy Ruley and Nicky DeVane would be picked up at their places of work, and no embarrassment to them was spared. It wasn't just class warfare being carried out by chippy, lowly paid public-sector workers, trying to grab some headlines along the way (although Vince suspected it partly was). It was meant to pull away ladders, tear off the old school tie and, most of all, loosen tongues. It was meant to give a clear message: their blue-chip lawyers and old-boy networks couldn't save them now. The bad old days of the police working almost as a private army for the upper classes, keeping the barbarians well and truly at the gate and not in the grounds, were supposedly long gone (although Vince also suspected it was not that long and not that gone).

A pack of squad cars jammed with uniformed coppers roared up Regent Street and along to Nicky DeVane's Beak Street studio. Inside the studio, the sinewy frame of Kevin Ridgeway, guitarist with the High Rollers, the new bad boys of the British pop invasion, was laid out on the floor and louchely grazing on an oily joint as he watched Nicky DeVane snap his model girl-friend, Minetta Fruitful. Luckily for them, alarm bells began to ring when the alarm bells were literally rung, along with the wail-ing of bellicose sirens and the heavy-booted footfalls of panting policemen clambering up the metal-grated stairs. And there were a lot of people there to be alarmed: hairdressers, make-up artists and stylists, with all their gofers and assistants and an assortment of hangers-on. Kevin Ridgeway and Minetta Fruitful didn't go anywhere without an entourage who were all well drilled in the disposing of incriminating evidence, the rapid concealment of stashes, and were thus able to extinguish and flush away anything that might have broken the butterflies on the wheel. So in this case, the law's heavy-handed (and clod-footed) tactics proved a bit of an own goal.

The second arrest didn't score at all. They nabbed Guy Ruley on the street outside his Cheapside offices as he was alighting from his chauffeur-driven gunmetal Bentley Continental. He had just arrived back in the country, after a private jet had taken him from Frankfurt to Paris, where his private helicopter was waiting to whisk him back to London. He had attended an urgent meeting with some foreign heads of state about a mining deal worth the kind of money that only heads of state and mining deals can muster.

Back at Scotland Yard, Detectives Philly Jacket and Kenny Block had given Dominic Saxmore-Blaine's written confession a good once-over, got the gist and were primed and pumped and raring to go. Vince thought it would be a good idea to split the redoubtable duo up, and Mac agreed, so Jacket would sit cracking the knuckles and brooding violently in the background whilst Vince shot questions at DeVane, and Block would be doing like-wise as Mac interviewed Guy Ruley.

But, after telling the two men about Dominic Saxmore-Blaine and the triple murder of their best friend Johnny Beresford, the Russian spy Boris Sendoff and Marcy Jones, nothing could have prepared Vince and Mac for what the two interviewees – dapper snapper Nicky DeVane and the minted mining magnate Guy Ruley – proceeded to tell them. It was unbelievable. It was a *joke*.

CHAPTER 30

In Interview Room 2, Nicky DeVane's spry little frame had sunk back into his chair. His big brown bedroom eyes were frayed, confused and scared. Philly Jacket stood by the door, cracking knuckles, as if to highlight the fact that there was no way out for the little feller. Vince meanwhile loomed over DeVane.

Vince: 'A joke? What do you mean a *joke*?'

DeVane, in a distraught and quivering voice, replied: 'The blooding, *that* was the joke. It was a stunt. A set-up. A prank. The whole thing was a bloody wind-up.'

Nicky DeVane shook his head even more vigorously in disbelief, as the full horror of it sank in and the real punchline of the 'joke' smacked him in the gut and knocked all the wind out of him.

'So don't keep this joke to yourself, DeVane. Share it with us. Now!'

'Yes, sorry, of course. The Russian spy—'

'Boris Sendoff.'

'Yes, Send − *off*. Well, there was no Russian spy. And he wasn't killed, for Christ's sake. The gun was filled with blanks. The man Dominic killed . . . or thought he killed . . . was an actor just playing the role of a Russian spy. He was *paid* to do it.'

Vince could see where this scenario was heading as soon as he heard there had been a joke involved. In a place like the Imperial, a joke or a prank was always going to have to veer heavily towards mordacity. Something sharp and lethal enough to cut through the booze, drugs and general debauchery of the place would be needed to raise a laugh from its jaded crowd. Vince looked around at Philly Jacket, who had stopped cracking knuckles once the news had sunk in. Vince raised a finger to say, *I'll be back*.

He swung out through the door of Interview Room 2 and stalked along the corridor to Interview Room 4. But before he got there, Mac had exited the same way out of Interview Room 4, and was marching towards him wearing the same perplexed look as he was. The two men locked eyes, each trying to see which one had the best answer.

Mac broke off first with: 'A *joke*?'

'You heard the punchline yet?' asked Vince.

'Yeah, the big Russian's not from Stalingrad, he's from Stamford Hill. He's an actor named Bernie Korshank.'

'What else have you got?'

Mac shook his head in the negative. And without further ado, they both turned on their heels and went back to their respective interview rooms, to get more. A lot more.

As Vince swung back into Interview Room 2, he found Philly Jacket pacing around the table, not only cracking knuckles but looking as if he wanted to use them. Nicky DeVane was still sitting, cowed, at the table Philly was circling, looking as though he'd been crying. Vince shot Philly a look that asked if he *had* used them. Philly shot a look back that said: *Much as I would like to, I'm not that bleedin' stupid.*

Vince sat down opposite DeVane, clasped his hands in front of him, and took a deep and loud breath that marked a new seriousness and urgency to the proceedings. He said: 'Tell me all about Bernie Korshank.'

'Like I said, he's an actor. I didn't know him. I'd only met him once, fleetingly, at the Imperial. Johnny introduced me to him. Of course, Korshank was right up his street.'

'Why "of course"?'

'Johnny was always coming up with different characters to amuse himself with. He liked to mix it with all sorts, the high life and the low life of London. Variety is the spice, he used to say. Aspers and Simon Goldsachs had no time for types such as Korshank, so they always warned Johnny to be careful.'

'Hold on,' said Vince. 'Why the hell should Beresford have to be careful of some actor?'

'I call him an actor in the loosest sense of the term. Believe me, he's no Larry Olivier. Actually, Bernie Korshank is a nightclub bouncer who does a bit of acting work on the side. He's had a couple of lines in *The Saint* and *Dixon Of Dock Green*. He always plays the heavy – and looks the part, I must say. He's a very frightening-looking man.'

Vince got the picture. He'd known a few of 'the chaps' who'd screen-tested in their time. And TV shows like *The Saint* always needed convincing 'faces' to fill a set and look the part.

'Okay, tell me about the gun.'

'As I said, it was loaded with blanks. Bernie Korshank had taken care of the bullet wounds with blood squibs, like they use in TV special-effects departments. Very realistic-looking.'

'Realistic? How do you know all this, since you were asleep in the bar, according to Dominic Saxmore-Blaine's story.'

'Yes, I was, but Johnny told me all about it the next day. He was pissed off that I wasn't there to witness it. He phoned to reprimand me, but he couldn't stay pissed off for long. He soon moved on to telling me how the prank had played out. Johnny the Joker, he loved practical jokes like this one. The more elaborate and the bigger the audience the better. He'd talk about them for hours.'

'The military coup, was all that part of the joke, too?'

DeVane's gaze dropped towards his hands, as if to inspect the outsized oval carnelian seal ring he was wearing. 'Sort of.'

Vince went in hard. 'What does *sort of* mean, DeVane?'

Philly Jacket cracked a medley of knuckles to accompany Vince's tougher tone. And Nicky DeVane quickly snapped back into the programme.

'That was just Johnny indulging his fantasy life. He'd always had a fertile imagination. Always been rather a fantasist and a dreamer, wanting a life of great adventure. One of his cousins was good friends with Ian Fleming, the author, and Johnny used to play cards with Fleming at his club, Le Cercle, and later at the Montcler. After Fleming died, Johnny started dropping Fleming's name, and telling people how he had based James Bond on *him*. Said it was no coincidence that they shared the same initials, JB. He even said that Fleming wanted him to do a screen test for the part. I joked that they probably wanted to save money by having him use his own luggage and monogrammed shirts. *He* said it was thwarted because the American producers wanted some chap who looked like a Scottish truck driver.'

'Sean Connery?' Philly Jacket piped up. 'He *is* Scottish, and he *was* a truck driver.'

'No,' corrected DeVane, 'he was a milkman.'

Philly: 'Or was he a gravedigger?'

Vince: 'He played a truck driver in *Hell Drivers*.'

Philly: 'Did he play a truck driver in *Hell Drivers*? I thought it was that feller who played *Danger Man* – Stanley Baker – who played a truck driver.'

Vince: 'Stanley Baker didn't play *Danger Man*. But he was in *Hell Drivers*.'

Philly: 'So who played *Danger Man*?'

Vince: 'The other feller who was in it.'

Philly: 'Sean Connery didn't play *Danger Man*.'

Vince: 'No one's saying he did. There was another feller in *Hell Drivers*, who played him.'

Philly: 'Stanley Baker, Sean Connery, and the other feller who played *Danger Man* were all in *Hell Drivers*?'

Vince (dry as you like): 'That's right, Philly, they were all in it. On account it's customary to have more than one actor in a film, so they can talk to each other.'

DeVane: 'Just like it's customary to have more than one truck driver on the . . . uh . . . um . . . motorway.'

Vince turned from Philly to look at DeVane. Philly Jacket peered down at him too. The looks directed by the two men were enough to finish off the faltering smile that had begun to unfurl on DeVane's lips as he realized he was still very much in a street called *Shit*.

With the showbiz interlude over, Vince pressed on. He wanted to know all about Beresford and the components of his rich fantasy life. Nicky DeVane, a naturally malicious gossipmonger, obliged. He sat up straight in his chair and knitted his fingers together on the table in front of him, just as he would with his girlfriends and camper colleagues in the fashion business before he settled in for what he routinely termed a 'good goss sesh'. He had a glint in his eye, and that brisk look about him had returned as he told Beresford's story.

After a hardly distinguished academic career at Eton, where Johnny had spent most of his time gambling and reading off-syllabus boys' own adventures that fired his imagination, such as the works of John Buchan and Rider Haggard, Beresford went on to Sandhurst with the express intention of joining the Special Air Services and becoming an action hero. In 1941, Johnny's father had served in the North African campaign with Sir David Stirling, the giant Scottish laird who had created the SAS. And, along with such larger-than-life real heroic figures as Blair 'Paddy' Mayne, he had helped turn that small elite military outfit into the stuff of legend, unparalleled for their bravery, their stealth and their sheer bloody ferocity when taking it to the enemy. They dared, they won, and young Johnny Beresford had wanted in.

But there was one problem thwarting the young man's planned warrior narrative. His feet just weren't up to the rigours: they blistered and bruised and bunioned and broke out in every sort of rash imaginable. March? He could barely walk as far as the NAAFI in his army boots. The fact was, Johnny just wasn't up to the footslogging demands of the SAS. He was six foot three inches of prime muscle-bound old-Etonian British bully beef, and born to lead, but his Achilles heel was not just his splitting and throbbing heels; it was his collapsed arches, his clawed ingrowing toenails, and skin that looked like bubble wrap after the first mile marched in full pack. Sir David Stirling, a dear friend of the family, insisted that there was nothing he could do, there were no strings to pull in that elite regiment as there had been at Sandhurst, where more time was spent mulling over maps than marching. You were only ever as strong as your weakest link.

Beresford viewed this as a failure, a slur on his manhood, so he left the army completely. And then he went about doing what he was best at, making money and having fun. But he tried to get his revenge. He used to thrash Sir David Stirling at cards in the Montcler at every opportunity, and thus took a small fortune off him. But deep down he knew that these were hollow victories against a man like Stirling. When he quit the army, he left not only his torturous boots and kit behind, but the best part of himself as well. He abandoned the heroic side, the leadership side and, in many ways, the innocent side. He was no longer a part of something greater than himself. He was now cast adrift in the thrusting world of dog-eat-dog capitalism, where every man fought for himself – not for the unit, the regiment, or for Queen and country. He made money, but to what end? So, with the help of booze, Johnny Beresford retreated into his childhood dreams and a world of heroic adventure. But there were no real coups to savour, no daring deeds with himself leading the charge and knocking out military installations in a matter of hours along with a select band of SAS chums, and taking over small countries off the coast of West Africa to be run by the elite of the Montcler set. Just as there had been no big Russian spy – just a bit-part TV player. It was Johnny Beresford indulging his fantasy life – a deadly fantasy life that looked as if it had cost him his real one.

As for the business with Dominic Saxmore-Blaine, Nicky DeVane dismissed it as a schoolboy prank. 'That's all it was supposed to be. Christ, Johnny had played the same one at school on more than one occasion, and no one ever got hurt.'

Vince leaned across the table to Nicky DeVane, and said calmly: 'The only problem with the joke was that no one bothered to tell Dominic the punchline. You knew it, Mr DeVane, so did you call Dominic to reassure him that the bullets he'd fired into a man were blanks? That the man he thought he'd killed was just play-acting? That it was all a big joke?'

The collapse in Nicky DeVane was palpable. If anyone had walked in right now, they'd have thought that Vince must have given Philly Jacket the okay to pummel DeVane where he sat. He looked as if someone had slipped the bones from his body.

But Vince didn't let up. He loaded up again and carried on firing into the contrite corpse that was Nicky DeVane. 'So no one told Dominic it was a joke, and in that seventy-two hours, Dominic Saxmore-Blaine turned himself into a real killer. To cover his tracks, he killed a woman he thought had been a witness to his crime. A young mother and an innocent woman, regardless of what she did to earn her money.'

'The girl . . . the girl in the papers?'

'That's right, Mr DeVane, the girl in the papers. Marcy Jones was her name. Don't forget that.'

'I'd seen her, of course . . . with Lucky at the Imperial. But she looked so different . . .'

Nicky DeVane now did something that no doubt his friends would have frowned upon: he began to sob uncontrollably. His shoulders juddered and his head shook, tears flying everywhere, like a manic lawn sprinkler.

Vince turned away from DeVane and towards Philly Jacket, who stood against the wall, hands turning over change in his pockets, eyes hooded, dripping contempt from a snarling mouth. Vince returned his attention to DeVane. He didn't know whether to put a comforting arm around the little feller, or slam him back against the wall and tell him to shape up.

What stopped either of these things happening (and more likely the latter) was a knock on the door, and Mac entering. A quick glance at Nicky DeVane answered the question he'd come to ask, but he asked it anyway.

'You ready?'

Vince gave him the nod and stood up.

'C-c-c-can I go now?' DeVane asked through plaintive sobs.

'Don't be fuckin' stupid!' barked Philly Jacket, before either Vince or Mac could reply.

They stepped outside and closed the door, hearing the scrape of a chair against the cold floor as Philly Jacket took the seat Vince had just vacated. Then the rumbling voice: 'So you're a photographer, eh? Small world. I got me a camera for Christmas . . .'

They stepped out of earshot of events in Interview Room 2, knowing that Philly Jacket was about to commit Chinese water torture with his tongue.

'Did you get any tears from Guy Ruley?'

'Not a bit of it,' said Mac. 'Dead-eyed and impassive throughout. He blames it all on Dominic Saxmore-Blaine. Said he always knew Dominic was weak. Said that's why he didn't want to be in on the joke blooding. Not just because he didn't think the kid couldn't handle it, but because he didn't think Dominic was worthy of joining their little dining club. A fag at Eton and a fag out of it, he reckoned. He thought he was a sissy boy.'

'Is that what he and Beresford argued about at the Imperial?'

Mac gave a little *comme ci, comme ça* nod, and said, 'Yeah, but it was mainly to do with some money that Beresford owed Guy. They were in a business deal together.'

'Yeah, Ruley told me about that.' Vince shook his head in mild disgust and major insight at how this lot operated, and opined, 'They wouldn't allow an inconsequential little thing like Dominic Saxmore-Blaine to spoil their evening. When it comes down to it, it's the money with them – always the money.'

'I'll finish up with Ruley,' said Mac. 'I left Kenny boring the hell out of him about his stock of premium bonds. Meet you in the Inferno in fifteen minutes. I'm dying for a snort. All this has left a bad taste in my mouth.'

'I need to break the news to Isabel.'

'Markham took a WPC and went to see Miss Saxmore-Blaine personally.'

Vince caught loud and clear the disapproval in Mac's tone at his use of the ex-suspect's first name. And he himself thought doing so a little strange, when he had always addressed her formally as Miss Saxmore-Blaine, even when she had insisted on being called Isabel. It was a reluctance he put down to not wanting to be drawn in by a beautiful woman, and led smack-bang into a dead end.

'I'm heading the case, Mac. I thought that was my job?'

'I think there was some concern that you might end up taking your work home with you.'

Before Vince could go through the routine of rustling up some indignation at his professionalism thus being called into question, Mac saved them both the trouble, about-heeled, and headed back down the corridor to Interview Room 4.

CHAPTER 31

Dante's Inferno was smoking. Philly Jacket and Kenny Block had broken out the cigars. The two detectives had purloined a couple of Montecristo No. 2s from the Supe's office. The senior officer in the room, Mac, took no part in the crime and just tamped and fired up his pipe. Vince breathed easy and innocently with a stick of Wrigley's spearmint chewing gum. A bottle of whiskey had been cracked open, and chipped teacups now brimmed with the murky amber liquid. The only thing that wasn't happening was a game of cards. No doubt that would come later. But the mood, on the surface, was celebratory.

To Philly Jacket and Kenny Block, it was cut and dried. Dominic Saxmore-Blaine did it: case – or cases – closed. Two birds with one stone. More gold stars for their clear-up rate. Commendations from the Chief of Police. A rock solid, copper-bottomed, take-it-to-the-bank, done-and-dusted deal. A clear-up of the twenty-four carat, no-questions-asked variety.

But all the time Block and Jacket were locking down the case with laudatory appraisals, Mac was looking intently over at Vince. Eventually he asked: 'You don't look convinced, what's up?'

The young detective was seated on his usual sagging pile of boxes, feet planted firmly on the floor, elbows on his knees, chin cupped on his knuckles, once again striking a Rodin-like pose. Mac, Philly and Kenny sat around the warm glow of the half full/half empty (depending on points of view and dispositions) bottle of Bushmills that sat magnetically in the middle of their makeshift table composed of eight stacked boxes.

Philly and Kenny looked round suspiciously at Vince, and Philly asked abrasively: 'What's not to like, Treadwell?'

Vince straightened up and told him. 'It's wrong.'

Kenny pulled a face like a bad smell. '*Wrong?*'

'I can't disagree with the psychology behind Dominic murdering Beresford,' said Vince. 'Beresford had turned him into a killer, twisted his mind so out of shape that there was no coming back. And if you think you've killed twice, and know for sure you've killed once, a third stiff's not gonna make a whole lot of difference.'

'Isn't that just what we're saying?' said Philly Jacket, after a quick eyeball consultation with Kenny Block.

'Exactly,' Vince replied. 'Psychologically it all makes sense. And motivation-wise, sure. Who wouldn't want to kill the man who had played that kind of joke on you, and turned you into a monster? But, logically, there are still too many anomalies for me.'

A unified groan went up from Block and Jacket. As far as they were concerned, Vince Treadwell was 'at it' again, looking a chocolate gift-horse in the mouth.

Vince continued. 'The two murders committed on the same night are too different,' he said, slowly climbing to his feet. 'You've got a frenzied, bloody attack with a hammer, then a cool calm assassination with a gun.' He began to leisurely circle the table, cutting through the dead air and the smoke that hung heavy in the room like atmospheric movie mist. 'The gun at Beresford's house, how did Dominic get hold of it? He confessed to dropping the weapon after he killed Bernie Korshank. So how did he get it again? Did little Dominic Saxmore-Blaine, all of eight and a half stone, really overpower the fourteen-stone army man who was now holding it? Did he find the gun in a drawer? Was it even the same gun used in the fake killing of the big Russian? And we still have the problem of the body being moved. Maybe Beresford wasn't moved very far, he was probably killed in the room we found him in, but, all the same, he *was* moved. Which makes it puzzling why you would bother unless you wanted to provide a distraction, to draw attention away from something? Dominic Saxmore-Blaine, the tearful frenzied killer, thinking like a cool, dispassionate assassin who is concerned about distracting the police. I just don't see it.'

Philly Block said: 'The little bastard killed Marcy Jones with a hammer, Treadwell. I don't suspect that was noted in his Oxford half-term report either.'

His partner backed him up on this supposition: 'Anyone who could do that is capable of anything. His mind was twisted. He was boozed up and flying on pills, he could have picked Beresford up and thrown him through the French windows for all we know.'

'Then why didn't Dominic tell us that?' Vince stopped pacing as if to give emphasis to his main point. He searched for an answer on the men's faces. None came, so he continued. 'After all, Dominic told us everything else. Think about his written confession: this was a man who liked to write, a student of English literature; probably had a novel in him if things had turned out differently. Lots and lots of pages spent on describing the murder of Bernie Korshank giving the performance of his life as the Big Russian in the Imperial Hotel. And on the murder of Marcy Jones, who got equal billing. Lots and lots of detail about both those murders, telling us how he did it and why. And yet when it comes to the killing of Beresford . . .' Vince gave an unconvinced shake of his head, and a weighty note of incredulity took up residence in his voice, 'his hero, his commander in chief, and also the author of all his woes and ultimately his death. All he got was a couple of sketchy sentences, with no detail about the gun and how Dominic got it. No detail about how he killed him, what room he killed him in, how many shots he fired into him. Or if he moved the body or not. No detail there. Nothing.'

In the silence that dropped like an atom bomb into the room, Vince slowly glanced around at the men seated about the table. Even with his lips wrapped around the stem of his pipe, Vince could see that Mac wore an almost imperceptible smile. Maybe it was worn more around the eyes than the mouth, but it was clear to Vince that the old stager was liking what he hearing. As for the other two, they didn't like hearing it, not one little bit. They could now see their neat little parcel with the bow on top getting unpicked and torn apart, and there was seemingly nothing they could do about it.

Vince continued: 'Dominic couldn't go into detail about the facts of Beresford's murder, because he didn't *know* about the facts of the murder. And if Beresford had told him it was all a big joke, and that was the motive for Dominic killing him, then why hasn't Dominic mentioned it? Why hasn't he written down that the killing of Marcy Jones was a big fat waste of time, because it was all a big fat joke from start to finish?'

Vince couldn't help but note how the pacifying pipe protruding from Mac's mouth could no longer contain the broad smile that had spread across his face with each damning premise that Vince had laid out.

Meanwhile, Kenny Block had both consternation and anger struggling for supremacy on his face, with anger clearly gaining the upper hand, since he looked as if he wanted to put his fist right through the table. But the table was made of cardboard boxes stuffed with old files, and with a bottle of good whiskey sitting precariously on it, the venting of his rage was stymied.

But Vince could see that Philly Jacket was thinking good and hard, and this soon led to a bright-eyed and confident synthesis when he offered: 'I know why. With all the booze, the pills, the dope, Dominic Saxmore-Blaine was obviously totally off his fucking nut by the time he got around to writing that confession. And maybe, just maybe, it was easier for him to believe it was all true. Because the truth was too hard for him to swallow: that he was just the butt of Beresford's sick joke. Like you say, Treadwell, Beresford was the little shrimp's hero, and now he had become the man's joke. It was all too painful to take. So he made it sound better: he wrote how he wanted it to be. How he wanted to be seen. He made it up, like a true writer.'

'So the lie became Dominic Saxmore-Blaine's reality?' asked Vince.

'Exactly!'

'Sounds good to me, Philly,' said Kenny Block.

Philly was on a roll. 'Maybe Dominic just believed it all anyway, like a true schizoid. Maybe he killed Beresford because he challenged his new twisted reality. It's obvious that Dominic Saxmore-Blaine was a schizophrenic psycho. End of story.'

Kenny Block picked up the bottle of Bushmills and brimmed Philly Jacket's cup. They raised and chinked their mugs, and then puffed contentedly on their Montecristos.

Mac looked up at Vince, still smiling. *Your call.*

Vince gave an impressed-seeming nod of his head. Then he said, with some deliberation, 'Given the exacting and pernicious hold Beresford had over Dominic, that's a scenario that had already crossed my mind. And it certainly works, Philly.'

Kenny Block, full of pride for his partner, who was still too glowing to respond, said, 'Bollocks! Say what you think, Treadwell!'

'I'm just not buying it.'

'Ha!' exclaimed Kenny Block. 'You should be glad Dominic Saxmore-Blaine did it! It frees the sister up, if you know what I mean.'

Philly and Kenny exchanged furtive knowing glances that suggested the point had been long thought out and discussed, and they had been dying to make it to the young detective.

Vince stopped lounging against the wall and tensed up. Mac stopped smiling.

'What do I care about the sister?'

Kenny Block stood up. 'Come on, Treadwell, everyone knows you fancy yourself as a bit of a ladies' man. This'll get the posh bint off the hook and out of the nuthouse so you can have your wicked way with her, give her one right up—'

'Vincent!' shouted Mac, who was now also on his feet, along with Philly Jacket. The two corner men were now in the ring, Mac pulling Vince off Kenny, whilst Philly was doing likewise with restraining Kenny. The contenders had each other around the throats – to stop each other from talking, presumably. As riled as they both were, and as much as they would like to, they still had enough sense to know that trading blows would have been un-acceptable. So a good cathartic grapple was called for. And it seemed as if Kenny Block had won, because Vince had let go of his throat and raised his hands in surrender. He choked out, 'Keh, keh, keh, Kenny! Geh, geh, geh, get off me!'

Kenny released his grip and Vince wheeled away from him with a big grin on his face. And, on getting some wind back in his lungs, he belted out: 'I've got it! Dominic must have known we'd get around to him sooner or later. Deep down he knew he was cooked. So the deathbed confession, it don't get much better than that, it has coppers lighting up cigars and cracking open the Bushmills. He knew he was going to kill himself, knew he wouldn't make the distance. That's because he knew he couldn't live with what he'd done. So why not take the blame for Beresford's murder too? He was protecting his sister! He was tak-ing the rap for her because his confession would, as you so eloquently put it, Philly, get her out the nuthouse.' Vince glared at his two tormentors, and added, 'So I could give her one, you pair of mugs!'

Mac, Block and Jacket were standing with their mouths slightly agape. Not at what they'd heard from Vince, although it did seem to trump the previous argument. It was because of what they saw, and Vince hadn't yet – because he had his back to the Chief Superintendent who had just walked through the door. Markham had never lowered himself sufficiently to enter the basement of the Inferno before. But it wasn't his new surroundings he was looking so disapprovingly at – it was Vince.

CHAPTER 32

'Hoist by your own petard, Treadwell.'

'It would seem that way, sir,' said Vince, who even now, and try as he might, was still unable to dislodge the note of irony in his voice. 'But as usual, sir, all is not quite as it seems.'

He was standing in Markham's office, gazing at the painting of the Queen again. Any feelings of warmth he might have held towards the woman had long gone, due to over-familiarity and a sense of impending doom every time he clapped eyes on her enigmatic smile.

'It seldom is with you, Treadwell. It seldom is.'

Vince had a rejoinder to this already lined up, but it would undoubtedly be the finish of him. Its sheer breadth and depth of drollness made him want to crack up when he thought about it, and it saddened him to think that it would never see the light of day. But it couldn't, it mustn't, so to stop him thinking about it he fixed on the most boring item in the room – and there was so much choice! Markham was sitting at his desk, and Vince noticed that his chair looked new. He'd heard Markham had problems with chairs, always changing them, could never get the right fit, up and down with ants in his pants. Rumour was that he had piles. At this precise moment, Vince couldn't help but hope that rumour was true. This new chair was grey, padded, modern, and it seemed to ergonomically accommodate the Chief's lanky frame nicely. Vince had seen these plush office babies before: you could adjust the height, they had a 360-degree swivel action to them, and they also rocked back and forth. As office chairs went, they looked like a lot of fun. But with Markham's size 14s planted firmly on the ground, the Chief Supe was hardly getting a wobble out of it, and therefore certainly not having fun.

'There's always a flashy little shout line where you are concerned, Treadwell, and *all is not as it seems* would seem to be it, in this instance. Only it's very much as it seems, this time. As I'm sure Mac informed you, I've been to visit, as you so eloquently describe it, the "nuthouse".'

Not before time, thought Vince. But he said, 'Again, sir, you would have to have been there for the first part of the debate with my colleagues to understand the, uh . . . the language I employed.'

'I got the drift, Treadwell.'

'How is Miss Saxmore-Blaine, sir?'

Markham, whose eyes seemed to constantly miss the mark when addressing Vince, as though he was too unpleasant a proposition to look squarely in the eye, hit the target this time, and he fixed his authoritative glare on him. 'As well as can be expected. I also found out that you were out with Miss Saxmore-Blaine at a supper club.'

'She said this?'

'Hardly matters where the information comes from, Treadwell.'

'Well, it sort of does, because it's not true. Sir.'

'You deny fraternizing with her?'

Vince said, 'Yes, sir.' Vince thought, *mind your own business, you stiff—*

'It wouldn't be the first time with you and the ladies, Treadwell.'

And hopefully not the last, you stiff— 'I'm a public servant and take my duties very seriously, sir.'

'Drop it, Treadwell. We know your movements after you left the club. And it's not the only occasion you've sought out Miss Saxmore-Blaine's company.'

'May I ask again where you got—'

'No, you may not. I shan't be entering into a dialogue with you about your actions, Treadwell. But needless to say . . .'

Markham then went into monologue mode. Vince zoned out, busy with his own thoughts, but he picked up the gist. He was off the case, a case that Markham now considered closed anyway. It was clear that Markham was going along with Dominic Saxmore-Blaine's confession to both murders. And clearly Markham was going with that because he had been *told* to go with it. Because it involved a stink, a stink that went right to the top. Any further up, and the Queen herself was likely to be asked to step down from her portrait on Markham's wall and start giving character references.

CHAPTER 33

It was around 8 p.m. when Vince got home. After leaving Markham's office – the monologue having dragged on longer than something out of Shakespeare, but not half so easy on the ear – he'd gone back down to the Inferno and found it empty. Mac and Block and Jacket had gone off to find the big Russian, aka Boris Sendoff, aka Bernie Korshank, to play out what they no doubt thought was the case's endgame. Vince hung around and waited for them to return – but they didn't. He'd talk to Mac tomorrow, knowing he wouldn't appreciate a call tonight, and that Mac was a great believer in sleeping on things. Vince wasn't, so the conversation with Mac that he'd been playing out over and over in his head was driving him nuts.

In need of distraction, he turned on the TV and found it was a toss-up between *Peyton Place* and, of all things, *Danger Man*. So he got up from the couch, turned off the box and went into the kitchen to stoke up the stove. He took down the French press from the cupboard, heaped in some fresh and reassuringly expensive Jamaican Blue Mountain Java, and made himself some strong black coffee. He didn't reckon on a lot of sleep tonight; instead he reckoned on a lot of pacing around the flat, trying to figure out the next move in this case. But, as he thought about it in his present state of mind, he knew he would get about as far ahead as a one-winged fly.

Saved by the bell as the phone rang. Vince grabbed the receiver off its cradle expecting, hoping, to hear Mac's voice. There was the sound of pips, then the sound of traffic in the background, before he heard: 'Vincent?'

He recognized the voice, and there was a pause as Vince thought of what to say. The girl had had biblical amounts of tragedy heaped on her, enough to bury her, so the usual telephone greetings sounded trite.

'Where are you, Isabel?'

'That's the first time . . . the first time . . . you've called me . . . Isabel.'

He thought the line must be breaking up. But it wasn't, she was.

'Can I meet up with you?' he asked.

'I'm outside your flat, in the phone booth on the corner. I hope you don't mind.'

'I don't mind.'

Vince poured her a large brandy from the bottle of Napoleon that had been left behind in the flat, along with two full bottles of Scotch. When he found this dusty bulbous bottle of Corsican brandy, his first reaction was to throw it away, bad memories; but he had kept it in the hope that maybe one day he'd get a knock on the door from someone who'd appreciate Corsican brandy.

'You won't join me?'

'I'm fine with this,' he said, sitting down in the armchair opposite her with his cup of black coffee.

Her eyes were clear, not red-rimmed and stained, showing no signs of crying. She was holding on, that meant. Underneath her DAKS raincoat, which Vince had hung up in the airing cupboard to dry because it was tipping down outside, she was wearing black slacks, black patent-leather boots, and a ribbed black sweater with three brass buttons at the shoulder. She looked, as ever, very beautiful, inherently stylish, soberly dignified and, dressed in black, ready for the impending funerals.

'I'm sorry about your brother,' Vince offered. 'I was planning on telling you myself, but . . .'

'Mr Markham was perfectly pleasant.' Vince didn't argue that point; now was hardly the time for personal beefs. She continued, 'It was strange. When he told me, for some reason, and God knows why, I didn't cry . . . I even smiled.' She looked at Vince for an answer to this mystery.

'You're in shock. I've heard of stranger things.'

Her eyes drifted away from him, and a bitterness entered her voice. 'I wonder if Asprey collected any money on Dominic?'

'Money?'

'Johnny . . .' she said, but as soon as she uttered the name, it sounded like a mistake she wouldn't be making again. All the warmth that surrounded her old dead lover was like a hangover, a habit, and one she wanted to vanquish immediately. Her tone became clipped, distant and businesslike. 'He told me Asprey has something called the Suicide Stakes, a list of people that he had written up on a sheet of paper, like horses in a race, with the odds next to each name. The odds were set on the likelihood of those people killing themselves. Asprey knew his crowd and, in his line of work, suicide isn't uncommon. People get into debt, and it then becomes a matter of honour. And for the gambling addicts it's a way out. Taking one's own life is almost seen as the right thing to do. I knew that I was on that list, but not worth betting on apparently. I was an odds-on favourite.

'It was all viewed as a bit of a joke, until money changed hands. The artist, Douglas Houseman, he used to play piano at the Montcler. Dougie suffered from depression. Along with a broken heart, and all the other slings and arrows that life threw at him. And if you don't have the armour for it . . . well, he killed himself. People didn't think that Asprey would actually collect on the bets. They thought it would be dismissed as bad taste. They thought wrong. Asprey collected his money, his blood money. Didn't bat an eyelid, apparently. A wager is a wager, something to be honoured. Above and beyond anything else, it would seem. Certainly above ordinary morality.'

'When I first mentioned the chances of Beresford committing suicide, you looked shocked. I take it he wasn't on the list?'

'He was, but at odds of a hundred to one. The only two not on the list were James Asprey himself and Simon Goldsachs. Asprey was running the book, of course, and Simon Goldsachs . . . no one dared propose him for the list as he was somehow considered indestructible. An immensely lucky gambler who always wins and, of course, he's as rich as Croesus. Money arms you against death, that's the reckoning.'

Vince stood up. The Jamaican Blue Mountain was percolating through his brain and a caffeine jag was kicking in. Fresh ideas were spiking and needed walking around the room. He went over to the window and inserted his fingertips into the Venetian blind for a glimpse of the outside world. The rain had a steady, relentless thrum to it.

He said, finally, 'If Beresford's luck at the tables was turning sour, maybe someone killed him and made it look like suicide just to collect on the bet? At a hundred to one, that's some payday. Enough to kill him and make it look like suicide?'

The rain got louder, a lot louder. Then he realized that the room had just got quieter, a lot quieter. He looked round and saw that Isabel's head was bowed, and her shoulder blades were hunched and trembling. The silence was due to her trying to control her breath, trying to keep it together.

Vince let out a muted groan that he hoped she heard. Because, as far as the insensitivity dial went, he was completely off the scale. He wanted to kick himself in the mouth. He'd forgotten Isabel's grief, forgotten her tragedy, and forgotten he was no longer in the hothouse of the Inferno with Mac and Block and Jacket, riffing on the case and dispassionately throwing out ideas and motives. He went into the bathroom and collected a box of tissues and placed them on the coffee table in front of her. Then he stood there feeling stupid, and looking about the same. 'I'm sorry.'

'This is silly of me,' she said in a jumpy voice, stoically trying to smile her way through the crying jag. She reached into the gaping mouth of the box, yanked out a handful of tissues, and then buried her face in them.

Vince propped himself awkwardly on the arm of the couch, at a safe distance from her, not imposing himself and altogether feeling bloody useless. But he had the idea that Isabel Saxmore-Blaine wasn't the type to cry. She didn't seem very good at it, seemed caught out, surprised and genuinely embarrassed by her reactions. He'd known some professional criers, some real teardrop merchants in his time, and it was always diminishing returns for those girls who would blubber at the drop of a hat, or the breaking of a date, the forgotten phone call, the neglectful comment. So when a crack squad of tears did eventually punch their way through Isabel's shutters, and make their escape down her hot cheeks, it was all the more heartbreaking.

Eventually she emerged from her Kleenex mask, and gulped down some shaky breaths to steady herself, then said in a measured tone, 'I don't understand you. Mr Markham told me that Dominic had confessed to the murder of Johnny.'

Vince found himself agreeing to this. He knew he was foolish to have said what he'd just said. Her pain was still too raw. Her brother was dead, so his guilt or innocence in the murder of Beresford seemed irrelevant. Vince apologized, said he was talking out of his hat.

Isabel forgave him and said, 'The heartbreaking thing is, Asprey would have been right to have Dominic on his list. Poor Dominic never really stood a chance. You see, when my mother took her own life, it broke my father's heart. He never really stopped loving her, even after everything she'd put him through. So I became a Daddy's girl, riding to hounds, shooting and fishing. Anything to be at his side; anything to please him. But it wasn't just for him, it was for me. I'd lost one parent, and I didn't want to lose another. I was always scared that whenever he left the house, I'd never see him again. Dominic, he got rather squeezed out. He wasn't good at sports, and was a quiet, shy boy who never really got on with my father.

'But Johnny made an effort with Dominic and, of course, Dominic looked up to him. That was one of Johnny's qualities, making people feel special by taking an interest in them. I knew Dominic wasn't his type, not really. Johnny did it for me.'

Vince saw her stoicism was again slipping. A nerve above her right cheekbone throbbed maniacally. Her jaw clenched, the pack of muscles holding it together expanding and contracting with each memory that shot through her like a poisoned arrow. And it was all aimed at Beresford, the man she had loved, the man she had grieved for, the man who had turned her brother into a murderer, and the man who had ultimately taken away his life. She wanted to scream, to throw something, but she didn't.

She took a sip of her brandy and let the pointlessness of it all wash over her, then said solemnly: 'And now I know it was all a cruel joke.'

'It wasn't just a joke on Dominic,' said Vince. 'From what I heard, the joke was on Beresford too.'

She looked up at him with a question mark in her eyes, and a fair amount of hostility there too. For her there was only one victim in this crime, and it wasn't Johnny the Joker. But she wanted to know more.

Vince eased himself off the arm of the sofa and sat down a respectable distance away from her. He then explained the whole story to her, as laid out by Nicky DeVane and Guy Ruley. Isabel had heard the bare bones of the pernicious joke from Markham, but not much about the motivation behind it. About Beresford and his machinations: the spy, the assassin, the dog-of-war mercenary ready to take over a small country and rule it with an elite cabal from the Montcler. Of course, it all made perfect sense to her. The bravura, the machismo, the gun he carried tucked in his cummerbund; the big jokes and boys' own fiction that had led to a flabby and debauched ex-guardsman slumped in a chair with a bullet in his brain, and a naïve young man with slit wrists taking the long cold nap in a crimson bath.

And then there was the girl. Yes, the girl from the wrong end of town. The girl who turned out to be in the wrong place at the wrong time.

'The girl, Marcy . . .' Isabel said tentatively. 'She had a daughter. What is her name?'

'Ruby.'

'That's a pretty name. What happens to her?'

'She's still in Great Ormond Street hospital.'

'Then what?'

Vince gave an uncertain shrug then said, 'She'll stay with her grandmother, I assume.'

On hearing this, Isabel's tears seemed to evaporate, the redness disappeared, and her eyes looked clear and determined as she declared, 'We must do something for her.'

Vince didn't answer this, but silently agreed. He got up and poured them both some fresh coffee. After some ensuing small talk about the contents of his flat, the artwork on his walls, the books on his shelf, his taste in music, she managed to steer the conversation around to a reluctant Vince himself, and proved an accomplished inquisitor. Her journalistic experience perhaps? But Vince detected, rightly, that Isabel Saxmore-Blaine was sick of her own life and the characters that inhabited it, and now wanted to take her mind off it and engage in a different narrative, so he obliged and yielded to her questioning, and told her all she wanted to know.

She wasn't surprised to learn that he had taken a degree in law, but was surprised that he hadn't chosen a different and more profitable path for exploiting it, like becoming a lawyer or a barrister. Vince explained that he liked his law a little bit more on the lively side, deriving more satisfaction from the thrill of the chase and the cut and thrust of frontline detective work. He joked that he enjoyed getting into punch-ups and kicking down doors too much to don a wig and get fat and rich by sitting on the benches.

But she saw something about him that told her this wasn't a joke. The way he carried himself, perhaps, with an athleticism, an agility. Or maybe it was something in his eyes, or just above his eye, his right eye to be precise – the thin white line slanting down across the black eyebrow, indicating a scar. He also bore a scar that sliced down through his chin, about half an inch long, accentuating his dimple. It was a very good-looking face, but she had decided that long ago, when she had first seen him properly, in the Harley Street hospital. Darkly romantic, like a good gigolo. But, unlike a good gigolo, it was a face that hadn't always been vigilant about preserving its looks. There was a surly toughness about him, a contained violence . . . and perhaps a hint of murder around the eyes.

The onset of night became unavoidable, and it seemed to crawl around the flat, closing down the day and their conversation for good. It was time for bed for both of them, whether they liked it or not, and that awkward *What next?* exchange came up. Isabel bluntly insisted that she didn't want to go back to the Harley Street hospital, or to stay with friends. And she doubted that she'd ever go back to her Pont Street flat. Vince offered her his bed for the night, while he'd take the couch. She took him up on his offer.

Vince's dreams that night were vivid: a naked Isabel came back into the living room and shook him, if not awake, then enough to raise him up from the couch and steer him like a grateful and gummy-eyed somnambulist to his own bed. It was, quite literally, a dream come true. Vince had suffered these dreams before: a beautiful girl entering the room, beckoning him forth to make love to her. A shadowy spirit figure and yet, oddly, possessing the face of a movie star – say Brigitte Bardot, or Sophia Loren, or the home-grown Julie Christie. On more than one occasion she had been some anonymous beauty glimpsed in the crowd that day, or a flirtatious but wordless brief encounter in a train or tube carriage. But never with this ending: the ending he'd wanted. The ending he'd been dreaming about.

Like a pair of stumbling thieves, they made their way into the bedroom. Vince may have banged an elbow on the door jamb, and stubbed a toe on the bedpost, but it wasn't enough to pull him out of his half slumber, his waking dream world. Once in bed, she folded herself into him and they began to kiss. She tasted good. Along with the sweetness of the brandy and the slipperiness of the lipstick (a winning combination in any man's book), there was the sharpness of salt; her face was still hot, flushed and damp with silent tears.

She manoeuvred herself on top of him. And just as she herself was moist and ready, his hard-on was already achingly old. It was the product of the dream he'd been fervently having about making love to her in the very bed he was now actually, dreamily, making love to her in. Or rather, she was making love to him in. She had ordered him not to move. Vince, never good at taking orders, willingly accepted these instructions, did *exactly* as he was told, and lay there supremely supine, as stiff as a varnished eel. Then Isabel's long body was laid fully along his; he could feel her against him inch for inch. Her legs rested hotly against his, her toes dug into the base of his shin. It seemed the only point of separation happened at round about the third rib up, where her back arched enough for Vince to see her breasts, tantalizing handfuls that were well and truly out of his reach. He was under strict instruction not to move – and therefore move he did not. He was tempted to be insubordinate, except her hands were firmly gripping his upper arms and pinning him to the bed. She began to build up a rhythm that was occasionally broken by stirring circular movements. He saw her long neck crane back, so he could admire the strong rim of her faultless jawline. Funny the things you only notice when you're half asleep and being right royally seen to – like how her elbows were double-jointed.

Her eyes were squeezed shut with enough concentrated vigour to crease and crinkle her taut skin. She was wrapped in her own world and he somehow felt a detachment from the proceedings, albeit a pleasurable one; like a voyeur, but not quite, because he knew that at any moment he could change what was happening.

But why would he do that, he asked himself. Things were going very nicely, thank you very much.

As her movements became more vigorous, again she issued a breathless and almost pained instruction for him not to move. That was clearly to be her role, and the more she moved, the stiller he became. He was enjoying this game. Her head dipped suddenly and her thick hair came down like a curtain and covered her face, a face that was now pleasurably twisted, a mouth that now crookedly gaped. Strands of damp hair danced on his face. It tickled.

Deciding it was time to break ranks and disobey orders, he raised his hands, which were braced at his side grabbing up fist-fuls of sheet, shook off her grip, reached for her hair and scraped it away from her face with some force, holding it bunched behind her head. She emitted a high-pitched exhalation, and he couldn't tell if this was due to the activity they were both so vigorously engaged in, or from the pain of having her hair pulled back like a Chinese doll. He realized it was a heady mixture of both. When she announced in a low-pitched growl that she was about to come, he didn't say a word. He was too busy trying not to come before she did. A concentrated effort, because the visuals were like nothing he'd witnessed before, the glorious sight of her was tearing him apart, so he closed his eyes.

When it happened, and their eyes eventually opened again, they found each other with their hands clasped around each other's throats. A long lascivious smile was lashed around her mouth and, after some jerky movements that looked as if she was wringing every last scintilla of sap out of herself, she rolled over on to her back and, sated, folded silently into him and closed her eyes. The dream was now over, and again she looked sad.

Vince woke up the next morning feeling as though he hadn't slept at all. He lay in the same position, flat on his back, feeling sure he hadn't moved out of it the rest of the night. Maybe subconsciously he had still been obeying orders, and was still waiting for Isabel's permission to move. If he was, he was out of luck, for she had gone. Maybe the whole thing had been a dream after all? A dream within a dream within . . .

In the living room, sitting on the tiled coffee table, was the brandy glass with her lipstick prints all over it. And on the couch from where he had been collected lay the twisted sheets. There was no note. He gave it an hour, made some coffee, then called the Salisbury Hospital. She had just checked out, no forwarding address or contact number.

Vince took a shower and washed away the sweet, sweet smell of dreamtime, before he cracked on with the day. He phoned Mac and found out that the case was officially closed. Detectives Kenny Block and Philly Jacket had located the 'actor' Bernie Korshank, who was working as a doorman at the Kitty Kat club in Camden Town. Korshank had verified Nicky DeVane and Guy Ruley's story. Vince told Mac he still wasn't satisfied, though there was no need to, because Mac knew how Vince felt about the case. There was a long pause in their conversation, which should have been filled with Mac saying something along the lines of, *The bodies are going into the ground next week. The case is closed, and you're already too deep in the brown stuff without a shovel, as far as Markham is concerned. So if you value your career, you'll let this one lie.*

But Mac didn't say any of those things. Because again there was no need. The older man knew exactly the stuff the younger man was made of, so such advice would have been all rather pointless.

CHAPTER 34

Marcy Jones was laid to rest at Willesden cemetery. It was a large turnout and the church was packed. The preacher was all fire and brimstone, and the congregation were with him every step of the way: speaking in tongues, praising the Lord, raising their arms to the great above. They seemed to be working beyond faith, assured in the knowledge that there was something up there to acknow-ledge their swaying and praying.

Half of Notting Hill had turned up to bury its now favourite daughter. With the help of a prodigious propaganda campaign that included posters on every available wall, and leafleting on every street corner, all put out and paid for by Michael X. Marcy Jones had reached almost saintly status. An innocent black girl used, abused and then slain by the white devils was the copy that went with the picture of Marcy Jones togged up in her nurse's uniform.

Tyrell Lightly was there, with Michael X and the rest of the Brothers X, again all swathed in the uniform of Black Power. They stood ominously scowling at a sore thumb that stood out in the congregation. But Vince Treadwell wasn't the only white person there; there were a dozen or so nurses and doctors from the hos-pital where Marcy had worked. But he was the only white face who had dared walk into Michael X's back yard and take his main man out.

Tyrell Lightly's eyes burned through the black shades he was wearing, and straight into Vince. As Vince turned to acknowledge the now goateed and uniformed gangster, Lightly rubbed the back of his long, guitar-plucking thumbnail over the fresh scar and lump that now permanently marked his sharp nose. It was the bony gangster's way of saying they still had unfinished business. Vince couldn't help but pull a quick smirk at his handiwork, but then turned away quickly. He wasn't there for a show of machismo and a staring competition, but to pay his respects. Little Ruby Jones recognized him immediately, and gave him a heartbreaking smile and a tentative little wave. This made it worth it, and neutralized the thirty or so scowls he was getting from the Brothers X.

When the preacher left his pulpit, Michael X took his place. No one in the congregation looked too pleased with this state of affairs, but the presence of the shade-wearing muscle gathered around the self-styled revolutionary soon quelled any dissenting voices.

But not all. With their hard-earned sense of Christian forgiveness and shared sufferance, the mothers and the grandmothers and the women in the congregation weren't scared by the Brothers. Michael X may have been top dog on the streets, but this was their domain and they took instruction from a higher power. And, as Michael X delivered his diatribe about the white devils and their legions of rapists and murderers and pillagers, the women in the congregation began to make their voices heard with a chorus of disapproval, and with shakes of their heads so forceful that the Brothers X soon looked well and truly intimidated.

It was clear that Michael X was deliberately hijacking the service, and Vince knew that the ire of X was aimed squarely at him. He felt that his antagonistic presence was also playing its part, so he decided to leave. Tyrell Lightly had been eyeballing him all the way through the diatribe, looking daggers and breathing bullets, and if that wasn't enough, as the detective left his pew Lightly laboured the point by making a knife gesture with his forefinger and then running it across his throat. But it wasn't that message that chilled Vince; it was watching the gangster slip his arm around his little daughter's shoulder.

As he left the church Vince knew they would meet again.

Michael X had to eventually leave the pulpit when the women drowned him out with an impromptu and full-voiced rendition of 'What a Friend we have in Jesus'.

From reading about the Beresford funeral in the paper, Vince realized it was a very different affair. In fact a very private and muted affair. Only the Montcler set and close family were in attendance, but strictly no one else. The exclusivity that permeated the Montcler cabal in life carried over just as effortlessly into death. If you weren't a member, you weren't getting in. He was buried in the family mausoleum, where the rest of the battling Beresfords had been honourably discharged to. James Asprey read a eulogy, something from *Thus Spake Zarathustra*. Isabel Saxmore-Blaine did not attend.

But three days after Beresford's funeral, Vince did receive a phone call from her, informing him of her brother Dominic's funeral, which he was cordially invited to attend. She didn't employ quite that level of formality in her language, but the distance evident in her voice wasn't completely explained away by the miles of phone line between them. This was the first time he'd heard from her since the night they had spent together, and there was no mention of it. Although Vince hardly expected her to review it in detail, he was at least hoping for an explanation of her flight from his bed without so much as a scribbled note left on the pillow; just to clear the air perhaps. Maybe she merely wanted it to be left shrouded in nocturnal uncertainty. Or maybe that dream sequence had been her idea of a nightmare. 'Don't move,' she had insisted, and he had remained corpse-like throughout. Sex and death had mingled too closely that night. Either way it wasn't up for discussion and, the more he thought about it, the more he agreed.

Isabel told Vince that the funeral would be another very private affair. She then told him – as if to stem any hope he might have that she wanted to see him, that it was her father who had requested his presence. To discuss certain matters. Then, polite and brusquely businesslike, she said her goodbyes and hung up in his ear.

CHAPTER 35

The Saxmore-Blaine country seat was in Wiltshire. The family owned a village, and beyond it as far as the eye could see. Which was pretty much what you always saw in the country: rolling hills with a patchwork quilt of wheat and maze and furrowed brown dirt.

Set in its wide acres, the fifteenth-century stately sandstone pile was a game of two halves. The front half was a fortified castle with castellated towers, turrets, embrasures and a crescent-shaped moat. And the back half was a Tudor manor house with a long, welcoming, mullioned window stretching across its front, and a Capability Brown garden. Architecturally this mixture was considered eccentric at the time, as if the original owners had decided to split the difference between their male and female tastes when they built their home. But the real eccentricity of it was that the wife had been allowed a say at all, and didn't instead get dunked as a witch.

The service took place in a private chapel inside the house. It was quick, perfunctory and not very well attended. Isabel stood with her father, the ambassador. Vince had noticed an oil painting of him in one of the hallways, dressed in his full panoply of ceremonial attire, with its gold brocade and rope and a chestful of multicoloured ribbons garnered during his war days. He was mid-sized in height, with a large but finely appointed head that was covered in thick silver hair. He wasn't in ceremonial uniform today, rather in morning dress. It was easy to see where Isabel got her looks from and, Vince suspected, when not on the booze or the happy pills, her fighting spirit. Isabel had told him that as a child she always wanted to be at her father's side, and there she was, practically holding him up, for there wasn't a lot of spirit in the old man today.

Once it was over, everyone filed wordlessly out of the chapel apart from the father, who sat in prayer with his thoughts. Vince started to follow the rest, half hoping he could make a break for it in one of the long corridors beyond. But Isabel stymied such a move when she approached quickly and hooked her arm around his, announcing, 'I could do with a stiff drink.'

In one of the more homely sitting rooms, which nevertheless stored enough grand antiques to make a skilled burglar salivate, Isabel poured herself a large single malt with just a spit of water. Not a drink he associated with her, but it did match the surroundings. He didn't know if this was called the Oak Room, but it should have been, for the walls were panelled in it and the furniture was made of it. There were coffers, chests, cabinets and bookcases, and taking up one entire side was a long, medieval and richly hued refectory table with fourteen pegged and dowelled chairs gathered around it. This room alone looked as though it had been responsible for the felling of a sizeable forest. Vince sat himself uncomfortably on a lumpy two-hundred-year-old haysack sofa.

And then his eye caught her. She stood above the fireplace, wearing a long gown that, due to its translucent and snug fit, made her look as if she was naked. It was a painting of Isabel's mother. The thick golden hair, jet-black eyes, a slash of red for a mouth – all very wild and strikingly vivid against the pale background of whatever indistinct setting she was posed in. Maybe it was Greco-Roman. Or maybe it was Mars. She wasn't wearing any shoes and was raised on tiptoe, coming at you full frontal, as though she was about to break the fourth wall and walk out of the picture. It was an odd composition, and Vince couldn't tell if the portrait was any good, as it all seemed a little out of focus. Not abstract, or surreal, just out of focus. The eyes followed you around the room, but covertly, never fully engaging. The painting was out of sorts with the rest of the room, out of sorts with the rest of the house. The subject didn't look as if she belonged in the English countryside at all, for that matter. And maybe that was the problem. The ambassador had taken her out of her natural environment, and she had wilted – or gone mad. So, in many ways, the artist had captured her true essence perfectly.

Isabel padded over to the fireplace and, like an actress hitting her mark, stood directly under the painting. He could see the likeness. She had some of her mother's structure – the colour, the vivid wildness – but she was more in focus and earthed by her paternal genes.

'Thank you for showing up.'

'You said your father wanted to see me.'

She stood there considering him. His last statement was as perfectly reasonable as it was perfectly true, and yet it seemed to annoy her intensely.

Vince sat there appearing relaxed but, of course, she didn't know how uncomfortable he actually felt, and not just because of the sofa he was sitting on. It didn't help that he was sure that somewhere in the guts of the old bastard sofa there lurked an ancient coiled spring that was about to finally give way, then shoot up through the upholstery and spear him in the last place he ever wanted spearing.

Her annoyance built in the uncomfortable silence, until she said somewhat tersely, 'Aren't you the least curious, Detective Treadwell, as to why I didn't contact you?'

'You left without an explanation or a number, so I had a feeling you didn't *want* to be contacted. You've been through a great deal, Miss Saxmore-Blaine, and I perfectly understand. But I'd just like you to know that whatever I can do to help you, I will.'

'Quite the Galahad,' she mocked, then took the first sip of her drink.

It must have whetted her appetite because she then took three more in quick succession, each one more voluminous than the last. Glass almost drained, she continued, 'Well, now I have the opportunity, I'd just like to say—'

Whatever she wanted say, she wasn't prepared to say it in the same room as her father, who had just entered. The ambassador boomed, 'Detective Treadwell?'

Vince stood up sharply, considering it a good opportunity to get off the hay-sack missile launcher. Isabel took the opportunity to sashay over to the booze table and re-brim her glass. As she passed Vince, their eyes met in wordless conference, in which they both agreed to resume this conversation at another time, in another place. She gave her father a comforting and accommodating smile, then said, 'I shall leave you two gentlemen to it,' and walked out of the room.

The ambassador's eyes were fixed firmly on his daughter as she did so, and it was the glass in her hand he was looking at with stern disapproval; like finding an unpolished buckle on the parade ground.

'My daughter didn't offer you a drink, Detective?'

'No. Thank you, anyway, sir, but not just now.'

The old man went over to the table stocking the booze, and poured himself one from the same decanter as his daughter. A single this time, and with more than a dash of water. 'I find, these days, that I prefer people who turn down a drink over those who never turn down an opportunity to have one. In my younger days it used to be the other way round.'

The ambassador's deflated and grief-stricken state in the chapel seemed have disappeared. In fact, he now seemed rather pumped up, back straight, head held high – all ready for life and its challenges again. Vince had the feeling the ambassador would now shed no more tears for his only son. Once he'd left that chapel, he'd left him behind and his grief with it.

Vince glanced up at a picture on the wall directly above the ambassador. It wasn't a portrait of the ambassador, but there was a striking family resemblance in the set of the strong jaw, the full head of silvery hair perhaps. The painting, circa 1850, featured a man dressed in Harris tweed plus-fours, standing on some grey rocks. There was a choppy ocean behind him, and a blue sky with some billowy nimbus clouds, and a single white double-circumflex to indicate a seagull in flight.

'Sir Arthur Saxmore-Blaine,' said the ambassador, following Vince's gaze. 'He was army, like most of the Saxmore-Blaines.'

'Was he an ambassador too, like most of the Saxmore-Blaines?'

'Not an ambassador – he was far too honest and blunt-speaking for that. But he was an explorer, a naturalist and an illustrator of some repute. The family owes him a lot. You know how this family made its fortune, Detective?' Vince shook his head. The ambassador gleefully told him: 'Shit.'

'*Shit?*'

'Shit. No other word for it. Shit. Good old-fashioned, good honest shit. Of course the Saxmore-Blaines were an industrious lot. After all, houses and land like this don't come cheap. They had made and lost other fortunes in the past. But none like Sir Arthur there had bequeathed. The joke is, he left us a pile – a pile of shit. And that shit was worth its weight in gold. Let me explain.'

'I'm wishing you would, sir.'

'You see the seagull behind him?'

Vince saw it. On further inspection, it looked a little out of perspective for the picture, more like an oversized albatross or a small glider. But once the ambassador had pointed it out, Vince figured it was emphasized because it wasn't just background; it was very much part of the story.

'You see, Detective Treadwell, seabirds were a favourite with my ancestor. He travelled the world studying and illustrating them. It took him to their colonies, as far away as Peru and the Christmas Islands, where they massed in their thousands for nesting and breeding purposes. And, as well as breeding and eating fish and what have you, the other thing they do is *shit*. Lots and lots of the stuff. What's shit good for?'

'Avoiding?'

'You're not a country man, Detective. I can tell that by your footwear, the cut of your suit, even by your colour and complexion. There's a touch of the Mediterranean about you. Of Italian extraction, are you?'

'I was left behind by the gypsies, so the story goes.'

'I wasn't being insulting, Detective, merely observant.'

'You'll have to forgive me, sir, but in the house I grew up in we didn't have five hundred years of ancestry hanging up on the walls. So my family lineage is a little murky.'

'Well, let me tell you what shit is good for in this neck of the woods. Fertilizer. And bird shit, seabird shit, is the best fertilizer there is. Guano, as it's referred to, has lots of valuable properties. Arthur discovered this, so he mined it for all it was worth. He laid claim to, and bought for a pittance, huge swathes of coastal land in places like Peru and Chile that were considered completely useless, due to being covered in birds and bird shit. He re-made this family's fortune many times over. Oh, we've tarted that fortune up over the years with property and farming and gilts and bonds, but it's the shit that underwrites it all. *Shit*.'

At that, the ambassador turned and raised a grateful glass to the wily old shit-shoveller in the portrait, then took a hearty swig of his single malt.

'But you're not here to hear talk about shit,' he continued, refocusing his gaze on the detective before him.

Vince got the feeling his host loved telling that story, and mined the 'shit' humour for all it was worth. Not wanting to disappoint him by missing this opportunity, Vince replied: 'I'm not here to talk shit.'

He was right. The ambassador smiled broadly, then he threw him by saying, 'Then why *are* you here, Detective?'

'You wanted to see me, I believe?'

'But that's merely your pretext. The real reason is you're here to see my daughter. I feel I interrupted something a minute ago.' Vince didn't confirm or deny the ambassador's remark, so the old man continued, 'She's a beautiful woman who attracts the wrong kind. I'm not saying *you're* the wrong kind, Detective Treadwell. But you are the wrong kind for my daughter.'

'Of uncertain extraction and without five hundred years of ancestry up on the walls, that kind of wrong kind?'

'You strike me as a good man, Treadwell, and an honest man. You're a policeman, so can't be all bad.'

'Oh, you'd be surprised.'

'I need calm in this house, calm for my daughter. I've read the papers. They're looking for a story, asking if I blame my daughter for Dominic. Well, I don't. Dominic was weak, always was. He was his mother's son, God rest her soul. Well, now they are together, with their Maker.' The ambassador glanced up at the painting of his dead wife, not lovingly, but as if to check it wasn't about to come crashing down. 'And if you read the papers, I assume you know all about her, too?' Vince gave no reaction, not wanting to assume too much. And certainly not wanting to mimic the ambassador, who seemed to thrive on assumptions. 'Well, they can go to hell! I blame James Asprey and that damned gaming house of his.'

'That's very blunt, very honest,' said Vince.

'I'm a retired ambassador, and being retired is a bloody relief, Detective, I can tell you that. As well as having the privilege of meeting some real first-raters, I've also had the misfortune to meet more pricks and horse's asses than I've had state banquets. And I've always held my tongue. So, now that the shackles are off, I've promised myself I will speak freely until my dying day.

'I knew Beresford's father in the army. Different regiment, different club, but a fine man, a fine soldier. In this case, the apple fell very far from the tree. The son wasn't fit to black his father's boots.'

The ambassador said all this with such vigour that Vince couldn't help but wonder if he was talking about his own son. There was a frightful symmetry between the two fates that had befallen and would forever link the houses of Beresford and

Saxmore-Blaine. The ambassador took some calming breaths, but couldn't rid his face of the twisted disgust it displayed.

'That place, it's the Devil's arcade.'

'What place is that, sir?'

'Why, the Montcler club, of course. I know many a decent man who's lost his fortune, and his soul, at those tables. And Asprey still lets them go on playing, drawing them deeper and deeper into his debt. Asprey and his ilk represent everything that's wrong with this country. No, sir, I didn't approve of Beresford – and I was right. He reaped havoc on my children, on this family, and, well, he's paid the price I suppose. But I shan't mourn him. To hell with the lot of 'em!'

The ambassador took the first sip of his drink. He didn't look as though he enjoyed it as much as his daughter did. Tough act to follow. But then again, he didn't look as though he enjoyed anything as much as his daughter, or his ex-wife for that matter. But the booze obviously worked in taking away some of the bitter taste in his mouth, and seemed to soothe his rancour. He finally stopped pacing and took a seat in a stern-looking high-backed armchair with leather-padded upholstery. It was as shiny as a saddle, and looked just about as comfortable.

'I'm not completely insensitive or deluded as to the ways of the world, Detective Treadwell, and my own place in it. And also as to my failings as a father. I want to make amends for that now. It seems the person who is most forgotten in this dreadful mess is the young woman my son killed. My daughter and I have discussed the matter, and Isabel will in due course contact her family to make arrangements for reparations to be paid to the daughter and her grandmother. I know what she did for a living, and I know that God will forgive her. I only hope that He will forgive my son.'

Vince gave a series of slow considered nods to this. The ambassador had declared all of this as a matter of fact, as if the Jones family had little or no say on the subject. But Vince didn't argue the point, as it seemed only right that reparations should be made. What's the point of having a shit pile of money if you can't do the right thing with it? And, anyway, what Vince was really considering was his next point. The one he knew he'd be making – and the real reason that he was there.

He hit him with it now: 'What if I told you, sir, that I don't think your son killed Beresford?'

The ambassador said nothing for what seemed like the longest time. For a man who talked, gave instruction and advice, smoothed over awkward situations, the silence seemed vacuum-ously long. He just sat there, elbows on the arms of the padded chair, both hands cupping the cut-crystal tumbler containing the single malt. Vince was certain the man had heard him, but felt duty bound to try again. He did some throat clearing to prime the ambassador that he was going again – then hit him with it.

'I said, sir, I don't think your son Dominic killed—'

'I heard what you said,' barked the ambassador. 'I am neither deaf nor a fool who blurts things out without considering them first. Kindly allow me that time.'

Vince noted the ambassador's emotion. Whilst keeping the cara-pace of calm, the man's voice had an uneven grating sound to it, like glass in a machine.

'But I'm also not a slow-witted buffoon who takes all day to make up his mind. And my answer to you is, of what possible use, or good, is that information to me now?'

Vince stalled. 'Well, I . . . I think I can clear your son's name. You see, there are too many anomalies in this case. Like the man-ner in which Beresford was killed and the fact that Dominic—'

'God damn you!' The ambassador slammed his flattened palm down on the side table next to him, felling a silver-framed photo which had a domino effect and felled some more clustered nearby. They were photos of Dominic and Isabel as children.

'My son is dead. And so too is Beresford. If there's any justice in this world, then that's justice enough for me. Let me make myself clear: I want this investigation ended. I want my daughter's name out of the newspapers, and my family's name, what's left of it, off the tongues of all those malicious bastards.'

'Your son is accused of a murder I don't think he committed, therefore I don't think justice has been done. I'm a little confused, sir. I thought you'd be—'

'Dominic killed a young woman, that much is clear. Killing Beresford, the man who set that horrendous act in motion, was a just killing – an honourable killing. My son deserves that honour.' The ambassador put his drink down on the table and stood up. 'I have no need to tell you, Detective Treadwell, that I know lots of people. Let's start with the Home Secretary, shall we, and work our way down to the Commissioner of Police.'

'I'm breathing exalted air, Ambassador,' Vince remarked drily. 'But the case is officially closed,' he added in a deliberately bemused tone. 'And even if it was still open, it's out of my hands now, because I'm officially off it.'

'From what I hear about you, Mr Treadwell, open or closed means little to you. You seem to have a curiosity that needs satisfying, whatever the official status. Tenacity is a quality I admire, but not in this case. It makes me sick to my stomach.'

Vince didn't bother with sounding bemused this time, as he saw that the ambassador had the measure of him. The ambassador then offered some avuncular advice to the younger man, but it was clear that he thought Vince was trouble, didn't want him consorting further with his daughter and had the power and influence to end his career. Vince listened, kept his counsel, and then watched as the old man strode out the room.

Vince got the picture: if Dominic was going to go down in history as the tawdry murderer of a prostitute, why not go down with an *honourable* killing of an ex-guardsman as well? His last act of righteous revenge. Vince was getting to understand the logic, for it was pretty much the same logic employed by Asprey and the Montcler set in their day-to-day dealings with the world. Those very same men the ambassador so despised. And the more Vince thought about it, the more it stank the place up like one of Sir Arthur Saxmore-Blaine's guano mines on a hot day.

A very old butler with a serious stoop went with him to the door and silently saw Vince out. He didn't bump into Isabel on the way out, in fact he didn't bump into anyone on the way out. The house seemed as empty as a graveyard at midnight.

CHAPTER 36

That night, Vince headed to the Kitty Kat club in Camden Town, which offered a mixed bag. It ran a not very busy jazz night for people who really didn't know or care that much about jazz. It had a burlesque night that did lively business. An open mic talent and comedy night, where you were unceremoniously gonged off if you didn't cut the mustard. But the most popular nights were Tuesdays and Thursdays.

Inside the Kitty Kat club, there wasn't much to distinguish it from any other red flock wallpaper and glitter-ball joint, apart from its clientele on a Tuesday or Thursday. Today was Tuesday, and men and women danced cheek to cheek, only not with each other. Fey young men foxtrotted with burly builders wearing full make-up. Bulldog dykes in business suits held their frilly-dressed ingénues tightly for the tango. The queer and dyke combination was fostered on the theory that if the club got raided, they'd all just swap partners, à la Adam and Eve, just as the Old Testament intended. Then all back to Adam and Steve and the twentieth century, just as soon as the Vice coppers had been slipped their envelopes and left. It was like a party game of musical chairs or pass the parcel.

The hostess who led Vince into the back room to meet Bernie Korshank was a pretty little blonde dyke doing a pretty good impression of Marlene Dietrich circa *The Blue Angel* (1936), in top hat, tails and fishnets. For some reason that Vince didn't ask about, because he really couldn't be bothered to get into it, she had a life-sized pink plastic lobster that she trailed behind her on a lead.

The back-room office was guarded by a metal-covered door with an impressive couple of locks on it. Inside, the walls were lined with boxes containing the club's most precious commodity, liquor. Bernie Korshank, seated at a desk, had just closed a book when Vince entered: *The Complete Works of William Shakespeare*. Complete enough, sonnets and all, for the hefty tome to close with a dust-raising thud.

Korshank lived up to his reputation, and to Dominic Saxmore-Blaine's description. He was a monolith of a man made up of a pylon of fused muscle and a palaeontologist's prize collection of bones. As a schtaraker, he looked straight out of the Lew Grade school of TV heavies. The big desk he was seated behind looked more like a tray propped on his lap. The chair he sat on had to be presumed, because Vince couldn't actually see it. He was dressed in his bouncer's uniform of a black tuxedo, single-breasted with satin shawl lapels. Such was his bulk that Vince reckoned it was a 'cut and shunt job': a canny tailor had used two tuxedos to make one, and you couldn't see the join. The clip-on bow tie sat on the desk next to a mug of tea. The open-necked shirt revealed thick tufts of shiny black hair that, given the size of his barrelling chest, suggested he was smuggling a grizzly bear past customs. He glanced up at Vince from behind half-rimmed glasses that looked stretched to breaking point over the broad and fleshy expanse of his face. He had a full head of thick jet-black wavy hair, heavily pomaded and brushed back from a narrow brow that furrowed down into a bulbous nose that looked as if it had cushioned many a blow. Swarthy beyond measure or description, but here goes: he had the kind of face that if you shaved it using a hundred hot towels, lashings of suds and a freshly forged razor stropped to within an inch of its life, in an hour's time he'd look as though he'd been dipped in soot and in need of another.

Korshank took off his glasses and rested them on the collected works of the Bard. The specs didn't lessen the impact of his face;

in fact, they added an archly sinister aspect. But, with or without them, Vince could see how the impressionable Dominic Saxmore-Blaine would have been terrified of this man. And how the task of felling a beast like Bernie Korshank would send you nuts – because there was simply so much of him. For the frail young man, it must have felt as if he'd committed mass murder.

Vince didn't take any chances with the big boy, and immediately showed him his ID. Korshank nodded and gestured for him to take a seat opposite. Vince sat down and gave a nod towards the tome.

'You rehearsing for a play?' he asked.

'Just reading. I likes to brush up. I spoke to you fellers already.'

The voice matched the body; big and blunted, it sounded as though it had been hauled up from the bowels of the earth. It was also slow and deliberate, as if trying hard to reach beyond the stalls with its distinct enunciation, but it was always going to be stymied by the European accent breaking in.

'What you doing here, copper?'

'Someone recommended the lobster.'

It had the desired effect: Korshank smiled. And, when he did, the effect was surprisingly pleasant, showing rows of squat gnashers, and comical creases around the eyes.

'That's Trixie,' he said. 'And no matter how handsome you is, copper, she ain't for you, and that's for sure!'

'I sort of figured I stood more chance with the lobster.'

Korshank suddenly stopped smiling and immediately the room grew oppressive. 'And, just in case you're wondering, I ain't no pansy.'

Vince immediately raised his hands and showed his palms in the international gesture of surrender, then got in quickly with: 'Absolutely positively not. I never thought it for a second.'

The big man seemed satisfied with this answer, and the dark clouds in the room dispersed. 'My boss got me working here on account of my acting, and mixing with theatrical types. He reckoned I'd be kosher with the queers, more tolerant. It don't bother me much what they gets up to, not like with some of the fellers.' The big man gave a philosophical shrug. 'But I ain't complaining. The boss has been good to me and we don't get no trouble in this place. So I spends most of my time in here, and it gives me plenty of time to read.'

'Sounds like a good set-up.' Vince brushed some imaginary lint off his trouser leg, then said, 'I was hoping you could tell me about what happened at the Imperial.'

'Like I said, I already spoke to you boys about it, and I don't need reminding.' But it was too late, he was already reminded. For a bit-part player it was a pretty convincing interpretation of sorrowful and solemn. Heavy-browed, burdensome, and Brando-esque, *à la On The Waterfront.* Vince believed the big feller wasn't acting, or certainly believed he couldn't act that well.

Vince prompted: 'It was an unfortunate turn of events.'

'If I'd have known the boy wasn't right in the head, you think I'd have done it?'

'Not for a second. No one's blaming you, Bernie.'

'*Bernie?*' The big fellow arched a shiny black eyebrow. 'What's with the *Bernie* all of a sudden? We skipped a chapter, copper. What happened to Mr Korshank?'

Vince, again with the international gesture of surrender, said, 'You're right. I'm sorry, Mr Korshank.'

There was a pause before Mr Korshank said, 'Forget it. Bernie's fine by me, copper. And I don't blame me neither. I blame Beresford. But he bought it, too.' He gave a listless shrug. 'So all's well that ends well.'

Vince looked down at the Bard's big book on the table, thinking that wasn't the play title he would have chosen to sum up events. But tragedy does play out as comedy second time around, so maybe . . .

'Talking about good reads, Bernie, I read the confession – Dominic Saxmore-Blaine's confession. There's a few things about it that don't play right. Like the ending.' The big man studied Vince intently. Undaunted, he continued. 'Must be one of the first things you look for in a good play script, how it ends, if it makes sense.'

'I ain't no writer. I just does what's put in front of me. Move here, move there, break a chair over him, hit him over the head with a bottle.' Looking at Vince's crinkled brow, Korshank reassured him, 'Don't worry, they're props made out of balsa wood, and the bottles are made out of sugar to look like glass.'

'Yeah, and the guns are loaded with blanks,' said Vince, bringing it all back around to the principal players. 'No, I'm sorry, Bernie, but I'm just not believing the end of our little story.'

Bernie Korshank rested his hands on the table as clenched fists. If his face looked as though it knew where the bodies were buried, the hands looked as though they had dug the holes that put them there. 'What you saying, copper, I'm a liar?'

Again Vince went palms-up in a placating gesture, and was tempted to take out the perfectly creased quarter inch of white hanky from his breast pocket and wave it about frantically. 'Easy, Bernie, that's not what I'm saying at all. All I'm saying is, I don't think Dominic Saxmore-Blaine killed Beresford.'

Bernie Korshank unballed his fists and weaved his fingers together again. Vince breathed easy at seeing him in the newsreader position; it meant the big man was not about to throw a punch, at least not imminently

'God rest his soul,' said Korshank. 'The kid was a squit of a man, nothing of him. But in my experience, a gun in a man's hand soon evens things up.'

'Yeah, but what was he doing with Beresford's gun in the first place? With real bullets in it?'

'He could have got hold of bullets. He had time.'

'How d'you mean, Bernie, he had time?'

'The gun, the kid had the gun. He must have got bullets for it.'

'Did you read the report, Bernie?'

He shrugged. 'They didn't have no report.'

'Two coppers, Detectives Kenny Block and Philly Jacket?'

Another shrug from the big man. 'Who can tell? Coppers all look the same to me. Apart from you. You'd do well in the movie business.'

'Yeah, and before you know it I'm dragging a lobster around on a chain.' Korshank laughed at that. Vince continued. 'These two coppers looked especially the same, right?' Korshank nodded. Vince cursed under his breath. A typical half-arsed job from Block and Jacket. Vince pulled up his chair and rested his arms on the desk. Korshank picked up that he was serious and drew in closer to the detective. It made for a comic silhouette, with Vince looking up, Bernie Korshank looking down.

'Okay, Bernie, in the report it says that Dominic Saxmore-Blaine confessed that he dropped the gun before leaving the room. Is that true?'

'Not to my knowledge.'

'Why do you say that, Bernie?'

'Because the gun was gone. You got to remember, my eyes were closed at the time. I was playing dead – and when I play dead, I'm dead. I'm gone, lights out, goodnight Vienna, a one hundred per cent stiff. Mr Beresford was paying me for the night's work, and I looked upon it as a professional engagement. Just as I would if I was working with Mr Roger Moore in *The Saint*. Which I have done, on two occasions. Once with dialogue when I said, "He's in there." I takes pride in my work.'

'I'm sure you do, Bernie. Tell me about the gun that night.'

'When Mr Beresford gave me the sign that the kid had gone . . .' Korshank gave a solemn shake of his head, and grief and guilt rattled in his voice, 'I have to admit . . . we both cracked up laughing. Then we tidied the place up, and I got changed into a new shirt. He thought the kid must have dropped the gun at the door. He was sure he heard him drop it, too. But it wasn't there.'

'So Beresford never had the gun?'

'That's what I'm saying! The kid must have taken it with him. Too scared to think, he just ran out of there with it. But Mr

Beresford wasn't too bothered. It wasn't his favourite gun, just a little revolver.'

'A snub-nosed Colt .32?'

'That's the piece,' said Bernie Korshank. Then, amongst his disgust, he tried to rustle up some irony. 'Yeah, he got it back in the end, though. With one in the head.'

Vince had one last question for the three-storey thespian: 'When Dominic ran out the room, did he leave the door open?'

Bernie Korshank shrugged, and Vince saw that he didn't have a clue. Because only three people knew that information – and two of them were dead. The third, well, that was yet to be discovered.

Vince said his goodbyes and his thank-yous to Bernie Korshank. At least he was sure he did, but he wouldn't have put his life on it, because his mind was now elsewhere. It was at the Imperial Hotel, his next port of call. He knew of three ways of accessing the upper floors of the hotel: there was the lift, the main stairs, and then there were the service stairs . . .

As he floated, heavy in thought, past the dancing fruits in the Kitty Kat club, he gave a distracted nod to Trixie, the Marlene Dietrich with her pet lobster, and made his way out of the club and into the clogged night air of Camden Town. His head was swimming with possibilities, and the case stretched out in front of him further than Camden's Parkway. He swung left into Arlington Street, heading to where he'd parked the Mk II, and clicked his fingers and smiled as an idea spiked, livening him up from amid the swamp of possibilities, motives and scenarios he was mired in.

If that fresh thought had spiked a moment or two earlier, Vince might not have felt the cosh that crashed into the back of his knees, instantly crumpling him, or smelled the chemical tang of the saturated rag as it smothered his muzzle and took him out.

CHAPTER 37

Everything about him ached. Everything about him throbbed. Everything seemed an effort. Which came as a surprise because, as far as he was aware, he wasn't doing anything. He was lying down. His eyelids, which also ached and throbbed, strained to open with all the ease of a pair of rusted old shutters. There was a lugubrious throb pulsing through him, but he couldn't locate or localize it, because it was all of him. His hands wanted to reach out and grip the parameters of the fold-out cot he was lying on, but they couldn't, as they had been bound together behind his back and were bloodless and numb. He felt beaten up, and wasn't sure that he hadn't been . . . His short-term, or maybe his long-term memory . . . he couldn't remember which was which, but either way it wasn't working.

The room was lit with furtive shards of light that sidled in from a door that looked as if it had been cobbled together out of ill-fitting wooden boards. It suited the room itself, which looked like it had been thrown together out of wattle and daub. Vince sniffed the air and could still smell the fumes from the chemical cosh that had taken him out – chloroform. But there was another smell, and it smelled like a mixture of wet grass and shit. And then there was the silence. No cars, no wailing sirens, howling boys, screaming girls, baying drunks, distressed derelicts. In fact no city. As he adjusted to the silence, other noises filtered through – the sound of crickets being the predominant one. The more he listened, the

276

louder they got. The crickets were making a real racket, drowning everything out. He was sure he wasn't in Camden any more.

Vince galvanized himself, and swung his feet around and off the cot and on to the flagstone floor. He felt the cold stones beneath his soles and realized he was shoeless. And that his feet were bound together as well. He then raised his upper torso up off the cot; it was all such a painful effort that it alerted him to the fact that his ribs and stomach muscles had taken a beating. All this sudden movement sent a rush of blood swirling around his body that all seemed to get dumped inside his head; a head that now felt on fire – and then it felt like the fire was being put out with a heavy wooden mallet. This pain led to a sustained and loud groan that alerted whoever was on the other side of the door, because they came swiftly through it.

There were two of them. They closed the door behind them on entering, but there was just enough light in the room for Vince to make out the broad strokes of shape, size and dress, but not any details or features. They were dressed the same, beige trench-coat style macs, black roll necks and black leather driving gloves. He had the feeling the gloves were worn more for knuckle work than for driving. That feeling was confirmed when a gloved hand gripped a hank of his hair, and a second gloved hand shaped like a clenched fist hurtled towards his cheek. It wasn't a knock-out punch, but it was an introduction to the way things were, had been and, Vince suspected, were likely to continue for the foreseeable future. Vince rode the punch as, for some reason, he had no fight left in him. It struck him as strange that he should have no fight left in him. When did the fight leave him? Had he already had the fight beaten out of him? Did he ever have it in the first place? He just couldn't remember, since this was just a morass of pain.

Then he realized he was naked. What he had initially thought was clothing, a dark fabric covering his skin, wasn't at all. It was bruising. It was dirt. It was grime mixed in with sweat and blood and shit. His own shit. It was as if he'd been dragged through a ploughed field, rolled around on the black and grimy stone floor and then kicked around like a football.

He was lifted from the cot and dumped into a wooden kitchen chair. He felt as though he'd been in this chair before. Everything now seemed familiar. Ghastly and familiar. The men in the mackintoshes he'd seen before, he knew them, they were . . .

'How's it going, friend?' said the one on the left. Or was it the right?

'Still not talking, friend?' said the one on the right . . . left?

'Friend doesn't want to talk to us.' Left, right, left, right . . .

'Friend's not friendly,' said the two-headed mackintosh monster.

Their accents weren't English, yet they weren't European either. The language was their mother tongue, but not of these shores. It sounded harsh, authoritarian, and used to getting its own way. But although the language was English, he still didn't know what the hell they were talking about.

He was about to ask them, when the next blow was delivered. It was a short jab to the right side of his mouth with enough force for Vince to let out an anguished yelp, but again not enough to clam him up with a broken jaw. Another landed on his left side, just to even things up. He felt his lip split, then sweet, tangy blood seeped into his mouth and trickled hotly down his chin. The flesh had split too easily. He realized that it split because it was a previous wound that hadn't had time to heal. There was a sickening familiarity to it all. And the memory of all the pain they had heaped on him was amassing itself now and washing over him. Long-term and short-term memory came flooding back, just when he didn't need it or want it. The cumulative effect was agonizing. He wanted to cry, but instead he started to giggle. High-pitched and hysterical, like a hyena on amphetamines. Yeah, that was it. It was animal. It was raw from pained naked flesh.

'The friend is laughing again.'

'What's the friend laughing at?'

One gloved fist glanced off his chin, the second came in from another angle. His eyes closed. More punches landed. A stinging slap to the left cheek, followed quickly by the full pelt of a back-hander across the right cheek. A hook to the jaw forced him to bite into his tongue, the salty and sweet blood was again in his mouth, he could feel loose flapping flesh.

'Friend mustn't go to sleep on us.'

'No, friend needs livening up.'

Vince opened his eyes to see that a box had been produced. It was a dull green colour, not much bigger than a shoe box. Once the lid was lifted, he could see it was an old military field telephone that worked off a hand-wound generator. Two leads were attached to the generator's red and black conductor valves, with a vicious-looking pair of crocodile clips just waiting to bite on to something. It wasn't long before they did. One of his torturers, which is surely what they were by now, attached the cables to his nipples. He wasn't even aware that he had nipples until these things were attached to them. The memory returned, and punished him again. Vince now had confirmation of why his skin was mottled with filth. He *had* been writhing around on the dirt covering the flagstones.

Two strips of black gaffer tape were swiftly placed over the electrodes to insulate them, and to make sure they didn't come loose. They were determined that Vince should feel the full blast of the shock. Without ceremony or any arch words, the crank handle of the hand-held generator was vigorously rotated. Vince saw a red needle jolt on the generator's small dial. Then came the current. On impact, his body torqued and twisted and stiffened. The current coursed through him, torching his nipples, numbing his chest, but it was a violent numbness like a sustained hammer blow. The electric anguish then shook him and threw him out of the chair and on to the floor, rolling and writhing around as if he was trying to put out a fire.

It was down there, on the soothingly cold stone flags, that he saw the colours. Bright fizzing electric colours, neon shards cutting through his brain. Pain became a spectrum of great and surprising beauty. Taking on a life of its own, turning into something indescribably and incandescently striking and sensual. A vivid and deepening ecstasy overtook him. And, when the shooting stars, neon glows, phosphorus rainbows and hallucinogenic firework displays were done, the blackout came.

Everything about him ached. Everything about him throbbed. Everything seemed an effort. Which came as a surprise because, as far as he was aware, he wasn't doing anything. He was lying down. His eyelids, which also ached and throbbed, strained to open with all the ease of a pair of rusted old shutters. There was an ache, a lugubrious throb that pulsed through him, but he couldn't locate or localize it, because it was all of him. His hands wanted to reach out and grip the parameters of the fold-out cot he was lying on, but they couldn't, as they had been bound together behind his back and were bloodless and numb. He felt beaten up, and wasn't sure that he hadn't been . . .

'The friend is laughing again.'

'What's the friend laughing at?'

Vince closed his eyes in readiness as the two men in the mackintoshes inexorably went about their business . . .

The cold bite of the crocodile clips as the electrodes were attached . . .

It was the blood that woke him. He felt it bubbling up in his throat. He was lying on his back, and he couldn't move, but he knew he had to otherwise he'd drown. He was surprised he had any blood or fluid left in his body, for he imagined his innards to be a blackened desiccated pit. His carrion flesh drained of blood. He rolled over on to his side and coughed it up. Each cough wrenched his body and ratcheted up the pain. Every bruise, cracked rib and piece of pummelled flesh cried out. He put a voice to his pain. At first a low blood-bubbling gurgle that turned into an angry growl, which then subsided into a wretched whinnying sound, accompanied by a sustained crying jag that he wouldn't have wanted anyone to witness. And finally a fuck-it-all-to-hell, full-throttled howl. The animal was dying. He knew it would be over soon. No one deals out this kind of punishment and leaves the victim to tell the tale.

The beams of light sliced through the slatted door. His tormentors, the mackintosh men, stepped into the room. They lifted him off the cot and placed him in the chair. Vince knew what that meant, more of the same. He didn't know how many times he'd gone through this. It seemed as if he couldn't remember a time without it. But he also knew he wasn't capable of withstanding much more of it, even if they were.

'One last time, friend.'

'Are you ready to talk, friend?'

'Who do you work for, friend?'

'Who's paying you, friend?'

'Who's your master, friend?'

'We're sick of you, friend.'

'We're tired of you, friend.'

'Are you tired, friend?'

'You want to sleep, friend?'

'You want to close your eyes, friend?'

Vince made a noise that might have resembled the words Yes, please, kill me now. He was ready to close his eyes. He wanted it over with, he wanted it done, he wanted out. And they accommodated. Again in unison, like some dreadful conjuring trick, the black leather gloves were pulled from the mackintosh men's pockets and slipped over nimble knuckles, and they went to work on him again. Pulling their punches to deliver the pain in small percentages, but they all added up, and he knew these were just the warm-up shots to get them into their stride. Once they were in it, the blows came in harder, heavier and faster. It was a mutual feeling; they'd had enough of Vince like he'd had enough of them. Vince felt his swollen blood-blistered lips pull taut, then break open with watery blood eddying down into the dimple in his chin. And just when it got to the point that he couldn't take it any more, hey presto, the green box was produced. The great livener!

There was also something new; a fresh prop was produced. A dirty-looking towel was wrapped round his head like a turban. The towel was heavy and slipped down over his eyes. It took a few moments for Vince to realize it was soaking wet. The cold wet towel felt good, soothing, but that wasn't its purpose. Its purpose was to be used as a conductor for what Vince reckoned to be the final killer jolt of juice that would fry him.

The electrodes were this time connected to each of his nostrils, a strip of gaffer tape wrapped around his nose for insulation. Panting out of his mouth, he closed his eyes in readiness. With the water on his face, his nose taped up and his eyes closed, it was a new sensation, like drowning. Drowning or burning. He was sure that, as a kid, he and his friends had discussed, if push came to shove, which kind of death they would choose over another. And he was sure it would have been a unanimous vote for the drowning over burning. So, to honour old playground friendships, Vince went along with the drowning and closed his mouth. His mind searching for prayers, looking for redemption? Looking for forgiveness? But he couldn't think of anything to say, or even think. But whatever thoughts were going through his head, they were quickly abandoned when he heard clattering sounds. Something was wrong. He heard the mackintosh men leaving the room and slamming the door shut behind them. Vince opened his mouth and gulped down some air.

There were raised voices, and other people now in the adjacent room. There was a panic setting in, shouting, threats. Then there was gunfire, three reports. Each seemed not to hit its intended target because Vince didn't hear the yelps and cries that usually accompany getting shot – no matter how tough you are. Or maybe they were dead. No, because there was more talk, though it was quieter now. The gunplay seemed to have got things under control. The sound of those interminable crickets returned, the volume slowly rising till he couldn't hear anything that was happening next door.

Vince shook his head vigorously to rid himself of the towel, a painful move because he could feel and hear the blood sloshing about as though in a barrel. He wrenched open eyes that were gummy with congealed tears, just in time to see two men emerge from the light of the adjacent room and take their place in front of him – their shooters drawn. Vince took them in. These men didn't share the uniform duality of the mackintosh men, for they were both wearing different coats. One had on a brown leather flying jacket, the other wore a check topcoat. But, on further inspection, things still didn't look too promising, for they didn't look like the Red Cross. One was compactly built with a tufty flat-top style haircut, a pug's nose, and what looked like shiny pink lines down his cheek, three of them about two inches long, looking like someone had raked a claw made of razors down his face. The other fellow was taller, younger and looked more alert, more in charge. He had thick wavy black hair swept back from a widow's peak. His black brows slanted sharply down over quick eyes that were as narrow as a Chinaman's. Everything about his face was shaped like a sharply suspicious V. His eyes scoped the room, burning through it, looking for more trouble. Vince got the feeling that he liked trouble, and was disappointed not to find more of it but just to find him here: naked, beaten black and blue, and for all the world looking as though he was about to die. Satisfied there were no more mackintosh men, they pocketed their shooters.

'They did a job on you, that's for sure,' said the tall one, looking Vince over. It was said in a tone of professional appreciation for the work done, not necessarily pity for who it was done on. The squat flat-topped one nodded in agreement. He too seemed to be weighing up and admiring the mackintosh men's handiwork, and looked as if he was about to break out in a smile and opine, 'Nice work.'

The tall one broke him out of his reverie by saying, 'Let's get him out of here.' They grabbed Vince under the arms, lifted him out of the chair and carried him through to the next room. His rescuers – or new tormentors – muttered words he couldn't comprehend, because his ears were howling due to the blood swilling around his head. But the expressions on their faces and the way they held him at a distance, like a soiled rag, spoke volumes.

In the next room he saw a big open fire that looked as though it was used for cooking as well as heating the place. Copper pots and pans hung over it, and there was a long wooden farmhouse table with chairs around it. And the most important detail, the one he was really searching for, the two mackintosh men. They were face down on the stone floor, their hands and feet solidly bound together with the same black gaffer tape they had used on him. Their mouths were taped too. He wanted to see their faces, get a good look at the bastards, so he'd know them, so he could hunt them down and return the favour. He wanted some answers. But most of all, he wanted to stop feeling like a wretched animal, to stand up straight like a man and get the smell of piss and shit and sweat and blood and fear off him. But he couldn't do any of those things. So he passed out instead.

He woke up in the back of a travelling car. A coarse tartan car blanket was covering him. He looked out of the window at bright lights and cars rushing by on a dual carriageway.

The dark-haired gunsel with the quick eyes was sitting in the passenger seat. Hearing Vince groan on waking, he glanced round. Vince saw a smirk on his cocky-looking face. The squat flat-topped one driving peered at him in the rear-view mirror. He too had a smug satisfied look on his face. Maybe having a beaten-up and broken copper on the back seat was their idea of fun.

The tall dark one said: 'What did they want with you, pal?'

Pal? Had 'Pal' now replaced 'Friend'? Was he out of the frying pan and into the fire or vice versa? Either way, the frying pan was travelling at speed, and he didn't fancy jumping out of it himself.

'Who do they work for?'

'Come on, talk to us, brother.'

Brother? Had that replaced 'Pal'? It would seem that you couldn't pick your own family any more than you could pick your friends, or your pals.

'Why won't you tell us?'

Vince stopped listening and started planning. His feet and hands weren't bound now. Flat-top had his hands squarely on the wheel, concentrating on the road, going at a steady 50 mph. The gun was no longer in the dark one's hand.

Vince suddenly sprang forward and threw himself on to the steering wheel. That sent the car veering to the right. The horn went off, along with a chorus of other horns from the cars swerving around them as they veered across the lanes to avoid them. Some were more successful than others. Brakes being slammed on, screeching tyres, the sound of crashing and crunching metal. Inside the car, alarm had set in. The cool cats with the shooters weren't smirking smugly now; they were screaming like schoolgirls going over Niagara Falls in a barrel. With Vince now covering the steering wheel, they yanked at his arms, pulled his legs, pummelled his back and tore at his hair. But still he stuck limpet-like to the wheel. There was a screech of tyres around the careering car as it broke through the barrier of the central reservation.

'Brake! Brake!' was the call going up from the tall dark one to the flat-topped driver, who in his panic had forgotten that he still had power over the pedals. He braked. He braked too late. The white lights filled the windscreen.

CHAPTER 38

Vince had been here before. The familiar pall of bruised flesh, bones that ached as if they'd had the marrow scraped out of them, and broken and twisted blood – or at least that's how it felt as it coursed through his body. Nothing was easy, everything hurt. A good motto that, he thought; he'd put it on his gravestone. He'd been out of it for four days. Not in a coma, just drifting in and out of consciousness. Splayed out on the bed, unable to move as his body tortuously repaired itself.

The doctors told him that, apart from one cracked rib, there was no lasting damage. The cut lip, cut eye and bloody nose would eventually heal to nothing. The bruising would fade. It had been a professional job, his torture, painful, but leaving no lasting damage. Nor had the electric shocks damaged any internal organs. Vince imagined his insides resembling a mixed grill of sizzled liver, fried heart, smoked lungs and devilled kidneys. Not so, said the doctors.

He was now sitting up in his bed in a private room in the hospital, with windows just big enough to shoot arrows through. Mac had brought him a bunch of grapes. Vince still had teeth, he'd checked, but he wasn't eating. A grape would feel like swallowing a cricket ball. As Mac polluted the room with the familiar pungency of his well-tarred pipe, Vince filled him in on what had happened to him, from his questioning of Bernie Korshank in the Camden Town club to being snatched and tortured somewhere in the countryside, to being dragged out of the farmhouse by the tall boy and flat-top. Then the car crash. The Wolseley 610 (stolen) Vince was travelling in had gone into a tailspin, probably due to the tall one pulling on the handbrake, resulting in them just missing the oncoming truck. The two gunsels had run off, abandoning Vince, who quickly passed out.

As the older detective listened, he never changed his expression, and seemed to barely modulate his breathing, even at what Vince considered the most breathtaking parts of his account. When Vince was done, Mac filled and tamped his pipe again before letting out a sustained 'Mmmm . . .' He then smiled as he broke the news: 'You're relieved of all duties pending an inquiry.'

It was delivered with the calmness of someone who assumed the recipient was expecting it. The recipient was indeed expecting it, but couldn't really bring to mind one single event that might have tipped the scales against him. But he knew such 'events' were there in legion, and bunched together like the grapes that Mac himself was now devouring. Take your pick of any number of indiscretions, disobediences, liberties and overstepping the marks he'd made on this case. But, deep down, Vince still knew he was right to have made them. They might punish him for his actions, but he could not chastise himself.

Once the news had been given time to digest, Mac asked: 'So who were they, Vincent, the two that snatched you?'

Vince gave a wary smile, then wished he hadn't, for he could instantly feel the sutures in his lip, and his cheekbones ached. He knew he'd have to talk like a ventriloquist and keep his expression in neutral for a while. Torture for him now would be merely some form of tickling. Vince said, 'Is this a police officer asking a civilian?'

'I'd like to think more of a friend asking another friend. You want them caught, don't you?'

'Spooks.'

'MI6?' asked Mac.

'They had an accent.'

Mac laughed. 'Russians out to exact revenge for comrade Bernie Korshank?'

Vince didn't laugh, and not just because his face ached. 'South African makes more sense – from what we learned from Dominic Saxmore-Blaine, and about their dealings in Africa.'

'The coup?'

Vince nodded, or gave what he thought was an approximation of a nod, seeing as he was as stiff as a park bench.

'Talking about Saxmore-Blaine, we got the autopsy report. That was no cry for help. He'd severed main arteries, both his wrists. But there was a third, his penis. He'd severed the artery on that too. Doc said it looked as though he'd tried to cut it off completely. It was hanging on by a thread.'

Vince didn't know if he had it in him to cross his legs, but mentally he did.

Getting off this uncomfortable subject, Mac said: 'Back to the South Africans. Did you get a proper look at them?'

'No, but I'm sure they were the two men I saw at the Imperial that time. Which means they were the same ones who garrotted Ali Azeem. I only spotted them from behind as they were leaving the hotel, but they were wearing beige macs, trench-coat style.'

'Macs are popular. I've got one myself. Sorry, Vincent, but we're going to need more than that.'

'They obviously didn't want me to see them, and they were professional, so I didn't. What can I say?'

'How about the two that saved you?'

'Get a sketch artist, I'll draw you a picture. Better still, show me some mugshots and I'll pick them out. I'm sure they'll turn up somewhere. Those two weren't spooks. And they were very English, very London. I've a feeling I've seen them before – or maybe just the type.'

'So you get snatched by spooks and saved by villains?'

'Hardly saved. They wanted the same as the spooks. Answers I didn't have for questions I didn't understand.'

'Think about this, Vince. Maybe you're not supposed to have the answers. Someone else will have them, but not you.'

'If you insist on being so enigmatic, Mac, I'll call the nurse in for my bed bath.'

'I've seen your nurse, pretty little thing; I'd take one myself.' Mac reloaded his pipe, loaded it with stringy-looking tobacco, tamped again and fired her up. 'I've told you that I play the markets, juggle the stocks?'

'With some success, I hear.'

'I've done okay over the years. I put my girls through a good school on it. I've made money because I've received good advice from one particular man, and I've taken it. I've known this fellow for over thirty years, and I started out with him when he first started in the business, as one of his first clients. And he's done very well for himself since. He outgrew my level of patronage a long time ago, but we remained friends and I've taken care of a few parking tickets for him over the years.'

'What else are friends for?'

'And this fellow has told me to steer clear of the Montcler set, because nothing is going to stick on them. Not now. They've got patronage from high up.'

'How high?

'Try the PM himself. Harold Wilson's looking to change the image of the Labour Party. Ditch some of the cloth-cap mentality and reposition themselves as the friends of big business. Cultivate middle-class aspirations, if you will. To do this, he wants to cosy up not only with the respected old-guard captains of industry, but with the emerging young bucks such as Simon Goldsachs. The days of this country making stuff out of pig iron and digging up coal are on their way out. Pretty soon, practically everything we buy is going to have *Made in China* stamped on it. It's the markets that are the way forward, and we're talking about making money on a global and grander scale. And the men who play at the tables of the Montcler – men like Simon Goldsachs, especially Simon Goldsachs, are leading the way.'

'They can make lots of money, but can they get away with murder?'

'No one's saying that, Vincent. But that little coterie at the Montcler have a lot of political firepower. They've got friends in both the Lower and Upper Houses. Practically every peer of the realm who likes to gamble, and most do, have dealings in the Montcler. Five or six key Cabinet members, a dozen or so in the Opposition. Even our own Commissioner has been known to play a hand or so. As for Beresford's joke with Dominic Saxmore-Blaine, about taking over a small country in West Africa, it's not looking so funny now.'

'It never did. Nicky DeVane told me that Beresford's father served with Sir David Stirling, the Scottish laird who organized the SAS.'

'Of course.'

'Beresford was a failed SAS man himself. He couldn't make the cut, but he still had the ambition.'

At this, Mac smiled and shaped his mouth for a silent 'Ahhhh'. It was clear that he and Vince were reading from the same manifesto. Mac said, 'Britain's no longer a real power on the world stage, as we don't have the firepower. It's America and Russia that are the top dogs now. They're the ones who came out as the real victors in the Second World War, and they're the ones who shout the odds. So what do we do instead?'

'Complain about the weather?'

'Private forces. And by that I mean privately funded armies going into countries that are strategically or economically profitable to us, and stirring things up among dissatisfied locals. That's what Stirling and his band did in the Yemen. It was public knowledge, if you bothered to look.'

'And you did?'

'Since this case came up involving the Montcler, and from what my friend in the City told me, I thought it was worthwhile getting into. Just to see what we're up against. From what I can tell, they're working on behalf of the British government with the implicit dictate that if it all goes wrong, they're on their own and the government can't be blamed. Big wars are too expensive, and failure too humiliating, but small privately backed ones where Britain benefits, and gets to reinstate some of its power and influence in the world, that's the way things are going. And the kind of men who can provide such backing gather around the tables at the Montcler.'

'Your friend told you all this?'

'He told me some of it. The rest gets backed up by history and economics. All of which I take an interest in.'

'So Beresford was killed because he was drunk and began opening his big mouth about the coup?'

'If there is a coup, then, yes, that seems as likely a scenario to me as any other. But I've got a feeling this is nothing you hadn't thought of already, right?'

Vince emitted a meditative humming sound, then said clearly, 'My money is on the two mackintosh men killing Beresford. If they are South African secret service, it fits in nicely. Maybe they were working alongside the British spooks?'

'Vincent, we could speculate like this till our heads dropped off.'

To get that on the way, there followed some considered nodding of heads from the two detectives as they surveyed the territory they were in. Sex, death and power; the messy prints of a British political scandal were all over this case. Like the Profumo stink-up of a few years back, but without the iconic photography and the snappy one-liners. And with far more corpses.

'So now, Vincent, the thing to do is for you to prove it's not all a joke gone wrong, and maybe bring down a government whilst you're doing it.'

Vince stared at the older detective, pipe jammed in mouth, and saw he was being deeply ironic with that last statement. His was a long gaunt face that suited irony.

'So what's the alternative, let them get away with murder?'

'There is no *them*, Vincent. Asprey, Goldsachs, Ruley, DeVane – it goes beyond *them*. You're up against the grey men. I mean the grey men stalking the corridors of Whitehall, making decisions and reaching out to their old-school-tie friends for support. They've got more power than the men at the dispatch box, because the men at the dispatch box come and go. But the grey men are always there, keeping the whole thing ticking over.'

With that, Mac finished off the last of the grapes he had brought, and was gone.

Vince did the only thing that was available to him – apart from throw off the sheets and do a jig on the bedside table – so he lay there and thought about Mac's lecture on the brave new world of post-war British imperialism. Mac was right: it was nothing that hadn't already crossed his mind. A mind that even he recognized, if left unchecked, became fertile ground for conspiracies and machinations. But it struck him as disconcerting that Mac, ever the most evenly balanced of men, should have espoused such a theory. If he, the voice of reason, thought something was rotten in the state of Denmark, you could bet your bottom krone that it was in fact a festering bubonic cesspit. Then he thought about Mac's friend in the markets, and wondered if there really was such a friend. Or if Mac had himself been called into some gloomy room deep in the bowels of Whitehall to face a crescent of seated grey men telling him to keep a lid on his young colleague before a nasty accident befell him. Again.

CHAPTER 39

Two weeks later, and Vince was out of the hospital. His body still carried the bruises but they were fading fast and he felt he was getting back to full fitness and form. But he had changed, for he didn't know if he could take a beating like that again. He felt totally raw; he felt as if his attackers had dipped into his reserve, helped themselves to that bit extra that gave him the confidence to go toe-to-toe with just about anyone, and also the knowledge that he could soak up a beating better than most and yet spring back to his feet again and dole out double. This feeling of uncertainty they'd left him with made him angry, and hungry — hungry for revenge, and to even up the score. He wanted to call them *friend* in return. He wanted to pound skin, hear bones break and have *their* blood-soaked pleas in his ears. He wanted to shock them in return, turn the handle and send them to hell with the entire national grid coursing through them.

It takes a beating like that to make you realize just what you are: a bundle of delicately put together humanity, 80 per cent water and a bag of soft tissues, breakable bones and painful nerve endings. The beating had aged him, thrown him ten years into the future and caused his step to falter. No bad thing, he was sure Mac would say. Maybe that's why the older detective, after reading the medical report and discovering there was no permanent damage, had put a wry smile on his face.

After a further two weeks convalescing at home, Vince was fully on his feet, pacing his flat and working up ideas. And the first one that struck him – the alpha in the pack, the one that had been jostling for his attention ever since his eyes had opened in the hospital and he was reasonably compos mentis – was to make a return visit to the Kitty Cat club in Camden Town. With or without his badge, he still wanted answers. And, whilst he wasn't too bothered about not having a badge to brandish to get the job done, he was worried about not having some other form of back-up to brandish when the job needed a little more emphasis. It was all part of the 'New Caution' he was adhering to.

So, before Vince went to Camden Town again, he made some phone calls, and was given the name of a fellow in Kings Cross called Shinny Vaccaro. Shinny was Shinny because he was small, about up to your shins being the reckoning. Of course he wasn't *that* small, but the underworld is a world of ready nicknames and gross exaggerations that, once given, tend to stick. Shinny Vaccaro was also an armourer, an underworld quartermaster. He had a good rep, since all his guns were clean, untraceable. He serviced the underworld, naturally, but he also serviced the other side – whenever clean and untraceable guns were called for. It took some greasing of palms and some straightening out, but eventually Vince met up with Shinny in a pub on the Gray's Inn Road.

Shinny was improbably tall, about six foot something, heavyset, ginger-haired, ketchup-cheeked and spattered with freckles. And he was obviously not Shinny Vaccaro at all, more like Mick O'Malley. Still, in the private bar he introduced himself as 'Shinny', and Vince got the mixed message that either he worked for Shinny or no one got to meet Shinny. Or maybe, just maybe, Shinny didn't exist. Either way, Vince wasn't much interested in the ins and outs of Shinny Vaccaro, and he came away from the meeting with what he wanted: a snub-nose Colt .38.

Vince parked the car in more or less the same spot he had parked it the last time he was in Camden Town, just off Parkway. As he made his way to the Kitty Cat club he was sure he could smell chloroform in the air. The sky was grey and bruised, and looked like crying its thunderous heart out at any moment. So there were a good few people stalking the streets in beige trench-coat style macs. His eyes searched for the two men. His fists buried in his coat pocket were balled and ready to go. The gun in his shoulder holster was loaded.

'That's a scary-looking face you're wearing, cock,' said Trixie, the Marlene Dietrich MC. She was sitting on a tall bar stool in the mirrored reception area of the club. As it was afternoon, she hadn't yet changed into her top hat, tails and stockings, but instead was in a pair of Levi's and a checked shirt. On the remark, Vince dropped the paranoid scowl he'd been wearing and pulled a convivial grin. His face no longer ached, but he still wasn't up to speed on smiling as readily as he once had, and maybe he never would be again.

'That's better, handsome.'

'You remember me?'

'Of course I remember you – the detective.'

'Is Bernie about?'

'Haven't seen him in yonks,' she said, retrieving a large cigar from a handbag sitting on top of the small reception desk. It was faux crocodile, and it held the faux lobster that she dragged around on a lead. She lit her cigar with the unwieldy blue petrol flame of a brass Zippo lighter, paying him careful attention as she did so. 'You look like you've been in a punch-up, lover boy.'

'I was. Just a shame I was sitting down with my hands tied behind my back when it happened. That'll teach me. So where's Bernie?'

She shrugged. 'We've got another feller working the door here now. She's not as sweet as Bernie, to be honest. I don't think she approves of us.'

'She?'

'All the men are shes and hers and all the women are hims and hes and cocks and pricks.'

'I see. Then how come you called me "cock"?'

She shrugged. 'Relax, you silly little tart. There's no rules to these things!'

He laughed. 'And this new doorman . . . she's a prude, eh?'

'And you're not?'

'Live and let live, I say, as long as it doesn't frighten the horses.' She laughed at that. 'Tell me, the new doorman, what did *she* have to say about Bernie?'

'Ha! You learn fast. *She* doesn't say a lot. Larry scares her, you see. She doesn't get Larry.'

'Larry?'

'Larry the Lobster, silly.'

Marlene Dietrich puffed a cloud of smoke in the direction of the plastic crustacean sticking out of her imitation-crocodile handbag on the counter.

'Of course, silly me.'

'Believe me, girl, I did question cunty about Bernie, but the dim bitch really didn't seem to know. You see, I like Bernie. We always chatted, about films, about plays we'd seen. My cock likes squiring me off to the West End for a spot of play watching and a good musical. *Don't put your daughter on the stage, Mrs Worthington, don't put your daughter on the stage.* I'll tell you one thing about Bernie, Officer Krupke, she seemed rather out of sorts of late, and no mistake. Not her normal self these last few weeks. Depressed, I'd say. She's a big old bird, I'll grant you, but she's a sensitive soul is our Bernie.'

'I need to talk to him . . . her. Do you have an address?'

She didn't. Or he didn't. But then it turned out she did – or he did. It took some persuasion, but Vince made it clear to Marlene Dietrich that Bernie Korshank wasn't in trouble. But he knew why Bernie was depressed, and Vince was in a position to alleviate that state of affairs with some information he had for him. Not all lies.

Marlene Dietrich's information was good and took him to a small flat in Stamford Hill. Bernie Korshank's wife was a small woman, very small – comically so, considering how big Bernie was. She was Polish and spoke in very polite but very broken English.

Everything had 'please' and 'thank you' before or after it. But it wasn't just her limited grasp of English that forced these mannerly platitudes, for they seemed genuinely heartfelt.

Vince got the impression that there had been real hardship and sorrow in her past. In her mid-forties, the war wasn't too distant a memory for her, and Poland and the Jewish ghetto had felt the deathly grip of fascism more keenly than most. And yet here she was, a survivor, just happy and relieved to be living on these free shores, in the Jewish community of Stamford Hill, another enclave but one that wasn't fenced off and starving, and about to be relocated to a death camp.

The flat was pink and peach and everything in it was chintz and busy, and cosy beyond belief – or desire for most men. It seemed as unlikely a milieu for Bernie Korshank as any Vince could imagine, since everything here seemed just too small, dainty and fussy for the big bouncer. Including the little Polish wife, who was maybe five foot at a stretch, even in high heels – and those were the kind of heels she looked as though she didn't possess.

Vince's eyes were drawn to the panoply of paintings that covered almost every inch of the walls, walls that were themselves already in full bloom with colourful floral wallpaper. The ornately framed paintings depicted places that looked as if they didn't exist except in fairy stories or on chocolate boxes. Country-scene idylls with waterfalls and pointy turreted castles in the background, and muslin-frocked and bonneted shepherdesses tending their sheep with smiles on their faces – the shepherdesses *and* the sheep. It was all quite an eyeful but, after what she might have seen over the years, who could deny her freedom to surround herself with such an idealized narrative of the world.

Mixed in amongst all the Disneyland on the walls was a sober black and white framed photo of her husband: a head-and-shoulders shot with Bernie in an evening suit and a matinee idol pose. The heavy features were lifted by a gregarious smile, and the inherent brutality and hardness of his visage softened by a smear of Vaseline over the lens. It was a professional job, and the professional who had done the job was Nicky DeVane. The dapper snapper's signature was clearly wrought in an elaborately scrolled and gilded font in one corner of the portrait.

But before Vince could fully take on board the implications of this photograph, he was hit with another eyeful. In a polished burr-walnut cantilevered frame, taking pride of place on the mantelpiece, was another black and white photograph, showing Bernie Korshank smiling and shaking hands with someone. Vince recognized the setting, for the shot was taken in Al Burnett's Stork club. Vince also recognized the man Korshank was shaking hands with. He recognized him from youthful mugshots dating from the last time he had taken a serious pinch, and from periodic newspaper headlines and articles, Pathé newsclips, book covers, and in the flesh once while under surveillance at a Lyons tea house in Piccadilly. Casting an anthropological eye over the picture, Vince thought it spoke volumes. In stature, the other man reached up to about Bernie Korshank's breast pocket; and yet the powerfully built Korshank seemed stooped and subservient next to the older man. And that was because the man was Billy Hill. *The* Billy Hill – *Boss of Britain's Underworld* was how his ghost-penned bestselling memoir described him. And the man's reputation was such that no one argued with the description.

Vince had a lot of questions he needed to ask, so when she offered him a cup of tea and a slice of Battenberg, he readily accepted. Out came the best bone china and then the chat. She told Vince that her husband was off on business in Tangiers, but couldn't – or wouldn't – say what kind of business it was.

Vince knew that Billy Hill had interests in Tangiers, because Tangiers was a very interesting place. Situated on the North African coast by the western entrance of the Straits of Gibraltar, where the Mediterranean met the Atlantic, it was a centre for smuggling cigarettes, booze, hash, dope and other contraband. Word was that Billy Hill had been visiting there since just after the war, busy organizing shipments of this *and* that. Tangiers and the International Zone had become a Mecca for smugglers, spies, speculators, subversives, gamblers, fugitives, counterpart French criminals, Arabic cliques and the literati, with American Beats experimenting with negative

morality and cut-and-paste prose. All of these could be found lurking in the twists and turns of the kasbah, where the market was
always in the black and everything was negotiable – from stolen
money, stolen bearer bonds and stolen documentation to counter-
feit versions of all the above. All thrived in the confusion, opportunity and intrigue that the International Zone contained.

As she served Vince up another dainty cake on a doily, and
poured him a second cup of copper-coloured tea, Vince wondered
if Korshank had confided in his wife about the business at the
Imperial. But considering the cosiness of the surrounding décor,
he realized that Korshank probably left the details of the world he
operated in at the doorstep. And Vince didn't have the heart to
bring it over her threshold either.

CHAPTER 40

Vince wasn't surprised to hear a girl's voice over the intercom, but he wasn't expecting to hear the voice that he heard. As he clanked up the metal grated stairs leading to Nicky DeVane's studio on Beak Street, he wondered if he'd got it wrong. That seductive and smoky voice hitting all the right notes and oozing class, maybe it belonged to another brittle blonde. Another long-limbed, highly strung and combustible thoroughbred galloping through life, causing chaos and heartbreak. There must have been lots of them in the world that Nicky DeVane inhabited, in fact stables full of them. Then he wondered if he was going to walk into a crime scene: Nicky DeVane corpsed out on the floor, with Isabel Saxmore-Blaine as the killer standing over him, holding a smoking gun. Revenge for her brother? Isabel genuinely committing a murder would have given the case a kind of baroque symmetry, but not the satisfying resolution Vince was looking for.

'Detective Treadwell.'

It was indeed Isabel who answered the door. Vince didn't bother to tell her that the 'Detective' part of his life, or certainly the title, was suspended. Minus a badge, he had no more right to call himself that than an Oxford Street store dick.

Vince followed her into DeVane's studio, noting that she was dressed in what Vince took to be her favourite outfit: black ski pants and a black sweater. Against the white walls and floor of the studio, she cut a dramatic figure, as if she was about to have her picture taken. Then, again, every time he'd seen her, she had looked capable of stepping out of a glossy magazine. No one looked this good, not in the real world. He believed it was called breeding. He *knew* it was called money.

'I heard what happened to you,' she said.

Vince awkwardly brushed the back of his thumb over his cheek. It was a redundant gesture, as there wasn't anything on it now.

'Do you know who was responsible?'

'We're working on that.'

Isabel persevered with more questions, but Vince was still working on putting it all behind him and forgetting. And anyway, it wasn't an episode he wanted to share, especially with her.

She finally got the message, made an assumption, and offered: 'Nicky's not here. He's in the Caribbean. He's shooting a swimwear collection, I believe.'

'Nice work if you can get it.'

She picked up on his tone, and rather agreed with the *old rope* analogy that passed wordlessly between them. But, out of loyalty, she put up a defence of the dapper snapper's profession. 'I know for a fact that Nicky works very hard on these shoots.'

'Yeah, must be a real slog to be surrounded by beautiful women, with all that sun pouring down on you, and nothing but white sands, blue seas and the finest hotels to break the monotony. May I ask what you're doing here?'

'Nicky's letting me stay whilst he's away. There's a small flat upstairs. Just until I get myself fixed up with a new place. As I said, I never want to set foot in my old flat ever again.'

They stood in a parallelogram of light in the centre of the studio, about eight feet away from each other. It felt awkward, discombobulating. The white studio with its arc and spotlights, and painted backdrops ready to fall into place, made Vince feel as if he was on a stage in one of those modern-dress versions of *Hamlet* that were all the rage these days. The white mise en scène representing the icescapes of Denmark, or maybe the character's inner life of emptiness, turmoil, adriftness or some such *stuff*. Either way, there they stood, like two stranded actors desperately in need of direction. Vince contented himself with a bit of stagecraft and put his hands in his pockets and shuffled some loose change. Isabel clasped her hands behind her back and moved from heel to toe like a ballet dancer, which was a natural enough manoeuvre for her.

'I'm thinking of moving abroad for a while. Maybe back to New York. I have some pretty good work contacts in journalism. Or maybe I'll spend the summer in Ibiza. It's one of the Balearic Islands in the Med. I'll just sit around smoking hash and splashing about in the sea.'

'Why doesn't that sound as much fun as it should do?'

'Because you're very perceptive, Detective. My heart's not in it. But right now I'd rather be anywhere than in London.'

'But why *here*?'

She frowned, as if his last utterance was a very peculiar thing to say, then went over to the far side of the studio. Against the wall was a counter set up just like a bar in a cocktail lounge, albeit a very stylized and futuristic one. The bar was all streamlined angles and sprayed silver, with red neon tubing encircling it like the rings of Saturn. It was a bar in which Robby the Robot or the Jetsons might have a drink at. It was obviously a prop for one of Nicky DeVane's no doubt exhausting photo shoots, with the space race and beyond as its theme. Models in metallic bikinis and kinky boots with fishbowls over their heads, colonizing other planets and making them just like home. Vince saw this as a very optimistic view of the world because the way things were going, what with the Cuban missile crisis still ringing in everyone's ears, and *Dr Strangelove* up on the movie screens, Vince didn't see a rosy future of jetpacks, teletransportation and very attractive green women as an acceptable alternative to the more earthly hues. No, instead he saw a scorched earth, nuclear winters and maybe, one day, them all rising out the primordial sludge only to screw it all up again. But that didn't sell toothpaste.

Once established at the bar, perched on one of the four chrome-tube stools that stood in front of it, Isabel plucked a very terrestrial-looking pack of cigarettes off the tin-foiled counter and sparked one up. By way of beckoning him closer, she asked, 'Why *not* here?'

Vince went over and joined her at the bar and said, 'DeVane was there with Beresford that night at the Imperial. He was part of it all.'

She took a long, loaded pull on her cigarette, and fired off a shot of disdainful smoke over his shoulder, just missing his ear. 'Nicky explained the whole thing to me. At the time it was happening, he had already passed out in the bar.'

'I think if Nicky DeVane could handle his liquor better, he'd have been up in that hotel room playing along with Beresford and his so-called Russian spy. Who I've met, incidentally: a frightening-looking man who has no doubt done some terrible things, and is more than capable of doing more. But, for all that, has a heart of gold, by all accounts. He's very cut up about what happened.'

'You think I need to hear all this?'

'Yes, I do, because I think Nicky DeVane was complicit in your brother's death.'

'Nicky is my dearest friend.'

'So you told me. He was Beresford's, too, and also a loyal follower. Then again, I think they were all complicit. The whole lot of them—'

Isabel cut in: 'Who are *they* and *them*, Detective Treadwell? Anyone who went to public school? Anyone from my social class?'

'So what happened to your brother and Beresford, it was all just a public-school prank that went wrong?'

Isabel crushed out her barely smoked cigarette on the tin-foiled counter. 'It was all Johnny's idea and his doing, and he's dead. I did consider transferring my hatred for what he did to Dominic on to Nicky and the others, but what would be the point? I try and live my life without harbouring resentments.'

'You know Nicky DeVane loves you, don't you?' Vince smiled. 'Of course you do. That gives him a motive stronger than most.'

Her head jolted back with a quick blast of derisive laughter. 'You think Nicky killed Johnny?'

Vince shrugged a pretty unconvincing shrug.

'Then call me a fool. Nicky might have had the motive, but he doesn't have the guts.'

'You'd be surprised what love can do – especially when it's obsessive and unrequited.'

'Maybe that's just your obsessive and unrequited little mind working overtime, Detective,' she replied tartly. Restless, she then dismounted the stool and moseyed over to one of the long windows. Arms folded, she leaned against its frame and looked out at the expanse of London that was available to her gaze. It was a choice stretch, a lively vein of vibrant inner-city life. Carnaby Street milled below, and you could pull up a chair and watch it for hours. Vince watched her, as she provided another easy-on-the-eye view you could waste some time on. Staring out the window, Vince was reminded of that time he first saw her in the Harley Street private hospital. Framed in the light of the window he had wondered then what it would be like to sleep with her. It had been an innocent thought, unshared with anyone. A lot had changed since then. He had slept with her, but, on reflection, nothing had changed. He felt as distant from her now as he had then; more so, in fact.

Still looking out of the window, she said: 'Anyway, I don't know why you're still concerning yourself, since you're not on the case any more, Detective Treadwell.'

Vince watched as her cheek dimpled and a medium-sized smile took possession of her lips. He sensed a victorious note in her voice, and it was like the crack of a starting pistol. A snide note, a false note, and Vince didn't like it, not one little bit. So he gave it to her with both barrels.

'Nicky DeVane took some photographs of Bernie Korshank: not just quick snaps but posed portrait shots. Korshank's an actor, of sorts. Those pictures must have taken up at least an hour of Nicky's time. You said yourself how hard he works, and yet in his statement he said that he had never met Korshank before in his life. Surrounded as he is with beautiful women, you wouldn't easily forget a mug like Bernie Korshank's. Nicky DeVane lied, and I want to know why.'

'The case is closed,' she insisted in a weary voice, her interest wandering again as she stared out of the window, seemingly spotting someone amid the platoon of ants bustling below who had taken her interest.

'And who closed it, your father?'

She didn't answer that. She didn't need to, for he saw the flush of entitlement. And Vince felt his own face flush with blood as anger swelled inside him. His jaw jutted, his fists balled; he wanted to pummel the wall beside her, then shake some life into her, anything to break her out of her torpor.

He did neither, just said: 'You're worse than your father. I can understand him wanting some make-believe honour for his son. But I had you pegged as a twentieth-century girl. I was wrong. You're toeing the line, flying the flag and not rocking the boat – not often you get to string so many clichés together like that, but freshness of thought wouldn't exactly fit this occasion.'

At this, her torpor was finally toppled. Her back straightened, her head cocked challengingly, her arms stiffened by her sides as if she was holding a couple of daggers in her clenched fists and was about to lunge.

'I think you're out to spread as much muck as possible,' she snarled. 'I think everyone who has been hurt by this case now deserves to be left alone to grieve. Your superiors have made their judgement, and I don't see what the hell is so special about you that you think you're above the rules!'

Lots of words struck a chord in Vince in that statement: *rules*, *superiors*, *judgement*. And he hated every one of them. 'So who does decide all this? Your father? James Asprey and his pals? I don't think so, Miss Saxmore-Blaine.'

'You're very naïve, Mr Treadwell. They've been making those kinds of decisions since time immemorial. And that's what you can't stand: the status quo.' Her eyes looked as though they had cross hairs superimposed on them. Her mouth looked as though it needed a muzzle. 'You don't give a damn about Johnny, or about Dominic for that matter. Underneath all the well-tailored veneer, the looks and education, you're just a common little spiv and a vicious little guttersnipe on the make. And on a downward spiral to nowhere, from what I hear.'

'Last time you had that look on your face, Miss Saxmore-Blaine, you were licking my lips and dripping sweat into my eyes.'

The smirk he wore was rapidly wiped off when her flattened hand cracked across his chops. He wasn't very proud of his last comment. It wasn't very gentlemanly. In fact, it was guttersnipe talk, and he knew it. Taking that as a good a cue as any, he about-turned and made his way to the exit.

CHAPTER 41

Vince went looking for Billy Hill. As detective work went, it was an impossible task, because if Billy Hill didn't want to be found, he wouldn't be found. An audience with the Pope would be easier to arrange at such short notice. But Vince's reckoning was that, if he put his name about enough, he hoped Billy Hill might want to find him.

His first stop was the Centurion club, just off Saffron Hill in Clerkenwell. In the murky main room, men sat huddled drinking espressos you could stand a spoon up in, with slices of lemon peel on the side. The coffee drinkers who frequented the Centurion weren't the Espresso Bongo crowd of Soho, with jazzsters, hipsters, pill-poppers and potheads enjoying a legal jolt and hanging out and shooting the shit. No, the coffee drinkers in the Centurion club were all of Italian extraction, and all ex-paisan of Charles 'Derby' Sabini and his Italian mob of Saffron Hill. And in their heyday, the twenties and thirties, they were all well versed in wielding a straight razor on the racetracks of England. They spoke in hushed tones so as not to be overheard, even when they were the only customers in the place. An atmosphere of suspicion hung heavy. In the back room of the club was one of the busiest bookmaking and lay-off operations in the country, run by a man named Alberto Dimeo, otherwise known as Italian Albert, or Dimes. Sitting in one of the booths was his mentor and fellow Italian from Saffron Hill, whose anglicized name was Bert Marsh. Vince had come across him previously, when he was working Vice in West End Central. Bert Marsh didn't make the papers, didn't push his weight around, and didn't seem to do much more than sit in the back of the Centurion and drink a chain of two-finger measures of bitter espresso coffee, in a huddle with other men of a similarly crooked disposition. It was hard to tell his role now; some said that he'd retired in the fifties and ceded control of the Italian end of things to Dimes, who was in turn in cahoots with Billy Hill. Others said he was still the power behind the power behind the . . .

But Vince knew it paid not to be sucked into the myth-making and barroom banter of villains. However, he certainly knew that Bert Marsh was a consummate fixer, someone who knew everyone, and therefore someone who could get the word around. So Vince bought him a cup of coffee . . .

Next stop was Soho. For the Cabinet club on Gerrard Street and The Modernaires on Old Compton Street. The two clubs were run by Aggie Hill, Billy's former wife. All clubs in Soho contained the occasional villain, but the Cabinet actually catered for them. The place was awash with Brylcreemed, dark-suited hoods with skinny ties around their necks and thick scars across their cheeks, along with frowns and scowls worn as precursors to imminent conflict. In London, all points of the compass gathered under Soho's volcanic neon glow, and with that came plenty of rivalry and needle. It was Friday night, and already things had kicked off. Some *right fucking liberty-takers* from Deptford were going toe to toe with some *right two-bob cunts* from Islington. Vince left at the first sound of breaking glass.

The crowd in The Modernaires on Old Compton Street was more mixed, a place for wives or girlfriends – but God forbid both on the same night. The girls wore their hair as high as structurally possible, and drank Dubonnet in their double-knits and diamantés, and slurred their vowels and cackled with laughter. En masse, they seemed a far more frightening proposition than the menfolk. And when one of them gave another one of them a *funny* look whilst jostling for position before the communal mirror in the Ladies, while applying fresh mounds of mascara, a prize catfight broke out. Painted talons ripped at brittle hairdos, and the cut and thrust and the sheer up-close nature of it put the men's set-to in the Cabinet club to shame. These women knew a thing or two about having a testosterone-fuelled tear-up.

Other clubs he hit were the Log Cabin club, Al Burnett's Stork club, The Bagatelles, Winston's, Churchill's (no relation) and The Astor. Next up were the spiel joints that he knew Billy Hill had interests in, which in Soho was just about all of them.

By the time this subterranean trawl was done, and he'd foot-slogged his way all around the not-so-square mile of Soho, Vince felt as if he'd smoked five hundred cigarettes and been soaked in a vat of booze. Not that he had drunk or smoked, but just had so much of it blown over him or spilled on him amid the Friday night revelries that, by the time he got in a taxi for home, the cabbie gave him a nod and a wink and said he looked as if he'd had a good time. He hadn't, but he'd done the trick. He'd put the word about that he was looking for Billy Hill. He had let it be known to every doorman, bartender, hostess, cloakroom attendant, cigarette girl, waiter, card dealer and shill. And none of them had given anything away – nothing concrete, nothing you could hang your hat on. Some said he was off in Tangiers, setting up new nightclubbing ventures. Others said he was in South Africa, mining a rich vein of profit in gold and diamonds. Others said he was busy buying up swathes of the Spanish coastline and developing high-rise tourist ghettos in places like Torremolinos.

Vince's last port of call for the night was the Moscow Road in Bayswater, the address of Billy Hill's sumptuous mansion flat. There was a pub opposite the block Hill lived in, and it was known that, on any given day, plainclothes coppers were regularly propped at the bar watching Hill's movements. It was all so obvious, and all so well known, that Hill sent his men into the pub to talk loudly at the bar about their boss's coming and goings. The pub soon became known as 'the Ministry of Underworld Misinformation'. If the rumour emerged that Hill had a meeting in

Myrtle Street in the East End, it was odds on he was really up on the North End Road in Fulham.

Vince told the cabbie to wait for him, got out and then bowled straight over towards the block of flats, where he was met by a uniformed and smiling concierge who opened the door for him. Vince asked if Billy Hill was in. The accommodating smile on the concierge's face immediately transmogrified into open hostility. Adroit at talking out of the side of his mouth, he asked, 'Who wants to know?' Obviously on Hill's payroll, Vince gave him all the required information, then headed back to his cab.

It was on Praed Street in Paddington, finally on his way home, that Vince had the stroke of luck that had thus far evaded him on this case. Sexy Sadie from the Imperial was striding along the street, or 'striding' as much as her restrictive red satin pencil skirt would allow. And she had a man in tow, a punter. Vince got out of the cab and tailed them. It wasn't much effort. A block away from where he'd spotted her, and just past a parade of shops and restaurants, she hung a left down an alleyway and made her way to a door that she and the punter disappeared through.

Vince approached, and decided the door looked a doddle. He'd seen better security on an outhouse. But, seeing as this was the age of the new caution, he remembered an old trick Mac had taught him about closed doors. Try opening them first. Vince turned the handle, pushed the door, and it opened . . .

Met by a steep set of carpeted stairs, with the glow of a red light awaiting him at the top, he silently climbed them. The landing was whorehouse red from the carpet to the wallpaper. Chinese paper lanterns decked the halls to give a feel of the exotic Orient, and dragon silks draped the doors. But this was more Chinese takeaway than the authentic world of Suzy Wong. He doubted there was a geisha girl waiting behind any of the doors. And all he could hear was the sound of loveless, joyless, muted sex. Rents getting paid, kids getting put through private schools, but mostly habits getting their fixes.

Vince didn't have to select a door, as one was picked for him. In shirtsleeves rolled up to reveal the ill-formed inky blottings of prison tattoos, about five foot eleven and medium build, but with one of those extended guts that looked as if it had been grafted on. He asked: 'Who let you in?'

'The front door was open.'

The man shook his head in weary annoyance, then said, to no one in particular, 'How many times do I have to tell them?' He focused back on Vince. 'So what can I do for you?'

'Well, I saw the light was on and I thought . . .' And I thought I'd come up here and slam you into the wall. Vince spoke the first part, then did the second. Before the gutted pimp even knew he was in a fight, he was sliding down the wall. He hit it with such force that the skimpy structure shook and alerted the pros and the punters that all was not well.

Sadie, as the last one in, was the first out. There was no *coitus interruptus* involved for her; she hadn't even removed her drawers or gone through her price list yet. Her punter, saggy and sad-looking, stood right next to her. He wore a winning combination of Y-fronts and socks, with just enough sartorial flourishes in the form of stains and holes to really gather some admiring glances from the ladies.

The pimp was now up on his feet, trying to look purposeful, and waving his hands around in front of him as if it meant something. It may well have done, just not to Vince, who said: 'Tell him who I am, Sadie.'

'Leave it, Freddie, he's a copper.'

Away from the grunts and groans, desperation and disappointments of the whorehouse, Vince and Sadie had found solace in a small hotel off Paddington Green. Its bar was cosy, with enough illicit liaisons going on there to make them both feel at home.

Sadie sipped a brandy and Coke, numbing and sweet just as her cravings demanded. The intervening weeks hadn't been kind to her, and she was desperate not to get pinched. Holloway and cold turkey didn't appeal. In the grip of her addiction, she was clearly on the slide. It had taken her swiftly and silently, without fight or complaint. She was a lot thinner than the last time he'd seen her, the sallow skin hanging over her small bones without much conviction. In her low-cut dress, the breasts were unavoidable; but where he'd once admired them for their plumpness, they now looked tired and pouchy. What with the perfunctory glacial eyes, everything was working like machinery towards a single purpose and her only real concern, that next 'angry fix'.

She talked. She *wanted* to talk, to unburden her woes. And Vince let her do so. This wasn't all heart on his part. It was quid pro quo. She told him that her boyfriend had OD'd. Her girlfriend had left her. Her habit had ratcheted up. And, since the debacle at the Imperial, her income had dwindled. And now she was back on Praed Street, tipping over half of her earnings to the pimp, Fat Gut Freddie. Poor Sadie, there was enough tragedy and tumult in her story to drag down an entire army of bright-eyed and bushy-tailed optimists and evangelists. Enough loss of innocence to wall up Eden and hang up the condemned sign. It was at times like these that Vince understood Bernie Korshank's little wife's taste in décor: the smiling sheep amid the country idyll. He might try and grab some of it for himself one day. Maybe go live on a farm and toil on the land. Or go further afield, to the Rockies in Canada, or the outback of Australia, the Amazon jungle. Any damned place to throw off the stench of the city and the hard-luck stories, before his heart dried up within his ribs and looked like a piece of cuttlefish hanging in a bird cage.

Once Sadie had exhausted her luckless narrative, she glanced back at Vince, with eyes no longer moist with self-pity but narrow, tense and full of suspicion.

'Anyway, you haven't come to listen to my problems, have you?'

'Dominic Saxmore-Blaine, you knew him?' She shrugged. Vince blazed her a pair of dark eyes, put an edge in his voice, and said, 'That wasn't a question, Sadie. Now, tell me, was he a punter?'

'Not one of mine, no.'

'How about Marcy's?'

Sadie looked away. It could have been in thought, but she could just as easily have been lost in a junkie distraction, a junkie musing, like considering the possibilities of the world existing on another plane – on her thumb nail, for instance. Vince judged himself to have already shown her enough patience. 'They're both of them dead, Sadie. What is there to protect now – their reputations?'

'Yeah, he was Marcy's punter. But more than that, I'd say. He'd sort of fallen in love with her, if you get what I mean?' Vince got it, since it wasn't so hard to get. Sadie added, 'Occupational hazard, dearie.'

'But also, with the right punter, an occupational goldmine, right?'

'It was for a while. Dominic started buying her presents, giving her money. Quite a bit of money, in fact. At twenty-one, part of his trust fund had started coming through. I told Marcy she was on to a good thing here, but she had to play it right. It's happened to me a couple of times, in my younger days. Before this shit took . . .' Her voice trailed off and she looked wistful.

'So what happened, Sadie?'

'That was it, not a lot. That was the problem. Nothing happened, not in the trouser department anyway. Little Dominic couldn't consummate the love affair. He couldn't get it up, the poor dear.'

An involuntary grin broadened across Vince's face, as the pieces of Dominic Saxmore-Blaine's shattered psyche began to piece themselves together. His deflated performance in the sack made perfect sense for the act of Grand Guignol he'd committed. The self-mutilation, the self-loathing, the sexual inadequacy – it was all so grimly obvious. An eye-wateringly dramatic gesture, so personal

313

and private, yet it demanded an audience. It demanded further investigation.

'What's so funny?'

Vince stopped grinning. 'Nothing's funny, Sadie. I was just thinking.'

'*Thinking?* I've not done that in a while. It doesn't pay, not in my line of work. Did I tell you I used to be a artist? Pretty good, too. I studied at Camberwell for two years, fine art. Sculpture was my discipline. That's where I met Greg, and we started—'

'Another time, Sadie. Tell me about Dominic and Marcy.'

'She tried it every which way with him. But nothing stirred, not a thing. Poor Dominic was traumatized, distraught. And so was Marcy, as you can imagine.'

'She was about to lose the goose that laid the golden egg?'

'You could put it like that. The poor love had already confided in her that it had happened to him before. He'd tried it with lots of working girls: thin ones, fat ones, redheads, blondes, brunettes, even an Oriental in Hong Kong. All the same result, nothing. Marcy assumed he was queer. Nothing wrong with that, she told him; just go with it if that's what he was. You can't change the clay you're made of. Dominic didn't like that at all. Which was a surprise to me, as I thought they were all at it in public school.'

'They are, but only when still at public school. So he stopped seeing Marcy, is that it?' Sadie nodded. 'And, of course, stopped giving her money and presents?' Sadie looked away. Not because of a junkie distraction this time – alternate worlds, parallel universes – but something akin to guilt and shame. 'Like you said, Sadie, you've been in this situation yourself. What did you do?'

'I didn't do anything.'

'You had Marcy's back. You were her girl.'

'Nothing like that.'

'No, nothing like *that*. But you did give her advice. You did show her the ropes. Come on, Sadie, she started out as a maid at the Imperial, then you told her how to earn some real money. You practically put her on the game.'

'No!' Sadie shot back loud and clear. 'No, I never!'

Vince looked around the lounge bar, where faces looked back at him. But they were all faces that wanted to mind their own business and didn't want any trouble. He turned back towards Sadie. She had guilt, all right. She had it good and deep. Maybe Marcy would still be alive if Sadie hadn't persuaded her to capitalize on Lucky Lucan's growing interest in her and go on the game. Which in turn led her to her liaison with the fragile yet lethal Dominic Saxmore-Blaine. Vince didn't pursue the guilt angle, as she looked as though she was paying the price for it already. Here was a heroin-ridden husk who looked as if she needed a fix ten minutes ago.

Vince said, 'So Marcy started blackmailing Dominic about not being able to do the business in the bedroom, right?'

'Something like that. First of all he gave her some money to keep her mouth shut. But you know how it is: money has a nasty habit of getting spent. So, yeah, I said she should ask him for some more.'

'How much?'

'Fifty pounds, sometimes more!'

'A week?'

'Why not? He had plenty of it. All his crowd did, and it was his choice. He wanted to keep going to the Imperial because his friends did. If he hadn't kept hanging around there, Marcy wouldn't have done anything. Makes you wonder why he did.'

'Like you said, because his friends did. Because he wanted to be one of them, wanted to belong. But he wasn't like them.'

Vince considered the six hammer blows that Dominic Saxmore-Blaine had struck against Marcy Jones's head, and they all made sense now. He had wondered about the number and the sheer ferocity of the attack. For a cold-blooded assassination, it was too personal; there had to be more behind those blows, and now he'd discovered what. Armed with a hammer, Dominic had at last attained penetration of a sort. It was the perfect Freudian storm. Dominic Saxmore-Blaine had found his excuse for killing Marcy

Jones. She had witnessed him running down the stairs, smeared in fake blood, after fleeing an assassination on behalf of the Montcler set and Merry Old England Ltd. Now he had his sanction, to rid himself of his sexual tormentor, his blackmailer, and become the man he wanted to be. For Dominic Saxmore-Blaine, killing Marcy Jones was a winning hand all round.

Sadie knocked back the rest of her drink, and shrugged. 'That's the way the cookie crumbles, I reckon.'

'Very philosophical.'

She noticed the edge in his voice, and had her retort all lined up. In a tone of ruffled defiance, she said, 'Forget it, copper, I don't give a damn about these men. They pay to use us. If the tables get turned, then they've only got themselves to blame. I've got nothing to be ashamed of.'

'No one's saying you should be, Sadie. Like you say, everyone takes their chances in a place like the Imperial, and you and Marcy were just a couple of working girls with mouths to feed, rents to pay, and big bad habits to assuage, right?'

She didn't answer, and Vince could see she was too busy working out ways to cut this conversation with the copper short. She desperately wanted to make a call. She wanted to burn up some brown, fill up a spike and lose herself, off the streets into the land of nod.

But, before that happened, Vince pulled her back to reality with: 'So Marcy's taking a good few quid off Lucky Lucan to stand there whilst he dresses up as Hitler and listens to Wagner. And she's also collecting the same off Dominic Saxmore-Blaine, for keeping shtum about him not getting it up. She's doing good business with those two alone, without even really having to put out.'

'That's right. Nice work if you can get it.'

Sadie's hand reached down to Vince's thigh, and began to work her magic. 'I'll do anything for you, handsome. Anything . . .'

Vince removed the hand. 'You've already done it, sweetheart.'

CHAPTER 42

On twirling the key in the lock of his front door and cracking it open, Vince knew that something was up. Either the mice had taken up smoking, and got scared of the dark and turned on the living room light, or he had guests. He padded into the hallway and, as silently as the hinges would allow, retrieved a cosh from the closet, and a knuckleduster hidden in a pair of plimsolls. His switchblade was already in his pocket. Why he needed this primitive artillery was simple: he'd forgotten his gun. He'd left it in the car, taped under the driving seat for security. With hands behind his back, like a visiting dignitary at a country fête, he moseyed on into the living room, clutching the cosh in his right hand whilst his left was adorned with the heavy jewellery of the knuckleduster.

The first thing he saw was a pair of Webley Mk IV service revolvers pointing in his direction. At about gut level. Outgunned and outnumbered, the hardware he was holding and the sharp pointy thing in his pocket might as well have been made out of marzipan. One gunsel sat on the couch. The other sat in the high-back armchair that was given to him by Mac when Vince had put his back out during the call of duty – kicking down a door probably. The chair looked austere, but was surprisingly comfortable.

'Lose whatever's behind your back.'

Vince slipped off the knuckleduster and placed it on the side table nearest to him, which held a lamp that was lighting the

317

room. He put the cosh on the table, too. For an instant he thought about sweeping the lamp off the table and pitching them into darkness. But he knew he'd be bent over with several bullets in his gut before the lamp hit the floor. These gunsels were good at what they did, and he knew this because they were the same two fellows who had taken him out of the farmhouse after taking care of the two mackintosh men. Vince knew this was no time for taking hot-headed risks. He also knew that you can catch colds by leaving your house without drying your hair properly, eating cheese at night gives you nightmares, and eating spinach gives you—

He swept the lamp off the side table, and the room fell into darkness. He bolted for the door, but it slammed shut. He immediately saw the glint of the Webley, *another* Webley, that told him there was a third man in the room, who had been standing behind the door. The two gunsels were up on their feet now, with their Webleys cocked.

Vince said, 'Okay, fellers, my mistake,' and stuck his hands in the air. They quickly went down again as a fist drilled into his gut. It was a sucker punch, and as good a gut shot as he'd ever taken. It knocked every puff of wind out of him. Vince doubled up, but wasn't given the time or luxury of having a good old wallow in his discomfort, as he was grabbed by the lapels and launched head first into the wall. What cushioned the collision was a framed canvas on it: the triptych of jazz players. The most expensive purchase he'd ever made, *ever*, was now lying on the floor alongside him, looking crushed and winded too.

As the overhead light was switched on, Vince looked up to see the two gunsels he already knew, and a third man, who he also recognized but couldn't quite get a handle on. Vince was about to ask *What happens next?* when the distant flushing of the toilet broke the thought. Then from the bathroom came the sound of the turning of a tap, and the flow of water, accompanied by the whistling of the tune 'Danny Boy'. When the washing and drying of hands was completed, the source of the music emerged from the bathroom. He came along the hallway, with the whistling of the tune getting louder and louder, and finally into the living room. There he stopped whistling.

This one wasn't carrying a shooter, however. He gripped a small plastic-faux tortoiseshell comb between thumb and forefinger, and was raking it through the thinning strands of greased black hair that lay flattened against his nut-brown scalp. A scalp that had neglectfully gone without its sunhat in the warmer climes of, say, Tangiers? Satisfied all was presentable, he glanced down at Vince and the crumpled heap of modern art on the floor. He looked reasonably contented with what he saw, but also rather nonplussed by the whole thing.

Then, to no one in particular, he said: 'Doctors tell me it's the prostate. I don't know. All I do know is that I'd give a million quid just to be able to take a good long hard piss.'

Billy Hill then glanced around and saw the side table with the cosh and the knuckleduster on it. 'I heard he carries a knife, too,' he said to the tall dark-haired gunsel.

'We got him covered,' the man replied confidently.

'That's what you said last time, bright boy, and he got away – gave you the slip.' Billy Hill then addressed the other fellow, the one who had slammed Vince into the modern art. 'This the same feller?'

'That's him,' he replied out of the side of his mouth.

Vince recognized him now. He wasn't wearing his blue uniform and peaked cap, but this was the concierge of Billy Hill's apartment building in Moscow Road.

'Go wait in the car,' said Hill. The concierge gave Hill the nod, pocketed the shooter and left the room. Hill looked down at Vince again, and asked, 'Can you get up?'

'I'm working on it,' said Vince as he climbed to his feet, not wanting to look any more poleaxed than he needed to.

The men arranged themselves around the room. Billy Hill was naturally drawn to the most throne-like seat there, the high-backed armchair, whilst his two gun-toting compadres sat side by side on the couch. Vince pulled up a chair from the small side table that operated as his desk and sat opposite them. Billy Hill shifted from cheek to cheek in his seat in a sustained effort to get comfy. He eventually gave a satisfied sigh. Then, looking squarely at Vince for the first time, he said, 'I like this chair. Think I'll get me one of these. Where'd you buy it?'

'It's not mine.'

'It's comfy, whoever's it is. I like a firm seat these days. You wouldn't think so, with my troubles, but I do. Like a park bench, for instance: I can sit on those things for hours, providing the view's accommodating. Nice duck pond or something.'

'Yeah. I guess I should give it back, though. A friend lent it to me when I did my back in—'

'That's enough, sunshine, I don't want your fucking life story. Got my own problems. Wait till you get to my age, the fucking aggravation of it all! Prostate the size of an apple. Doctors sticking their fingers up my arsehole, and I don't even like people pointing at me, so imagine how I feel about that!' Billy Hill shook his head in irritation and then gestured to the painting lying on the floor. 'What is this shit anyway?'

'Modern art.'

'Expensive?'

'Enough.'

Looking at the work, Hill developed a disapproving grimace on his face, as if the prostate had enflamed further and gone from apple-size to a grapefruit, or maybe a prickly pineapple. 'Well, if you hadn't have got cocky, it would still be hanging on the wall. Though why you'd want it up there is beyond me.'

Billy Hill, now reaching into his sixties, looked every bit like a gangster. A movie-star, old-school gangster in a double-breasted grey-flannel suit with a faint chalk stripe running through it, and a brightly embroidered tie that verged on being a kipper, which featured, against a crimson background, a Polynesian woman in a golden grass skirt sporting a hat made of fruit, like Carmen Miranda. His shoes were black Oxfords, with mirror finishes on them, and if Billy Hill did look down and see his reflection, this is exactly what he would see: a pair of heavily hooded eyes that were blacker than the exit holes in the muzzles of the two guns now pointed at Vince. Add to that a nose that was pitted like a strawberry, and a solid fighter's chin that looked as if it could, and had, taken a fair few punches in its time and had never let him down. It was a lined and sombre face, though you couldn't tell where the natural lines of age ended, and the old razor scars began. But in the world where he grew up and plied his trade, such scars were considered as natural as the lines on your face.

The sheer Humphrey Bogart-ness of Billy Hill was uncanny, and for a moment Vince felt as though he was in a film. He couldn't make out which one though, since they were all winners. The Burberry trench coat currently draped over a chair, with a brown felt fedora resting on top of it, all completed the Bogart look. But this was no time for Vince to romanticize Billy Hill or confuse fact with fiction. There were enough minions and syco-phants ready to bow and scrape to him, like the two gunsels seated on the couch. They were like a Dobermann and a bull terrier ready to tear into Vince at the slightest trill of their master's voice. And it was a raspy old voice, though not through barking orders or shouting to make itself heard, for Billy Hill didn't need to do that, since people hung on his every word, every gesture. It was raspy through the constant irritant of Player's cigarettes, a packet of which was gripped in his hand, along with a gold Ronson lighter. He lit one of them up and took a long gratifying sip, as if swilling the smoke around his gums, then blew it out of one corner of his mouth with what seemed like weary disgust.

After getting his much-needed nicotine hit, he looked at Vince with a slow, appraising gaze, then said: 'You've been making your-self busy.'

'It paid off.'

'You could have seen me a long time ago. My boys offered you a lift home, but you did a runner.'

'I thought I was out of the frying pan and into the fire.'

'Nice way to treat two good Samaritans who saved your life and was just offering a lift to the hospital. Feelings were hurt. Right, fellers?'

The bull terrier nodded. The Dobermann said, 'Messed up a nice car there, brother. A Wolseley 610.'

'I fancied a walk and didn't want to get my blood on your upholstery. Sorry it got smashed up, but it wasn't yours in the first place. It was stolen. I'm glad to hear you both got home all right.'

'No problem, brother. We just stole another one.'

Vince said to Billy Hill, 'To be honest, if you already knew who I was, I'm surprised you bothered. Wouldn't it have been easier just to have let them kill me?'

'We all make mistakes,' said Billy Hill. 'Okay, copper, I'm here now. So what can I do you for?'

'How did your boys know where to find me?'

'Bernie called me straight after you left the Kitty Cat club. And if you're worried about Bernie, he's in Tangiers taking care of some business for me. I thought it was best because of that shit with the Montcler feller, Beresford, it upset him. Don't get me wrong, Bernie Korshank ain't soft — he was excavated from the side of a mountain! But he's got his sensitive side, too. He's a theatrical.'

'Yeah, I saw him throwing the Saint down some stairs the other night.'

Billy Hill shrugged. 'He probably had it coming.' Vince frowned, genuinely not knowing if Hill's last statement was meant to be a joke. If it was, it was delivered beautifully — as dry as chalk. The old gangster continued, 'We'd been taking an interest in you since the first time you came to the Imperial. So when you went on the missing list, we had a pretty good idea who snatched you. We'd been taking a pretty keen interest in them, too.'

'Why the interest?'

'In you or them?'

Vince shrugged. Either way would do.

322

'They'd been to the Imperial, cosying up with brasses and buying them drinks, expensive drinks, and asking them all sorts of questions. But never taking them upstairs. Then they came into the Kitty Cat, but they didn't look like a pair of irons – just sat at the bar. So our interest was up. This was all before Scotland Yard got involved.'

'Always one step ahead, eh, Mr Hill?'

'Call me Bill. Most of you chaps do. As for being one step ahead, you better believe it, my fine friend. My liberty depends on it. Anyway, Mr Smith and Mr Jones here' – he gestured towards the faithful retainers seated on the couch – 'followed them to the farmhouse. Those fellows didn't look like farmers, neither.' Billy Hill shifted suddenly in his seat. It wasn't Vince's line of questioning making him uncomfortable, but something deep in his bowels. 'It's the weather that does it,' he explained. 'Every time I come back to this poxy country it gets irritable. The prostate needs a hot climate.'

'I could do with a holiday myself.'

'From what I hear, Treadwell, you'll now be able to take one. The case is closed – and, even if it was still open, you're off it. Maybe it's time for you to start listening to your superiors.' Billy Hill acquired a glint in his eye, pulling a spry smile that exposed a sturdy set of ivory smoker's teeth. 'I know a gaff in the kasbah that could make you forget all about that beating you took. Dusky maidens, my young friend, dusky maidens.'

'I have a funny feeling I'm back to listening to my superiors right now. Come on, Bill, throw me a bone.'

'Then you'll lay off?' Billy Hill didn't wait for the detective to answer. 'I don't think so. I don't think you're the laying-off type.' He looked around at the two on the sofa. 'Pretty cute, ain't he? He gets us around to his flat, doesn't offer us a drink, not even as much as a cup of tea. And has us answering questions, for a case that he's not only not working on, but is officially closed. This boy gets just what he wants!'

The tall dark one said, 'You want me to shoot him, Bill?'

'No! I want to offer him a job.' Hill's eyes were firmly fixed on Vince now. 'I'm impressed. You don't handle yourself like a copper: all mouth and no trousers hiding behind a badge. You got brains, and I hear you can handle yourself too. Good with your fists. Can use a blade. Not scared. Yeah, you've got bollocks, chutzpah, or call it what you will.' The wily old gangster's eyes narrowed into a dissecting look. 'I see violence in you, boy.'

'What's your point?'

'I could use a man like you.'

'I'm fixed just fine right now,' said Vince, knowing the job offer was just to throw him off track.

'I'm not just trying to throw you off track. I'm serious.'

Spooky, thought Vince, one step ahead and a mind reader. This omniscient old gangster really did know how to chill the spine.

'Thanks, Bill, I'll give it some thought. But whilst I'm still working for the other side, and knowing you're not one to volunteer information to the likes of me, and you're not going to tell me how you're involved, maybe I can offer some more free thinking? My deduction?'

Billy Hill fired up another Player's, did some shifting in his seat to settle in, then gave him the nod.

And Vince laid it out: 'Before gambling became legal in 1960, you got to know James Asprey. The young Eton and Oxford man was bound to fall under your gaze when he started to ply his trade as a bookie, setting up a one-room office behind Oxford Street, in the West End. By the time he started his modest book in '52, you had everything and everyone in the West End tied up.'

Billy Hill remained unmoved and unaltered by this information. Vince ploughed on: 'Then we've got the Imperial Hotel connection. The way I see it, your name's not above the door, Bill, but you run that place. Yet you're not in the hotel business for the fun of it and, let's face it, the Imperial lost its gloss in the '30s. You're not a pimp either, but you do take a cut from the working girls' profits for their use of the place. And with your man on the reception keeping an eye on the cut, it's a very profitable hotel. By the way, your man on the desk, Ali . . . that's where I first saw the mackintosh men, the day Ali was killed.'

'The mackintosh men?'

'That's what I call the two who snatched me.'

Billy Hill's face flashed with anger at this news. He crushed out his cigarette in the small side plate he was using as an unofficial ashtray. 'They killed Ali?' Vince gave him a solemn nod. 'He was a good man, Ali,' continued Hill. There was a mournful meditative pause, as if to assess his loss. Then he quickly sprang back to life as a thought struck: 'Apart from that poxy-looking syrup on his head!'

'Yeah, that was quite a rug he *almost* wore.'

'Don't think he didn't earn a good whack working with me, because he did. He could have bought top-of-the-line syrups for every day of the week!'

'I reckon the mackintosh men must have been trying to get information out of him.'

'Like I said, a good man. Ali wouldn't have stood for that. He'd have put up a fight.'

'Well, he picked the wrong one with them.'

Billy Hill shot a glance over to the two sitting on the couch. They shrugged and shot him a defensive look back. Hill then returned his attention to Vince. 'A missed opportunity – we should have taken care of those bastards when we was taking care of you. Should have shot the pair of them!' He shook his head: he was deadly serious about the lost opportunity, and it grated. He then looked at Vince and barked impatiently, 'You think I've got all night?'

Vince cracked on. 'In the mid to late fifties, Asprey was making quite a name for himself, becoming the man for big-money gambling parties – rummy, poker, Kalookie, but mainly chemin de fer. Chemmy was his game: fast, addictive, and favouring the house more than other games. James Asprey needed an address to run his chemmy parties, since he'd outgrown privately rented flats and the rooms at the Ritz. But somewhere west of Regent Street, for the area most of his punters would come from. The Imperial was perfect. That big dining room became one of the biggest gaming rooms in London. And the fully stocked bar. Brasses if the urge took them. The place had an edge about it.

'And most of all, it had you. After all, gambling was illegal when Asprey started and, for all his rich and powerful friends, it would still leave him open to the criminal fraternity. So why not go to the top man? A reasonable man. A man you could do business with. And that's how you met the Montcler set – at the Imperial Hotel. What happened next is anybody's guess. But if it's crooked and there's big money involved, all roads inevitably lead to the great Billy Hill.'

The old gangster made a play of weighing up the detective's assessment. After some arching of his eyebrows, pursing of his lips and some acquiescent and concurring nods of his head, he looked pleased with this appraisal. Especially with the last part. Vince knew he'd like it, and that's why he dared to say it.

Billy Hill said, 'Smart as the lash, Treadwell, and just about right on every count.'

Vince continued. 'Asprey, amongst other things, is a snob. And being a snob is a twenty-four-hour job; and they don't give it up for anyone. Asprey wouldn't have anything to do with you personally, Bill.' This was met with a glacial, hooded-eyed look, meaning Vince's goodwill account had just been wiped out. His stock had fallen. Vince could feel the room frost over as he now crept across the thin ice. He tried to warm things up. 'Asprey would be too scared to have anything to do with you, Bill, because Asprey's smart enough to know he's a snob, and smart enough to know that he couldn't hide it from you. James Asprey himself comes from middle-class stock, and they always have something to prove; they're always chippy and they make for the worst snobs. So he sent Beresford in to deal with you, his house player and his second in command. The Beresfords were proper aristos, feudal lords, as old as the hills they owned. Johnny Beresford wasn't a snob; he was Johnny the Joker, a raconteur, full of hail-fellow-well-met bonhomie and charm. He was easy in his own skin and knew how to mix.'

Billy Hill agreed, and picked up. 'Beresford used to run the games at the Imperial. Asprey used to run the smaller games, mostly in private flats. We're talking serious money, with serious connections: heads of multinational conglomerates, heads of state, lords, prime ministers – and I heard rumours of a president. Fellows that really couldn't afford to be caught gambling. Especially in a place like the Imperial. So I only met Asprey a couple of times, formally and with other people around. But I could tell, right off the bat, he was a real prick!'

Vince considered this. In lieu of a beard, he stroked the scar on his chin. The needle Hill had with Asprey was obvious. The way Vince pegged it, Billy Hill didn't give a monkey's about Asprey being a snob. But he did give a monkey's about coming off second best, and not taking a cut from the serious money. That clicked into place for Vince. When gambling became legal, and Asprey opened up the Montcler club, he didn't need Billy Hill's services any more. So Asprey severed all connections. All the high-rollers from the Imperial followed Asprey to the Montcler, to mix in with the really high-rollers who previously couldn't afford to be seen gambling. The Montcler club changed all that. To be seen gambling in the Montcler was a positive boon. It meant so many things on so many levels. Not only that you had money, but you had enough of it to lose. To be a card-carrying member was pure social enhancement and elevation.

'What's on your mind, bright boy?'

'That you killed Beresford. Either as a warning to Asprey, or in revenge for getting cut out of his business.'

Vince watched as his house guest took this in his stride. He was a gangster after all, and Vince was a detective. So accusations and denials weren't that unnatural, all part of the game.

After unflinching consideration, Billy Hill said: 'I grew up dirt poor in the Seven Dials, a family of thieves, never had nothing unless it was stolen. Now I have more money than I know what to do with. I'm as rich as Croesus. And the worst thing about having all this money is that my accountant, crooked as he is, tells me that even if I lived as long as Methuselah, I wouldn't even put a dent in it. So I had no reason to put the squeeze on Asprey. I'm retired and I got all the pensions I need.'

'It's never just the money with men like you, Bill. It's the thrill of the chase. Getting one over men like Asprey – especially men like Asprey. Showing them the true nature of power, and who's top dog. That's what you thrive on.'

'Ha!' Hill barked, followed by a throaty chuckle. 'You've got me pegged, smart boy. What can I say? Happy now?'

'Happier.'

'You're a mendacious and tenacious little prick, Treadwell! You think you know me? Well, I know *you*. And I know you won't let this go until you get some answers. So to get you off my back, and out of my business, I'm going to *give* you some answers. And then, from here on in, no more. First off, I didn't kill Beresford. He was a pal of mine. He was a real classy act. He was also a cheat. A real classy cheat, if you will. And he cheated for me. We had the best card scam in London. Untraceable. And we made a lot of money. For me to kill Beresford would—'

'Would be to kill the golden goose?'

'Pure gold, Treadwell. Twenty-four carat!' Billy Hill laughed again, followed by an excavating clear-out of his throat, then he said: 'Got anything to drink?'

CHAPTER 43

Vince was woken up by the bell. He scrambled into a pair of strides and a T-shirt and padded barefoot into the hallway. On his way to answer the front door, he looked into the living room and saw, on the coffee table, three drained glasses and a decimated bottle of Napoleon brandy. The remnants of a night spent with Billy Hill and his boys. He also had a fleeting recce of the mullered painting, now resting lamely against the wall instead of displayed on it boldly. Vince gauged the damage to be repairable, but he shuddered at the further expense involved.

Whoever was at the door wasn't going away, but was thumbing the bell with a determined urgency. Vince didn't know what time it was, but it felt industriously early. So he opened the door, expecting to find someone in uniformed service such as the laundry delivery, his postman wanting him to sign for something, or the milkman wanting him to settle up. Instead he got Isabel Saxmore-Blaine. She didn't look as if she'd just tumbled out of bed either. She looked primed and ready, sleekly dressed and as shiny as the polished buttons on her navy reefer-style coat. He didn't know how he felt about her standing there. Even amongst all the pain he'd been put through recently, he could still keenly feel the sting of that slap on his cheek. He invited her in with a mock grandiose sweep of his right hand, and she silently accepted with a pleasing smile across her painted red lips.

She took Billy Hill's vacated seat in the living room, and Vince perked them some coffee. Then they sat in silence, savouring the strong brew. She broke the silence and commented that the coffee tasted good, the best she'd ever had, in fact. He told her why: it was Jamaican Blue Mountain, the best you could get. And he needed it. He hadn't hit the hay until about 5 a.m. The clock in the kitchen had since told him it was 8 a.m. Three hours' kip was not nearly enough after all the schlepping he'd done around dirty old London Town; and all the talking and listening and garnering that he'd done while sitting with Mr Hill.

Isabel glanced down at the almost-drained bottle of booze on the table, with the three empty glasses to which she gave a special scrutiny. To Vince it looked as if she was searching for lipstick traces on them. A vanity on his part, perhaps, but to the naked eye there was very little else to view on them. She then turned round to look at the busted painting, and said, 'Looks like quite a party you had last night.'

'Just the four of us – more of a soirée, I'd say. What can I do for you, Miss Saxmore-Blaine?'

'I've come to apologize for my behaviour the last time I saw you.'

He yawned (completely involuntarily) and gave a purposeful nod.

Undaunted, she continued, 'I was in a bad space, not just physically but emotionally. I was operating on anger not reason. And you were an available target.'

Maybe it was because he wasn't fully awake, but these words sounded strange to him, like an overly constructed babble, the sort of words you pay a shrink reassuringly large amounts of money to spew at you. He suppressed another yawn. But he did manage another nod. It was a thoughtful nod, like Freud listening to a patient sprawled on his couch.

'And I want to make it clear to you that, yes, of course I want Johnny's killer found. And, yes, if Dominic is innocent, of course he must be proven to be so.'

'Why the change of heart?' he asked, adding quickly, 'Not that it's not welcome.'

'I suppose I was retreating into the past, knowing how all this would affect my father. I knew how he would . . . how he would view it. I thought it was only right that I stand by him and by his wishes.'

'Just like you've always done?'

'Exactly.'

'I can understand the change of heart, as it's not a very tenable position any more.'

'Don't be brutal, Vincent. I'm being as honest as I can.'

'I'm not being brutal, just frank. Because the longer this goes on, the harder it will be to find the killer. But I do appreciate your honesty. Brutal honesty, that's what's called for, agreed?'

'Agreed. And I'm also sorry for the way I treated you. You gave me shelter that night, and I didn't even thank you.'

Vince yawned again, lavishly this time. But this one was forced, and it was forced to disguise the tawdry smirk that he was pretty sure was crawling scurrilously across his face; because there was a good gag in there somewhere, but he wasn't about to drag it to the surface and wag it about.

Isabel sat on the edge of the armchair, her back as straight and as upright as a bookcase. Averting her gaze from him, her poised head was tilted towards her hands resting together on her lap. But, coy as she looked, Vince sensed that she wanted her last statement batted back. At last she wanted some recognition for what had passed between them.

He obliged. 'As it turned out, not a wholly altruistic act on my part. And I'm also sorry for my comments, the last time we met.'

'Yes, and I apologize for slapping you.' A smile gently tugged at her lips. 'I'm glad you weren't unduly troubled by it.'

Vince smiled back; he liked this game. 'It was a strange night, Miss Saxmore-Blaine, but a highly enjoyable one.'

'Call me Isabel. I think you've earned the right, don't you?'

All pretence was now gone. What had been denied until now played itself back to them, and set free uncontainable smiles at the thought of that uncontrollable act. Deep down, Vince knew that

Isabel wasn't made up of that stultifying, life-denying reserve that puts a thick layer of frost over everything it touches. It was the first time he'd seen her really smile. A magnificent and heroic effort had been put into a couple of earlier efforts, but tragedy had weighed her down as inevitably as gravity. For the first time, he saw the warmth and innocence in her face, the potential for joy. But the admittance and the smile meant more than just the freeing of emotion; it was the turning away from stale ideals, from an inherent sepsis of thought that would have allowed Beresford's killer to go free, and her brother to be found posthumously guilty of a murder he had not committed. The carapace of her class had now been thrown off, along with its burdensome expectations and stagnant immobility. So there they sat, grinning at each other like a couple of Cheshire cats on a hot tin roof.

CHAPTER 44

Isabel returned to the bedroom holding two mugs of Jamaican Blue Mountain coffee. Vince watched her attentively; there was a lot to watch. She was naked and, among her many attributes, his eye was instantly drawn to her vagina. It was so well groomed that it really did deserve to be on show, a travesty to cover it up. She wore her pubic hair trimmed short, shorter than most he'd seen. It gave the perfectly formed V a shiny, velvety appearance, and you could clearly see the deliciously pouty lips that were now swollen and moist, like an inviting mouth that you just wanted to kiss. Vince now fully understood why women didn't like bushy beards on men, and, in that moment, he vowed never to grow one.

It had been different this time. They were both fully awake, for a start. But semi-conscious though she was at the time of their last liaison, Isabel was well aware of how it had played out, and she was also well aware of her emasculating tendencies in the bedroom. She liked to take control of the proceedings, and had clearly left more than a few cocksure sack artists sprawled, spent and shame-faced on the sheets as she had her wicked way with them. So she happily yielded to Vince, and let him take the lead this time.

Isabel handed him his coffee mug, got under the sheets, and said, 'So, tell me, what did Billy Hill want with you?'

'He didn't want anything. I wanted him.'

Isabel looked wide-eyed in astonishment at this revelation, as if Vince had summoned up the Prince of Darkness himself. 'Why would you ever want him in your home?'

'Because Beresford was a friend of Billy Hill's.'

After the initial shock of this revelation, she then nodded in meditative accord, as if it all made perfect sense to her. 'I knew Johnny liked to play with fire, and he mixed with some very questionable characters, so I suppose seeking out the company of a real-life gangster would be considered quite a coup. I assume he's also a killer, not that I know anything about him. Only what I've read in the papers. So is he a killer?'

Vince shrugged. 'If he is, thus far he's got away with it. But someone will always be around to do what Billy does. And if anyone has to do it – which they do – I'd rather it was him. But, officially, he's supposed to be retired.'

'Unofficially?'

'He offered me a job.'

'Doing what, beating people up?'

'Why do you say that? I have other attributes.'

'What other attributes do you need, to be a gangster? I thought it was just bullying on a grand scale. Did you accept the job?'

'What kind of a girl do you think I am?'

'The kind that would probably make just as good a gangster as he would detective. Binary opposite attraction, and all that.'

'You forget that, pending an inquiry, I'm no longer a detective, so might well be in the market for a job.'

'My father knows your Commissioner.'

'So I heard. Could he put in a good word?'

'He advised my father that I should keep well away from you.'

'I never knew the Commissioner cared.'

Isabel took a sip of her coffee, and made an 'Ahh' sound that could have indicated she was enjoying it or she was getting bored with Vince's cool indifference to his career as a cop. She then placed her mug on the side table and said, 'I'm being serious, Vincent. Don't you care?'

Sensing her annoyance, Vince unlaced his hands from behind his head, and turned over on his side to face her. 'The disciplinary hearing is out of my hands. There's not a lot I can do about it, apart from turn up and tell the truth, so I don't see the point in getting worked up about it.'

'You have a record of violence, true?'

'What else did he say?'

'That you're intelligent, resourceful and just what the Met needs. But you've also been disciplined for being reckless and going into situations you shouldn't.'

'Wow, you memorized my record?'

'No, but I was paying attention when my father told me. Do you deny it?'

'Not the first bit.'

'You told me that you liked kicking down doors, remember?'

'I was joking. There's a lot more to this detecting malarkey than just kicking down doors. First of all I have to find the right door before I kick it down. And I object to being described as violent.'

'You may object, but is it true?'

'No, your honour, it isn't,' he replied, sitting up and leaning over to the bedside table to retrieve his cooling coffee for a voluminous swig. 'I won't deny that the job can get a little rough around the edges at times, but to say I'm violent suggests I go around doling it out unnecessarily. I don't. I just give as good as I get.' He put his mug of coffee back on the bedside table, and drew in closer to Isabel, his hand reaching under the sheets and cupping her breast. She looked down archly at this impertinent gesture, and raised one eyebrow like a question mark. He gave her nipple a circular rub with his thumb until it was fully extended and chafing with ticklish friction. She expelled a high-pitched yelp, and her face creased with laughter until it got too much for her and she rolled away from him.

'You see, you really would make a good gangster. You're an awful bully, Treadwell!'

'I'm the number one nipple-tweaker in the London underworld.'

She stopped laughing, demanded that he be serious, and said, 'Did Billy Hill kill Johnny?'

'He says not.'

'But he would say that, wouldn't he?'

'He would, but it's up to me whether I believe him.'

'And do you?'

'Yes. Knocking off someone of his social standing would bring down a lot of aggravation. And anyway, he was making too much money with Beresford in a card-cheating scam they were running.' On releasing that little nugget, Vince searched her face for more evidence of shock. There wasn't any, but there was a wry little smile. 'You don't seem surprised,' he added.

'I'm not,' said Isabel, 'because it makes perfect sense. With Johnny and Asprey, gambling was never just about having fun, sportsmanship or even winning. It was more than that. For them to win, others had to lose. And that's the part they really liked – beating other people. Johnny couched it in militaristic terms, said it was about the victors and the vanquished. Rather predictably, Asprey used evolutionary and zoology analogies to put that point across: survival of the fittest, primary species dominating – it was all about the same thing.'

'Still, it's quite a risk if you get caught. And it's not as if they had nothing to lose, themselves.'

'It's the gambler's mindset. They thrive on risk. Believe me, if they had all the money in the world, they'd still try and work out ways to bilk a few people they secretly despised. It feeds their sense of superiority and entitlement. What else did Billy Hill say about it?'

'Not a lot. No details about how the scam worked – who it was done to, or who else was in on it. And no mention of James Asprey or the Montcler club.'

'You didn't ask him?'

'No.'

'I suppose not, with two men holding guns on you.'

'Nothing to do with that. I didn't ask because I knew he wouldn't tell me. Billy Hill's not in the business of helping coppers solve crimes. He just wanted me off his back, and himself out of the frame. Beresford's dead, so nothing more can happen to him, and his reputation may now be as shot to pieces as he is, so nothing to lose there. But if others were involved in the same scam, Billy's not about to implicate them. And there's no evidence, either way.'

'So this is what Johnny's death comes down to – cheating at cards?'

Vince didn't answer. Vince didn't know.

CHAPTER 45

The rest of the day passed gently and pleasantly enough. Isabel said she owed him lunch, after the meagre meal Vince had sprung for after her night in Jezebel's. They ate at a new restaurant in Chelsea that was pulling in the in-crowds. It featured pornographic chess sets. Bashing the Bishop was taken literally. All the pawns were porns, featuring every position available – or certainly sixteen of the best. The King and the Queen were hard at it, and not just with each other. There were rutting rooks, and the Knight's sword was fully drawn.

But, chess sets aside, there were other interesting characters assembled around the main room. At the bar sat two well-known and well-behaved West London 'Faces'. There was a famous actor currently making inroads into Hollywood, accompanied by a stunning-looking redhead and surrounded by some lesser mortals in the same profession, who were all hanging on his well-rounded words. Also some bohemian-looking artist types, who wore their hearts and professions on their paint-spattered sleeves, and talked loudly about art between gulps of red wine, drags on roll-ups and forkfuls of rice from their dishes of *blanquette de veau*.

It was a Johnny Beresford and Isabel Saxmore-Blaine type of place, decided Vince, simply because there were lots of Johnnys and Isabels seated around the place, or approximations and facsimiles of them. And maybe that's why the conversation between them became stilted. Or maybe it was because Vince was tired and still too preoccupied with the unresolved case to make small talk. Either way, she had to coax some conversation out of him, and Vince could tell that it had really dried up when she came round to discussing their hobbies. It turned out that Isabel had lots of them, from country sports through the entire gamut of urbane salon culture. Vince, it turned out, had none to offer in return. Zero. She didn't believe him, pointing out the broken artwork on his walls, the books on his bookshelf, the record collection. Vince eventually piped up that he had plans to learn a musical instrument – the alto sax. Isabel said that she played the piano, to Grade 6.

It was dark by the time they made it back to the flat Isabel was renting just off Flood Street in Chelsea, where she tentatively invited him up for a nightcap. He made his excuses, he was tired, not at his best and needed to get home, all of which was true. They'd done a very memorable morning, an entire afternoon and the best part of an evening together, and it was now time to call it a day. There was a tacit understanding between them that they both knew how to not outstay their welcome.

But as Isabel scraped her key in the door, there was something urgent she needed to ask him. 'Do you think it would be possible for me to meet Marcy Jones's family? Or is that the worst idea in the world?'

Vince could think instantly of a hundred and one reasons why it would be impossible for her to meet them, but then his mind scrolled back to Marcy's funeral: to her mother and her aunts, and all the bonneted Christian women out-singing and, in their own way, out-muscling Michael X and his mob with their display of Christian forgiveness. Forgiveness was a concept Vince had grappled with and lost, but wielded in those women's hands, it was a mightily powerful weapon.

'I know where they'll be tomorrow morning, if you want to find out.'

On the walk back to his flat in Pimlico, Vince decided to take the scenic route via the embankment. There was some genuine

London fog swirling around in the damp night air, obscuring and abstracting and making everything just that little unreal, and Vince wanted to take it in. The lamps lit alongside the darkly running river glowed orange, like a landing strip for some monstrous seabird, creating a Turneresque Thames that was alive with possibilities and yet soaked in history and horrors. This was the city of his imagination. Along the embankment couples linked arms, tramps huddled around bottles and expensive cars rushed confidently past.

Vince reached into his jacket and gripped the butt of his gun. He didn't look round, but was aware of the tap-tap of two pairs of footsteps behind him, measured in their stride as if not wanting to catch up, not wanting to overtake, but wanting to stay right behind him. Vince stopped. Whoever they were – and he had a pretty good idea – he didn't want to lead them directly to his home. No, he wanted to leave them here, on the embankment of the Thames. He wanted to leave them lying *in* the Thames, if he had the chance. Behind him, the sound of shoe leather against the stone pavement petered out, too. Before turning round to face them, Vince transferred the gun from his shoulder holster to his right-hand-side jacket pocket. He judged they could not see this manoeuvre by what light was available to him: very little beyond eight or nine feet. The fog was doing a good job in providing cover for both parties involved. The conditions were perfect to kill someone.

There were low voices, and, somewhere wrapped in the night, he was sure he heard the words *See you around, friend*.

Vince pulled the gun out of his jacket and started to move back towards them, towards that voice. He passed a seated young couple locked in a kiss. Passed three men wearing football scarves and carrying rattles. Passed a man walking a snappy terrier . . .

Vince stopped. He listened, and all he heard was his own breath, jagged through fear. He slid the gun back into its holster.

See you around, friend.

He knew that voice would never leave him.

CHAPTER 46

Suited and booted in his Sunday best, Vince picked up Isabel on the King's Road and they drove off to St James's Methodist church on Lancaster Road in Notting Hill Gate. She too was in her Sunday best: smart, demure and respectful-looking in a dark blue suit.

God was doing good business. It was a full house, completely packed. The congregational composition was pretty much as it had been for the funeral, mainly black families with a smattering of white ones; but all unified under the one roof, and all singing from the same hymn sheet. Vince had never seen so many smiling faces. No wonder they all liked this place, he thought. He was beginning to like it himself. If he hadn't habituated himself with a stack of newspapers and a lie-in on a Sunday morning, he could see himself pitching up here and having a good singsong, and getting to know the parishioners, volunteering himself, getting baptized, and . . . what cut the fantasy short was spotting the reason why he was here in the first place.

The Jones family had taken up all of the first three pews: Cecilia Jones and her three sisters and their husbands, and children and various other offshoots of the family. Compared to the women in the congregation, all the men seemed second-bested in church. The sermon was delivered by a man but, even elevated in his pulpit, he clearly knew that it was the women who ruled the roost in this place. After the service, Vince left Isabel still seated and went over to the family, where he was warmly met — especially by Ruby.

Isabel watched as Vince talked with the family. She had recognized Ruby immediately from the images she had seen of her dead mother in the newspapers: a posed photo of an angel-faced black girl in her nurse's uniform; a vision of innocence and virtue and esteem. Isabel took several deep breaths to try and quell the debilitating anxiety that now took hold of her. Her cheeks flushed and she felt hot tears brewing behind her eyes. She edged out of the pew and along the aisle, as quietly and swiftly as a church mouse – though not even that, because they at least belonged there and she didn't. She felt herself an impostor, an enemy. Once out of the church, she stood by Vince's car and wept. She soon felt an arm around her shoulder, and she drew into him. He kissed her on the forehead, then took her hand.

In the drawing room of Cecilia Jones's house in Chesterton Road, Isabel was sitting with the ladies, seven in all including herself. They drank piping hot tea and ate homemade cake, which was a darkly rich confection of rum and raisins. Vince ate two slices of the delicious thing, and Cecilia said she'd give him the recipe to hand on to his wife. With his mouth still full of the sticky rummy cake, he didn't correct her and nodded to indicate his delight at this opportunity to hand it to the fictitious Mrs Treadwell.

Apart from Vince, the only other man present was the minister, who was there to serve as a spiritual policeman to the proceedings. Although forgiveness was the aim of them all and the order of the day, faced with so much to forgive they potentially needed someone on hand to guide them through it. The minister's presence, as it turned out, wasn't necessary. Once the cake had been snarfed and the tea drunk, Vince made his excuses and left the women to it, as all thought it best he should. His plan was to get the newspapers, and then sit in the car and catch up on the world news and the football results. But as soon as he shut the living room door, he saw Ruby sitting on the stairs.

'Do you want to see my new room, Mr Treadwell?'

The newspapers could wait. The world could wait. Even the football results could wait.

'I do, but only if you call me Vince. All my friends call me Vince.'

She offered him her hand, he took it, and she led him up to her new room, which was much the same as the old room, since all her toys had been transported from Basing Street to Chesterton Road. Vince got on his knees with Ruby, and she went through the names and history of each doll, teddy bear and toy in the room. All apart from one, a blonde Barbie doll in a red plastic raincoat with a matching peak cap. She sat in a moulded red plastic MG sports car with a white interior. It looked brand new, untouched and expensive. When Vince asked Ruby about the Barbie, the little girl's head dipped and Vince realized something was wrong. He put the tip of his forefinger on to her chin, and raised her head, to reveal eyes glazed over with a sheen of tears.

'Who gave you this doll, Ruby?'

Her hand shot up and swept his finger away from her chin.

'You can tell me,' he assured her.

After a protracted pause, she leaned forward and cupped her hand against his ear and whispered . . .

CHAPTER 47

Vince got into the Mk II and retrieved the Colt .38 that he'd taped under the driver's seat, and tucked it into his waistband. The switchblade hidden in the glove compartment he slipped into his jacket pocket. Tooled up, he got out of the car again and slammed the door shut. He wanted to run but held back, taking a calming breath. He knew he'd be needing all his strength and all his restraint as he strode towards the Portobello Road.

Midday Sunday, he was hoping to find Tyrell Lightly standing outside one of the pubs with his cohorts, shooting the shit and watching over their corners, as they were wont to do. Or even spot a Brother X, not that he expected too much from them, but the word that Vince was after Tyrell Lightly might have filtered back and flushed him out. In Finches bar it was the usual lazy Sunday afternoon crowd. But then, the place was full of the usual lazy Sunday afternoon crowd on any day of the week. Knots of men stood there nattering away about nothing in particular, while hangovers were getting the hair of the dog, darts were getting thrown and time was getting wasted until lunch was served.

Vince headed on down Oxford Gardens to Michael X's head-quarters. The one-stop community shop that advertised itself as being open twenty-four hours a day was closed. Vince rang the bell, banged on the door, called through the letter box and got no response. He thought he saw brief movement from behind one of the curtains covering the windows, and he could have sworn he glimpsed a sudden fleeting eclipse when he peered through the spyhole in the door. But if anyone was in, they weren't answering.

He then did the rounds of known haunts and hangouts, just like he had done when he first went in search of Tyrell Lightly. The drinking club in Powis Square, where he'd last located Lightly, had been closed down and a For Sale sign was now attached to a pillar of the portico. Vince headed down to Westbourne Grove to the Calypso club and the Fiesta. Business there was brisk, but again no Tyrell Lightly. History repeated itself, unsurprisingly: the daily grind of criminality in most cities is all about history repeating itself. The quest for the quick and illicit pound could be as dull as the dullest nine-to-five – just with longer hours. So it wasn't such a surprise to find the drug dealer Vivian Chalcott plotted up in the Walmer Castle, sitting in a snug, on his own, reading the papers, and minding his own damn business with a pint of Guinness patiently losing its head before him.

Vince stood over him, casting a long and impatient shadow, till Chalcott lowered his paper and peered up with alarmed eyes, a glistening white foamy moustache covering his thin bristly moustache like a morning frost. His business today was no longer his own, and he knew it.

'Tyrell Lightly. I need him, Vivian. And need him now.'

The Cellar Door was an aptly named one-room drinker with a pool table, and was situated in the cellar of a second-hand furniture shop on the Golborne Road. Vivian Chalcott had given up Tyrell Lightly, again, without too much of a fuss. He didn't like Lightly. He'd heard the rumours about his predilections, and Vince now confirmed them. Vivian told him the news that Tyrell Lightly was out of favour with Michael and the Brothers X. He was back in his pimp gear and no longer wearing the uniform of X. Vivian put it down to Lightly holding out on some deals, cutting up rough with the whores, trying to carve out some business of his own and generally rude-boying his way all over town and pulling cowboy stuff as if he was still back in the yards of Trenchtown.

So here Vince was, descending the steep rickety cellar stairs leading into the Cellar Door club, while listening out for the voice of Tyrell Lightly, or at least the mention of his name, amid the bar-room chatter and West Indian patois that blended so effortlessly with the chinking of the glasses and the potting of pool balls. As Vince reached the foot of the stairs, if there had been a piano in the place it would have stopped playing. All eyes were fixed on him; Vince counted about ten pairs of them. Someone uttered a heavily question-marked 'Pig?'. Vince was hearing that word a lot lately.

Two fellows playing pool moved in front of him, blocking his view. They looked as if they'd been living in the place all their lives, seldom coming up for air. Behind them, Vince heard the unnerving click of pool balls, knowing full well that three of them swung around inside a sock could do a lot of damage.

Beyond the pair of pool players, a door creaked, and he was sure someone had slipped out of the place. There was music playing on a transistor radio, something chirpy and innocuous by the Dave Clark Five. It got turned up full pelt and soon became oppressive white noise. And, as if on cue, the pool cues that the two players wielded for sport were now gripped to inflict violence.

The player prodded the tip of his cue into Vince's chest and asked, 'The fuck d'you want, white boy?'

Vince looked down at the little round blue chalk mark on his shirt. The player prodded Vince again in the chest, and this time the chalk mark appeared on the narrow strip of his black knitted tie. It looked as though the pool player intended to make a habit of this and turn Vince's shirt and tie into a matching polka-dot ensemble. Men were now laughing. It was clearly an appreciative audience. Encouraged, the pool player cued up again for another shot at Vince's chest. Vince's forearm shot up and carved the pool cue away with a circular sweep. By the time his hand had returned home he was holding the .38 snub-nosed revolver, which he stuck into the chest of the pool player. Realizing that little blue chalk marks were soon going to be replaced by big red bullet holes, the player dropped the pool cue to the floor. His partner followed suit.

Vince pulled the gun out of the pool player's chest, took aim and fired a shot into the radio on the bar. The white noise died and the radio toppled off the counter. At this, there was some sucking of teeth, some muttered curses, but otherwise muted resignation ruled the roost. A gun going off in a joint like this wasn't such a shock to the system; a poetry recital going off would have produced a more startled reaction. Vince then barked out simple instructions to these occupants of planet shit-hole: 'Get the fuck out of here and close the cellar door behind you!'

There was no immediate movement, just a bristling silence as everyone considered and weighed up the white boy (with the gun) in the room. Were they really going to stand for this in their own back yard? This moody-looking malcontent coming in for one of their own? These fleeting thoughts, these crossings of minds, didn't last that long, and certainly not long enough for Vince to feel the need to repeat his instruction. Even with the maths stacked up against him, the .38 was always going to be the great equalizer in this equation. For those gathered in the Cellar Door, it was turning into a no-brainer. Maybe it was something in the intruder's eyes, the bloody-minded intent evident there, but he certainly looked as though he'd take out at least three of them before they got near to him. There were no volunteers to be those first three. So the bottles and glasses that were about to be hurled at Vince were now put on the bar, pool balls were put back on the table, knives being thumbed in pockets were left safely sheathed. And up the stairs and out the cellar door they all trooped, the .38 tracking their movements every step of the way.

Vince then darted up the stairs and shifted the heavy bolt on the door securely into place. He knew he had to work fast, for they'd be back, bigger, uglier, angrier. And he knew that a gun set firmly against Lightly's head would be his passport out of there.

347

Without its occupants, Vince got the true hellishness of the place. It was a brick cellar, with the walls painted a dull rusty red. Everything was painted this colour, including all the furniture, which looked like all the stuff they couldn't sell in the second-hand shop upstairs. At one end of the room was the bar, and to the side of that bar was a door, which looked uncharacteristically closed. Vince had never been in this dive before but he'd have betted pound notes for peanuts that this door was usually left ajar. He went over and opened it with ease.

There was a bare brick passageway beyond, and Vince moved through it with the gun extended before him. To the left was another door, half open, exposing a toxic-looking toilet for catching dysentery on, and a small handbasin for contracting leprosy in. He moved further down the passageway that seemed to be looming into the black hole of a tunnel. Never a big fan of dark enclosed spaces that hid people who potentially wanted to kill you, as he edged forward his footsteps got increasingly timid. Further in, and the solid block of blackness ahead of him beat against his eyes. He half expected to hear a whistle and then see the bright headlights of a train getting bigger and bigger as it hurtled towards him.

He gingerly tapped away with his foot as if he might be at the edge of a precipice. He then felt a drop of a good . . . couple of inches, and stepped down into what he thought must be the widening expanse of another room beyond. Vince's eyes adjusted enough for him to get some vague sense of his surroundings. His hand groped the wall alongside the entrance to this new room, and, on the black coalface it resembled, he struck gold – the light switch.

On the throwing of the switch he was faced with a wall of furniture. Stacks of chairs and tables and cupboards and wardrobes and filing cabinets, all piled up almost to the ceiling. This was obviously a storage room, or a burial ground, for the shop upstairs: a final resting place for all the old crap they couldn't sell. And somewhere amid its wreckage, Vince reckoned, was Tyrell Lightly.

A nice little hiding place, a needle in a haystack. Vince cocked the .38.

'There's only one way out, Lightly, so let's get it over and done with, eh?'

Vince thought he heard the creak of wood nearby, something moving about, and it wasn't woodworm. But he didn't hear the words *I surrender* or see a white flag poking out from the top of the pile of furniture. So he took aim and sank his first slug into the centre of the heap. The shot echoed around the cavernous room.

'Coming out now?'

It wasn't so much a creak from the pile of furniture this time, more of a groan, as though it was a big sentient creature and Vince had just shot it in the gut. And there was movement too. He detected a slight swaying at the peak. But not so much as a squeak emerged from the real living organism hidden in its bowels.

Two more shots: one to the left of centre, one to the right. More groans from the woodpile that was now visibly shaking, and looked for all the world as if it had had enough and was about to up sticks and march on out of the place. But it wasn't just the furniture that was making noises now. There was heavy breathing, then panting like a dog, a whinnying sound that grew and grew until it could be held no more and burst forth into a full-throttled cry of pain.

Then the furniture pile that had taken three slugs finally collapsed and came crashing down. Vince's first reaction was to dive to the ground and make himself as small as possible as the whole shebang came tumbling down. It sounded a lot worse than it was, and he felt the first few bumps, but nothing major. It was like diving under the weight of a crashing wave, where all the mayhem was above.

But he did feel the footfalls of someone scampering over him. And he did feel a warm liquid drip down on to his cheek. He climbed out of the pile.

Once the dust had settled – and there was dust, eye-clogging, choking and coughing spitfuls of the stuff – he saw that the gun was no longer in his hand and Tyrell Lightly was no longer in the room. And there was a banging noise from outside – the sound of the cellar door being kicked in.

Vince made his way back through the darkness of the tunnel and into the light of the club itself. There were shiny studs of fresh blood against the dull red of the floor. He saw Tyrell Lightly crawling up the stairs. His eyes were wide open, his mouth was gaping, his nostrils flared, the combination forming perfectly rounded circles all over his face. His expression was that of a contortionist trying to turn his face inside out. And Vince saw why, and winced himself, for the bullet wound was located around the man's crutch.

Tyrell Lightly was already halfway up the stairs as Vince grabbed him by the scruff of his purple velvet collar. He was about to drag him downstairs and throw him on to the pool table when the door burst open and half a ton of Brother Xs appeared at the entrance.

Michael X surveyed the scene, and saw Vince with his hands round the throat of Tyrell Lightly. Vince shook his head, because the scenario all seemed dreadfully familiar. He was half expecting to see the big black hooker rise up from the floor and smack him right in the mouth. It never happened.

Instead, Michael X added a new twist, by producing a sawn-off shotgun from the inside of his black leather coat. Then, without ceremony or commentary, he took aim and fired off a shot.

CHAPTER 48

With a clothes brush in his hand, Vince stood before a full-length mirror in his bedroom, giving the pitch-black dinner jacket he was wearing the once-over. He looked the part, although he wasn't certain what the part would be. But he knew it was his last roll of the dice, as far as this case was concerned, and he couldn't think of a more apt place to roll it in than at the Montcler club.

When the intercom buzzed, he looked at his watch and saw that his 'date' was an hour early. No date in the history of the world has ever been *an hour* early. It was Mac, though, and Vince buzzed him up. Then he paced the hallway, waiting. It wasn't like Mac to pay social calls on a Saturday night, and he'd never even been to his flat. When they did meet up outside office hours, it was usually somewhere neutral like the pub. But Vince had to remind himself that, now he was a civilian, the normal rules didn't apply.

Mac looked grave. He did grave very well. With his pipe in his mouth, his penchant for grey flannel and the monochrome professorial look, he always had that air of late forties post-war austerity about him. He was definitely pre-rock and roll. There were no colourful frivolities about him, and he looked especially pre-Elvis tonight. He turned down the offer of a drink, and even of having his coat taken, and headed straight into the living room. There he did the very thing that Vince had been doing before he answered the door – he paced. Mac paced like a pro. There was a real determination in his pacing that made Vince look like a dilettante. He paced up and down on the Moroccan rug in the middle of the room. Vince feared for its voluptuous nap, which looked as if it was going to be trodden into the ground and reduced to tarmac.

'What's wrong, Mac?'

'Two days ago a body was found on the sidings of the railway tracks going up to Wembley Central. Cause of death was immolation, they think.'

'Wouldn't they know for sure?'

'The body was in a sack, and burned almost to a cinder. But there were puncture marks and deep cuts all over him. He was partially flayed, and he'd been castrated. Buckshot was found in his lower abdomen. Any one of those injuries could have killed him.'

'Dental records?'

'Very distinctive. Half his teeth had been removed. Worth their weight in gold if you get my drift?'

Vince got his drift, but still wasn't volunteering. He looked at Mac with a gaze open to interpretation. Sort of blank, sort of knowing, sort of goading.

Mac got the goading part loud and clear, and said: 'Last Sunday you were spotted in Notting Hill, running all over the place asking for Tyrell Lightly. You own a Colt .38?'

Dry as you like, Vince responded, 'Give me a minute and I'll check my receipts. Why do you ask?'

'Because, along with all the other possible causes of death, they found a .38 slug in him.'

'You think I did that, Mac?'

'I think *someone* did. And I think you know who.'

Vince shot back with: 'So I'm an accessory to torturing and murder?'

'Well, let's put it this way, I think you know a lot more about it than me and the rest of the *chumps* down in Scotland Yard.'

And Vince did. A lot more.

Michael X had taken aim. His target was laid out for him: the expanding mass of red oozing from Tyrell Lightly's crutch area. And by the time Michael X had aimed the gun, Vince was pretty much using Lightly as a human shield. A cowardly act? The only other option was to put himself in front of Lightly, thus well and truly in the line of fire. You got medals for that kind of bravery, and one day Vince would like to step up on the podium and collect one. It's what coppers dreamed of, it's what most decent-minded people dreamed of, doing the right thing and getting a medal pinned on your chest for doing it. But not for Tyrell Lightly.

In the split seconds he had available, Vince had weighed it up and made a judgement call; and there was no way in the wide, wide world of unlikely scenarios that he was ever going to take a bullet for that lowlife. Vince was then pushed out of the way as about ten of the Brothers X clambered down the stairs and proceeded to jump all over Tyrell Lightly. When he was sufficiently flattened, they scraped the battered bantamweight gangster off the floor and on to the pool table. A blue-baize pool table that was about to run red and become an operating table. Already Tyrell Lightly looked as if he'd just had a bucket of blood and offal dropped into his lap. It was only after Michael X had taken off his leather jacket and rolled up his sleeves and had the thin paring knife in his hand that he remembered he was in the presence of one of Her Majesty's police officers. Michael X said something about protecting his people and dispensing justice.

Vince looked at the butchery on the pool table (true to the rules of 8-ball, Michael X nominated the pockets they'd be going in) and realized it was too late to save Tyrell Lightly. His quick little eyes were already glazing over with death. A death Vince knew deep down he was complicit in; a death he had let them get on with. And, more importantly, a death he didn't think would be discovered. *Fuck*! Just why the Morons X decided to leave the body to be discovered on a railway siding was anyone's guess . . .

'I don't know who did it, Mac.'

Mac expelled, even for him, a ludicrously protracted 'Mmmmmm' before he said, 'I wish you'd given that a little more thought before you answered. Because right now it doesn't feel like I'm talking to a colleague. A partner. Or even a detective in the Metropolitan Police Force.'

'Right now I don't have a badge.'

'You forced their hand, and you know it.'

There was a pause as Vince searched for an argument. But what was the point? He knew that Mac knew it as well as he did, so he let the silence serve its purpose.

Mac said, 'You can get the badge back. It's not over.'

'So what do *they* want?'

'They want Michael de Freitas. All this Malcolm X Black Power stuff getting exported from across the pond is making people nervous. To them it stinks of communism.'

'Revolution?' said Vince, with a snort of derision. 'Come on, Mac, Mikey de Freitas, whatever he chooses to call himself, is no Malcolm X. And even if he was, look what happened to *him*. What killed Tyrell Lightly was good old-fashioned gangster stuff. I heard Lightly was going it alone. He got sick of taking orders off Michael X and dressing up like a boy scout. He wanted to wear his flash suits, deal his own drugs and cut up hookers. He paid the price.'

'Any other rumours about him?

'That's all I heard.'

'You heard a lot. What were you doing in Notting Hill last Sunday, anyway?'

'Isabel Saxmore-Blaine wanted to contact Cecilia Jones. Her family wants to make reparations to the Jones family.'

'Throw some money at them, eh?'

'What's more crass, Mac, for them to do that or for them not to do that?'

'Why come to you? Isabel Saxmore-Blaine's father is in good with the Commissioner. I'm sure the correct arrangements could have been made.' But before Vince could answer, Mac expelled a protracted 'Ahhh' of enlightenment. He then looked Vince up and down, as if noticing him in the dinner jacket for the first time. 'Going up in the world, Vincent. You weren't kidding, were you?'

'About what?'

'Eaton Square. When you first copped an eyeful of Beresford's house. You said you'd marry into money and—'

'And you'd be my butler? Yeah, I remember.'

'And now you're all dressed up and doing the town. Maybe you're more suited to that lifestyle than being a copper? A good-looking, smart young feller like you gets plenty of opportunities, so be a fool not to take them, no? Maybe I'll read all about it in the society pages.'

Vince didn't answer. Instead he watched as Mac's eyes narrowed on him. It was a look of reappraisal and the eyeing up of a potential new adversary. It made Vince feel sick.

'You didn't tell me where you're going tonight, Vincent?'

'No, I didn't.'

'I'll see myself out.'

Once Mac was gone, Vince took his place on the Moroccan rug for some pacing. Exhausted, he then slumped down on the sofa, hands in pockets. He felt a growing sense of unease after the older detective's visit. The easy friendship that had always passed between them had ebbed and flowed, but on the whole it was a constant. It was a back covered, a hand given, a trust upheld. It was built on solid mutual respect. And now it seemed fraught with betrayal and secrets and lies.

The phone rang.

'Are you ready?'

'I'm ready.'

CHAPTER 49

The Montcler Ball, held for its members and their guests, was only in its second year but had already established itself as the hottest ticket in town. And one of the most expensive. All the proceeds went to charity, a charity of James Asprey's choosing. The charity benefiting this year, as indeed it did last year, was a wildlife fund and game reserve in Africa that was devoted to the conservation of rare breeds. The reserve was also contractually obligated to provide Asprey's private zoo with healthy animals. For Asprey, charity began at home. When a society journalist had noted that the Montcler Ball's charitable donations revolved around Asprey's interest in stocking his zoo, the scribe got sent a yak turd through the post.

Vince picked Isabel up, and off to the ball they went. She wasn't wearing a normal ball gown, because this wasn't a normal ball. It was a fancy-dress and masked ball. The ladies especially were encouraged to be inventive, and the fanciest-dressed of them would receive a prize. The theme was beasts of the fields and birds of the sky. Last year the theme had been pirates. Asprey loved pirates almost as much as he loved animals. He saw an affinity with his set and the likes of Blackbeard, Captain Kidd and Henry Morgan. High-risk buccaneering business types. Vince thought the affinity was tenuous, since asset-stripping was hardly the same as swinging through the yardarm with a cutlass gripped in your teeth. And Isabel dismissed it altogether as a tiresome conceit since, compared to Vince's profession, and his penchant for punching people and kicking down doors, they were mostly overindulged pussycats. Vince took the backhanded compliment in good grace.

And, talking of pussycats, Isabel had of course come dressed as one. In an all-in-one black satin catsuit, with thigh-high patent-leather boots fitted with a spiked contortionist's heel that elevated her to a good six foot. She wore an elaborate hooded cowl over her head with pointed pussycat ears. Her lips were painted a deep and bloody red. Her nails had been dipped in the same bloody colour, which gave the effect that she had just feasted and left the butchered carcass lying on the green of Berkeley Square.

Vince's mask was that of a wolf. He'd wanted a monkey mask to go with the monkey suit, but it was Isabel who had picked it, since she considered Vince to be the archetypal wolf at the door. Although he could just as well have been an albatross. Either way, a masked ball was, quite literally, the perfect cover. Because there was no other way Vince and Isabel would have gained entry into the club. The only reason she had the invites tucked in her black patent-leather clutch bag was because it wasn't her name on the card. It was the name of an acquaintance: a female acquaintance who hated Asprey (although *he* didn't know it, because *she* had kept it secret), and had been surreptitiously looking for a way to bring scandal, or worse, to his door ever since her father had lost everything at Asprey's gaming tables. So when Isabel explained the situation and her intentions, the woman was more than happy to give up her ticket.

Since Beresford's funeral, the remaining Montcler set had laid low. James Asprey himself had been in Africa setting up his wildlife foundation and collecting animals for his expanding zoo. Simon Goldsachs had been spending time between his home in Paris and his newly furbished apartment in New York (Goldsachs was keen to conquer America and had been making his presence felt on Wall Street; he'd already started buying up stocks of a well-known tyre company and had consequently found himself seated before a Senate committee looking into his 'hostile' practices). Lord Lucan, in light of his involvement in the case, had for once warranted his nickname and been lucky enough to escape a public scandal, but privately was said to be desperately trying to keep hold of his marriage and his money, both of which meant staying away from the gaming tables. Guy Ruley was said to be relocating his engineering and other business interests abroad, and selling up his country pile in Buckinghamshire.

But, for Vince, the most important member of the set would be there tonight: Nicky DeVane. On a photo assignment for *Vogue* magazine on the private Caribbean island of Mustique, and still reeling from the scandal, he had decided to stay there until things had cooled down. And now he was back, lured by an invite to the Montcler masked ball. DeVane, who was still labouring under the delusion that his friendship with Isabel was a cloudless one, had called her to say that he was back in town. She had then called Vince. She didn't view this as a betrayal of her old best friend, because she no longer considered Nicky DeVane as her old best friend. After meeting up with Cecilia Jones and the good women of the congregation of St James's, things had changed in her world. They had offered forgiveness not only for her but also for her brother. It was a generosity of spirit that had shone an uncompromising light over her life and all those who inhabited it.

And Vince, in keeping with the wild animal theme of the party, had already identified Nicky DeVane as the runt of the Montcler litter. And in a move that James Asprey would himself have fully understood and appreciated, Vince intended to stalk him, separate him from the pack, and then pick him off.

Arriving at the Berkeley Square building, the animals came into the Montcler club two by two. They were the finest, strongest, noblest of their breed. Whilst the wolf mask completely covered the top half of his face, Vince had never held much faith in disguises. Masks might work in comic books, but Vince reckoned that Leonard, the perennially dinner-jacketed gatekeeper of the Montcler, didn't bother to read comic books. He read cards and rolls of the dice, he read eyes, twitches, tics, demeanours and the signs on people's faces, and he'd have seen through their disguises in a hot second. So they avoided Leonard and went down to the basement entrance of Jezebel's, where tickets were taken with a less suspicious scrutiny.

Vince and Isabel had a quick prowl around the nightclub. The fancy-dress party was in full swing down there, too. Most of the men's outfits were monkey suits and masks – tigers, lions, gorillas, and more tigers, more lions. All big cats and primate alpha kings. Let's face it, no one wanted to turn up as a gazelle or a wildebeest – which was just asking for trouble. But if Isabel thought she was going to waltz off with first prize, she was in for some stiff competition – it was a jungle out there. And it provided the perfect opportunity for the ladies to get out their furs, furs of every description: the A to Z of alpaca to zebra – and not forgetting the 101 dalmatians. And if they weren't in furs, they were in a full plumage of feathers: Day-Glo birds of paradise, petrol-blue preening peacocks, black and white penguins. Isabel sniffed around the place, but couldn't sniff out the scent of Nicky DeVane and the rest of his pack. So Vince and Isabel made their way over to the cast-iron spiral stairs situated behind the ladies' cloakroom that linked Jezebel's nightclub to the gambling club upstairs.

It was more of the same upstairs – *lots* more. The waiters were all black guys dressed up as Zulu warriors. So authentically were their costumes and so warrior-like was their demeanour that, when Vince swiped a glass of champagne for Isabel off one of them and asked where he was from, he was surprised to hear, in dulcet tones, that he hailed from Tulse Hill.

In the grand saloon, a fifteen-piece band played swing and hotsy-totsy jazz tunes, with a line of bongo players in the front row beating out a jungle rhythm. The few men who had broken ranks with the monkey suits were all wearing Safari khakis and pith helmets. Vince half expected to see a Berkeley Square beefcake in a skimpy Johnny Weissmuller chamois loincloth. Or maybe, he thought, that was to be James Asprey's big entrance: the ape man – the great white king of the jungle, swinging in on a vine from the balcony. Nothing doing. Not even a Doctor Dolittle.

At a squeeze on his shoulder, he glanced round to see Isabel poised at his side. She was just so implausibly and off-the-scale sexy that, whatever the outcome of tonight, kitted up in that outfit, this evening was never going to be a waste of time. It would always be eminently memorable, and something to play back in his mind on those cold and lonely nights.

'Nicky's here,' she purred in his ear. She directed Vince's gaze towards the entrance, and there he was, flanked by the two models Vince had seen him with the first time he'd visited the Beak Street studio. Isabel explained how they were always on show when Nicky DeVane wanted to attend an event and impress others. The taller the better, and one on each arm, to bookend the dapper snapper. He suited the sobriquet tonight, garbed up to the nines in a gold lamé suit with black leopard spots expertly stitched on to it and trimmed with ocelot fur – as was the mask he was wearing.

His Praetorian guard of praying-mantis models, with their bulging eyes and stick-thin elongated limbs, were not however dressed as predatory insects. They too were both on the feline fancy-dress tip: one-piece catsuits, just like Isabel. Vince saw Isabel's fur bristle at the sight of them, as if her claws were drawn. But, as far as he was concerned, it was no contest. Isabel had the curves, while they just looked like a pair of mangy moggies in desperate need of a good feed.

Vince and Isabel kept their distance and watched as DeVane launched himself into the room on a propellant of privilege and gleaming bon-vivant confidence. He went about doing the rounds of hail-fellow-well-met handshakes and noisy theatrical kisses. But Vince noted that the reception he was getting was somewhat cool, and his mask may have been slipping. A couple of feathered birds DeVane clearly knew flew right past him without offering him a peck. A pride of lions gave him a swerve when he offered his paw. Vince then saw the unmistakable white dinner jacket of Leonard approach DeVane, who was by now looking uncertain and diffident. Leonard didn't assuage his fears. Wearing a simple and skimpy Zorro-esque black mask, and looking more like a bank robber than a masked-baller, the professional meeter and greeter glared at the little guy in the lamé suit, and crooked a finger indicating for him to follow. The blood drained from DeVane's face. He made his excuses to the two models, and trailed off after Leonard up the grand staircase.

Vince said to Isabel, 'Why don't you go down to Jezebel's, and I'll meet you there later?'

'Do I have to? I'm rather enjoying this. I'm imagining we're Nick and Nora Charles.'

'Not in that rig, you're not. One of the points of going undercover is not to be noticed, and you're far too eye-catching for that.'

It was true, everyone was looking at her. All the men thought they recognized her, because all the men *did* recognize her. The fantasy life and sexual ideals of most men is a pretty slim volume, and Isabel Saxmore-Blaine, in a skin-tight catsuit and thigh-high boots, pretty much ticked most of the boxes most of the time. So, without complaint or question, puss-in-boots-galore high-tailed it back down the spiral staircase to Jezebel's nightclub.

Vince followed the gold lamé suit up the stairs to the top floor, where Asprey had his office. Also located on this floor were the 'drawing rooms' for the more private games, away from the constant call of *card* and *banque*, and the chatter of the shoe being passed and chips being thrown in.

Vince sat down in one of the wing-backed green leather armchairs by the fireplace, where it provided him with a view of Asprey's office. On the table in front of him was a pack of cards and an impressive-looking backgammon set inlaid with fruitwoods and ebony. Vince looked around the room, noticing every table had the same set-up. There was no such thing here as a quiet break away from the gaming tables, because every flat surface was a potential gaming table, ready to snaffle you up in adrenalin and debt.

Leonard had sat DeVane down at one of the three chairs gathered around a card table positioned in the antechamber just before Asprey's office. DeVane was left there for a full ten minutes. As anxious and antsy as he looked, he didn't get up to have a pace about, or even fetch himself a stiff drink. He obediently sat at the table, contrite and consumed with anxiety, like a naughty schoolboy who had been told to wait outside the headmaster's door until a fitting punishment could be thought of and meted out.

'Fancy a game, old boy?'

Vince realized an old silverback gorilla had just sat down opposite him. He weighed about 300 lb, was put together like a sumo, and huffed and puffed as he laid out the backgammon board in front of him.

'Of course, no gambling tonight. Aspers is quite insistent. And if Aspers insists, we merely follow.'

Vince recognized this old silverback gorilla. The full-face furry gorilla mask he was wearing was now pulled up to his forehead, exposing the jowly countenance and whisky-river proboscis of Sir Peter Benson, the newspaper proprietor.

'But what do you say to a pound a point, just for some interest? Sod the monkeys and lions! I puts me money on the human race when it comes to charitable causes.'

'Why not,' said Vince with a wolfish grin. Not much of a backgammon player, just like he wasn't much of a chess player. Steeped in philosophical and war-like strategic ponderings as the games were, he held them in much the same regard as he did snakes and ladders. What attracted Vince to this game was the fact that the old Fleet Street gorilla provided him with perfect cover. He just hoped that whatever happened would happen fast, for the silverback was a sedentary old beast who looked as though he could hardly put one gout-ridden foot in front of the other, but could move around a backgammon board in a fashion as swift and assured as a chimp up a tree. No sooner was the board laid out than one of the Montcler's liveried footmen was at Sir Peter's elbow, brimming his crystal tumbler with something aged and alcoholic from a silver-cuffed decanter. Sir Peter took it upon himself to start the game. He threw a three and a six.

Vince's peripheral vision was taken up by what was going on in the antechamber. Two men had now come through. They weren't wearing masks. They were wearing scowls. James Asprey and Simon Goldsachs.

The silverback threw a five and a four.

Asprey and Goldsachs sat down at the table opposite DeVane, and well and truly faced him down. Vince watched as the photographer's slight frame got smaller and smaller in his chair, squirming, diminishing. You didn't need to be a lip-reader to work out that DeVane was getting it in the ear, up the arse and just about in every other available orifice. And, all the time, James Asprey and Simon Goldsachs were taking turns to speak. And as one spoke, the other held DeVane gripped in a commanding glare. Vince was reminded of the interrogating double act of Philly Jacket and Kenny Block, a formidable pair who had it down cold. He was then reminded of the two mackintosh men, another cold and deadly double act. It seemed bad news was travelling in twos these days.

Asprey was a study of invariable disdain, measured and systematic. As his wide mouth let forth a calm yet sustained torrent of abuse, the rest of him remained coldly and pitilessly unmoved by the obvious distress he was causing DeVane. It was like watching the autopsy of a lifeless corpse slowly being taken apart limb by limb, organ by organ, dissected and discarded. And when Asprey's deliberating and detached beasting had abated, there was no respite for the dapper snapper in the gold lamé suit that must have now seemed about as cool as a clown's outfit.

The silverback told Vince to pay attention. He threw a one and a three, and cursed.

Goldsachs then took over. And it was a hostile takeover. It was a different approach from Asprey's. Goldsachs got right in DeVane's face: leaning across the table, he looked as if he was going to eat him. But it was those eyes that did it for him, those terrible eyes emitting tractor beams of indignant disgust. Goldsachs finally waved him away with a dismissive hand as though he was swatting a fly from a sandwich.

The silverback roared. Something had happened in the game that he was very pleased about. Vince looked pleased for him, too, although he had absolutely no idea what had happened because he wasn't paying the slightest bit of attention.

He turned quickly to see the hot glow of Nicky DeVane's lamé suit making its way out of the drawing room. Vince stood up.

'What's going on?' asked the old silverback.

'Sorry, Sir Peter, nature calls. And much as I'd like to cock a leg and take a piss on the carpet, this is only fancy dress.'

Sir Peter chuckled heartily. 'Oh, yes. Rather! Rather!'

Vince picked up the pack of Montcler playing cards from the table and pocketed it. He then followed DeVane as he proceeded down the stairs, shakily, as if he'd aged fifty years in five minutes. Without picking up his two models, who were now in conversation with a couple of horned rhinos, he then headed for the spiral stairs that connected the Montcler to Jezebel's.

Vince followed. He didn't need to keep a distance, because DeVane was preoccupied, and mortified, and clearly everything was just a sickening blur to him. Once downstairs, he headed straight for the bar and took up residence on a stool, ordering up a cocktail called a Long Island ice tea. Vince watched as the bottle-spinning barman created this highball of hard liquor: rum, gin, vodka and tequila all went into the mix.

'Poor Nicky,' said Isabel. 'He looks like a man whose world has just caved in on him, and he's been pulled out from under the wreckage and given a blood transfusion – but they forgot to put any fresh blood back in.'

Vince agreed. They were seated on a couch that had a clear view of DeVane propped at the bar. Vince had already told her what happened upstairs, and Isabel had described it as a 'mobbing up'. In light of what he'd witnessed, it didn't need that much explaining, but explain it she did. 'It's an Eton term. It's what happens at school when your friends decide to turn on you.'

Vince reached into his jacket pocket and took out the pack of cards, broke the seal and took the cards out. They were the same as any other pack of cards, just customized with the Montcler seal and house colours on the back: red and green. And with something else that set them apart, made them just that tad more classy, that little more special. The cards had a gilded edge, so when piled up and viewed from the side they looked like a little block of gold, like an ingot. Vince allowed himself a cautious smile at this observation.

'What are you doing?' she asked.

'Playing patience.'

They didn't have to be that patient, as Nicky DeVane wasn't nibbling his drinks; he was sucking them down. He was now on his fourth highball of the powerful firewater that was meekly, and misguidedly, called a Long Island ice tea. The inhabitants of Long Island must have been a pretty raucous crowd, making Vince wonder what they put in their morning coffee: nitro-glycerine and TNT?

At the bar, Nicky DeVane began to talk. Loudly. And the talk was of James Asprey and Simon Goldsachs. Before long, DeVane was up on his feet, digging in his heels, and complaining to all those around him about his treatment at the hands of those bastards. Who the hell did they think they were? DeVane made it clear that he knew things, he knew things about them, things that could bring them to their knees! The bartender attempted a quiet word with him, but DeVane volleyed with some more loud ones. The bartender put through a call.

Within minutes, Leonard was down from the gaming club and at DeVane's elbow, an elbow that was still hoisting more booze down his throat. He told DeVane that he had to leave the club, and he had to leave now. A taxi was waiting to take him home.

Vince reached into his pocket and pulled out his keys and handed them to Isabel. 'I'll meet you back at my place.'

'Where are you going?'

Vince nodded towards DeVane, whose tight little frame was surging upwards with rage and remonstrating with pointed fingers at the dead-eyed, immovable, implacable Leonard.

Isabel looked at her old friend, with his booze-mad eyes and his angry spittle-propellant of a mouth, and got the message. If she felt any pity for him, she wasn't showing it. She was all business and on with the programme. She took the keys, collected her coat from the cloakroom, and left the club as stealthily as a cat slipping out the kitchen door.

Nicky DeVane was meanwhile being ejected from the club by Leonard, and Vince followed. As he stepped out from under the club's striped canopy, he saw Nicky DeVane negotiate both the kerb and the waiting cab. Leonard stood watching too, and the two men glanced at each other. Vince could almost hear him wondering, *Who is that masked man?*

Then Leonard's cold eyes caught fire and he said: 'Goodnight, Detective Treadwell.'

'Goodnight, Leonard.'

Leonard, no doubt in a hurry now to inform his superiors about-faced and went back into the club. Vince made his way over to DeVane, who was just about to close the cab door when Vince jumped into the taxi beside him.

'Shift up, Nicky,' he said to DeVane with the reassuring conviviality of an old friend. And, in the conspiratorial tone of a kidnapper, he instructed the taxi driver: 'The Criterion.'

'Good idea!' said DeVane. 'I could use a drink!'

'I'm right ahead of you, Nicky.'

'Who are you? The big bad wolf? Well, I'm no little Red Riding Hood – or the three little piggies for that matter, or . . . Who are . . .' Vince then took off his mask. 'Ah, the detective. I've got some bloody stories to tell you!'

Vince smiled. 'Again, Nicky, I'm right ahead of you.'

CHAPTER 50

The bar of the Criterion International Hotel was big, badly lit, modern and very anonymous. If there were other people in it, they didn't register any more than the plastic palms, the innocuous piped lounge music or the velour décor. Once seated at the long bar, DeVane ordered up another Long Island ice tea. Vince slipped the barman a folded five-pound note and told him to keep them coming, but keep them light on the spirits and heavy on the Coke and soda. He didn't want DeVane living up to his reputation as a lightweight and taking a nap in the bar nuts, just as he had done at the Imperial.

'Ahhhh,' Nicky said, taking his first sip as if he'd just sailed through the desert using his tongue as a rudder. 'Now, do tell me, Detective, what can I do for you?'

Vince took the pack of cards out of his pocket, split the pack and gave them an expert shuffle, folding them into each other one way, then making them arc and fold into each other the other way. He then fanned them out like a choreographed troop of Busby Berkeley dancers.

'Oh, bravo, maestro. I see you've done this before.'

'I'm not much of a card player,' said Vince. 'To be honest, I find sitting around waiting for your luck to show up rather dull. But I did learn a couple of tricks. It impresses the girls, eh, Nicky?'

'Quite so, Detective.'

'That time I went to your studio, I saw you doing a neat little card trick, too. The girls looked impressed.'

367

Nicky smiled at the thought, then quickly looked around him, as if he had mislaid something. 'Where are they?'

'The girls? You left them at the Montcler. It's okay, we don't need them now.'

DeVane discharged a town-drunk hiccup, then said, 'What on earth were *you* doing at the ball?'

'I have high friends in low places. Tell me about the card tricks you know.'

'Card tricks? I've forgotten most of them. I used to do magic at school. Never much of a lad for sports, but I was one of the youngest to gain entry into the Magic Circle. At school it was a marvellous way to avoid bullying and buggery. And, eventually, as you say, Detective, a way to get the girls. Vince, isn't it?' Vince nodded. 'May I call you . . .'

'I'd be offended if you didn't.' Vince handed him the playing cards. 'Show me a trick, Nicky.' DeVane, happy to be asked, picked up the pack of cards and gave them a confident shuffle.

Vince then said: 'Show me the trick Johnny Beresford was pulling with Billy Hill.'

On hearing this, DeVane fluffed his shuffle, and the cards cascaded from his hands and the smile fell from his face.

'I know all about Beresford and Billy Hill, and the card scam. You lied to me, Nicky. You lied to me under police questioning, which is a bit like lying under oath. You told me that you didn't know Bernie Korshank, that you'd only met him once, briefly, at the Imperial. You lied, because I know he came to your studio and you took his picture. You were so proud of your work, you even signed your name in the corner.'

DeVane looked flushed, but not in a good way. 'Yes, I'm sorry, I did know him. I met him through Johnny. Silly of me to lie, but I panicked, you see. I didn't mean to—'

'Yeah, you panicked, Nicky, because Bernie Korshank works for Billy Hill, and that puts you in the frame with him.' Vince watched as a big tear bellyflopped into DeVane's drink. He almost felt sorry for him. It was a bad night for the dapper snapper, and it was getting progressively worse. Vince felt so very sorry for him that he upped the ante. 'I spoke to Billy Hill. He came round to see me, and we chatted. Affable fellow. Even reasonable, up to a point.'

'What did he . . .'

'I know you were in on the card scam with Johnny Beresford.' Vince *didn't* know, but he suspected. But now he *did* know, because there was no denial from DeVane. 'I could haul you in right now for card cheating at the Montcler, and let's see where it leads us. You think you've been ostracized now? Wait until that shit hits the fan – and the papers.' Nicky looked up at Vince with sodden and quizzical eyes. 'I saw what happened, Nicky, with you and Asprey and Goldsachs. I saw them *mobbing up* on you.'

'I'm finished with them,' he said, sniffing back more tears. 'They can go to hell.'

'But it's not *them* you have to worry about, Nicky. It's Billy Hill.' Vince let that sink in, then watched as the anxiety and self-pity on the man's face turned into unbridled fear. 'If I put you in the frame with Billy Hill, maybe he'll dispense his own justice. He'll shut you up just like he did with Johnny Beresford.'

The tremulous voice asked, 'You think . . . Billy Hill killed . . . Johnny . . .'

Vince didn't think Billy Hill had killed Beresford, because Billy Hill told him he hadn't. And Vince had believed him. But for the purpose of turning up the heat on the already broiling DeVane, he gave as non-committal a shrug as he could muster without falling off his stool, and said, 'I'm not interested in card cheating, Nicky. It's murder I'm interested in. Always was, always will be. And I think you know more than you're telling me.'

'I know nothing.'

'I think you know *everything*. Asprey's washed his hands of you. You've been hung out to dry. But I can help you. I can keep your name out of the card cheating, and away from Billy Hill. So if you know what's good for you, you'll tell me everything. *Everything.*'

Nicky DeVane looked as drained as his glass. As one of the only two customers sitting at the long bar, Vince easily caught the attention of the complicit young barman, who was reading a copy of *Playboy* that he had stashed under the counter. Again he went in heavy on the fizz and light on the firewater. Nicky DeVane took on board some heavy slugs of his drink and, along with them, Vince's words. He knew he was backed into a corner that could potentially turn into a dead end. Because he knew Billy Hill was bad news. And now, he thought, that the news had just got worse: Billy Hill had lived up to his underworld reputation as a ruthless operator and killed Johnny Beresford. These were the thoughts running through Nicky DeVane's head, because these were the thoughts Vince had put in his head. And this is why Nicky DeVane now told Vince *everything*.

'Johnny was scared. A friend of his, Hugh McGowan, used to own the Hideaway club in Soho, until he got muscled out by two brothers from the East End. A deeply unpleasant duo. You may have heard about it?'

'Everyone heard about it, Nicky. It was in all the papers.'

'Quite so. Well, Johnny had warned Aspers that you had to be careful with these people, Billy Hill and his ilk. You couldn't just use them and discard them. It's like a Faustian pact. So, to get Billy Hill off his back, he told Aspers about a card scam he'd been working on. It was called the Gilded Edge.'

Vince picked the Montcler playing cards up off the bar and fanned them out, their gilded edges glistening under the available bar light. Nicky eyed the cards and said: 'Aspers liked the sound of it. He certainly liked it more than just giving Billy Hill money. And it was a way for them to "win" more money, which they needed.' Vince's eyebrows arched in surprise at this, and Nicky DeVane clarified. 'Things weren't as rosy in the garden as they seemed. Johnny's luck in business had soured some time ago, and he had recently taken some heavy losses in certain big investments. And Aspers had sunk a fortune into turning a country pile he'd bought in Canterbury into a private zoo. He used to joke that feeding monkeys doesn't cost peanuts. So they could both do with the money.'

'And not forgetting greed.'

'Quite so,' conceded DeVane. 'Anyway, Aspers gave the go-ahead, but he laid down the ground rules. They were only to cheat certain players, obviously ones that they didn't care too much about. And if they got rumbled, well, one of them would have to take the fall. And that *one* was to be Johnny, since Aspers would plead total innocence and ignorance of the matter. He wouldn't know a thing about it. Fair dos, thought Johnny, what good would it do to drop them both in it?'

'What indeed,' deadpanned Vince. 'So what was your part in it, Nicky?'

'For the scam to work, Johnny needed someone else to go along with it and read the cards with him, and share the luck, as it were. To be honest, Vince, me and Johnny had been rigging games and cheating at cards since Eton. We used to subtly bend the corners of the pack: a high-value card would be bent upwards, low-value downwards. It was an old magician's trick I learned in the Magic Circle. What you do is hold the cards lightly, and shuffle gently so as to maintain the bend at the edges. Of course, it was never guaranteed, but it gave you odds of about 60 to 65 per cent. Enough of an edge to come out on top.'

'What were the odds for the Gilded Edge?'

'Bigger and better. Johnny had twenty/twenty vision, so I'd say at least 80 per cent, maybe more. Johnny and Aspers made a lot of money that way. Certainly enough to satisfy Billy Hill with his cut.'

'And your cut?'

'I got a flat fee. When my father died, I got clobbered with death duties, and it paid those with change to spare.'

'So you, Johnny Beresford, James Asprey and Billy Hill. Who else knew about it?'

Nicky DeVane pursed his lips in a gesture of serious thought, then gravely replied, 'It was top secret. I *mean* top secret. Loose lips sinks ships, and all that. I never talked to anyone about it – not even to Johnny. We just did what we did, and he would give me an envelope with my payment once a month. Sometimes it was more than I expected, sometimes it was less, but I never questioned it either way. And I never discussed it with him, even when we were alone together. I did mention it once, in a roundabout sort of way, and Johnny gave me such a baleful look that I never mentioned it again. It was the great unsaid. If it ever got out, it could have ruined us all. Plus the fact Billy Hill was involved, so there was the added factor of fear.'

'How about Simon Goldsachs – did he need the money too?'

DeVane detected the irony in Vince's voice and replied, 'God, no. Simon's aiming to be the richest man on the planet . . . wouldn't surprise me if he gets there. But I assume that he knew. He does have a share in the Montcler, after all, and he and Aspers are as thick as thieves. As you witnessed tonight.' DeVane looked bitter, then took another swig of his drink, swilling it around like mouthwash before sucking it down. 'It was the things Simon used to say, in a roundabout sort of way, that made me think he knew all about it. Simon was always warning Aspers to be careful with his animals, saying that wild animals could never be fully tamed or trusted. But it was the way he said it, very analogous, so I always thought maybe he was referring to Billy Hill and his ilk. And if you're right about him killing Johnny, it was good advice.'

'How about the other two, Lucan and Guy Ruley?'

'Lucky?' DeVane asked, before shaking his head dismissively. 'As you know yourself, he's far too unbalanced. A degenerate addict of a gambler, so he could never be trusted.'

'Guy Ruley?'

DeVane gave a listless shrug that seemed to sum up his attitude towards Ruley, then qualified it with, 'I've never got on with Guy. Never had much to say to him. Simon Goldsachs gets on with him, respects what he does. Something in mining and engineering . . . all sounds very . . .'

'Practical? Useful?'

'Boring.'

'Ah.'

'Guy was a couple of years below Johnny and me at Eton, but I never considered him one of us. Not really.'

'Why's that? He's in the Montcler team photo, has the money, went to the right school.'

DeVane went to hoist his drink, then stopped halfway between the bar and his gaped mouth, and he said rather apologetically, 'Oh, Vince, I'm afraid you might think I'm a frightful snob if I tell you.'

'Don't worry about it, Nicky. You're an aristocrat, and it goes with the territory. I'd be disappointed if you weren't, and it would kill the American tourist trade.'

DeVane thought about it for a second, then let rip with an impulsive peal of laughter. 'Quite so, quite *bloody* so!' This outburst of laughter must have set something off, because he suddenly looked queasy and uncomfortable. 'Oh, Vincent, you must excuse me, but I need to get to the little boys' room post-haste,' he said, dismounting from his stool with some effort. 'When I get back I shall tell you all about how the Gilded Edge works . . . I'm surprised you haven't asked already, Vince.'

Vince picked up the loose cards on the bar and packed them into a tidy block, and said, 'That's the thing about good tricks and puzzles. I like to work them out for myself. And I think I've got this one beat.'

'Bravo! I shall look forward to hearing it,' replied DeVane, before he toddled off to the gents with a stiff and unsteady stride.

Confident he had their card trick sussed, Vince sat at the bar, making busy with the cocktail sticks. One in his mouth, and one dislodging a small piece of grey grit from under the forefinger amid his otherwise perfectly clipped and kempt phalanx of nails. That operation took up the fat end of a couple of minutes. He then gathered up the cards from the bar and did some fancy shuffling that brought the young bartender over to initiate some conversation. He was an English Lit student studying at London, and was only reading *Playboy* because it contained an interview and a short story by Vladimir Nabokov. The young bartender's story was upheld by the thumbed and annotated copy of *Lolita* that was stashed along with the jazz mag. By the time Vince eventually got up and made his way into the gents, Nicky DeVane had been absent for about fifteen minutes.

Vince found the aristocrat sitting on the throne in a cubicle, out for the count. Vince shook him, gave him a couple of wakening slaps across the chops, and even considered shoving his head down the toilet and flushing the chain, but decided against it. Nothing was going to stir him out of his current stupor. It substantiated the account of his behaviour at the Imperial, as an unreliable lightweight.

Vince told the young barman that his friend, the Honourable Nicholas no less, was sleeping it off in his private chambers. He then slipped him a couple of quid to keep an eye on him, and picked up the pack of cards from the bar. Nicky DeVane had never got around to telling him about the Gilded Edge card cheat, but as Vince left the Criterion, wishing the young bartender good luck with his exams, he wore a sanguine and solid grin on his face.

Ten minutes after Vince had left the Criterion bar, two men entered it. Both were of medium height and build, and were attired in dinner jackets. And they both wore rhino masks.

CHAPTER 51

Vince got a taxi back to his flat. The cabbie wanted a conversation, but Vince didn't; he was busy. His head was still spinning with all the information Nicky DeVane had revealed.

And with all his own theories slipping into place like tectonic plates, the path was becoming less crooked and uneven as, conversely, the fault lines and cracks in the suspects' stories and motives began to appear. He was so caught up in the case, and lost in thought, that when he knocked on his own front door and had it opened by Isabel Saxmore-Blaine, still in a catsuit and thigh-high boots, he stepped back in surprise before he stepped in. He'd forgotten about the fancy dress ball they'd just attended, and now thought he'd died and gone to heaven.

Vince told Isabel everything that Nicky DeVane had told him. She had questions, but he had more and wasn't too interested in playing catch-up, as the clock was ticking. He explained that he needed to get into the house in Eaton Square, and reckoned he knew a way in. When he and Mac had first checked the place over for possible ways of entering not involving the front door, they had realized the house could easily be accessed through the back garden. That just meant getting in through the—

'I have a key.'

Isabel cut him dead with that statement. Then she looked suitably sheepish, as well she might. If that little fact had been floated earlier, her claim of innocence would have been thrown further into jeopardy. She confessed that she found a spare set, and had another set clandestinely cut. Beresford – controlling, fastidious, territorial – would have been apoplectic had he found out that she was prowling the premises uninvited and unsupervised. But Isabel had her reasons: she suspected he was seeing someone else. Not just an informal fling (which their liberated and louche arrangements had allowed for) but a full-blown affair with a model he had stolen from Simon Goldsachs; a woman who Isabel suspected had probably been procured for them both by Nicky DeVane. So with the green-eyed monster mocking her every move, she had searched through drawers, ransacked laundry baskets, plundered suit pockets and ogled his address book. Not her finest hour, she now admitted. Vince didn't care, so long as she had a key.

They drove to Isabel's new flat to pick it up. Vince asked her if she wanted to change out of the catsuit and into something more appropriate. She refused, stating that he hadn't changed either, so why should she? And, anyway, she thought the outfit was highly appropriate for their venture, and most enjoyable. Vince couldn't argue with that, and got the comic-strip connotation, and went along with it. So the masked detective and his catsuited sidekick roared off in the growling Jag and headed for Eaton Square.

There had been changes to the house since Vince and Isabel's last visit. The olfactory senses were no longer assailed by the cloying odour of lilies. There were no flowers anywhere now, and the air smelled vapidly old and empty. With its occupant's death, it seemed something of the house had died with him. Most of the portraits featuring proud generations of battling Beresfords, were removed from the walls now; the finely struck collection of Paul Storr silverware was under lock and key; and all the antiques – from the heavy oak furniture to the dainty porcelain – were boxed up and put in storage until their fate had been decided. And that went for the bricks and mortar, too. The place had been the Beresfords' town residence since it had been built, but Her Majesty's Inland Revenue Service had been forensically fine-combing the Beresford finances, and they had been found wanting. Death and taxes, both guaranteed, and the former didn't negate the levying of the latter.

In the basement den/study things seemed relatively untouched, though. The Escalado horse racing game was still set up on the billiard table, with all the little jockeys and gee-gees lined up expectantly for the next race. All the cups and trophies were still on the shelves, along with the photos of Beresford and his friends.

Isabel asked, 'What's down here that wasn't down here before, Vincent?'

'Nothing. It's always been here. Just hidden, sort of.'

Vince went over to the side table that stood before the window that looked out on to the rising bank of the garden. It was a hefty-looking Regency side table in polished rosewood, and had a sturdy central-column pedestal that flared out into four carved-paw feet. Innocuous-looking enough, it looked as if it folded out into a small dining table. A silver condiment set, for salt and pepper and oil and vinegar, and the stack of six cork table mats rested on it.

'Beresford was playing cards when he was killed,' said Vince. He then pointed to the green leather armchair positioned in front of the TV. 'Then he was moved over to this chair, and the gun was put in his hand to make it look like he had shot himself.' Vince kneeled down to take a look underneath the table. To one side of the central support column he quickly discovered a small brass catch, shaped like a trigger, and gave it a pull. Isabel, without prompting, removed the condiment set and place mats and put them over on the desk. Then they both moved the table away from the window. Vince slid the top aside until it was open, unfolding into a table over twice its previous size. And that manoeuvre revealed that the underside of its polished surface was covered in green baize. It formed a card table that could comfortably accommodate eight players, and underneath the table top were concealed sectioned compartments stuffed with games and goodies. And clues. All of which Vince greeted with a broad smile.

Isabel said, 'I never knew this was a card table, but then again

I've only ever been in this room about three times. And one of them was when I discovered him dead. But it's hardly a surprise. He was a gambler.'

'Simon Goldsachs had a similar table in his study, which held a secret too. Grand plans for a paradise off the coast of West Africa. A Shangri-la where he and his friends could get away from the riff-raff.'

Vince rifled the compartments and took out gaming chips and money, including a roll of about five hundred pounds secured with an elastic band. There were also packs of playing cards still in their virginal cellophane wraps and stamped with the Montcler seal. And one other pack, which was already opened, and not a Montcler pack but a plain deck of Waddington playing cards that you could buy in any games store.

Vince picked up one of the Montcler packs, unsheathed it from its crispy plastic, broke the seal and opened it. He pulled up a couple of chairs and took a seat at the card table.

Isabel joined him. 'I thought you didn't play cards?' she said.

'Not with a stacked deck, I don't, and these are stacked. Marked.'

Vince began to deal out the cards, separating them into high-value and low-value, with six being the dividing number.

'Nicky DeVane never told me how their card scam worked, not properly. But he revealed enough. And Billy Hill gave me some clues, too. He said it was a twenty-four carat gold cheat. The rest I figured out.'

Vince put the two separate stacks of cards next to each other on the green baize. He said, 'Take a look at them, and what do you see?'

Isabel looked at the cards, then shrugged impatiently. 'Just two piles of cards. So what?'

'Take a good look at the gilding around the edges. Now what?'

Isabel looked intently at the two blocks of gold sitting on the table. She looked good and hard from all angles before she said, 'They're in different shades of gold?'

'Bingo!' said Vince, banging his fist with exclamatory zeal on the table. 'The low-value cards have been gilded in nine carat gold, so they look dull, almost coppery in comparison to the high-value cards, which have been gilded in twenty-four carat. They look almost yellow: got a real glint to them. It's simple enough to do; a home gilding kit could probably do the job. But once they're shuffled . . .' Vince shuffled the cards, 'and mixed in together, they look the same as . . .' Vince then took out the pack of cards he had taken from the Montcler club that evening and rested them next to the 'marked' pack, 'they look the same as the legitimate deck.'

Isabel's eyes narrowed in on the two gold blocks, and she examined them with a forensic intensity. Vince looked at his watch, and muttered something like 'We haven't got all night'. Isabel raised a hand to shut him up and then, in her own sweet time, eventually purred, 'Mmmm . . . well, my darling detective, I for one can see a slight difference. The marked cards look more grainy.'

Vince leaned in for a closer gawp and saw it too. 'Of course there's going to be a *slight* difference, because there *is* a slight difference. But it's only noticeable to the trained eye, and to those in the know. And you, my sweet, are now in the know.'

She looked at the grinning detective, and gave a concessionary little wobble of her head to acknowledge the fact.

'You're a tough crowd to please, Miss Saxmore-Blaine.'

'I'm just playing devil's advocate, Mr Treadwell.'

'And you play it well. But the difference is only noticeable by close comparison, and the people being cheated are never going to see the right and the wrong decks placed side by side.'

Vince picked up the marked cards, gave them another quick shuffle. He dealt out a hand, five cards, and fanned them in front of him as if he were playing a game. He was holding the Jack of clubs, the seven of hearts, the three of spades, the five of clubs and the nine of diamonds. It was a beast of a hand – a crippled claw, a hook – but it would serve its purpose.

'Take a good look at the top of the cards, and tell me what you see?'

Isabel sat back in her chair, at a respectable playing distance, and studied the top of the cards he was holding. She then concluded: 'I see nothing. I can't tell the difference.'

Vince looked perplexed. 'Are you playing devil's advocate again?'

'You do want a rock-solid case, don't you?'

'Fair enough, Clarence Darrow.' Vince laid the cards face down on the table. He got up and went over to the partners' desk and picked up a tall and industrial-looking anglepoise lamp, unplugged it and brought in over to the card table and plugged it back in. It gave off an illuminating 100 watts of dusty light.

He said: 'All casinos have bright lights, as bright as possible. Not only the 150-watt bulbs in the chandeliers, but the overhead table lights too. It's an unforgiving light that not only keeps everyone awake and playing, but it also helps prevent cheating. When you sit down at a gaming table, there are no dark spots, no hiding places. It's as if you're in a ring of fire.' Again Vince held the cards like he was playing a hand. 'Guy Ruley told me you're a good shot. Is that true?'

'I've twenty/twenty vision, the same as Johnny. To tell you the truth, I used to miss a few just so he wouldn't go into a frightful strop. To bag more than him, anyone would think I'd just shot his balls off.'

'Concentrate on the top of the cards, Isabel.'

It didn't take long before she said, 'I see it. Just a glint, but I see it.'

'Tell me the order of them, high or low . . .'

Isabel read out the sequence, 'High, high, low, low . . . high,' and she got it spot on. A smile tore across Vince's face, and he said, 'Beresford had it down cold, had it practised. So long as the other player didn't hold his cards too close to his chest or cover them up, he could read them. And no one in the Montcler would be that guarded, because no one would expect cheating. Because you were sitting among gentlemen, playing with Johnny Beresford and other like-minded men of honour.'

Isabel expelled a whip-cracking 'Ha!' at that remark.

Vince qualified: 'Well, the Montcler isn't exactly some two-bob back-room spiel in Bermondsey; it's in Berkeley Square, for Christ's sake!' He stood up, feeling invigorated, and went over to the shelf holding the collection of silver-framed photos of Beresford and his friends at play. To Vince's eye, the one empty picture frame looked like a big gaping mouth asking the questions *who?* and *why?* He reached into his inside jacket pocket and pulled out the photo that he had carried around with him since the case had started. It was creased, it was smudged, it was ripped at the corner, it was in bad shape. But as he slipped it back into the frame, it closed that gaping mouth and finally answered the questions.

Isabel came over and joined him. She looked at the series of photos with all the interest of a stranger. Vince wondered if it struck her as odd that she appeared in none of them. But he knew that thought must have struck her a long time ago, and then been washed over and conveniently forgotten in the miasma of booze and pills and emotional detachment that seemed to exist between herself and Beresford.

Looking at the men gathered in the photo, Isabel said: 'Which one killed Johnny?'

'He killed himself. He died by his own hand. But they're all guilty. One is more guilty than the others, but they all had a hand in it.'

'Johnny the golden boy. It almost seemed as if the Montcler club was created for him, and him alone. The first amongst equals . . .'

'Maybe at one time it was like that. But in every group there's always a pecking order. But it's not set in stone and, with time, that order can change. Stocks rise and fall. I think there's a new order emerging.'

CHAPTER 52

The Ruley residence was situated in rural Buckinghamshire. By the time they arrived there, it was just before dawn, when darkness was at its ripest, deepest and most oppressive. A sickle of moonlight hung poignantly in the pitch-black sky, with not even the twinkle-twinkle of little stars to illuminate the scene. The house was secluded, set in its own ample and wooded acreage, so without specific directions you would never find it. Isabel knew the way, since she had been to 'Chuckers' before, with Johnny and the rest of his gang for the occasional shooting party. The house was unofficially called Chuckers because Joseph Ruley, Guy's father, had built the place from scratch just after the war, and had designed it specifically to resemble the Prime Minster's country residence, Chequers, which was in the same county and not that far away. A massive pretension on his part that didn't go uncommented on. Joseph's wife – Josephine, no less – was also partly to blame, because of her unrepentant northernness and penchant for referring to everyone as 'Chuck'.

Vince slowed the engine and parked the Mk II in a small lay-by. Upon doing so, an argument ensued. Vince told Isabel he was going to break into Chuckers, and hopefully catch Ruley by surprise, and that she was to wait in the car. Isabel contended that she had been in the house and knew the layout, and therefore should accompany him. Vince said that he'd work it out, but she wasn't keen on being left in the car, away from the action. He opened the glove compartment and took out a pocket torch; he didn't need to shine it on those exquisite features to see that they were now arranged in petulant annoyance. Vince assured her that he wouldn't be long. He then wisecracked and said he didn't realize cats were afraid of the dark.

She turned slowly towards him and held him in a withering gaze that could have turned the verdantly lush and damp Buckinghamshire countryside into a barren and desiccated wasteland, and said that if he wanted a compliant little pet, he should have got a Poodle. But she eventually agreed to wait inside the car. And Vince, with his tail now between his legs, quickly got out of the vehicle and made his way along the country road towards the house.

The mock-Elizabethan mansion was gated, but nothing that couldn't be got over. He eventually found a way into the grounds by slipping under some rotting wooden fencing, all without snagging his dinner jacket on anything, which he considered a satisfactory result. The grounds of Chuckers stretched out before him, with kempt lawns and lots of privet hedges that sectioned off the extensive gardens into a maze-like grid construction. There was a long terrace of greenhouses that well served the grounds. The house itself, just like the real Chequers, was medievally busy, its roof serrating the dim skyline with pointed arches and turrets and chimney stacks.

The long mullioned windows made it easy to see that there were no lights on in the house, or seemingly any signs of life, or even any furniture inside the place. This was borne out by the three removal vans parked on the gravel drive. It was clear that Guy Ruley, reported to be leaving the country soon, had put his plans into motion.

Vince made his way around to one side of the mansion, where a small path descended to what he assumed were the servants' quarters. There he saw a way in. Some of the leaded windows in this part of the building were in bad shape and in need of repair. On one window, the lead was long gone, and the panes were held in by chipped and crumbling putty.

Vince took out his switchblade and began to work away, and in no time at all he had removed two rhomboid panes of glass. A hand was slipped in, a handle was turned, the window was opened, and Vince soon found himself crouching in a large white porcelain sink. He climbed out of the sink and on to the flagstone floor of the scullery. Overhead there were pots and pans hanging from S-shaped hooks, like a row of giant chimes. He was very careful not to disturb them and send them clattering into an alarming cacophony.

With the torch illuminating his path, he made his way stealthily through the house. The deeper he got into it, the more he saw how it was emptying out – just like the house in Eaton Square. Packing boxes and tea chests sat everywhere in the middle of empty rooms.

He padded along a wide hallway, his footfalls muted in the deep nap of a forest-green carpet that was bordered in red, and reached a door at the end. There he killed the light and pocketed the torch, put his ear to the door and heard the strained and panting breaths of exertion. Vince eyed up the door though he had no intention of kicking it in because he had no reason to believe it was locked. But it presented other problems. It was a big carved oak door with black metal fretwork fastenings and riveted cross panels. It looked as if it weighed a ton and was the kind of door that was specially built to creak and whine: a natural-born squealer that would give him away as soon as it was tugged. So, on turning the big twisted iron hoop handle and releasing the bolt from its holding, he gave it a swift firm pull and caught it by surprise. Not a peep was emitted, just the hushed whoosh of air being sucked out of the room.

Vince stood at the doorway and scoped the huge oblong space, which looked like it served as a refectory It was already stripped bare, and Vince could just make out the lighter panels on the walls indicating where paintings had just been removed. There was an arched stone fireplace that you could park a car in, and tall French windows looked out on to the grounds.

In the room itself, a solitary lit candle sat in a four-branched silver candelabra resting on the floor in the centre. Near that stood a chair which had a shirt, jacket, trousers and other items of clothing draped over it. Guy Ruley himself was lying on his back on a wooden bench. He was bollock naked. His outstretched arms held aloft two impressively heavy-looking dumbbells, which he lowered with a gasping count of, 'Forty . . . four . . .'

Vince didn't like that count of forty-four. He would have preferred a single figure, or at least taken something still in the mid-twenties.

On lowering the dumbbells to his chest, Guy Ruley let them drop to the floor, the heavy rug soaking up the dull 40 lb thud. He still lay on the bench, and breathed heavily and rhythmically. Whilst the single candle burned brightly in its branched candelabra, it wasn't the main source of light in the room. Through the French windows Vince saw the grounds were lit up with footlights. Not unusual to see in large grounds with an impressive garden display to show off, but these footlights were of the bright halogen variety, arranged on a flat patch of grass, and forming a large circle.

'Detective Treadwell?'

Vince turned his attention back to the centre of the room, and to Guy Ruley, who was now standing up, flexing his muscles while engaged in some kind of stretching activity.

'What can I do for you, Detective?'

'You can put your pants on for a start.'

Ruley looked perplexed, then made a play of looking down at himself, as if he hadn't noticed he was in the altogether.

'Do I have to?'

'It might be an idea.'

'Surely my roaming around as nature intended is not a crime. It is my house, after all. But you, on the other hand, being in my house uninvited, that *is* a crime.'

'True. But at least I'm dressed for the occasion.' Vince gestured to his dinner suit.

'How did you get in here?'

'The door was open.'

'That I doubt.'

'And yet here I am.'

'Here you are, indeed. Without so much as a warrant . . . I warrant.'

Vince, dry as you like, replied, 'Boom–boom.'

Guy Ruley stopped smiling, and punning. 'What are you doing here?'

'We need to talk.'

Ruley went over to the chair that held his clothes, picked up something white and skimpy and slipped it on. Vince had seen more material on a sticking plaster, but what civvies Guy Ruley chose to wear was not his call. Guy Ruley then took the trousers folded on the seat of the chair, gave them a vigorous wind-cracking shake and stepped into them, too. He then sat down on the chair, and looking not the least perturbed at having a detective break into his house whistled a tuneless little tune, unbunched his socks and rolled them over his feet. Finally he trod into his shoes – croc-skin loafers.

Guy Ruley looked Vince up and down and said: 'Looking very smart, Detective. I heard you were at the ball. We did all wonder why. The case is closed, and even if it was open, you wouldn't be on it. And yet here you are.'

Vince said, 'The business deal that you and Beresford fell out over. The one you argued about at the Imperial. That was no business deal. That was about Johnny cheating at cards. That was about Beresford cheating *you* at cards. Am I right?'

Guy Ruley laced his hands behind his head, stretched out his legs in front of him and crossed his natty and knotty reptile-skin covered feet. Superciliousness, supremacy and snideness all gathered around Guy Ruley's neatly formed and generically hand-some features. His refined mouth crimped into a smirk.

Vince played along, gave him what he wanted, issued an imploring little smile and said, 'Humour me.'

386

'I knew Johnny was cheating. He was winning too many hands. And he was getting sloppy. He couldn't deny it.'

'But you were off bounds, surely? You were at Eton together.'

'Three years below him. But it felt like a lifetime.'

'His fag?'

'No, that pleasure was Nicky DeVane's. No matter what the little shit says, he was Johnny's Gunga Din. I was viewed with too much suspicion, seen as a recalcitrant, if you will.'

Guy Ruley yawned, stretched again, then briskly stood up and went over to the French windows. He gazed out at the lighted circle on the grounds. The darkness before the dawn had reached it apogee, and it would be lighter from here on in.

'So why the needle, Ruley?'

'Come on, Treadwell, this is all rhetorical. You dig around, that's what you do. Very good at it, too. That's why you're here. Why do you think, the *needle*?'

Vince stayed where he was, in the centre of the room, as he didn't suspect Guy Ruley was going to make a dash for it through the French windows, and he'd have to get past Vince for the only other exit.

'My guess is, you can't change the clay from which you're made, no matter how hard you try or how much money you throw at it. That's the theory in some circles. And certainly the ones you move in, Guy. You were at Eton, but you never belonged. As far as your running mates in the Montcler went, they all came from a long line of breeding. But I have to admit I found your past the most compelling. Isabel said your father was a scrap-metal merchant who made it big, though she was sketchy on the details.'

'Bitch,' said Guy Ruley, without any modulation in tone.

'Don't get uppity, Guy. I think she meant it admiringly. Her family made their fortune through bird shit, so I wouldn't get too put out of joint. The name "Ruley" was deceptive. From what I read, your father was a fresh-off-the-boat Irishman who arrived in Liverpool penniless.'

'Simple, he changed it from Riley. As a young man he'd picked up a record for stealing lead off roofs. Then copper piping in condemned houses. All under the name of Joe Riley. Then he changed his name by deed poll, and eventually arranged to have his criminal record removed. My father had friends in high places by then.'

'From stealing the lead off roofs, he then disappeared for a few years, and turned up rich. How did he manage that?'

'He made his first real money when the First World War came along. After the war, which he deserted from, there was lots of scrap metal to be had. Lots of armoury got left behind, trucks, guns, even tanks. Everything had a value. The Great War was a dirty war, and there was dirty money to be made. Chaos breeds opportunity, and he capitalized. He returned from Europe with a small fortune, then turned it into a large one. Scrap and ferrous metals led to smuggling and smelting gold bullion, and munitions and gun running. During the Spanish Civil War he infamously armed both sides. He had no affiliations.'

'And with the money, he sent you to Eton and built this place, Chuckers. It looks old, but scratch the paint and you can't disguise the new brickwork. And that must have been the same at Eton. Never quite disguising it.'

'I made my way, had my father's resilience.' Guy Ruley turned round and faced Vince. Hands out of his pockets now, chest jutting bullishly, as if to show he was built of tougher stuff. 'So there you go, Treadwell. You think I killed Johnny because he cheated at cards and because I never quite fitted in?'

'But you did fit in, eventually. In fact, your stock is on the up. University degrees in engineering and physics gave you an edge over those floppy-fringed boys who read classics. You've got real skills that are useful to men like Simon Goldsachs.'

'What do you want me to say, Treadwell? Getting warmer?'

'A lot warmer, I'd say, Guy. Try a small energy-rich country on the west coast of Africa. Lots of civil engineering needed to get the infrastructure in place, and then get the oil and minerals up out of the ground. That takes skill. The kind of skill and connections you have in abundance. My guess is that your stock in the Montcler had risen. And as for Johnny Beresford, the ex-guardsman, playboy adventurer and fantasist, his had plummeted.'

Ruley stepped back over to the chair. 'All very intriguing, but I have an alibi. I was out the country at the time of Johnny's demise.'

'Conveniently so, if I may add. But Ireland's not that far away. A man of your resourcefulness would have no problem slipping in and out of the country unchecked.' Vince nodded towards the circle of light beyond the French windows. 'A privately hired helicopter could have whisked you back into London to kill Beresford, and then whisked you right back out again.'

'Proof?'

Vince reached into his jacket pocket and pulled out the playing cards – the plain pack of Waddington cards. 'I found these in the drawer of Beresford's card table.' He searched Ruley's face for clues, a tautness of tension around the mouth, an involuntary pulse, a glimmer of revelation in the eyes. But all he saw was that Guy Ruley was a good enough poker player not to give his hand away with twitchy tells or showy signs of uncontrollable guilt; and he was clearly loaded with more steely reserve than one of his old man's scrapyards.

Vince continued. 'There were six decks of cards in that drawer, and these were the only ones unsealed. And not a Montcler deck, so not tampered with. These were the cards that you and Johnny Beresford played with the night he ended up dead. Which means there's only two sets of prints on them, yours and his.'

'Assuming they're a fresh pack and hadn't been played with before.'

'Let's assume.'

Vince was close enough to hear that Guy Ruley's breathing was now laboured and arrhythmical. The fitness fanatic's heart was pumping faster than a fat octogenarian forced to take the stairs. Vince knew he had him.

'Dominic Saxmore-Blaine killed Johnny Beresford,' said Guy Ruley, slipping into his shirt. 'That's the way people want it. People with more power than you.'

'Yes, it's all written down in black and white. His mind twisted because of a practical joke that was played on him. What did Beresford call it, the joke . . .'

Ruley buttoned up his perfectly tailored, bespoke shirt. Fastening the top button around his muscled neck proved to be a perplexing challenge; a neck, as Vince suspected, that was now tensing up and throbbing with hot blood at simply the mention of the practical joke.

Vince prompted. 'You forget?'

Still Guy Ruley said nothing. He laced his red tie through his collar and tied a knot, yanking it tight.

'It was called the blooding,' Vince reminded him. 'Just like in fox hunting. On your first kill, blood is smeared on your face, and you get to join the hunt. Be part of the pack.'

Maybe it was the stiffness of the collar, or maybe it was the tightness of the knotted tie, but Vince watched Guy Ruley's aspect change. It looked flushed. It had been all cold surface, hard, undaunted and in control of the facts. Now it wavered, pitched into uncertainty, drenched in emotion. Vince himself smelled blood.

'Johnny the Joker, that's what you called him, Guy, when we first met. Always joking around.'

'Everyone called him that.'

'But I heard it from you first. It stuck in my mind.'

'Your point, Treadwell?'

'Nicky DeVane said that Johnny the Joker had played the same joke he played on Dominic before, at school – at Eton. And no one had got killed. Nicky was wrong, and my guess is you're lying. You haven't forgotten that name, the blooding, because he played the same joke on you. And someone did get killed, just twenty or so years later.'

Guy Ruley let out a snort of derision so poorly executed that Vince considered snorting one back in a derisive response.

Instead, he said: 'Dominic Saxmore-Blaine wasn't a well boy. He had his mother's mental frailties. And you, Guy, were just an impressionable schoolboy when it happened to you. And it left its impression on you. It twisted and it turned you, just like it did Dominic.'

Vince could see it now, for the pain of that memory was suffused over Guy Ruley's face. Buried and blunted for all these years, but now it was spiking and breaking through. Ruley lowered himself into the chair. His powerful body was suddenly as weak and uncertain of itself as that of a pimply and pubescent schoolboy.

He sat awkwardly in the chair, and said: 'It was more or less the same stunt Johnny pulled on Dominic. I had just turned thirteen, the age boys become men in certain cultures. Johnny didn't use the fox-hunting analogy you used. Though true enough, it would be far too parochial and unadventurous for him. I think he got it from one of his Rider Haggard novels, about killing a lion as a rite of passage.

'It was the end of term. We had a place we used to meet, in the copse near the school, and we'd been drinking. Bottles of stout were the tipple back then. Black, potent stuff it was, especially at thirteen. Johnny had paid one of the local lads from Slough to play the victim. I was spun the story that he was a no one, a little guttersnipe thief who had it coming to him. Our attitude towards him was rather like John Betjeman's attitude towards Slough in general, reckoning that it wouldn't be missed.

'Nicky DeVane was there too, as always, at Johnny's side. Even then he had a flamboyant way of wearing his tie, his boater worn at a jaunty angle. So when the little twerp insisted that he'd done it at my age, killed a boy I mean . . . well, I sort of had to. It was peer pressure more than beer pressure, I can assure you.

'The gun was a starting pistol. Even then, Johnny reckoned he knew all about guns. He said it was real enough, and belonged to his father. Of course, I hadn't even seen a gun back then, let alone handled one. Ironic really, considering my father had armed most of the world at one time or another, and had used plenty in his time, but he kept me away from them. Wouldn't even let me go shooting grouse, no matter how genteel the company. He saw killing for sport as obscene. Funny that . . .

'Looking back all those years ago, Treadwell, to that day in the woods, maybe I should have known it was a *joke*. The boy died very theatrically. He was a right little ham, a worse bloody actor than Bernie Korshank, I'm sure. Jumping about, clenching his heart, moaning and groaning and rolling around, then finally dying face-down. But the blood on his shirt looked real enough. It was from a joke shop, I was told later. But how was I to know what death looked like? I was at Eton for Christ's sake.

'After I'd shot him, I left Johnny and Nicky to it, to get rid of the body. They were going to bury him in the woods and no one would find him, they assured me. It wasn't until I returned to school the next term that they told me the truth, that it was all a joke. Johnny gave me the whole summer to think about what I had done . . . They say the summers of your youth are the longest. How very true. But none like that . . . the longest summer ever. I wanted to die every day of it. I even tried.' Guy Ruley raised his left arm to reveal a small white scar, about an inch long, on his wrist. 'I did it with a shard of glass from one of the greenhouses. I didn't have the guts for it, though, and I said the cut was an accident.' Guy Ruley's arm flopped down by his side, as if he'd just performed one of his vigorous weight lifts. 'I guess I didn't want to get anyone else into trouble . . .'

Vince considered what he'd just heard. From all the grand designs, vaulting ambitions, enormous piles of money, dreams of world domination, it all scrolled back and reduced to the sticky psyche of a thirteen-year-old schoolboy. And the playing fields of Eton.

Vince said, 'So that's what you and Beresford argued about at the Imperial.'

'Yes. He had it all set up with Bernie Korshank, but I told him Dominic wasn't up to it. And that it was a cruel childish joke, and that he wasn't a bloody schoolboy any more. Johnny laughed it off, said it hadn't done *me* any harm. I left the hotel, didn't want any part of it. My London flat isn't that far away, so I walked home. I wanted some fresh air, to sober up, get the stench of that place off me. But I couldn't let it go. I had no special feelings for Dominic Saxmore-Blaine, believe me. He was one of Johnny's little sycophants. I knew he was weak, though. Maybe that's why I couldn't stop thinking about it, and how it felt to me. And Johnny's words . . . about how it hadn't done me any harm . . .'

'So you went back to the Imperial?'

'Too late.' Guy Ruley gave a slow, regretful nod. 'By the time I got there it was over. Dominic must have just left. The door to the suite was open. I saw the gun on the floor, by the entrance. I saw Johnny and Bernie Korshank, and they were laughing, having a drink. Korshank still had his bloodied shirt on. It looked so real . . . just like the blood from the joke shop. They didn't see me.'

'And you picked up the gun?'

Guy Ruley sat up straight in the chair, as if realizing he was no longer a slouchy teenager, but a fully grown man on the receiving end of a questioning. He forced some bravado back into his voice as he said, 'Yes, perfect. As you deduced, Treadwell, Ireland's not that far away. It had all been arranged, and I'd flown back to London on a private helicopter. Then I'd driven to . . .'

CHAPTER 53

Guy Ruley had arrived at Johnny Beresford's house in Eaton Square at a little past – or perhaps a little before – midnight. He carried with him a tan pigskin attaché case. The private meeting that had been arranged between Johnny Beresford and Guy Ruley was a matter of the gravest urgency and secrecy. Guy certainly didn't expect Isabel Saxmore-Blaine to be in the house, and he didn't realize she was . . .

. . . Johnny woke up from his stupor not knowing that Isabel was upstairs asleep in the bedroom. He assumed that, after she had hit him over the head with the champagne bottle, she had fled the house and gone home to her flat in Pont Street. Without having time to attend the gash on his forehead, he heard a knock on the door, and answered it to find Guy Ruley.

. . . Johnny, with that big convivial grin bolted on to his face, welcomed his visitor: 'Come on in, sport!'

. . . Guy Ruley entered the house, unsmiling, and unresponsive to Beresford's bonhomie. Because this visit was no smiling matter. But that was Johnny's way, come rain or shine. Always charming, always smiling, *Johnny the Joker*. First thing Johnny Beresford did was explain the gash on his forehead: an argument with Isabel. Guy, however, didn't want to hear about Isabel Saxmore-Blaine. He had no sympathy and very little interest in the tiresome imbroglio that was Johnny and Isabel. Guy couldn't resist the comment that, leaving that scenario aside, and even without the gash on his head, Johnny still looked like shit. The man didn't argue the point, just carried on smiling. Rain or shine. Rain or shine . . .

. . . They went downstairs to the basement, the private den. Johnny topped himself up, poured himself a large single malt. He offered his guest one. Guy said he didn't need one, said he could imbibe Johnny's intoxicating vapours from where he was standing. He told Johnny to get on with it, as the clock was ticking and Guy had a flight to catch back to Ireland . . .

. . . Johnny Beresford opened up the rosewood side table that morphed into the green baize of a card table, and the two men took their positions opposite each other. Guy took his attaché case and put it on his lap; the snap of the locks being released produced a sharp businesslike sound that pulled everything into focus. Guy Ruley took out a fresh pack of cards from the attaché case. It was a pack of Waddington playing cards. No fancy embellishments with this pack, no minted blocks of gold hauled up from the vaults, or pretentious privateers flying their personalized colours. Just a plain pack of cards, a guaranteed clean deck. The game is poker. The style is seven-card stud.

. . . Their games were very different. Guy Ruley played with a new-found freedom, with the spirit of a man who was no longer shackled by reputation, by fear or by the past. He had found his own *style*. He played in silence, with a sheen of stilled serenity, imbued with confidence and a cold steel in his hand. On the opposite side of the table, Johnny Beresford knocked back brimming tumblers of Scotch, and laughed and joked and jawed his way through each hand. He played his usual game, full of zeal and panache. But its edge was blunted. It was somehow a parody of itself, and a sloppy one at that. Johnny Beresford was all rousing raises, bullshit bluffs and thoughtless folds. He was full of fizz and twang and entertainment, he was the joker and the wild card . . .

. . . But all the time, and on every hand, Guy Ruley won. He won big, he won convincingly. The victor and vanquished sat opposite each other . . .

. . . 'What do you say, sport, another hand? Just the one? Come on, you owe me that, no?'

Vince said: 'And Beresford's price for losing the game?'
  Guy Ruley said: 'Another game.'

. . . Guy Ruley reached into his jacket pocket and pulled out a pair of black calfskin driving gloves and slipped them over his winning hands. He then opened the pigskin attaché case again, reached into its guts and pulled out a snub-nose .32 Colt revolver, and a single bullet. The next game was to be Russian roulette . . .

Guy Ruley said: 'But you're right, Treadwell, it wasn't the money. It wasn't even about the honour. I was taken back about twenty years ago. I wanted to see real fear in Johnny the Joker's eyes. I wanted him to know what it felt like.'

. . . Johnny Beresford took some quick, deep, staccato breaths, as if he'd just taken a wintry plunge in the English channel. It had been agreed. He was to take one shot to the temple. One pull of the trigger. A five-to-one shot. Beresford loaded the single bullet into the chamber of the gun and spun the barrel . . .
  . . . Guy then told him that, instead of him taking the one shot, he was to take three shots. Three pulls of the trigger . . .
  . . . Johnny the Joker laughs. When he sees that Guy is serious, and he realizes that there is no humour to be had in the room, he tells Guy to fuck *off*! This isn't what they had arranged, what they had agreed on . . .
  . . . Guy Ruley again reaches into the attaché case and takes out another gun. It's the exact same model, a .32 Colt. On seeing

the gun, the blood drains from Johnny Beresford's face like the knuckles of a clenched fist . . .

. . . Guy told him that *his* gun was fully loaded. A full complement of bullets, one in every chamber. So it was Guy's six against his one, if he wanted to take his chances . . .

. . . Johnny Beresford banged his fists on the table, leaving a balled imprint on the green baize and sending stacked chips jumping up into the air. He reiterates and remonstrates that this is not what they had agreed on! The gentlemen's agreement! . . .

. . . Guy aimed the gun squarely at Johnny Beresford's head, cocked the trigger and said the rules had changed. And, anyway, he was never much of a gentleman – like his father before him, who Johnny had never failed to remind him was a working-class guttersnipe on the make. But don't get Johnny wrong; he was never a snob. He could mix with anyone – just as long as the anyone he was mixing with knew their place. Trouble was Guy, like his father before him, never knew his place. Always wanted to rise above it, always wanted more. He was the new order. The new way of doing things. But, as Guy saw it, it was the same as the old way. He was just stacking the deck in his own favour, giving himself the Gilded Edge . . .

. . . Six chambers, three pulls of the trigger, one bullet. Johnny Beresford, the great gambler and master manipulator of the odds, tried to work out those most simple of numbers. But this wasn't a horserace, a hand of cards, the roll of a dice or even a punt on the markets. It was his life! Numbers, fractions, liabilities, probabilities, they became meaningless and abstract. All he knew was that he didn't like these odds. He didn't like the new rules he had to play by. And yet he knew there was nothing he could do about them. He was, perhaps for the first time in his life, powerless . . .

. . . *All the king's horses and all the king's men couldn't put Johnny the Joker together again* . . .

. . . 'Come on, Johnny. Let's do it!'

. . . He picked up the gun. He put it to his head . . .

. . . 'Do it, Johnny. *Do it!*'

CHAPTER 54

'*Bang!*' exclaimed Guy Ruley, with one hand shaped like a gun and pressed to his temple as he pulled back the imaginary trigger. He held his gun-shaped hand there for a moment, maybe imagining the imaginary bullet shooting from his finger and tearing through the soft grey matter of his head, beating around his skull trying to find an exit, then running out of steam and lodging somewhere in his brain. Maybe in the part that stored all his childhood memories.

Guy Ruley then decommissioned his hand, and used it to lift his jacket off the back of the chair. With his other hand, he picked off some specks of lint, and he continued, 'The gods weren't with Johnny that night. They'd stopped smiling at him long ago. The first pull of the trigger got him. Without the ability to cheat, Johnny was finished, a spent force. And he knew it.'

Vince admired the cut of the jacket that Guy Ruley had slipped on, even though he thought it hung rather heavy. Then he asked, 'You said it had all been arranged, but who with?'

'Johnny's fate had been discussed over a perfectly civil lunch with James Asprey and Simon Goldsachs. Aspers, of course, knew about the Gilded Edge, but professed not to have known about him cheating on *me*. And, of course, he offered to pay back all the money I'd lost. I said it wasn't about the money. Aspers, contrite – or as contrite as he is ever likely to get – fully understood. Said he didn't expect anything less from me.'

'What did Goldsachs have to say about it?'

'Simon professed to know nothing about it, said the running of the Montcler was purely Aspers' affair. Simon knew the scandal could ruin Aspers, and would reflect badly on himself, if the story broke. So in recompense they said that Johnny must give me satisfaction, whatever I wanted. But it must be settled amongst ourselves, amongst gentlemen. And of course, being a *gentleman*, Johnny agreed.'

'Makes perfect sense. In the eighteenth century you and Beresford would have settled it with duelling pistols. This time around it's Russian roulette.'

Guy Ruley paid little attention to this comment, as he was now checking his watch. He then directed his gaze over to the lit circle on the lawn. Vince knew something was coming, and coming real soon.

And then it came, the first thing anyway. Guy Ruley lightened the load in his jacket by pulling out a gun: predictably enough a snub-nosed Colt revolver. The brand was known in America as the detective's gun. There was a certain irony there.

Guy Ruley said: 'Tenuous as the fingerprints on the cards are as evidence, it was a slight oversight on our part.'

'I'm equally embarrassed. Not spotting that the side table morphed into a card table was a dreadful oversight on my part.'

'Hand me the cards carefully, Treadwell. I'm in no mood to play 52 pick-up.'

Vince considered the next move. They were standing about fifteen feet apart. At five feet less, he might have been able to pull it off. But, as it stood, Vince did as he was told. He tossed them over to Ruley, who caught them with his left hand and pocketed them.

'Now what?'

'We wait.'

'We can play a quick hand. It's a clean deck.'

'I hear you don't gamble, Treadwell.'

'I don't. We can play for fun. Just until your ride turns up.'

'Ah, you see, Treadwell, my friends and I don't play for fun. Now, if you'd said that: winner walks free, loser accompanies you down to Scotland Yard, you might have got a game. But as it stands, it's pretty much game over for you, Treadwell.'

Ruley put a little more conviction into getting the drop on Vince. He raised the gun so it was pointed firmly at where all his major organs were stored.

'There's enough other people know what I know.'

'Your little playmate, Isabel Saxmore-Blaine? Now there's an unreliable narrator, if ever there was one. You know, Treadwell, it may be fun for you servicing the upper crusts, but she's bad news, take it from me. Aspers and Simon Goldsachs both blame Isabel for Johnny's downfall. I blame her too. Not for his death, of course, but for making it all look like murder again. It was all arranged, and the whole thing should have been so simple: Johnny Beresford, a gentleman down on his luck, discredited, dishonoured, depressed with his lot, retires dignified to his study, has a stiff drink and blows his brains out. An age-old scenario. Until little Miss Saxmore-Blaine stumbled drunkenly and melodramatically on to the scene, and made it look like murder all over again.'

'What the bloody hell is all this?'

Guy Ruley turned sharply to find Isabel Saxmore-Blaine standing in the doorway. To any man, seeing her in that get-up, she was an assault on the senses. She was car-crashingly, distractingly dangerous – so much so that she should have come equipped with her own private lighthouse. And on seeing the catsuited figure with her hands on her hips, accentuating her curves and somehow, in the half light, making her look like a pornographic egg timer, Guy Ruley did a flurry of double-takes before finally settling his wide eyes on her.

With the gun no longer trained on him, Vince made his move – he ducked down, sprang forward and tackled Guy Ruley around the waist. Ruley fell backwards, squeezing the trigger and sending a bullet rocketing up into the ceiling and hitting a metal light fitting, which in turn sent it ricocheting straight back down into the wooden floor. Close enough for Vince to see the varnished wood splinter in white shards.

Ruley was still holding the gun in his right hand. His left hand now gripped a hank of Vince's hair and he was pulling his head back, about to stick the hot snub barrel into Vince's mouth.

Vince still had his arms wrapped around Guy Ruley's waist, his hands pinned to the ground under Ruley's substantially muscled weight. He was also looking down the barrel of a gun. At the other end of the gun he saw the toothpaste grin of Guy Ruley. He watched as Ruley's forefinger tightened around the trigger—

Then he saw the pointy toe of a patent-leather boot swing into view and kick away the hand that was about to pull the trigger. There was a mighty clap, a shocking energy and a bright white light. The gun had gone off again and the bullet just missed Vince's cheekbone. He could feel the heat of the metal, smell the burn of powder, the eye-stinging blast of cordite.

The next thing he knew, his hands were free and working furiously at trying to rub away the blinding flash that was seared into his burning eyes – and his ears needed some attention too. The report of the gun had set off a ringing that would have sent Quasimodo reaching for the aspirins and earmuffs. Kneeling on the floor, Vince knew he couldn't stay sequestered in this sensory torture chamber for long. That boot of Isabel's that had kicked away the gun would now have to answer to Guy Ruley.

Vince opened his watery eyes and saw, through the webby mist, that an unearthly white light had filled the room and was shining in through the French windows. For a moment, he thought the bullet had hit its intended target – his brain – and he was on his final journey, going towards the great white light of lore. Vince ran his hands quickly around his head checking for bullet holes and blood. He didn't find any.

The ringing in his ears had subsided enough to let in a heavy whirling sound, which also emanated from outside. He realized it was the work of the rotating propeller blades and headlights of a helicopter hovering over its mark outlined on the lawn.

Vince turned away from the windows and scanned the room. It was like seeing everything in photographic negative – monochrome, murky and unreal. He wobbled to his feet, the deafening blast having done something to his sense of balance. He felt like a ghost unable to join the real world. He saw a shape in front of him that seemed to be floating spectrally around the room. He then heard a scream, and the hazy shape separated, as part of it fell to the floor. The bigger part, about 65 per cent of it, now came towards him. Vince then felt the full force of a very human fist as it was slotted into his mouth. It wasn't much of a punch. As Vince suspected, the bigger shape – Guy Ruley – wasn't much of a fighter. But it was enough to send Vince back down to the ground. Once down there, he crawled over to the supine shape lying on the floor – Isabel. He held her and peppered her face with kisses; somehow hoping, in lieu of smelling salts or medication, that it would revive her, or certainly comfort her.

Isabel groaned, and groggily uttered: 'He hit me, Vincent. He hit me . . .'

'I know, but you're okay. And I'm gonna hit him right back. Wait here.'

Vince climbed to his feet and staggered over to the white light pouring in through the French windows. He was still locked in the sensory straitjacket, and feeling the effect of Guy Ruley's sucker punch – one that he suspected could be repeated at any moment. All things being equal, he knew he could take Guy Ruley apart; one good shot to the jaw would send his pumped and bulked-out body to the ground. But all things weren't equal, since he could hardly see his hand in front of his face, and was pretty sure he couldn't hit the backside of a behemoth with a banjo.

He went after Ruley, through the French windows and over the paved patio that looked as if it was full of people, but was in fact full of marbled classical statues, down a small sloping embankment, and on to the flat grassy lawn with its circle of landing lights. He felt the whirlwind of the helicopter blades hovering above him. Maybe it was this new sensory blast, but things before him became clearer, and his vision began to drift back into focus. He saw the helicopter wasn't a commercial bird but a big, robust military type, maybe painted over in green camouflage or battle-ready grey. With two big rotors, one up front and one at the back, it was more than capable of carrying a platoon of men.

Vince couldn't see Guy Ruley, but he watched as the helicopter lowered itself, kicking up a minor tornado on the lawn, sending ants scurrying and worms tunnelling. He saw that the cast of night had now gone, dawn was happening and a carroty light was breaking through the morning mist.

The negative in his vision was developing and a harrowing picture was emerging: the pilots in the cockpit of the helicopter were the mackintosh men. Vince stood transfixed, for they still held that power over him. Their image burned through him as he committed their faces to memory. He could now make out every feature. Kitted out as fly boys in multi-zipped jump suits they weren't in their customary mackintoshes but Vince knew it was them; gut animal instinct told him so, and he could almost smell them. In a blink, one of the mackintosh men disappeared from view. Vince then saw what looked like a rope ladder being released from the side of the chopper.

Guy Ruley shot out from the darkness beyond the circle of lights and ran towards the ladder, which he grabbed and began to scale. Vince, who was about twenty-five yards away, sprinted towards the ladder, and as it began to rise he also grabbed it. His hands just managed to get a grip on the second-to-last rung of the ladder before it took off out of reach, like the tail of a kite.

The helicopter rose further and further, till they were now a good fifty feet above the ground. Vince tried to climb further up the rope ladder, or at least to get a firm footing on it. Because, somehow, he had ended up upside down, with his legs above him. He felt like one of those Olympic gymnasts doing an impossible and hernia-inducing routine on those suspended rope rings – but with the added obstacle of flying through the air, not having a mat to land on, and being totally useless at it anyway. Upside down, the blood was rushing to his head as he watched the ground and the circle of lights disappear and the broader sky loom into view. Using all his strength, and feeling every muscle and sinew in his body put in a shift, he tried to turn himself round on the rope ladder. Such was the gut- and groin-wrenching strain that he was sure his testicles had done a full retreat and were now lurking somewhere around his tonsils, steadfastly refusing to come down until their 'master' had sorted himself out. Vince did the boys proud, and managed to get himself facing in the right direction. With everything in place, he began to haul himself up the ladder, taking the rope rungs in scaling fistfuls.

Vince had one objective only: to get into that helicopter, get at the mackintosh men and make the glass cockpit run red like an open bottle of ketchup in the spin cycle of a washing machine . . . *then land the helicopter*. Vince hadn't thought it through properly yet; he was still too busy hanging on for dear life as the chopper pitched this way and that in a concerted attempt to ditch him. But, despite its best efforts, he held firm.

Vince wasn't even thinking about Guy Ruley now, who was just an obstacle that stood between him and his real quarry – the mackintosh men. But he was wrong to not think of Guy Ruley, because Guy Ruley was definitely thinking of him.

Ruley yelled out: 'Treadwell!'

Vince looked up to see Ruley positioned near the top of the ladder. Again with that white toothy grin behind the barrel of a gun. The same as it was in Chuckers, but now they were well and truly off the ground, eighty feet off it and counting . . . ninety . . . ninety-five . . . one hundred . . .

From being able to see practically nothing, Vince was now able to see *everything*, acutely and relentlessly. The black hole of the gun barrel was expanding, and like all black holes it was sucking everything into it. Then there was the big bang that sent the bullet on its way, and plummeting down towards its target: Vince's head. As it took its explosive trajectory and tore into his flesh, Vince felt the initial searing pain and felt the bullet lodge in his arm. The left arm to be precise, the left bicep to be even more precise. A bullet wound is always a very precise thing, and Vince was feeling every scintilla of it: its depth, its breadth, its sheer *unbelievable* pain. His first reflex was to do what Guy Ruley wanted him to do, and let go of the ladder. The second reflex overrode the first though: to hang on for the ride and don't die.

The helicopter had settled at around two hundred feet, but it was clear that it wasn't going anywhere until it had dropped its unwanted cargo. Vince saw one of the mackintosh men crouching in the hold.

And then he heard the clarion call: 'Kill him! Kill him!'

Guy Ruley had stopped smiling. But he hadn't stopped aiming. And with the mackintosh man's barked instructions stiffening his resolve, this time he looked fully adjusted to his role of executioner, and fully engaged and locked on to the target dangling beneath him. And the dangling target realized, pointlessly, and far too late, that he should have jumped when he had the chance. Forty feet was always going to be better than a hundred. He tried to kick some life into the rope ladder, get some swing into it so he wasn't any longer such a sitting target. But nothing moved: it and he remained stubbornly un-pendulum-like. He felt like a big fat fresh conker on the end of a piece of string, waiting to get smashed to pieces by the gnarled old champion that had been soaked in vinegar then stored in the airing cupboard for the last year before being brought into the school playground—

Bang!

The gunshot cut through everything. Time slowed, the helicopter engine stopped, and the propellers froze as the dead body fell through the air and hit the ground with a wince-inducing thud.

Vince looked down to see Guy Ruley spread out on the lawn below him.

Illuminated by the ring of lights, he was centre-stage, cutting a tragic figure. For his body lay chest down, but his head, attached to its broken neck, was facing in the opposite direction and looking straight up at Vince. But Guy Ruley was dead before he hit the deck and got all twisted out of shape. He had a bullet through his eye.

Vince looked around and saw Isabel Saxmore-Blaine just outside the ring of lights. She was still standing in the shooting

405

position, the gun wrapped in both hands and extended upwards. Encased in the catsuit, she looked a powerful and lethal presence. The huntress, the crack shot. All in black, like a shapely coffin.

Vince thought he heard her shout 'Jump', but couldn't be sure. Then his view of Isabel was suddenly swiped away as the helicopter took to life again, and lunged at an alarming angle before it began a quickening ascent. Battling the sudden G force, Vince looked up and saw that the mackintosh man was no longer crouched in the hold. To Vince, the solid rope ladder now felt like a length of spindly thread as the helicopter dragged him through the firmament. It was not so much like holding a tiger by the tail as a fire-breathing dragon that was now in full flight and soaring towards the heavens. All around him was sky, pure blue sky. Then the helicopter changed direction again, and swooped and plunged towards the ground before straightening itself out.

Vince now saw Chuckers, its hard ochreous brick getting closer and closer and closer . . . and before he knew it, he was dancing over the rooftop of the wannabe great house. The chopper had lowered itself enough for Vince to scrape along the roof of the house and, by their reckoning, be dislodged by one of the many obstacles in his path. But Vince held on, using his legs as shock absorbers to kick himself away from the bunched chimney stacks, the pointed arches, the turrets and towers with their cherubs and gargoyles and satyrs. And soon the tiles were falling freely as Vince's feet and arse skimmed along the roof, surfed the mighty rising and falling pediments, and twanged the spiky TV aerials and assorted rusty weathervanes.

The helicopter, after traversing the full length of the roof – twice – dropped down towards the long terraced greenhouses at one side of the house. As the chopper slowed to a hovering stop, Vince grabbed his chance with both hands and began to scale the rope ladder. Battered and bruised though his legs now were from crashing into and kicking away the assorted roof paraphernalia, they felt as energized as Jesse Owens' in '36, as Vince took the ladder two rungs at a time. Reaching the top, he gripped the lip of the hold.

He was just about to haul himself further into the belly of the chopper when he was met with the sun-mottled face of a white man from a hot climate, a pair of ruthlessly cold blue eyes, and the words: 'Goodbye, friend.'

Vince felt the rope ladder fall away, and the heel of a thickly treaded army boot stamp down on the crown of his head. Then his eyes closed as gravity did its thing, and he fell backwards and . . .
down
down
down
down
down
down
Crash!

EPILOGUE

Vince opened the door to Mac. Before the older detective had stepped over the threshold, he gave Vince the once-over, looking approvingly at his suit. It was grey flannel and it belonged to Mac. He'd lent it to Vince for the disciplinary hearing. Mac had quoted: 'In the words of Mark Twain, "Clothes make the man".'

'The rest of that bon mot is, "naked people have little or no influence in society". I do have suits of my own, Mac.'

The two men made their way into the living room.

'Trust me, Vincent, you turn up at the hearing wearing one of your sharkskin jobs and looking better dressed than that lot, and you may as well turn up in the buff. They'll suspect everything they've heard about you is true.'

Either the suit was making him itch, or Vince was just uncomfortable with the whole premise of trying to be someone he wasn't – namely, Mac. Vince clearly didn't hold with Mac's theory; he saw it as a self-defeating gesture, like donning sackcloth, a sign of humility and guilt. But he kept shtum, didn't want to hurt Mac's feelings. And if it made the older detective happy, then he could suffer the indignity of grey flannel for a couple of hours.

In the living room, Mac took his seat in the high-backed chair and lit the pipe that was already plugged into his mouth. Vince remained standing, pacing the floor and kicking up imaginary divots on the Moroccan rug.

'Relax, Vincent, and take a seat. You look like you've got ants in your pants,' said Mac, with a wicked grin plastered across his mouth that made the pipe wobble up and down.

'Very funny.'

Vince didn't have ants in his pants, but he did have glass in his arse. And, even though it had been a couple of weeks since he'd had it removed, he still couldn't sit comfortably, not without a big billowy cushion planted under his backside.

As the mackintosh man had hissed 'Goodbye, friend' and kicked him away from the helicopter, Vince had plummeted about thirty feet down and crashed through the roof of the greenhouse. His fall was finally met by the relatively soft landing of a wooden trestle table holding a thick earthy bed containing *Rumohra adiantiformis*, to give them their Latin botanical name – or ferns to the layman.

The mackintosh men had made their escape (a temporary reprieve, he'd assured himself). The only men who knew about the Gilded Edge, or at least had admitted its existence to Vince, were now dead. Nicky DeVane had died that same night. His death was similar to that of both his 'friends'. Like Beresford, he had seemingly died by his own hand. And like Guy Ruley, he took a drop from the end of a rope. But there were no bullets in the head for the dapper snapper. Nicky DeVane had hanged himself in his own studio, found dangling from one of its white beams in his gold lamé suit.

The young bartender at the Criterion had told the police how two men wearing dinner jackets and masks, stating they were friends of DeVane's, and obviously fresh from the Montcler Ball, had come into the bar and taken him home. No one knew who they were, or could identify them. Some said rhinos, some said hippos. Whilst the official verdict was suicide, Vince thought otherwise. The mackintosh men were certainly his prime suspects, with their dinner jackets hidden under the military jumpsuits. Vince suspected that they had been present at the Montcler masked ball, it being perfect cover for them just as it had been for him.

Vince knew that the dapper snapper was too wasted to kill himself that night – and also too short. He wasn't capable of throwing a rope over the high beam to hang himself. But his death was fitting, and maybe inevitable. In the fabled 'Suicide Stakes', Vince didn't know what odds James 'Aspers' Asprey would have fixed on his old friend Nicky DeVane, but he reckoned they were short. And, after the Montcler Ball, he was probably odds-on favourite for the drop. Vince had witnessed it himself, the big cats, Aspers and Goldsachs, mauling the little man, tearing him limb from limb. Nicky DeVane was already dead in the eyes of the Montcler set, the set that held sway over London's high society. And for Nicky DeVane, to belong was everything, to be ostracized was oblivion.

Mac looked at his watch – time to go. He stood up and asked Vince, 'You ready?'

Vince shot his cuffs, gave a nod, and they headed towards the door. Before they were out of the living room, Mac's eye caught the glinting cobra rising up in its stand by the record player, and asked: 'Can you play that thing?'

The alto sax had been delivered to Vince's flat two days ago. It was a gift from Isabel Saxmore-Blaine. It was her parting gift, before upping sticks and going to New York. She was leaving London to escape her new-found notoriety, or, as the newspapers' salacious headlines had described her: 'The crack shot aristo-*cat* with the *purr*-fect pedigree and nine lives, who saved a Scotland Yard detective's life.'

Unwanted as her new fame was, it made her an intriguing party guest, and the invites poured in. She had moved from social pariah to must-have guest faster than a bullet from a gun. None of this interested Isabel, apart from one offer of a fresh opportunity to kick-start her career in journalism. A certain 'happening' NYC pop artist, who had previously made the mundane soup can such a prized and iconic image, wanted to do her portrait – a silk screen of her in her now trademark outfit of the catsuit. He had also offered her a job editing a new arts and celebrity magazine he planned on launching. Art and celebrity and death seemed to be becoming irreversibly entwined in this artist's aesthetic. And, right now, Isabel Saxmore-Blaine, swathed in black like some avenging angel, seemed to encapsulate the whole vibe. The girl was *IT.*

Isabel said that she'd send Vince a signed original of the screen print, to replace the broken painting he still had leaning against his wall. Vince told Isabel that the indelible image of her, in and out of the catsuit, was now as much part of him as his right hand. Was he sad to see her go? Like he'd reasoned when he first met her, there was something immensely unknowable about Isabel Saxmore-Blaine. He reckoned that the dreamtime they'd spent together was as close as he would ever get to her, and she would always remain the great unknowable. But they would meet again, he was sure. Vince knew he'd be seeing New York City one day. It was on his to-do list, because it was his kind of town, as much as it was anyone's kind of town who possessed a pulse and a dislike for grey flannel.

Before they left the flat, Vince answered Mac's last question. He picked up the alto sax and blew a note. Just the one. But as brief as it was, what a sweet, sweet sound it made.

ACKNOWLEDGEMENTS

While I consider this book to be an unalloyed work of fiction, some of the characters who make an appearance are, or were, real. And a strand of this story is based on some events that may or may not have happened – allegedly.

These were some of the books and TV programmes I enjoyed for my extensive research, which I took extensive liberties with, and then played hard and fast with the facts: *The Gamblers* by John Pearson (Arrow); *Michael X* by John L. Williams (Century); *Billy Hill: Godfather of London* by Wesley Clarkson (Pennant Books); *The Real Casino Royale*, a Channel 4 documentary based on *The Hustlers* by Douglas Thompson (Pan); *The Mayfair Set*, a BBC documentary by Adam Curtis.

And finally, many thanks to Peter Lavery for his edits and encouragement.